CRITICAL PRAISE FOR RON FAUST:

"Faust is really impressive. The scenes are VIVIDLY DRAWN and his descriptions of violence ALL TOO REAL. A VERY ENJOYABLE READ."
>   —Ken Goddard, author of *Prey* and
>   *Balefire*

"Ron Faust has written a beautiful and powerful book ... OF THE KIND AND QUALITY WE ONCE GOT FROM JOHN D. MACDONALD AND EARLY WILLIAM FAULKNER.... He writes of nature and men like Hemingway, with simplicity and an absolute dominance of prose skills."
>   —Bill Granger, award-winning author
>   of *Hemingway's Notebook* and
>   *The November Man*

"IN THE FOREST OF THE NIGHT takes us to Central America for a close examination of the tempest of revolution and, ultimately, the barbarity and resilience of the human being. THIS IS POWERFUL STUFF."
>   —W. Michael Gear and
>   Kathleen O'Neal Gear, co-authors
>   of *People Of The River*

IN THE FOREST OF THE NIGHT

RON FAUST

TOR

A TOM DOHERTY ASSOCIATES BOOK
NEW YORK

This is a work of fiction. All the characters and events portrayed in this book are fictitious, and any resemblance to real people or events is purely coincidental.

IN THE FOREST OF THE NIGHT

Copyright © 1993 by Ron Faust

All rights reserved, including the right to reproduce this book, or portions thereof, in any form.

Cover art by Richard Andri

A Tor Book
Published by Tom Doherty Associates, Inc.
175 Fifth Avenue
New York, N.Y. 10010

Tor® is a registered trademark of Tom Doherty Associates, Inc.

ISBN: 0-812-51381-9
Library of Congress Catalog Card Number: 92-43175

First edition: March 1993
First mass market edition: April 1994

Printed in the United States of America

0 9 8 7 6 5 4 3 2 1

To Robert Gleason

And when he had opened the fourth seal, I heard the voice of the fourth beast say, Come and see.

And I looked, and behold a pale horse: and his name that sat on him was Death, and Hell followed with him. And power was given unto them over the fourth part of the earth, to kill with sword, and with hunger, and with death, and with the beasts of the earth.

Revelation 6:7–8

PART ONE

THE TOWER

CHAPTER

1

Dr. Martin Springer and the other two prisoners were confined in the bell tower of the old Church of San Pedro de los Mártires. It was a cubical room with thick ceiling beams, an iron lockbox and iron hinges on the seven-foot door, and whitewashed plaster walls. The stairway beyond the door was hardly more than a steep ladder. Hemp bell ropes hung through holes drilled in the floorboards. They could look down a thirty-foot shaft and see their guards in the room below. Sometimes the soldiers amused themselves by ringing the three bronze bells, swinging on the ropes, and Martin was half deafened for hours afterward.

"Bastards. I'll get them." Rodolfo Palafox would lie flat on the floor and try to spit or urinate down on the guards, who danced away, laughing and shouting, "Spit, traitor, piss, corpse!"

One night the guards brought in a simpleminded village girl who was not more than fifteen, and in the lantern light they drank cane alcohol and repeatedly raped the girl and grinned up at the prisoners, crying, "Spit, queers, piss, dead men!" Their leader, a sergeant, was not seen after that. The priest said that he had been summarily shot for counterrevolutionary activity, that is, for permitting the abuse of the village girl.

Two days later Father Perecho joined them in the bell tower, bringing several bottles of sour red wine, cigarettes, and some special foods—butter, cheese, white bread, and a charred quarter of pork. And in his soft lisping Spanish he talked about God's mercy, sweet and infinite; the pure holy Mother; the travails of Jesus; the certainty of justice and love in the True Life that will inevitably follow this false and ephemeral life. Death, you know, is the beginning, not the end. Once reconciled to death a man of faith would cease to regard it as a misfortune.

The young priest directed most of his long monologue to Major David Cabrera. Cabrera understood. Martin and Rodolfo Palafox understood too, and left most of the wine and food for the major.

"Father, will you hear my confession in the morning?" Cabrera asked.

"Of course."

"Judas goat," Cabrera said when the priest had gone.

Until then the major had not really believed that he would die in Tepazatlán; he expected to be ransomed by his family and friends. Men of his class were rarely executed.

Cabrera was shot the following morning. Martin watched from the south port. They escorted Cabrera into the walled churchyard and the young lieutenant read from a document that stated that the revolutionary tribunal possessed not only the right but the duty to kill its enemies. In the name of Justice; in the name of History; in the name of Future Generations.

Father Perecho absolved the man of his sins; the lieutenant established the legality of the execution; and the firing squad, most of them adolescents in oversized camouflage fatigues, fired a salvo.

Pigeons, alarmed by the cracking rifles, swirled out of the belfry's attic. Blood roses appeared on Cabrera's tunic. He collapsed in a boneless half-pirouette. The lieutenant drew his pistol and, like an assassin, went forward to administer the coup de grâce. There was a popping noise and Cabrera's head moved. No one knew what to do next. Soon Cabrera's face and torso were dotted with flies. He looked like a bundle of dirty rags in the dust of the churchyard.

But Cabrera had died in the flamboyant Latin American style, refusing a blindfold and contemptuously giving the order to fire. Until then Martin had not understood the ancient notion of "dying well." It wasn't only the major's pride, his display of courage, that was impressive: Martin saw that the man had turned his own execution into a kind of theater, had almost cynically exploited his death in order to vindicate his life. Cabrera had created a myth for his family, his comrades, his descendants, all who had known him or might someday hear about him.

"David Cabrera was very brave," Father Perecho gravely told them.

"Yes," Martin said. "I saw."

"But perhaps he was unrepentant."

"How can you permit the killing of men on Church property?"

"I have no choice. These people do whatever they wish. They wouldn't mind at all killing me."

"Then maybe it's your duty to be martyred."

"Who would that help?"

Construction on the original Church of San Pedro de los Mártires had commenced in 1595 and in 1603 the building had been consecrated. The stone blocks were quarried in a western province, transported overland many miles, and then floated down the Rio Negro on great rafts. That is what the priest told Martin. The tower had been connected to the church at that time, behind the sacristy, and its bronze bells had been cast in Seville. In 1758 an earthquake had reduced the church and rectory to rubble, although—"miraculously," Father Perecho said—the Romanesque tower had remained standing. The church was rebuilt partly with the old stones and partly with new blocks cut and hewn at the original quarry. The reconstructed church had been erected twenty yards northeast of the old site and so now the tower stood alone as a campanile. The new structure was larger than the old, and a pair of transepts had been extended out of the nave, giving it a cruciform shape.

"I wish I could show you the inside," the priest said. "But don't you think it's beautiful, Martin?"

"Yes," Martin lied. He thought it was heavy, cold, and ugly.

From the four glassless tower ports Martin could look down over the village and out to much of the surrounding countryside: the fields and trees, the viscous Rio Negro, and in the distance smoky blue mountains massed like thunderheads on the horizon. Vultures perched in the tall flowering trees of the village plaza, and skeletal mendicant dogs—each seemed to have a crippled hind leg—skulked along the narrow streets. It was always hot in Tepazatlán, always beautiful, always cruel. The children had bellies swollen from hunger and worms. Some of the old people stared up toward the bell tower with silvery glaucous eyes. And high in the trees the vultures spread their wings like frayed black laundry.

In his notebook Martin had written: *Of course it's banal to make vultures symbolic of evil. Even so, every morning they fly off to scavenge the battlefields and cornfields, the blasted villages, and they return with full gorges. They shit liquefied human beings on the statue of General Vargas.*

And after the execution of Major Cabrera, he wrote: *"The priest, in his black cassock, with his long neck and beaky nose, his badly cut tufted hair, reminds me of the vultures. That is unfair. He is no doubt a good man, as 'good' is defined in these pestilential gardens."*

The guards were subdued for a while after the executions of their sergeant and Major Cabrera, but they soon regained their raucous cheer. "You're next, Palafox!" they yelled. And, "You are next, gringo! Sleep well."

"No, you're next!" Rodolfo would scream. "You're next!"

Martin could look out beyond the churchyard walls to the village plaza and see the equestrian statue of General Vargas. It was a huge bronze, green with verdigris, that depicted the general astride a powerful stallion. And there were trees and shrubs in the park, banks of flowers, flagstone walks, an octagonal bandstand, and a marble fountain from which Indian women drew water into earthenware pitchers.

It rained every afternoon. Spiders of lightning scuttled through the smoky clouds. The raindrops looked like mushrooms as they burst on the streets and on the church's slate roof.

CHAPTER

2

Katherine nearly fainted when she stepped off the air-conditioned airplane. Hot, it was hot, a viscid sticky heat that was almost too dense to breathe. You had to bully your way through the air. And the colors, primary reds and blues and yellows, intense, intense, like the heat and the strangeness and the danger, piercing tropical colors, oh Martin, what a place to die in!

The customs functionaries, mestizos with straight black hair and insinuating eyes, stamped her passport, her birth certificate, and a bank statement that had got mixed up with the other things. Stamp stamp stamp, purple ink, leers. She had cramps. The curse or maybe a kind of prophetic dysentery. There were gaudy airline stickers pasted on her lovely Vuitton bags.

The customs vandals opened the luggage, lingered sensuously over her lingerie. Martin! *"Está bien,"* one of them finally said. *"Pase, Señorita."*

"Señora," Katherine said with a smile. Damn that smile, they'd probably turn up at her hotel room door at three A.M.

A loiterer with one milky eye and a crippled leg
snatched her two bags from the table and scuttled crabwise
across the customs shed and through an open door.
"Thief!" she cried, hurrying after him. *"Pícaro!"* No, that
meant rascal. Well, he *was* a rascal. She entered the terminal and bumped into a child peddler, spinning her around
and spilling her box of chewing gum onto the floor. *"Lo
siento,"* Katherine said. Was that right? Didn't that mean
"I feel it"? The *pícaro*, with his awkward lunging gait,
was now almost to the exit door.

"Mrs. Springer?" A tall man in a lightweight beige suit.

"What? Yes. That man—"

"It's all right, Mrs. Springer, he's a porter."

"Porter?"

"He's taking the bags to my car." He wore tinted
aviator-style sunglasses. He spoke with a soft, deep-South
accent.

"I don't feel well," Katherine said. "I'm sick."

"I'm sorry. My name is Robert Harley. I'm with the
U.S. Embassy. I'll take you to your hotel."

"Yes," she said. "Please."

Mr. Harley placed her bags in the trunk of a Chevrolet,
tipped the rascal with some dirty orange currency, and then
drove out of the airport grounds and down a long winding
road.

Ahead she could see the skyline of the city rising
against the green mountains beyond. They were in the
country now, though; hovels with corrugated steel or
palm-frond roofs, corn and bean fields, people, dogs, bur-
ros, cows, goats, palm trees that rose up and up then burst
into green tatters. A turquoise-blue sky. Now a bridge,
mucky water down below, probably swarming with snakes
and alligators and God knew what else. Corpses. More
fields and some jungly green hills, little shack villages,
billboards advertising hotels and restaurants in the city.

He had turned on the air-conditioning and it was reasonably cool in the car now.

"Mr. Harley, do you have a cigarette?"

"No, ma'am, I don't smoke. Shall I stop for some?"

"I don't smoke either, not really. Not for five years. Martin and I quit together. But since . . ."

"There are some stands ahead."

"We quit for health reasons, of course, but also because it looked bad, a doctor and his wife who smoked cigarettes."

"I've never smoked. I never understood the filthy habit."

This Mr. Harley seemed a complacent fellow, smooth, judgmental, vain. The vapors of his expensive aftershave contributed to her nausea. Katherine did not care for fastidious males—really, a man ought to be a little rumpled and not smell like a damned flower shop. Harley was immaculately shaved and barbered and manicured. A dandy. He did not sweat.

He slowed the car and eased off the pavement to a small refreshment stand. It was open on the sides, with a dirt floor and a roof of dried palm fronds. The counter was heaped with fruits and vegetables. Some desiccated strips of meat were cooking on a charcoal brazier.

"Would you like a glass of orange juice?" he asked.

"Is it safe?"

His smile was small, male, and superior. "The juice is freshly squeezed and therefore clean."

"But the glasses aren't clean. No."

He ordered a package of Dulce Superior cigarettes from the man behind the counter. Sitting on a wicker chair in the shade, a girl was feeding a baby with—was it possible?—Pepsi-Cola. Yes, a nipple had been slipped over the bottle and the baby, cheeks puckered, was sucking mightily. The Pepsi Generation. Oh, God. The heat, the sun, the vindictive sun, and the oily smoke from the fire was increasing her nausea. The tires of passing cars hissed on the asphalt. The cooking meat looked like appendixes and smelled spoiled. The girl with the baby intercepted Katherine's glance and smiled. "Cute baby," Katherine murmured. Now she noticed a dog sleeping by the girl's feet. A dog that looked like a piglet. She smiled at the girl, the baby, and the pigdog. Oh, God.

They returned to the car. The Dulce Superior cigarettes burned with a faint crackling. The tobacco was dark and strong but not unpleasant tasting.

"Incidentally," Mr. Harley said when they were back on the road, "you didn't ask to see my credentials."

"You didn't offer them, either," Katherine said. "Incidentally."

"You must be more careful. This isn't Wisconsin, you know."

"It isn't? It really isn't? My."

"Would you open your window a crack, Mrs. Springer, and let some of the smoke out of the car?"

"Have you heard anything about my husband?"

"We have hopes that he's still alive."

"Hopes, that's very nice."

The car entered a four-lane boulevard. The farm country was behind them now; not far ahead she could see the slummy outskirts of the city and, beyond, some tall buildings and the domes and bell towers of the cathedral.

"Would you like to see a little of the city?"

"No, not now. I'm very tired."

"I've booked you into the Hotel Nacional. It's quiet there, very pleasant. Your husband stayed there for a time. There are more modern hotels if you prefer."

"The Hotel Nacional sounds fine."

The boulevard led directly through the business district. Office buildings and hotels and restaurants and shopping arcades and green parks. It looked like an ordinary small city. There were few signs of war. Some armed soldiers on the street corners, here and there a jeep; but no smoking ruins, shell scars, broken windows, tanks, slain children. They stopped at a red light.

"What do you do at the embassy, Mr. Harley?"

"I'm the assistant commercial attaché."

"Do you know Martin?"

"We met once at an embassy reception."

The light changed and he drove forward.

"Why did you meet me at the airport? I mean, it was very kind and all, but the assistant commercial attaché. . .?"

"Right now we're operating with a reduced staff. We're targets of the terrorists, as you can imagine."

"Yes."

"Mrs. Springer, I've been briefed by our military attaché. He says that we have fairly reliable evidence that your husband is being held prisoner in a little town called Tepazatlán. That's in the west, in communist-controlled territory."

"But he is still alive?"

"He was at last report."

"A prisoner? But why?"

"Listen carefully, Mrs. Springer. We have some friends on the other side. We pay them. They work for the communists, they fight for them, but they do us favors, if you understand. Those kind of people can't be trusted completely. But money can purchase their temporary allegiance. Do you understand what I'm saying?"

"You have spies in the other camp."

"Yes, as they have in our camp. We're trying to arrange a rescue of your husband by one of our friends."

"Yes," Katherine said. "Please."

He turned right and drove down a narrow side street. There was just enough room for two vehicles to pass.

"We think your husband witnessed a massacre of the

entire population of a village. We would like to free Dr. Springer, for humanitarian reasons, of course, but also because he has a story to tell the world."

"I don't care about the pretext, Mr. Harley. Just get my husband out of there."

"You must not repeat anything I've told you."

"All right. But you've told me very little."

"This town is filled with informers. Anything you say about what I've told you, even a hint, could jeopardize your husband. As well as our friend."

"But there is a chance for Martin?"

"I won't claim that our friend is a good man. That would imply a moral quality." He smiled briefly. "But he's very competent. Yes, there's a chance."

Katherine looked straight ahead through the windshield. There were pushcarts and food stands and peddlers and beggars and people gathered around charcoal braziers, eating roasted corn and meats, and a legless man who moved along on a kind of skateboard. And there were children everywhere, fuel for this war or the next.

"I'll keep you informed," he said.

"Yes, please."

"Call me anytime at the embassy. I'll give you my home telephone number too."

"Thank you."

"We think that Dr. Springer witnessed a brutal massacre, an atrocity that the world should hear about."

Damn the world, Katherine thought, damn propaganda. I just want my Martin back.

Katherine was awakened by her own cries of distress. She reached for the bedside lamp but it was gone.

This was not her bedroom; the dimensions were different—the quality of the silence—and there were alien smells and an unfamiliar heat. The Hotel Nacional, yes. She lay quietly, orienting herself: It was, she remembered, a high-ceilinged room with a double bed, an ornately carved armoire, a dresser, a writing desk and chair, a television (which did not function) in the corner, a dinette near the balcony doors, and a floor lamp. The end table containing the telephone and reading lamp were on Martin's side—the other side—of the bed. She could hear the ticking of water in the bathroom, like a fast clock, and the contrapuntal beating of her heart. She thought of snakes, scorpions, spiders, intruders. The dream, that ghastly dream.

Katherine slid over on the bed, fumbled in the darkness until she found the lamp switch. There. Her body was clammy with sweat, she was thirsty, she was frightened. The heat, my God. The air conditioner, like the television, was not working. The dial of her alarm clock read 6:40. But 6:40 A.M. or 6:40 P.M.? It couldn't possibly be evening. Why was it so dark? Ah, because, remember, heavy blackout drapes covered the French doors.

On top of the dresser were bottles of Coca-Cola sitting in a cardboard ice bucket. The meltwater and the Coke were as warm as blood, the cola too sweet and sticky, but she drank one down, hardly breathing, and then opened the other. As she drank she stared at a painting on the wall: a bird, perhaps an eagle but looking more like some mythological dragonfowl, sat perched above the crucified Jesus. There was a thick, coiled snake in its beak. Jesus was yellow-orange and looked ironical.

The tiles were cool on her feet. How could anything be cool when the temperature was about one hundred and ninety degrees? Another painting on the opposite wall, another Christ, but this one looked like a hungry Fidel Castro. And one more oil painting, a geometrical landscape that was either very primitive or very modern.

Katherine pulled the drape cords, and light—an unusually pure light—flooded the room. She opened the French doors and stepped out onto a small balcony. The wrought-iron railing was only thigh-high and looked fragile, and her room was three floors above the street. Be careful.

The air smelled fresh although it did not seem much cooler outside. But fresh and sweet; she could smell flowers from the little park across the street and from farmland beyond the city. The shadows were long and dark. Below, women were sweeping the wetted cobblestones; uniformed schoolchildren walked down the sidewalk; three men who wore sandals and straw hats lounged on the corner, smoking cigarettes and spitting. Peasants, spies, day laborers, revolutionaries, idlers, assassins?

And then she noticed that during the night, somehow, the equestrian statue in the park had been destroyed. Chunks of bronze and reinforcing rod had been scattered all over the grass and walks, and the ground around the pedestal had been scorched. She saw what appeared to be a hindquarter of the horse lying on top of the bandstand's roof. There were broken windows in shops on the east side of the square. And there, near the beds of bougainvillea, could that possibly be the hand, forearm, and part of the rider's sword? How comical, how grotesque. Joint-severed bronze limbs were scattered all over the park. She had slept through the explosion; the noise had been incorporated into her dream.

Now she noticed the man. An American, she was sure, not just because of his reddish steel-wool hair and fair skin, but because of his posture, the way he moved, his casual swagger. A big man going to fat, going to seed, but still jaunty and not unattractive.

Whoever, the fool had retrieved the nearly intact head of the rider and now carried it across the park and perched it upon the rim of the fountain. He lit a cigarette and stood back. Cocked his head. Exhaled smoke. Shifted his position and began talking to the head. Katherine could hear his voice but was unable to understand the words.

Then she noticed that the three corner lizards, the men wearing straw hats, were staring up at her. Round mahogany faces grinning. And then she realized that she was wearing only pants and bra. It had been so hot, she'd forgotten—dolt!—and she hurriedly retreated into her room.

She drank some water out of the cardboard ice bucket and lit a Dulce Superior cigarette. The dream.

In the dream she and Martin were riding in an ancient mustard-yellow bus that spewed a horizontal tornado of smoke from its exhaust. The bus was crowded with silent brown people. Martin too was silent; he did not respond to her urgent pleas, she was unable to communicate her dread. It was very hot even though all of the windows were open. She was sweating, everyone on the bus was sweating except for Martin; he was pale and dry. "Please, Martin." And then the bus stopped and Martin, without a glance or word, rose and walked down the aisle and down the steps. When the bus pulled away she found herself sitting on the long rear seat between two stolid men, looking back over the dusty road. Martin's figure gradually diminished. And then the dark sky was webbed with cracks, light filling every fissure, and there was a great reverberating crack of thunder, a deluge of flame, and Martin lay alongside the road, charred and smoking.

CHAPTER

3

Tepazatlán was a base for the antigovernment militia in that province. Supplies were brought in overland at night, and by river traffic, and occasionally a battered olive-drab helicopter flew in just above the forest and settled on a bean or corn field. Soldiers rapidly unloaded the crates of ammunition and rations and then the helicopter rose up through its dust cloud and darted away.

Martin knew that soon the helicopter would carry orders for his execution or release, although he dared not expect the latter. One life, his life, meant nothing in the brutality and chaos of this small war. Mercy, pity, justice were not the issues: he was a nuisance now and a potential embarrassment in the future. Logically—and Martin bitterly conceded the logic of his murder—logically it was in the best interest of the insurgents that he simply and forever vanish. It was a political decision.

He and Palafox did not talk much during the daylight hours; it was very hot then, a swampy suffocating heat that deadened the body and paralyzed the brain; and it was better to simply lie on the straw pallets in that fly-buzzing heat or stand by one of the campanile's window ports and in a stupor stare out at the village. And too it seemed that in daylight they were seized by an inexplicable shame; it was impossible to confide then.

Every afternoon the clouds massed overhead and then at three or four o'clock the sky convulsed and it began to rain. One day lightning struck the tower's roof (half melting the vane and blowing off dozens of ceramic tiles): Martin had felt the static electricity accumulating, prickling the flesh on his scalp and arms, and then there was an incandescent glare and the simultaneous thunderclap. He and Rodolfo waited out subsequent storms in the center of the room, exchanging mirthless smiles.

It would rain for an hour or two, flooding the churchyard and streets, and then the sky would clear. They usually napped in the coolness that followed the rain.

At night they talked. Moonlight gleamed on the wet streets, dogs barked, the air was sweet with the fragrance of night-blooming flowers. On some nights there was a breeze that evaporated their sweat and kept the mosquitoes away. They talked and were silent, talked again, smoking loosely packed cigarettes that burned like fuses. Martin, a nonsmoker for five years, had gone back to cigarettes.

"Are you really a doctor?" Rodolfo asked one night.

"Yes."

He looked skeptically at Martin's untrimmed hair and beard, the filthy jeans and khaki twill shirt, the worn jogging shoes.

"You don't look like a doctor."

"What do doctors look like?"

"They're older. They're rich men. They look rich."

"Some doctors are young and not rich."

"Are you poor?"

"No, I have considerable money and property."

"Why would a rich man leave his money and property and family to come here?"

"I wanted to help the poor."

"Aren't there any poor in the United States?"

"Yes, many."

"Well?"

"Mostly, I think, I just wanted to get away for a year or so. I had never really been free. It's a long and difficult process to become a physician. And then it takes time to build a good medical practice. And too, Rodolfo, I married young and started a family. Yes. The fact is I wanted to escape for a year and have a great adventure."

"Is this your adventure?" Rodolfo asked. "You and me—are we having a great adventure?"

Martin smiled.

"That's crazy. Only rich people have adventures. Poor people have troubles."

"I couldn't foresee this."

"So. So, Martin, did you help our poor?"

"Some. A little."

Not very much: in the remote areas down here, without the miracle drugs and modern medical technology, a doctor was often no more effective than a shaman. Martin had practiced nineteenth-century medicine on aborigines and peasants whose lives (and many of whose diseases) were medieval. What good did it do to diagnose, say, tuberculosis, if the isoniazids or streptomycins were unavailable, or cost more than a man earned in a year? And a child with a gutful of worms kept the worms in the absence of an effective vermicide. And how useful were your surgical skills if there was not an aseptic room in the province and the only anesthetic was a bottle of cheap rum or, if you were lucky, a bottle of chloroform? And how could you practice preventive medicine when the people were so monumentally ignorant? They contracted tuberculosis and anthrax and brucellosis from unpasteurized dairy products, and giggled when you told them to boil milk. They thought you were mad when you told them that bubonic plague was caused by the bite of a flea. To them a bacterium was a creature less credible than ghosts or dragons or spirits.

Martin talked freely during those long hot nights. He was going to die soon: there was no reason to fear self-exposure or sentimentality or remorse.

"Of course I should have stayed home with my family. What will they do without me? To abandon them as I did, even if it was to be only for a year, was quixotic—no, stupid."

He talked about death. "I'm a doctor. Death is as familiar to me as to any man, but I understand it no better. It seems so illogical. We say that death is natural, inevitable, but secretly we don't mean it. The whole idea of death is outrageous, it offends consciousness, it insults life."

And he said, "I've been happy although I wasn't always aware of it at the moment. It seems to me that I was not quite strong enough and smart enough to impose a design on my life. I wish I could have another chance. I've learned. Still, I probably would not change much. We can try hard to change and we usually fail. Our choices are absurdly few, really."

Martin frequently talked about his family. "Kit—Katherine, my wife, is beautiful. I wish I had a photograph to show you. My son Peter is eleven years old. He's a pretty good athlete but not a good student. My daughter Mary is nine. Very pretty, quiet, bookish, artistic, I suppose. They're both healthy children, they will turn out fine with or without me. I only wish I could be with them for ten more years. Just ten. Peter would be twenty-one then and Mary nineteen. Adults. And Katherine . . .

"But they'll have the farm and there'll be enough

money. I earned a lot of money and I made some very good investments. No, they'll be financially secure. But I won't be with them. They'll go on without me. That's hard to believe, hard to take. I can understand why some suicides first murder their families. It doesn't seem right that the world should continue without one. It almost seems as if your family is being . . . disloyal. Isn't that a queer notion? Katherine would almost certainly remarry. The children would have a stepfather. What will he be like? I can't bear to think about these things. I can't very well imagine the future without me."

Martin felt that his Spanish was not adequate for the summing up of a life; his listener was too unsophisticated to understand that particular life even if expressed in the clearest of language. He wished now that he had talked to Major Cabrera. He was sorry that he could not talk to Father Perecho, but it was elucidation he sought, not absolution. Finally, on the last night, Martin realized that there was no language and no listener for what he wished to say.

Major David Cabrera had been the son of a rich landowner, an educated man, a graduate of both the national university and the military institute, and a career officer in the army. David fought to preserve and perhaps enlarge the privileges of his caste. He had been captured—kidnapped—by a team of "terrorists." Rodolfo Palafox was Cabrera's opposite, an awkward peasant lad from a remote rural village, shrewd rather than intelligent, a repeater of slogans but with no ideology beyond that of the full belly and the whole skin. Cabrera had despised Rodolfo because he served the communist cause and because—paradoxically—he apparently was a traitor to that cause, and finally because Rodolfo was devoid of that military sense of honor that to the major was more important than life.

Rodolfo was nineteen years old. He was a thin boy with

big eyes, knuckly hands, and a weedy mustache. He had
been accused of disobeying orders in the field and deser-
tion. Each charge carried the death penalty. But Rodolfo
was optimistic to the point of stupidity: He seemed to
think that the Revolutionary Council was merciful; or that
he would be acquitted of both charges; or that he might
succeed in one of his wild escape plans; or that he would
be saved by the intercession of Jesus or the Virgin or one
of the saints—*someone.*

"It will be all right," he said, "when they understand."

Each morning the guards emptied the cess-bucket and
returned it along with another bucket filled with fresh water. They had always been thirsty when one gallon had to
be shared among three men, but now that Cabrera was
dead they had enough to drink, though with little left over
for washing.

They were given two meals a day, morning and evening,
usually beans and rice and tortillas. Father Perecho
brought them cheap cigarettes.

Cabrera, the week before his execution, had thought of
an escape plan. There was no glass in the window ports;
each was barred by round iron rods embedded vertically in
the cement. If they removed the two center rods there
would be enough space to crawl through. And late the
night of their escape, while the guards below were sleeping (drunkenly, they hoped), they would draw one of the
bell ropes up through the hole in the floorboard, secure it
inside the tower, and lower themselves to the churchyard.
"It will work," Cabrera said. "We can do it." They would
make their way through the courtyard, Cabrera told them,
down the silent streets and then across the fields to the
river, where they might succeed in stealing a boat. A good
plan, Martin thought. He trusted Cabrera's daring and
competence. But one morning the eldest of the guards,
Herrera, tested all of the window bars and found the loose

ones. They had been beaten, not too severely, and had been denied food that day.

Often, awake or sleeping, Martin had a vision of Major Cabrera sprawled dead in the dusty churchyard. It was an accurate mental photograph: the major, diminished by perspective and death, the blood, the flies, the shadow of the tower diagonally bisecting the yard, and the swift shadows of the alarmed pigeons. There seemed to be a concealed significance in the scene; it possessed an emotional power that far transcended the event.

Sometimes in sleep Martin felt the bullets tear through his chest. His heart quivered, close to fibrillation it seemed, and then kicked strongly again when he awakened. He understood that soon it would not be a dream; he would not awaken. This certainty separated him from the priest, the soldiers, the villagers, even his family, all of humanity except Rodolfo Palafox, who endured similar dreams.

One night Rodolfo awakened and said, "Is that you, Martin?"

"Yes."

"I dreamed that I was dead. I was in a hole and they were throwing dirt on top of me."

That was no dream, Martin thought. "Go back to sleep," he said.

"Don't smoke all of the cigarettes, Martin."

CHAPTER

4

One morning Father Perecho arranged to have Martin released from the tower for a few hours.

"Would you like to see my church?" the priest asked when they had emerged into the courtyard.

"All right," Martin said.

"It's small, but this is a small, remote parish."

Martin was dizzied by the sudden opening of the world; the sky, infinitely deep and blue, gave him vertigo. He missed the compact solidity of floor, four walls, and ceiling.

"We'll walk through the streets for a time. I imagine you'd enjoy some exercise. We could eat at a café, if you're hungry."

Martin hesitated. This temporary liberty frightened him as much as captivity. He had adjusted to confinement. For weeks he had been free of the terrible necessity of choosing.

"Are you all right, Martin?"

"Yes."

"You are very pale."

"I'm all right. Really, I'm only fatigued. I don't sleep well."

They crossed the churchyard and exited through a gate that was painted the same color, red oxide, as barns in Martin's area of the Midwest. The street was convex and paved with uniform smooth, oval stones that had been removed from the river. Some of the women on the sidewalk crossed themselves as Father Perecho passed. A lame dog rose out of the shade and limped away. Two young soldiers, armed with automatic weapons, followed them. They were mischievous and half contemptuous, behaving like schoolboys who no longer respected their masters. Twice Martin heard them refer to Father Perecho as the *"maricón."* The queer.

"A fine morning, isn't it?" Father Perecho said.

"Yes."

"I thought it would be good to leave early, before the heat."

"Yes, yes, a good idea."

"This way, Martin."

At first the priest had addressed him as "Dr. Springer" or simply "Doctor," but he'd gradually become less formal. Martin continued to call the priest "Father," partly out of irony—Perecho was a gentle, rather foolish rural boy of twenty-four years.

The street narrowed and they walked between continuous walls set with doors and iron-barred windows. Colored splinters of broken glass had been cemented into the tops of the walls and glowed with a jeweled radiance in the sunlight. Each door, Martin knew from his tower view, opened into a flowery patio. Palms and fruit trees rose above the pastel-colored walls. Inside, caged birds whistled and shrieked.

"You're not a Catholic, are you, Martin? A lapsed one, perhaps?"

"No."

"You aren't Jewish. Protestant, then?"

"I'm pagan, Father. I believe in the great god Pan."

"Martin, don't jest—your soul is in peril."

"So is my ass," he said.

Martin enjoyed teasing the priest even though the young man was so somber and ardent, so simple really, that he hardly understood that it was a game. Father Perecho seemed to regard levity as a sure manifestation of heresy.

The street curved to the left, narrowed even more, and then abruptly opened into the plaza. Trees erupted skyward, frozen explosions of green dotted here and there with vultures and raucous black birds like starlings. A roofed colonnade shaded the sidewalks on all four sides of the square. They passed a bakery, a barbershop, a farm implement store, a closed movie theater, and then the priest stopped before a café.

"Are you hungry, Martin?"

"I'm always hungry."

"Then we'll eat."

The café was about fifteen feet wide by thirty feet deep. There was a wooden counter, some tables and chairs, holy pictures clipped from magazines and pinned to the pastel-green walls, and helices of black-dotted flypaper hanging from the ceiling. They sat at one of the tables. The soldiers remained outside, peering in at them through a dirty window.

"Well. What will you have, Martin?"

"Coffee."

"Coffee, yes, I think I shall have coffee too. What else?"

"Eggs?"

"Eggs, yes. And ham and beans and tortillas."

"Orange juice?"

"Certainly. All right, then. And cigarettes."

Martin nodded warily. He was determined to save his gratitude until he learned in what moral coin the priest intended to exact payment.

"Ah, Martin, I wish you hadn't come to my unhappy country."

"So do I."

"It's so senseless, so futile."

A stout woman with a face as round and pocked as the moon appeared, took their orders, and returned to the kitchen.

"What have you heard?" Martin asked.

"About. . . ?"

"Yes."

"They are taking a long time to decide what to do about you and that is a good sign."

"Yes," Martin said, not believing it.

The woman brought them glasses of orange juice, half-filled mugs of coffee, a pitcher of warm cream, cigarettes, and a box of wax matches.

"Father Perecho, I want to write a letter to my wife. Will you see that it is mailed?"

"It is very difficult," he said softly. "You understand."

"There are things I want to say to her. About our lives together, and the children."

"Ah," the priest said with false cheer, "and how many children do you have, Martin? Boys or girls?"

"I want you to see that she receives the letter."

"Of course, if it passes the censor."

"Damn the censor," Martin said. "Damn your timidity."

"Please." The priest glanced over his shoulder. Outside the two soldiers were chatting with a pair of coquettish teenage girls.

"Father Perecho—"

"My position here is very delicate. They let me stay with my church and parishioners because I don't meddle in politics. But if they thought I did anything against them . . ."

"I'm not asking you to martyr yourself, I'm asking you to see that a letter is mailed. That's all. It isn't much."

"It's madness, all of it. Are greed and hatred and power the easy way for mankind, Martin? History seems to indicate that. But it doesn't make sense. Shouldn't love and peace and cooperation be the easy way?"

The woman came with their plates of food, refilled their coffee mugs, emptied the ashtray, and departed.

The priest met Martin's eyes for the first time since the letter had been mentioned. He expelled a breath and said, "I don't know when it will be mailed. I'll have to wait until someone passes through whom I can trust."

"All right," Martin said. "Thank you."

"But you must not mention this letter to anyone."

"I promise."

The priest smiled anxiously.

Martin also smiled. "Don't let your eggs get cold, Father."

After breakfast they wandered through the twisting back streets. Martin was soon disoriented. It was very hot now. Dogs lay panting in the shade. The shadows had retreated to the north side of the street and seemed to be slowly draining into the cracks between sidewalk and wall. A blind man, led by a child, stopped them and Father Perecho bought a lottery ticket. Again old women crossed themselves as the priest passed, and old men removed their frayed straw hats. The soldiers, a dozen yards behind, laughed at the superstitious respect for the *"maricón."*

"Martin," the priest said. "Martin," he mused. "Were you named after Martin Luther?"

"I don't know. I could be."

"Martin Luther burns in hell," the priest said.

Ahead now Martin could see what appeared to be another park; but no, it was a cemetery enclosed by an iron-spear fence, with a pair of fluted columns rising on either side of the gate. A scene of the Assumption had been carved into the marble lintel. The priest led him through the gate and down a cobblestone road, past what must have been the caretaker's quarters, derelict now, and then onto a path that tacked among the graves. The cemetery had been neglected; the little marble city of tombs and monuments and statuary was half concealed by weeds and tangled thickets of shrubbery. Some of the stones had been overturned. A parasitic moss, hanging in ragged clumps, seemed to be killing the great trees.

"The war, the chaos . . ." Father Perecho said helplessly. "We don't have the money to keep things up. And there has been much vandalism—even some of the tombs have been looted."

There were some absurdly proud monuments scattered here and there, structures worthy of a minor pharaoh: a columned temple in the Grecian style, a forty-foot-high obelisk, heroic statues built over underground crypts. This was a poor province in a poor country, Martin thought, but there are always rich among the poor, rich perhaps because of and not despite the general poverty.

They passed the statue of a landowner named Perez, and a marble—mostly veiled by weeds—of the Virgin and Child. Then they proceeded through a humble section of the cemetery, and beyond to dozens of new graves, bare dirt mounds marked by crude wooden crosses or rock cairns.

The priest stopped at the foot of the most recent grave, last in a long row.

"David Cabrera," he said.

Martin nodded.

"Perhaps someday his family will remove the remains to their private cemetery."

A low mound, reddish soil, pebbles and pieces of root mixed with the earth.

"Let's go," Martin said.

They walked among other graves, older ones, some of them concave and overgrown with thistle and briar. Small earthenware bowls lay at the head of several graves.

The priest noticed his interest. "The Indians cling stubbornly to some of their old superstitions," he said. "The

Church has been unable to completely eradicate all of their pagan beliefs. They come here at times to leave food and water for their dead."

And then, after a pause, he added: "All of this is consecrated ground."

The path led to another iron fence. The gate was secured by only one of the three hinges and lay askew. Beyond the fence were more graves.

"Beyond this fence is unconsecrated ground. You understand—suicides, Protestants, unbelievers, one Jew, as I recall, are buried here. The section used to be maintained by the municipality but now we, the Church, must do what we can. It isn't much."

Martin lit a cigarette and leaned against a tree. Small white butterflies floated like snowflakes through the air. It was quiet except for the ticking and buzzing of insects. There was no breeze. Martin could see the church tower rise above the rooftops to the south. The two soldiers were resting in the shade of a nearby tree.

"If it happens," Father Perecho said, "if the worst happens, and of course we must pray that it doesn't—but if it happens then you must be buried on that side of the fence."

"Father, it doesn't matter where or if I'm buried. Leave my carcass out for the dogs and swine, I don't care."

"Martin, please. You don't mean that."

"I want to go now."

"First I'll show you the church."

The church was narrow, deep and high, built of roughly hewn stone blocks. Thick, age-blackened beams supported the vaulted roof. There were small round stained-glass windows high on the east and west walls, and a stained glass dome directly above the altar. An old woman, her head covered by a faded rag, kneeled in the center aisle. She did not hesitate in her prayers as they passed.

Each of the transepts contained a small chapel. The

nave was separated from the elevated chancel by a mahogany railing. Flames from votive candles were reflected on the tarnished brass pipes of the organ. The priest genuflected before the altar. The soldiers, quiet now, tired and bored from the long walk, sat together in one of the pews.

"Soldiers stole our silver candelabra, our tapestry, and our beautiful gold reliquary."

"What was the relic?" Martin asked.

"A sliver of the True Cross."

"Really?" Martin smiled.

"I believe that it was authentic," the priest said defensively.

Father Perecho was silent for a time and then he said, "Martin, let me baptize you into the Church."

"Ah," Martin said.

"Please."

"You lied earlier, didn't you?"

"Lied? No."

"You said that word hadn't yet arrived. When are they going to do it?"

"I'm sorry. Soon, I'm afraid. Notice has arrived that you are to be executed. It's just a matter now of waiting for the written authorization. I'm sorry."

"Written authorization. The fucking bureaucrats. You've been through this with other men. About how long do I have?"

"I don't know."

"Guess."

"It varies."

"Tell me!"

"Two days, possibly three."

"I would like to go home to the tower now," Martin said. "Home" was the word he used but the priest didn't seem to notice.

CHAPTER

5

Dix awakened early as always and still tired as usual. He showered, shaved, dressed, and went outside. There was a small park across the street from his hotel and he often went there early in the morning to read the city's lying newspapers, have his shoes shined, smoke, drink coffee from a paper cup, and contemplate the statue of the late General Vargas. But the night before last the statue had been blown up. The park was not the same without the noble general and his even nobler stallion.

The lemon trees in the park bore a lime-green fruit. The lemons here were green, orange skins a mottled yellowish-brown, and the egg yolks were blood-red. And the exiled and deceased generals remained splendidly mounted until their revolutionary successors arrived to exact justice. Dix did not think that the other General Vargases would be able to maintain their bold seats for much longer; statues of him were being demolished in cities and towns all over the country.

And urban guerrillas were causing trouble here in the capital. You could hear the crackle of small-arms fire a couple of nights a week now, sounding like popping corn in the distance. Recently a bomb had destroyed a government armory on the edge of the city. Less than a month ago three American military advisers had been killed at a fancy whorehouse on the other side of the river. Most of the journalists had called it a "popular social club" in their reports. Some of his colleagues had described it as murder. Dix had not agreed. The Americans were soldiers, weren't they? They wore uniforms, carried arms. They had taken sides. "Although," he'd said, "I can't wholly approve of killing either civilians or combatants in a whorehouse. I mean, what ever happened to the old concept of sanctuary?"

This was in Mason's suite at the Hotel Cristóbal Colón. There had been an impromptu party. Dix had been drinking ginger ale but everyone assumed that he was drunk.

"It's barbaric to kill a man who's got an erection."

Most of the old hands had laughed, but a couple of the young ones, the idealists, had become indignant. They'd accused him of being burned-out, bitter, cynical. "Evil," said a girl with dry hair and thick legs.

"You're precociously menopausal, honey," Dix said.

Furious, almost in tears, she described some of the horrors she'd seen. These kids saw a bloated, stinking, maggoty corpse for the first time and lost their equilibrium. They had discovered injustice. They had peered into the abyss. They became moralists. Dix assumed that he had once been like them, but he didn't know for sure; he couldn't remember his youth with fidelity.

"Evil is live spelled backwards," Dix had said.

Now a couple of shoeshine boys, entering the park from the south, saw him and began running, calling out, "*Limpiar, Señor* Deex? Shine, mister?" They arrived at the same time, one ducking around the fountain and the other vaulting a bench, and then they began jabbering at each other, competing good-naturedly. Dix settled the dispute by giving each of them a shoe. So what if they turned out different shades of brown? You did not have to go around with scuffed shoes in any Third World country. These boys were healthy and cheerful. So many of the children were sick. You could pity them but love would kill you. And you could overtip them the cost of a pound of beans. Some of the idealistic foreigners refused to overtip or give to beggars because they did not want to "spoil" the people. Poverty, no doubt, was an integral part of their beauty. "Anyway," they said, "you can't help them *all*."

Dix knew that he was being unfair to the idealists but he enjoyed being unfair. A real sense of fairness tended to complicate life intolerably. He'd realized many years ago that he was not an especially good man, and this under-standing made him halfway content with his life. You did what you could, maybe a little less. That was mediocrity. Mediocrity wasn't so bad: *mediocris*—halfway up the mountain. Only heroes did more than was expected of them. Failed heroes, soured heroes, were the dangerous ones, the destroyers. It was enough to be a witness.

Dix sat quietly and reflected, had his shoes shined, glanced at the newspapers, and smoked three cigarettes. This early-morning ritual restored him to himself. Each night was a kind of exile; each morning a difficult repatri-ation.

He saw a woman walk down the hotel steps. She hesi-tated on the sidewalk, glancing east and west, then turned and walked briskly toward the business district. Beautiful, tall and slender, elegantly dressed, a natural blond with, no doubt, man-killer blue eyes. Yes, violet eyes, lavender eyes, cobalt eyes, ultramarine eyes. "Ache," Dix said. He had seen her in the hotel lobby last night and figured her for a TV anchorwoman from some medium-sized market, down here for a long and informative weekend. She would pose in front of the National Palace or the cathedral, dressed in a safari outfit, and explain to the homefolk what this conflict was about.

It was almost eight-thirty and there were more people in the park, more shoeshine boys, peddlers of chewing gum and chocolate and flowers and lottery tickets. Men were arriving with pushcarts from which they sold fruit juices and flavored ices and toxic meats. A pair of cops, dressed in khaki and wearing huge pistols on their belts, strolled slowly with cop-authority down a walk and mounted the stairs to the bandstand. It was their duty to ensure that the important foreigners who stayed at the Hotel Nacional were not offended by importunate whores and maimed beggars.

"What are you doing, Dix?"

Dix jerked, turned. "Jesus, kid, don't sneak up on me like that."

"I wasn't sneaking."

"You're going to surprise an armed man like that someday and dress your mother in black."

"I'm sorry, Dix," Burke said, smiling. "It never occurred to me that you might be armed."

"I am armed with righteousness."

Timothy Burke walked around the bench, removed his backpack, cameras, film and lens containers, and sat down. He looked one day dirtier and poorer than he had yesterday morning. And, Dix thought, he was four or five inches taller than any man needed to be. He wore round wire-rimmed glasses and, in his left ear, a small gold earring.

"Who were you talking to?" he asked.

"Talking?"

"I heard your voice while I was walking over."

"Oh. Well, probably I was talking to myself. Or to the ghost of General Vargas."

"*Buenos días*, General," Burke said, casually saluting.

"You know, Timothy, I miss that statue. Did you ever take any photographs of it?"

"No."

"There's a tradition in equestrian statues that says if the horse has two feet off the ground—the pedestal—the officer died in battle. One foot off the ground and he died from wounds received in battle. If all four of the mount's hooves are touching the ground it means that he died in bed."

"What does it mean if the rider has only one spur?"

"One spur?"

"General Vargas, in the statue, had just one spur, on his right boot."

"I never noticed that. You remember just one spur?"

"Sure."

"You photographers are fiendishly observant. Eventually your objective and subjective senses merge and you're crazy. Well, one spur means that the general died in the embrace of a Swedish masseuse in a plush Miami Beach hotel."

"Right," Burke said. "Two spurs, two Swedes."

"Exactly."

"Dix, did you see that foxy lady come out of the hotel a few minutes ago?"

"Am I blind, son? Am I senile?"

"I talked to the desk clerk. The lady's name is Katherine Springer."

"So?"

"Dr. Martin Springer's wife."

"Oh? Well. Interesting. Listen, kid, why don't you take a few candid photographs of her. There might be a story in it. You know, anxious wife of missing physician arrives in tragic war-torn republic."

"Et cetera," Burke said.

"Et cetera. Come on, I'll buy you breakfast. And you

can shower and shave in my room. Unless showering and shaving are opposed to your Irish scruples."

"I'm out of thirty-five-millimeter stock, Dix."

"I'll loan you some money for film. As long as you understand that I get first shot at buying any good pictures."

"I'm a very good photographer."

"I know that, kid."

Burke was a free-lance. Some of the reporters and photographers tried to help him by giving him a place to stay when they were out of town, spare film or a small assignment, a hot meal, and Burke always accepted with the grace of those to whom poverty is emblematic of some obscure superiority. He was very talented and very cocky, and everyone enjoyed his company, probably, Dix thought, because they enjoyed observing a son of a bitch in the playful puppy stage.

"Did I hear you say something about breakfast?"

"You're like a son to me."

"Twice orphaned," Burke said mysteriously, smiling his slow private smile.

There were flowering trees and shrubs in the Hotel Nacional's patio restaurant, and half-tame birds fluttered down to peck crumbs from the flagstones. Finches bathed in the fountain's basin (which received its stream of water from the mouth of a marble porpoise that was balanced on its tail), and hummingbirds, iridescent blurs, irritably chased one another among the scattered tables.

Mrs. Springer was sitting alone at a table next to a bougainvillea-covered wall. A cigarette fumed in the ashtray. Her hair was free, her back was straight. She wore a white sundress and white high-heeled shoes. Now she lifted her coffee cup, held it halfway between the table and her mouth, and then lowered it without drinking.

Dix covertly watched her from beneath the portico. She

really was a splendid woman; the cool, aristocratic blond type. Ache.

He took several deep breaths, crossed the patio, and approached her table.

"Mrs. Springer?"

Yes, her eyes were blue, indigo now in the shade of the awning. The skin over her cheekbones and along the ridge of her nose was sunburned. A swimming pool lay beyond the wall; he could smell the chlorine.

"I'm sorry to intrude. I'm a friend of Martin's." A lie: he'd seen Martin around town from time to time but they had never passed beyond the banalities.

"You know Martin?"

"We hung around together while he was in the city."

"Sit down, please."

He pulled out a chair and settled into it. "My name is Dixon Stenstrom."

She did not offer her hand.

"I hope Martin is all right," he said.

"Are you with the embassy, Mr. Stenstrom? The hospital?"

"Call me Dix. And may I call you Katherine? Martin talked about you so much that I feel we're old friends."

"Martin talked about me?"

"Oh yes, Katherine this and Katherine that." More lies, but what the hell. "I'm a correspondent with the United Services Syndicate. Your *Milwaukee Journal* and the *Capital Times* in Madison subscribe—you might have read some of my pieces."

"I saw you in the park the other morning. You were talking to the severed head of what's-his-name."

Dix smiled. "He needed my counsel."

"And what did you tell him, Mr. Stenstrom?"

"I said, 'General Vargas, sir, not all the king's horses and all the king's men can put you together again.' And I said, 'Sir, I personally mourn the symbolism—it should have happened while you were alive.' I have the head in my room here at the hotel, sitting on the television stand. I keep it as a *memento mori*."

"Most of us don't require reminders of death."

The waiters here wore black trousers, white shirts with collars the size of gull's wings, and short red jackets. Ghostly, so unobtrusive you couldn't think of anything else, they drifted around the table, emptying ashtrays, removing cups, hovering. Dix suspected that it was contrived so that they could see Katherine close-up and smell her hair and perfume.

"Have you eaten breakfast?" he asked.

"I'm not hungry. I'll have more coffee, though."

"The orange juice is freshly squeezed. When was the last time you had real orange juice? And you ought to try the bananas and cream. This part of the world is famous for its bananas, of course. Bananas and tyranny. And the cream is thick and rich, not like the ooze we get in the States."

"All right," she said.

He ordered, then turned back to her and said, "Listen to the racket of the birds. Whistles, chirps, electronic beeps. It sounds like an aviary with a couple of cats loose. At night the place stinks of jasmine. Now they're hummingbirds, but at night bats fly above the tables. I hate bats. They have vampire bats here, you know. Actually, Katherine, I'm not a lover of nature. I don't know why God didn't make the planet three-quarters ocean and one-quarter city."

He halted, embarrassed by her blank cool gaze. "Actually . . ."

"How long have you been here, Mr. Stenstrom?"

"Nine months. Eternity."

"Then you must understand the situation well."

"The situation is dismal. Simply put, it's the bad guys against the bad guys. The government is absolutely corrupt and cruel. The rebel leaders are absolutely corrupt and cruel. Both sides wage war mostly by killing innocents. Both sides talk piously about their noble ideas, but neither side has any. The U.S. government is in tight with the ruling thugs here, because the ruling thugs are anti-communist thugs, free-enterprise thugs, *our* thugs. The U.S. State Department is master-pimp for the whorish regime. That's about it."

"As a reporter you must know many of the important people involved, on both sides."

"Well, sure. And they aren't impressive."

"I mean, you have contacts on both sides."

"I like to think that I'm an objective witness, Katherine. To me there isn't our side and their side. It's all just a stupid, deadly game."

Dix could see that she was impatient with him. She wanted something that he hadn't delivered. She shook a cigarette loose from the package and permitted him to light it, but she denied him the gift of her attention, her gaze. Ice princess. The fine hairs on her arms were golden. She did not paint her fingernails. One of the straps of her sundress had slipped over her shoulder.

A waiter brought their food. She drank half her orange juice and pushed the banana slices around in the dish.

"Do you know a man named Robert Harley? He's with the embassy here."

"Sure."

"He's the assistant commercial attaché."

"Well, actually, he's not. Harley is the number-two CIA man here. Everybody knows it. Harley goes on pretending."

"The embassy is trying to help Martin."

"I hope that's true. But, Mrs. Springer, I don't think you should rely on them."

"I feel that way too."

"It isn't likely that your interests and their interests will coincide."

"You're a reporter, Mr. Stenstrom. I suppose you're looking for a story."

"Always, yes."

"Does 'off the record' mean anything?"

"It does, you'd be surprised, it does."

"I think you're full of crap, Mr. Stenstrom." She smiled. Her smile ignited his own. He was eager to become her accomplice. "I never wanted to be full of crap," he said. "It just happened."

"One morning you woke up . . ."

"Full of shit."

"Yes. That's how it happens."

"What do you want, Katherine?"

"Off the record, for a while at least? Until Martin is safe?"

He nodded.

"Say it."

"Off the record. Cross my heart and hope to die."

"Dix, I want you to introduce me to a leader of the Revolution."

"Come on," he said.

"I want to offer a ransom for Martin's return."

"You don't know what you're doing. You have no idea."

"Can you arrange a meeting?"

"I guess. Christ. But think about it. Talk to the embassy people."

"I've talked. I'll tell you about that. But, Dix, you must know—I can't trust Martin's life to the State Department clerks. I can't sit here in this hotel and wait and wait and wait while Martin's in danger. I have a considerable sum of money. I want to buy his freedom."

"How much money?"

"I must make some telephone calls. I'll let you know."

"You know that Martin is alive, then?"

"We have to act as though he were, don't we?"

Dix poured some coffee into his cup. He didn't want any more coffee, but he needed to escape her eyes—her fanatical intensity—for a moment. He added cream, a spoonful of the coarse-grained sugar.

"I want my husband back, Dix."

"I'll see what I can do."

She waited until he again engaged her eyes and then she reached across the table and placed her hand over his.

Dix knew that he was being manipulated but he didn't care. Beauty must be served.

"Be true," she said. "Okay? Dix, okay?"

CHAPTER

6

Wounded and fatigued fighters were brought to Tepazatlán for medical treatment and rest. A Cuban doctor had established an infirmary in the municipal building. The less seriously wounded and the merely exhausted wandered the streets, listlessly played soccer or baseball behind the schoolhouse, or just sat for hours in the plaza. But one day about twenty of them got drunk and blew up the statue of General Vargas. The general had been a leader of the corrupt old regime, a member of the oligarchy, and his statue was clearly an insult to the Revolution.

Martin watched from the bell tower as the men became drunker and wilder. They were possessed by a crazed gaiety. They sang obscene songs, bath naked in the fountain, gambled with dice. There was a fistfight. The villagers—shoeshine boys, old benchsitters, peddlers of ices and roasted corn—gradually drifted away. Even the dogs and vultures left the park. One man emptied his automatic rifle into the sky; there was a great cheer and others took up their weapons and sprayed the treetops. Leaves and twigs and bits of bark rained down. There was a continuous rat-

tle and the ejected brass cartridges flashed golden in the
sun. An explosive device, perhaps a grenade, was detonated in the marble fountain and a thirty-foot geyser of
water erupted. A pair of officers entered the park and
were immediately surrounded by the soldiers, whose mood
swiftly changed from merry to bellicose. The officers
smiled frequently, and gestured with their hands, and then,
walking a little faster than was dignified, they left the
plaza. The soldiers cheered derisively.

A little later Martin saw them gather around the statue
of General Vargas. He could not tell what they were
doing. Their actions were a comical pantomime. But apparently they had rigged the statue with plastic explosives. Something went wrong and the charge detonated
too soon. The statue disintegrated. There was a bright
flash and the horse and rider dissolved in a cloud of dust
and hurtling rubble. Bodies were levitated with a slow
loose-limbed grace. In the instant before the noise
reached him Martin could hear the buzzing of flies and
Rodolfo's snores, small flaws in the vast silence. And
then the concussion arrived, a thunderclap, and screams,
and soon after the scene was frozen except for falling
leaves and billowing dust. Rodolfo awakened screaming.

Later the doctor and the priest moved among the dead
and wounded men. Father Perecho's voice carried clearly
to the bell tower. "I absolve thee," he said in Latin, "in the
name of the Father, the Son, and the Holy Ghost."

Martin sent word to the doctor, saying that he would
like to help, but there was no reply.

That night Martin lit a candle, placed it on the window
ledge, and got out his notebook and pen. He must write to
Katherine now. Nothing elaborate, a brief farewell that
would not be too painful for either of them.

My Dear Kit:

I do not expect to live for more than a day or two. There is not the time, I haven't the will, to explain. You may learn the truth someday.

As I write this I can see the night sky—even the most stupid of us can almost comprehend infinity while observing the stars. What can I say? Words are only the shadows of objects and ideas and emotions.

Do you remember that day many years ago when we skated twenty miles down the Wolf River? It was a very cold winter and the ice had frozen so smooth and clear that we could look down fifteen feet to the bottom. You claimed to have seen a gigantic fish. I carried brandy-laced coffee and sandwiches in my backpack, remember, and we ate lunch beneath some birch trees while a hawk carved pinwheels into the soft, incredible sky. Your cheeks were red and puffy from the cold. Your eyes teared. Your ankles hurt. We watched air bubbles flowing along beneath the ice. You laughed, spilled coffee on your new parka, remember, and I smoked the cigar that Mac had given me. Do you recall, you said, "This is a perfect day."

I mean that now is the time to be grateful, to bless our happiness together and repudiate sorrow, to celebrate the days and nights we shared. You understand, Kit, don't you? I know that you do. Grief is a waste, mourning a folly, melancholy a disease.

Raise our children to be bright and strong. Strong, not powerful, not hard. It seems to me that most of humanity's unnecessary suffering is caused by weak men. Weak leaders and weak followers. Teach the kids that they are to be neither masters nor slaves.

The constellations have revolved a few degrees since I came to stand by this window. The stars are a clock and I have learned to estimate the hour by their positions. The moon has risen and illuminated clouds which stretch and flex like swans. It is beautiful. Dogs are barking out in the night. The dogs are frightened of strange noises and quick shadows and so they bark. I suppose it's possible that there is an animal moving around in the darkness, and they can smell it, sense it, but it's more likely that they too are afraid of death, nothingness, and that is what they bark at.

All my love,
Martin

It was a sentimental and awkward letter. But what could you say, what was the right tone? He snuffed out the candle flame with his thumb and forefinger.

CHAPTER

7

One evening Father Perecho came to visit them with a wicker basket filled with food: cheese, fruit, bread and butter, beer, and a large slab of barbecued kid.

"Here is death's emissary," Martin said.

"The opposite of that," the priest said mildly. "You could call me a herald of eternal life."

"Tomorrow morning?"

"Yes."

"Both of us?"

"Yes, both. I'm sorry."

"It's absolutely certain?"

"The papers arrived an hour ago."

"Did you see the papers? Maybe there's been a mistake."

"No, Martin. I'm sorry."

Martin had no appetite but he managed to force down some food out of compliance with tradition. The condemned man ate a hearty last meal. Like Major Cabrera, he was showing off. Martin felt trapped in a difficult role in an ancient ritualistic drama. He had a part he must play.

His mouth was dry but he moistened the food with swallows of beer. There was no taste; he felt that he could just as easily have gulped wads of newspaper and rags.

Rodolfo ate gluttonously, as though unaware that he would be extinct before the meal was fully digested; and he teased the priest, saying that he had never eaten as well in his entire life, and that there were many people in his village, the country, maybe the whole world, who would gladly change places with him. Was Jesus fed so generously before *his* execution? ("He had a last supper," Father Perecho said dryly.) Well, if there was food in heaven he, Rodolfo, intended to eat like this always and leave beans and tortillas to the priests and politicians and rich landowners.

Martin did not admire him as he'd admired Cabrera: Rodolfo's courage seemed connected to stupidity or insanity. He was cheerful, sly, insolent, superior. Superior to the priest, to Martin, to death itself.

The priest seemed baffled and annoyed. He glanced inquiringly at Martin from time to time, blinked nervously, toyed with his rosary; and all the while Rodolfo ate and drank and chatted as if this were no more than a pleasant Sunday picnic.

"Did you buy the food, Father?"

"Yes."

"Church money or your own?"

"The Church's. I have no personal funds."

"Sure, I believe that."

"Believe it, it's true."

"All the Church gave me until now, Father, was little crackers and sips of wine."

"You're talking about Holy Communion," the priest said.

"Ah, but now the Church is finally, for the only time in my life, filling my belly."

The priest left soon afterwards.

There were no rains that day; the thunderclouds gathered, boiling and veined with lightning, and then dispersed.

At dusk two of the guards entered the tower, one bearing a rifle and the other a bottle of El Presidente brandy. A gift for the dead men, the tall gringo and the pisser. They joked harshly, but they had chipped in for an expensive brandy and that gesture was a denial of their hard faces and cruel wit. Martin thanked them. They seemed ashamed of their kindness. "We'll see how gringos die," one of them said. "We'll see how pissers die," the other said, and they laughed and left the tower.

Later Martin stood by the south port. There was no breeze and it was very hot. Lights burned here and there in the village. He could smell woodsmoke. Somewhere in the maze of back streets an infant cried. Bats flew erratically over the rooftops. Above he could hear the burbling of pigeons as they settled in for the night.

Every now and then he was seized by the realization that tomorrow he would die. This was his last night. He would see the sun rise one more time. That certainty penetrated his heart like a knife blade, sickening him, amputating hope. It was not an idea—the imminence of his extinction—that he could hold for long. He could apprehend it intellectually, as an abstraction, but without real belief. A rational thesis: tomorrow morning I shall die. Tomorrow morning I shall stand with my back against the wall and stare into the muzzles of eight rifles, and the weapons will recoil, puffing wisps of smoke, and I shall cease to be. But he did not wholly believe it; these thoughts were accompanied by a desperate hope and a sense that somehow he was exempt. And then once again, for an instant, he would believe, he would *know*, and he was overwhelmed.

Rodolfo sat on the floor, staring at nothing, muttering to himself, occasionally tilting the brandy bottle to drink.

Constellations, collections of remote suns, hung suspended in the indigo sky.

Martin lit a candle, placed it on the window ledge, and got out his notebook and pen.

What surprises me is the triviality of our last hours. No revelations, no conversions, no interior revolutions. Rodolfo will drink and smoke, and later he'll probably shadowbox, as he does almost every night. And here am I, writing in my notebook. Futile, ridiculous. Even the approach of death can't liberate us from our habits, ourselves. There is food left; I may eat later, and drink some of the brandy if Rodolfo leaves any.

And before morning I'll have to urinate, defecate, and I suppose I'll wash my face with the little water that's left before they arrive to lead us down the stairs. I know that neither Rodolfo nor I will die with the courage, the style, the grand defiance of Major Cabrera. Like Cabrera, I'll refuse the blindfold. Unlike Cabrera I will not ask permission to give the order to fire; that's beyond my strength. I hope I'll be able to walk, I hope my legs will support my weight. I hope I have a voice. I hope I do not shit my pants *before* they shoot me; I'll certainly shit them at death, by reflex.

There's no wind tonight and the mosquitoes have found us. (Us. I'm glad that Rodolfo will die with me, that I won't be alone. Is it possible to be more selfish? I know that Rodolfo feels the same way. We make it slightly easier for each other.) It's hot, my clothes are soaked with sweat, the dogs yap and howl, I can hear the distant percussion of explosives, and a drunk down in the plaza is singing "La Paloma." I remember reading that when the Emperor Maximilian was executed in a courtyard in Querétaro, a Mexican band played "La Paloma." A light, pretty little song. Maximilian was very brave, as I recall. His executioners—and presumably the band—had admired him. I wonder if—

Martin could not write any more.

He had started his journal upon arriving in the country. He'd thought he might someday write a book about his adventures.

He tore a page from the notebook, held an edge in the candle flame, and when it was burning well he tossed it out of the window. It was ash before reaching the ground.

He burned more pages that way. Small, brief flares in the night. Maybe someone would alert the guards. So shoot me. He tried folding some pages into paper airplanes, igniting them, and sailing them out into the darkness. They did not burn long. It was best to loosely crumple the pages, hold them in the candle flame, and then toss them between the bars. He found that if he made several balls in advance, lighted them right and left and tossed, lighted more, there might be three or four little fireballs in the air at once. Some still burned after reaching the ground.

"What are you doing?" Rodolfo asked from the darkness behind him.

"Signaling the fleet."

"Sure," Rodolfo said. "Sure, man." He was drunk. He wanted to talk. "Do you know who that priest reminds me of?"

"Be quiet. I want to think."

"Is there a heaven, Martin?"

"What's your guess?"

"There must be a heaven."

"Well, there you are."

"Tell me."

"No, there isn't. There is nothing."

"That can't be true."

"Sure, there's an afterlife, Rodolfo. And it's exactly as you've always imagined it. You'll be there very soon. Try to be patient."

"Don't be mean. Talk to me, Martin. Will you? Please? You understand things."

"I can't help you. Anyway, I have my thoughts too, you know. There are people and places I want to say good-bye to."

"Martin, talk to me. I can't stand to be alone."

"All right," he said. "All right."

Rodolfo fell into a drunken sleep several hours later. It was cooler now, with a breeze out of the north, and silent except for the barking of dogs. The stars had changed positions. Martin found that it was much too painful to think about Kit and the kids, his life, which now seemed to have been as brief and insubstantial as a dream.

It did not hurt quite as much to think about a place, the farm, where he had been happiest. That had been his only true refuge, the geographical point where he had felt whole and at peace. Home, in fact.

The farm was twelve miles from the town where Martin practiced medicine. It was situated on some gentle rolling hills above a small lake. In summer the shallow water around the shore was thick with reeds and cattails and lily pads. Red-winged blackbirds nested in the marshy area on the west end of the lake. The fishing was good; you caught panfish and bass and pike, and were sometimes surprised when a snapping turtle took the bait. In bed at night, with the window open, you could hear crickets and owls and the barking of a fox.

A hired man and his moronic son worked the arable land, growing corn and wheat and soybeans. The place lost money every year—a tax deduction. It was really a kind of play farm, a calendar farm. There were no rusting machines in the yard, no smells of manure or silage, a few riding horses but no commercial livestock. Great oaks shaded the house. Well away from the house, at the rear of the yard, there was a canted red barn, sheds and stables, slatted corncribs, an iron-grid windmill (used now as a tower for the TV antenna), and a concrete silo that looked like a medieval donjon. The orchard produced many bushels of apples and pears each fall. There were ninety-five acres in all. Poplars grew along the fence lines, and there was a thirty-acre wood of oaks and sugar maples and black walnut trees. Each summer a pair of red-winged hawks nested in a dead oak.

In autumn the leaves were ignited by sunlight into gold and amber and orange flames. The lake had a hard mineral aspect then. Waterfowl, ducks and geese, paused there on their flights south, and blackbirds swarmed over the fields.

Silence prevailed in winter. Silence and smoke. Thick braids of smoke issued from farmhouse chimneys, automobiles trailed swirling clouds of exhaust and snow, and the lakes and creeks were sometimes invisible beneath rising fogs of mist. The trees were bare. The lake frozen. There was not much color in the land during winter, grays and blacks and whites, and the crows were wriggling black dots on the snow. Horses steamed in that cold. Trees froze with reverberant cracks. The children came in from play with wet eyes and scarlet cheeks. Fence lines diminished with perspective to dark points. Withered yellow grass and corn stubble thrust up through the snow. The eye was drawn to any object that moved, a crow, a dog, a rabbit, a fisherman crossing the icc.

At night Martin and Kit and the children sat around a big fire, eating apples and walnuts.

Rodolfo had awakened. "Martin? What are you doing?"

"Thinking."

"What about?"

"A place. My family."

"What time is it?"

"Late."

"How late?"

"About four o'clock."

"So soon!"

"Yes."

"Tell me about the place and your family," Rodolfo said.

"All right."

"Sit down close to me. Talk to me. I'm afraid to die, Martin."

"So am I."

"Would I like the place and the people?"

"You would, Rodolfo, you really would."

CHAPTER

8

They were on that serpentine road that descends the coastal foothills to the sea. The right headlight of Dix's Volkswagen stabbed up into the trees that lined the road; the left, with a dim and yellowish light, illuminated less than fifty yards of asphalt. The broken white centerline flashed past like tracer bullets. Canted, shock-sprung trucks passed with their horns blaring.

"These people are in love with vehicles and guns," Dix said. "I don't know which kills more of the populace."

Katherine, smoking in the darkness alongside him, did not reply. She had spoken rarely since leaving the capital.

Flakes of broken glass and the eyes of dead animals were reflected in the headlights. Now and then the figure of a man, dressed in white cotton shirt and trousers, appeared briefly and then vanished, flicking on and off so swiftly that you couldn't be sure you hadn't imagined him. Where were the men walking to at this time of night?

They rounded a hairpin turn and below could see a small constellation of lights concentrated on the coastal plain, next to the vast black plain that was the sea.

"Is that it?" Katherine asked.

"Yes."

"What time is it?"

"A little after ten," he said. It seemed much later, more like the dismal still hour that precedes dawn, when your mouth was chalky and your eyes gritty, and your most profound truths turned into pious lies.

"Don't get your hopes too high," Dix said. "Maybe he'll show up and maybe not."

"Just who is he?"

"I really don't know. I talked to a man who talked to a man who ... This character calls himself Cortez. That's not his real name, of course."

"I still don't understand why he or someone else couldn't have met us in the city. It doesn't make sense."

A walking man flickered in the headlights and then was reabsorbed by darkness.

"Another hallucination," Dix said. "Did you see him?"

"This entire country and everyone in it are hallucinations," she replied.

They came down out of the last hills and the road curved south toward the lights. He could smell the rich salt and iodine odors of the sea now, and sense on his skin an even greater humidity. Jungleland, bananaland.

"This village used to be called Playas de los Muertos," he said. "Then, when there was a prospect of tourism, foreign and native, and the hotel was built, they changed the name to Playas del Oro. From the sands of the dead to the sands of gold. That's the mentality of the Spanish-speaking peoples—everything is either death or gold."

Most of the lights belonged to the hotel complex; the crooked dirt back streets of town were dark except for an occasional window or trembling neon. There were small groups of men on every street corner, lurching shadows, and some of them were drunk and hostile. Dix heard himself and the "puta" with him being cursed.

"Roll up your window and lock the door," he said.

They emerged onto the busier and better lighted main street and then drove south past the hotel complex and its cluster of shops and restaurants. Some of the people on the sidewalks were Americans.

Several hundred yards south of the hotel but still within its aura of light, Dix pulled the car over and parked. Evenly spaced royal palms lined the esplanade. The beach sloped down and away into a green-speckled darkness. The soft sea air was like a balm on his skin, his nerves.

"You can roll down your window now," Dix said.

They sat and listened to the dull cracking of the surf. A car passed heading north, briefly illuminating the interior of the Volkswagen.

"What now?" Katherine asked.

"We wait for Cortez."

"I'm not so sure that this is a good idea," she said in an accusing tone.

"Right, but remember that it was *your* idea."

"You should have insisted that we meet in the city."

"Mrs. Springer, you asked for a meeting, they didn't."

"It's hot. Can we wait outside in the breeze?"

"My instructions were to remain in the car."

"Your fidelity to instructions is to be commended," she said.

"Do you want to go back now?"

"No. I guess not."

Katherine removed her sandals, drew her bare feet up on the edge of the car seat, folded her arms around her knees, and stared sullenly through the windshield. She wore jeans and a cotton blouse. She looked like a teenager now. Dix supposed that she was spoiled. No doubt she had led a sheltered life as the beautiful wife of a successful doctor. She was in her early thirties, the mother of two children, and yet at times seemed virginal, untouched.

"Do you want a drink?" he asked.

"No. All right, yes."

He opened the glove box and removed a liter of dark rum, unscrewed the cap, which was shaped like a small cup, poured it full, and gave it to her. He drank directly from the bottle, a tentative sip at first, and then two big swallows. It was like arriving home after a long absence. It was as though he had lost the most interesting part of himself a while back and now found it again in this bottle.

She handed him the empty plastic cup and he was about to screw it back on the bottle when he thought, hell, why not, one more in honor of the reunion—hello, friend.

"Here comes someone."

A man strolled down the esplanade toward them. His short-sleeved white shirt was worn outside black trousers, and the leather heels of his shoes clicked on the concrete. A young man, thick black hair combed in a pompadour. He glanced into the car as he passed.

"He'll be back," Dix said. He felt fear now but not as intensely as he would have without the rum. One more drink would set him up well.

He watched the man in the rearview mirror: he proceeded forty yards down the walk and sat on a bench. His white shirt seemed to glow in the darkness. A match flared, went out, and was replaced by a glowing orange coal. He'll come over here when he's finished the cigarette, Dix thought.

"He's so young," Katherine said. "Do you think. . .?"

"I'm sure of it. One of them."

"This is like a dream."

"No it isn't. It's real, damn real."

"I don't know if I should giggle or be scared out of my wits."

"The latter."

"May I have some more rum?"

"Sure," Dix said, grateful because now he would be able to drink without appearing to need it too much.

They each had a cupful of the rum. In the rearview mirror Dix saw a spray of sparks as the man flicked away his cigarette.

"Okay," he said.

The man stood up, looking both ways down the boulevard, then walked toward the car, but more rapidly than before, in haste now and with evident purpose. He stopped and, resting his palms on the car's roof, looked down at Dix.

"You are Dix?" Deex.

"Yes."

"I am Cortez."

"Okay."

"The man lifted his shirt front so that Dix could see the revolver thrust into his belt. "I don't die alone," he said. "You understand?"

"I understand," Dix said, and it occurred to him that he was probably less frightened than this young man.

Now Cortez leaned down and gazed at Katherine. It was a stare that seemed fueled by loathing, but in a respectful tone he said, "Good evening, lady."

"Good evening," Kathcrine said.

"I am Cortez."

"Are you really? I am Katherine."

He reflexively lifted his right hand a few inches before denying the impulse to salute or remove a hat or tug at his forelock.

A car went by, heading south, and Cortez turned anxiously to watch it move down the boulevard. He had a sloping forehead, a fleshy hooked nose, a receding chin, and in profile looked, Dix thought, like a figure in a Mayan fresco. He was in his middle twenties and very thin—no, emaciated.

"Okay." Cortez got into the backseat of the car. "Drive that way—*derecho*."

Dix started the car, drove across the centerline, and headed south. Far ahead the taillights of the car that had passed them vanished around a curve. Cortez smelled of cheap hair oil and cheap aftershave. After a few blocks a motorcycle with two men mounted on it pulled out of a side street and followed them.

"My friends," Cortez said.

The road ran straight for two miles and then curved leftward, following the southern arm of the bay. The motorcycle behind them had no muffler and backfired with a fusillade of loud cracks whenever it slowed. Some low, thickly treed hills obscured views of the ocean.

"Don't be afraid, lady," Cortez said.

"I'm not afraid," Katherine said. There was no fear evident in her voice or posture.

"Slow this automobile," Cortez said. "You see that light?" (A large orange reflector, fixed to a tree trunk, glowed in the headlights.) "There is a road. Drive down."

It was a narrow muddy lane bordered by shrubs and trees that scraped the sides of his car and formed an arch overhead. The motorcycle, crackling furiously, followed a few yards behind.

"Where are we going?" Katherine asked.

"Don't worry, lady. A place I know. A place to talk."

The road opened into a clearing in which Dix could see a dozen scattered huts, miserable shelters built of poles implanted vertically in the ground and roofed and walled with palm fronds. Beer cans and broken glass were reflected in the headlight beams. He stopped the car. A naked man appeared in the doorway of a hut, stared toward the car for a moment, urinated, and then went back inside.

Dix set the emergency brake, turned off the engine and lights, and waited for a command. The motorcycle was silent and dark now too. Dogs barked, a baby cried piteously, somewhere a man was drunkenly singing, and beneath and through all those sounds came the periodic drumming of the surf.

"Pues," Cortez said. "We go."

"I have a bottle of rum," Dix said.

"It's okay."

"I'll bring it."

"Okay, okay, we go."

Dix, clutching the rum bottle by its neck, opened his door and got out. One of the motorcycle riders carried an unlit lantern; Dix could smell the kerosene. The other man walked with a limp. The five of them went down through the tiny village. Shadowy dogs, paroxysmal with rage, advanced and retreated. The baby was still crying. The drunken man still sang a love song. No lights burned in the huts. Dix expected to be taken to one of the huts but Cortez led them through the village and down to the beach. The sand was deep and wind-rippled.

The moon was high now and ignited the sands of the beach and cast a silver filigree over the ocean. Breaking waves glowed with a green bioluminescence, and green froth rolled hissing up the slope.

They reached a *palapa*, four poles set vertically into the ground and roofed with palm fronds. Inside there was a picnic table. One of the men lit the kerosene lantern and hung it from a nail. Dix and Katherine sat on one side of the table, the three men on the other side.

"Pues," Cortez said.

Dix placed the bottle of rum on the table. "A drink, gentlemen?" He offered cigarettes around; only Katherine refused. She was still sulking. They smoked. Dix saw that the other men would not drink first and so he unscrewed the cap, tilted the bottle, and drank. The limping man was short and thick-bodied and his sweaty face looked as though it had been chiseled out of cedar. The other man was older, maybe forty, with hands that had been deformed by labor. A peasant.

The breeze evaporated Dix's sweat and dryly rustled in the palm leaves overhead.

"Es su mujer?" Cortez asked.

"No," Dix said. Then he thought that he should have said yes. If she was not his woman then she was anyone's? Anyway, what an odd question: She was the wife of Martin Springer, the man she hoped to ransom.

"What did he say about me?" Katherine asked.

"Nothing. Small talk."

"I'm the only *mujer* here, Dix."

He gestured toward the bottle. The three men drank, first Cortez, then the Limping Man, and last the Peasant. Dix resisted the urge to wipe the bottle's mouth before drinking. Only a third of the rum remained.

"How goes the Revolution?" he asked.

"We win the fight," Cortez replied. "You will see."

"I believe it."

"You believe we will win?"

"Yes, eventually you'll win." Which, he thought, will signal the commencement of the counterrevolution.

"Are you communists?" Katherine asked.

Cortez looked at her. He did not reply immediately. Again Dix thought he saw malice in his expression, some private malevolence, but his voice was empty of emotion.

"Yes. Yes, we are communists if communists believe that the people should not starve. We are communists if communists believe that men should not be slaves. We are communists if communists believe that fascists should not stick bayonets into babies. We are communists if communists believe that truth and justice are possible in this world. Then yes, we are communists."

He seemed exhausted by the effort required to recite this catechism in English.

Morose, he rested for a time, and then pointed up toward the collection of huts. "Babies die of—of shit. *Cómo se dice?*"

"Dysentery," Dix said.

"Yes. Babies now, this night maybe, die of dy-sen-tery so close to you now, lady. Babies are sick but there is no money for doctors or medicine. Babies have no food—do you hear that tiny baby crying? And you, lady, you have expensive earrings, you have expensive gold watch, you have expensive diamond ring, and the babies they go without food."

Dix looked at Katherine and saw that indeed she wore small ruby earrings, a gold wristwatch, and next to her wedding band a ring with a diamond as big as a cashew. Was she crazy, coming to a meeting like this wearing valuable jewelry?

"Babies suffer," Cortez said. "Babies die."

Cortez looked at her watch and diamond ring.

"Like hell," she said.

The Limping Man and the Peasant looked back and forth between Cortez and Katherine; they did not understand the words but the mood was clear.

"You're wonderful, Cortez," Katherine said with a bright, false smile. "You're a hero to devote your life to succoring the poor, miserable babies. I would sacrifice my jewelry to the cause if I were a saint like you. I'm not. But I do admire your compassion and devotion to the little suffering babies."

"Easy, easy," Dix told her. Jesus. She talked to these men as if they were naughty members of her Sunday

School class. Dix drank some rum, drank again, then slid the bottle across to Cortez.

"Who can account for the misery of the world?" Dix said. "Who was it—Ivan Karamazov?—who declared that he could not believe in God as long as one innocent child suffered?"

Cortez drank, then the Limping Man, then the Peasant. The bottle was empty now. Good-bye friend. It was going to be a long tough night without booze. But then Cortez told the Peasant to go up to the village and find something to drink. The man obediently arose from the table and started walking toward the huts.

"Pues," Cortez said. "Did you bring the money?"

"Did I bring the money? No, I didn't bring the money. Did you bring my husband?"

"He is safe, lady."

"Where?"

"Here." .

"Here?"

"Yes."

"In this area?"

"Yes. He is happy. He says hello."

"How nice. So sweet. How much money do you want?"

"One million dollars."

"Is that all? Why, that's not enough to feed the starving babies for very long. I'll write you a check for five million."

"Katherine . . ." Dix said.

"Ten million! So that bad men will stop sticking bayonets into babies."

"Katherine, for Christ's sake!" Dix lit a cigarette and pushed the package across to Cortez and the Limping Man.

Above, the dogs were barking at something or someone, probably the Peasant. And below the swells lifted, speckled with green, turned concave and crested, with green foam hissing along the rims, and then crashed down, entirely green now, glowing with the same color as fox fire or the luminous dial of a clock. Each wave collapsed with a crack and then a prolonged roar. The foam advanced to within a few yards of the *palapa*. It was a hot night, blue and gold, with the palm trees silhouetted like black paper cutouts. Our bodies will voyage out on the tide, Dix thought. We'll be food for crabs.

"Pues," Cortez said morosely.

The Peasant returned with two bottles that contained a cloudy amber liquid. The bottles were sealed with corks. There were no labels. Home distillate. It smelled like naphtha and burned like phosphorus in the mouth, throat, esophagus, and belly. Jesus. Keep it down. Killer juice. Dix realized that he was more than half drunk. He'd thought he was too scared to be much affected by alcohol. Cortez and his friends were not yet drunk but they were resolutely working toward that state.

"Don't drink anymore," Katherine said. "Please, Dix?"

Cortez pushed one of the bottles toward her.

"Take a sip of the napalm," Dix said. "Show them that you're a good sport."

"Good sport! My God!"

She refused to drink or even fake drinking, of course. Of course. If only she would relax, loosen up a little, make friends, they might be able to pacify these citizens. Her coldness and scorn were a provocation. They were not *bad* men. They loved their mothers, respected their fathers, protected their sisters, revered the Holy Family and all the saints. No doubt their eyes teared at baptismals and weddings and funerals. And if they had coin to spare they might very well give to lepers and hydrocephalics.

The Limping Man, grinning, reached across the table

and half affectionately, half aggressively, ruffled Dix's hair. *"Qué dice, hombre?"*

Dix smiled at him, a tough masculine smile, he hoped, but it felt like a novocaine grimace.

"This is ridiculous," Katherine said. "Let's go."

They were cockroach poor, hungry half the days of their lives, ignorant, stupid, angry men who were getting drunk. They had weapons and the group irresponsibility that incubates crime. And they were infused with the narrow patriotism that justifies banditry and murder. Basically decent men, maybe, but this was a society ruptured by civil war, blood-drenched—you read about last night's atrocity in this morning's newspaper. Oh, shit, Dix thought. Deal around me.

"Let's go," Katherine said. "Now. Please."

"Not yet," he said.

"Now, please."

Cortez impassively watched them.

"Not just yet. I got to figure."

Cortez, drunk, seemed to have retreated deep within himself. He was not interested in their dispute. The Peasant sat quietly, like a docile child, but his eyes shone now and his mouth worked as if he were tasting something deliciously sweet. The Limping Man was more animated, squirming, smiling at each of them, happy at the moment but eventually a bad drunk—Dix knew his drunks.

"Can't you see?" Katherine said. "Oh Dix, can't you see, Dix?"

Now the Limping Man wanted to arm wrestle. No way. If Dix beat him the man would become sullen; if he lost the man would become arrogant; if Dix flatly refused the test the Limping Man would feel that his manhood had been slighted. Ignore the dumb challenge.

Cortez lifted his chin. "I live in the United States three year," he said. "I know your country. Yes, they call me 'nigger.' They call me greaseball. The Ku Klux Klan beat me up. The fascist police want to castrate me. Their dogs bite my legs."

Dix stared at him. What? What?

"Capitalists stole my nine-year-old sister. They make her fuck in your dirty movies."

What? The kid has been crazed by Party pamphlets.

Cortez nodded gravely. "Then they kill her."

"I wonder if her mouse hole is surrounded by blond fur," the Limping Man said to the Peasant.

"What did that man say about me?" Katherine asked.

"Nothing. A joke. Don't be so sensitive."

"Dix, what did he *say*?"

One of the bottles was empty now, the other two-thirds full. It didn't taste quite as bad now. It was killer juice, though—sugarcane distillate aged one day—but welcome at the moment. I'll go back on the wagon tomorrow, he thought.

"Please-don't-drink-any-more," Katherine said in her icy princess tone.

"I sympathize with your revolutionary goals," Dix told Cortez. "Liberty. Equity. Justice. Love."

"Revenge," Cortez said. "Blood." He nodded solemnly and took a cigarette from the package on the table. Dix struck a match for him.

"I want the world to be right," Cortez said drunkenly. "Why can't it be right?"

"Dix," Katherine said. "For God's sake!"

"We'll make things right," he told Cortez. "By Christ, we will make them right, Cortez. Okay? Okay?"

"Okay."

"Dix," Katherine said. "Give me the keys to your car."

"Gringas are all whores," the Limping Man said.

"Did you ever fuck a gringa?" the Peasant asked.

"Twice, I think. Maybe once."

This is almost funny, Dix thought. Almost. The Marx Brothers go psycho. Groucho, Chico, and Harpo rape, maim, and kill on a jolly Latin romp.

"The keys, Dix," she demanded.

"Stay cool," he said.

"The car keys, you bastard. I'm not hanging around for the gang rape."

"Listen," Dix said to Cortez. "We got to talk. About the money, about her husband."

"There is plenty of time."

"No. We've got to settle about the ransom."

"Later, man."

"Now. Look, let's take the bottle and go for a little walk. Okay? We've got to settle things. The lady is rich—do you understand?"

"Later, later."

"Now, goddamn it!" Dix said, hearing a high desperate note in his voice and thinking, that's not the way, but continuing, "Jesus, Cortez, do you want to be rich or not? Get up, come on." He snatched the bottle off the table and walked away. Come on, Cortez, come on, baby. He looked over his shoulder. Cortez was rising, following now, probably pursuing the bottle more than him. Come on, baby.

They stopped and faced each other fifty feet from the *palapa*. Katherine and the two men were frozen in the amber lanternlight, an awkward tableau. The sea was to Dix's left, rising, sizzling, crashing down with a carbonated green radiance. The water smelled like dead fish.

Dix drank, passed the bottle to Cortez. "Listen, pal, you can't get a million. No way, my friend. She can't raise that much so fast. Three hundred thousand dollars, no more. Tomorrow."

"I don't know, man."

You frigging penny-ante creep, Dix thought, you

cheapjack hustler, you rickety tubercular home for worms.

"Look, my friend, do you want the money or not? Say so now. If you don't, we'll walk. Three hundred thousand dollars tomorrow morning. It's in the bank. So, do you know Medina? Do you know Cintron? They're good friends of mine, they have to have their share. I have to have my share. Hey, do you think I'm one of the suckers? If we don't profit from this you'll be crucified. They know I'm here. You can't keep it all, Cortez. She gives me the six hundred thousand, I give you half. Don't be greedy. Hey, come on, man, are you stupid? Do you understand what I'm telling you?"

"I understand," Cortez said dully.

Dix glanced toward the table. The Limping Man had moved around the table and now sat next to Katherine. He smiled at her.

"Cortez, what do you want? Three hundred thousand dollars or nothing? It's your choice. Make it fast."

The Limping Man put his arm around Katherine's shoulder; she twisted out of his grasp and stood up.

Dix drank from the bottle, three long swallows. It burned no more than ordinary good whiskey now; he was anesthetized.

"Dix!" Katherine cried. The Limping Man was pawing her.

Cortez watched them for a moment and then shouted something to the Limping Man, who released her and returned to his place.

"Okay," Cortez said.

"You've made the right decision, kid. Call me at the hotel tomorrow morning."

"Give me some money," Cortez said.

"What?"

"Some money. For tonight."

"Oh, sure." He removed his wallet and withdrew all the currency—thank God he'd cashed a check this morning. Maybe the kid was smart enough to understand that the ransom was bullshit, and he was willing to settle for this little extortion. "Here's two hundred dollars. Take your horny friends to a whorehouse."

They shook hands.

"Pleasure doing business with you, kid."

He and Katherine walked slowly up the beach. Dix would not permit himself to look back to see if they were following. He could taste stomach acids, vomit, in the back of his throat. Dogs barked. The baby cried. "I'll drive," Katherine said. The car would not start. She flooded the engine. Dogs, their snarling faces the embodiment of evil, stalked around the car. It started then, finally. Katherine did not speak until they had rounded the curve and ahead could see the gaudy carnival lights of the hotel complex.

"You son of a bitch," she said.

"Look, this whole thing was your idea."

"The booze wasn't my idea."

"Well, it's over. We're safe."

"Revolutionary leaders," she said scornfully. "Cheap crooks, jackals."

"I don't understand it. I know that my contact in the capital is genuine. I'm sorry. I really am sorry. I don't know what happened."

"I'll tell you what happened. Your contact turned you over to his relatives or friends for the fleecing. That's what happened, Dix old boy."

"Let's forget it. It's over."

"And you got drunk. Are you crazy, getting drunk in a situation like that?"

"Katherine, Jesus, you didn't understand them. They were very dangerous."

"You *made* them dangerous. You started them drinking, you got drunk yourself. You're still drunk."

"I'm sorry. Leave me alone. I'm very sorry."

He slept most of the way back to the capital. It was not a deep sleep; he wanted to remain partly aware, and not snore or drool or cry out.

Back in his room at the hotel, Dix showered and then stalked around naked, leaving footprints on the tiles. "I am sorry to inform you, General," he told the pitted bronze head of General Vargas, "most grieved, sir, indeed, to notify you that you have been court-martialed. For cowardice, Major Vargas, for drunkenness, Captain Vargas, for failing your knightly vows, Sergeant Vargas."

He sat on the edge of the bed and lit a cigarette. "Ah, well," he said. "It's hard, very hard, Corporal."

Dix thought, I'll have to buy sunglasses for my bleeding eyes. And aspirin for my hemorrhaging brain. Two Bloody Marys before lunch, to steady the hand, and maybe—no, definitely—three or four beers to reduce the velocity of descent. And then back here for sixteen hours of sleep. Go back on the wagon.

"Stand back, you poxy hunchbacks," Dix said, rising and hurrying into the bathroom.

CHAPTER

9

A bird had entered Katherine's room. She saw it when she awakened. It was perched on the floor lamp's shade. Katherine had left the French doors open last night because of the heat. The air was cool now and she could tell by the light that it was early, just after sunrise. The bird was about the size of a cardinal and had a similar thick, seed-cracking beak. Its body was bright yellow, its wings and head (as if hooded) an iridescent purplish-black. Legs and beak were flesh-colored. Some kind of finch, probably. Now she watched from the bed as it ruffled its feathers.

Katherine made a clicking sound with her tongue. "Go on," she said. "The doors are open. You can find your way out."

She thought about last night. Dix drunk, the three stupid men who had dignified their criminality by calling themselves revolutionaries, the interminable drive back to the capital while Dix slept and she wept.

"Go!" Katherine said to the bird.

I will not cry anymore, she thought, and then she cried for a time.

Martin, she thought. I must stop pitying myself and think always of Martin.

The finch panicked when she got out of bed, and flew around and around the room, chirping. Poor little bird. She went toward it with her hands cupped; it flew into a wall and fell fluttering to the tiles. It huddled there, crouched small, feathers crooked. Katherine threw the blouse she had worn last night over the bird. It did not struggle. She slipped her hand beneath the cloth and took the bird in her hand.

"Poor thing, are you hurt?" With her left hand she smoothed its neck feathers. She could feel its warmth and rapidly beating heart. Its feet curled lightly around her ring finger. "Huh, sweetie, okay?" She gently kissed its tiny head. The bird writhed, twisted in her hand, and bit her lower lip. "Sorry, baby." She carried the bird out onto the balcony and released it. It fell almost to the street, fluttering, recovered, and flew off toward the park.

Katherine went into the bathroom and looked at her reflection in the mirror. The cut on her lip oozed a single dark drop of blood. She wiped it away with tissue and another drop formed, and then another.

Katherine carried the blood-speckled tissue into the other room and sat on the bed. Perhaps, she thought, the bird was a symbol: an occult message informing her that Martin was now free. He had been imprisoned, as the bird was confined in her room; but, like the bird, Martin had been released. What was the meaning of her small wound, the blood? Had Martin been hurt? No, she refused to believe that.

Katherine had not been superstitious until recently. She'd always been scornful of those who required the consolation of the supernatural—intrusive gods and mystic auguries and prophetic dreams. And yet now, since Martin's disappearance, she was constantly the prey of such irrational obsessions. Numbers were especially powerful: yesterday she was dismayed to learn that the hotel's street address was 849. She was represented by the eight, Martin by the nine, and the four was a hostile agent keeping them apart. And eight, four, and nine added up to twenty-one, an ill-omened pair that arithmetically combined to make three, a numeral that had the stink of the grave about it.

Numbers combined with alphabetical letters were doubly significant: a headline in yesterday's English-language newspaper had read, D. R. MARTINEZ TO DIE. Katherine was sickened even before she found the formula. D. (Domingo) R. (Rafael) Martinez was scheduled to die for his "anti-democratic" actions. So then: Dr. Martin/ez to die. Phonetically, the *e* and *z* became "is." Thus: Dr. Martin Is To Die. The original headline contained fifteen letters, which was fairly benevolent, but if you counted the punctuation you got eighteen, one and eight (I am eight, one is the devil), numbers of dreadful portent.

It was all crazy, of course, madly primitive. She would never tell anyone about her obsessions, even Martin, or her compulsions—the way she had to have every object in the room in its certain place, at the correct angle to all the other objects; or how she refused to speak her children's names to strangers for fear that she would be relinquishing a terrible power ... It was insane, Katherine knew that, but she could not turn off the continuous flow of fearful calculation.

She dabbed at her sore lip with the tissue. Damn. She was exhausted, she'd slept only an hour or two last night, but there were things to be done. I've got to do all I can to help Martin. Katherine missed Martin, she missed her children, she missed her mother, she missed the farm, she missed ... No, I will *not* cry!

She wept for a while and then got the hiccups. Hiccuping, laughing miserably, she went into the bathroom to shower. It is up to me, she thought, and she was terrified. I'm not strong, the world never made me be strong, and I'm afraid that it's too late now to learn how to be strong.

Martin, you Sunday supplement saint, you left us alone.

CHAPTER

1 0

Dawn lay just beyond the horizon now. Light was coming to the east coast, sweeping in over the ocean and up the beaches and across the coastal marshes and along the lowlands toward the capital. Even now a pink light was glowing on the glaciers of the higher volcanoes. Night prevailed here in Tepazatlán, but the moon was down, and there was a cool freshness in the air, a momentary autumn. The dogs had ceased barking an hour ago. And now, out in the darkness, a cock crowed. Strutting bully cock. Other cocks around the village answered its challenge. Chickens heralding the dawn.

"I'm sick," Rodolfo said.

Martin did not reply.

"I'm really sick, man." The coal of his cigarette pulsed in the darkness. "I'm so sick I think I'm going to die." A short laugh, a cough.

By now light would be penetrating the capital, reflecting off the high windows, creating shadows, evaporating the mist. Moving light, now illuminating the corn and cane fields west of the city, etching coconut palms, crawling up the forested slopes—insinuating light.

"Oh, I am so sick, hombre."

"You drank too much," Martin said.

"I drank too much. Of course I drank too much. I drank it all. Why not? Tell me why I shouldn't drink it all?"

"I'm sorry, Rodolfo."

"You're sorry. What good will that do me? You're sorry. The priest is sorry. The firing squad is sorry. Jesus is sorry."

"They'll be coming soon."

"He tells me that they will be coming soon. He thinks I don't know that. Shit. Shit, man, don't you think I know that they'll be coming soon?"

"Courage, Rodolfo."

"Courage, he says. He says, they say. Mother, father, priest, sergeant, majordomo, patron. Be a good boy, Rodolfo. Eat, work, sleep, Rodolfo. Courage. Vote, Rodolfo, fight, Rodolfo, and die, Rodolfo. Thank you very much. Marry, have babies, Rodolfo. Oh, yes, thank you. Starve, Rodolfo, starve your babies. Thank you. Kill, Rodolfo. Thank you. Die, Rodolfo. Thank you for this opportunity. Thank you, thank you, thank you. I thank you all for this fucking life."

False dawn: the eastern sky was slowly being infused with a weak light. Stars gradually faded, details emerged from the darkness; trees, buildings, the empty plaza, and finally the distant mountains.

"Thank you, thank you all very much. I wish I could return all the shit they've given me."

A yellow light shone up through the bell-rope holes in the floor. Martin lay prone and looked down into the room below; a lantern had been lighted and hung from a nail; two of the men were up and moving around, drawing water for coffee, slicing bread; the third still lay cocooned in his blankets.

"Do you think it will hurt?" Rodolfo asked.

Martin got to his feet. "No. They can hardly miss our vital organs at that range."

"Well, what if they do miss? What if they flinch? What if each one of them leaves it up to the others to kill us?"

"They shot well enough at Cabrera."

"But what if they only wound?"

"Don't worry. Dead or wounded, the lieutenant will promptly shoot you at the base of your skull."

"I want it over. Let it come now if it's going to come. What are they waiting for?"

Martin could smell coffee and frying bacon. He was lightheaded from fatigue. His eyes were gritty and his tongue tasted sour from the night without sleep.

"I'm sick. I have a headache."

"Shut up," Martin said.

The village was awakening: he could hear the clatter of a milk cart's wheels on the cobblestones, a woman's voice floating on the air, and farther away, the abrupt rumble of a car motor. Violations of the predawn hush. A dark figure walked diagonally through the park. Above her, inky blots in the trees, the vultures were stirring, stretching their wings, moving crabwise along the branches. They were not ready to fly; they would wait for the sun to heat the earth and create the thermals which enabled them to rise and glide with such gentle grace.

"Do you have any cigarettes?" Rodolfo asked.

"No."

"Do you think they'll give us breakfast?"

"I thought you wanted it over."

"A little coffee—some bacon and eggs. What would it hurt them?"

"Could you eat now, Rodolfo?"

"I'm hungry."

The sun was rising now. You could see it move in relation to the horizon. The clouds were stained. The sunrise looked like bloody lacerations in the flesh tones of the sky, arterial bleeding. The sun appeared elongated as it separated from the land, then it regained its disk shape and, while climbing, lost color. Soon it was silvery, blurred around the edges, and you could almost see the firestorms raging inside. Fusion holocausts.

Martin turned away. Black flecks floated across his field of vision. A retinal sun the size of a dime continued to burn after he closed his eyes. He folded his arms on the window ledge and lowered his face into them. Rodolfo was right; they were taking too long. These extra minutes were not a gift but a torture. Martin did not believe that he would be able to control himself much longer.

He heard a sound in the churchyard, lifted his head and stood quietly for a moment, then moved to the south-facing port. The red gate in the wall had been opened. The young lieutenant, his back straight, his boots, belt, and holster highly polished, was crossing the yard. He moved briskly. His bootheels kicked up dust. A man of pride, dignity, with a sense of duty. Of proper ceremony. He crossed the yard and entered the back door of the church. To pray? No, probably to alert the priest.

Now other uniformed men—boys, really—came through the gate. Yawning and sleepy-eyed, scratching, they straggled into the churchyard. One of them coughed. Another carried a half-eaten tortilla. Their rifles were slung over their shoulders on leather straps. Kids, six of them. No, here came another, and one more—eight. They milled aimlessly around the churchyard for a moment and then relaxed; a couple of them sat down, the others remained standing. Cigarettes were passed around, matches flared, smoke uncoiled slowly in the still air.

"What's happening?" Rodolfo asked. He was sitting on the floor with his back against the wall. His legs were splayed. Near him were the empty brandy bottle, bits of food, crushed cigarette butts. The flesh around his eyes was puffy. Each hair of his beard stood out against the pallor of his skin.

Now the back door of the church opened and Father Perecho and the lieutenant emerged. They were quarreling in whispers. The priest's cassock trailed in the dust. He carried his breviary. His hair had been wetted and still showed the comb tracks.

The boy soldiers gathered into a sloppy kind of attention, but the two men ignored them and walked toward the base of the tower.

"Are you ready?" Martin asked.

"Ready! You want to know if I am ready? Are you crazy? Of course I'm not ready!"

They heard voices in the room below: Father Perecho, the lieutenant, the guards. Now men were ascending the stairway. They reached the landing. A clink as the iron key was fitted into the old iron lock. The tumblers turned. The door swung inward, creaking. Two of the guards, bearing rifles, entered warily and then separated.

"Don't be difficult," one of them said.

"Get up," the other said to Rodolfo.

Rodolfo tried to rise, fell back, and then, using the wall for support, struggled erect. His cheeks were wet but he was not crying now. He was unsteady, still drunk, and seemed surprised to have so little control over his body.

"You first," a guard said to Martin, gesturing with his rifle.

"Martin?" Rodolfo said.

Martin crossed the room, passed through the doorway, and paused on the landing. Another guard, aiming a rifle at him, was standing at the foot of the stairs. Beyond him were the lieutenant, his pistol drawn, and Father Perecho. Their bodies were foreshortened by his perspective; they looked squat, dwarfish.

Martin descended the stairway. He reached the floor and was commanded to place his hands behind his back; he complied and handcuffs were locked around his wrists.

"Over there," the lieutenant said. "Sit down."

Martin walked a few paces and sat on a wooden bench. Now the other two guards descended the stairway. "He's drunk," one of them said. "He wants you to hear his confession."

Father Perecho nodded. He hesitated for a moment, as if gathering nerve, and then climbed the steps to the bell tower.

"What was he drinking?" the lieutenant asked.

"Brandy."

"Where did he get it?"

"I don't know."

"He's your prisoner. I want to know where he got the brandy."

"What does it matter, for Christ's sake!" the guard said.

The lieutenant flushed angrily but did not speak. He was in his middle twenties, Martin thought, thin, with a bony face and a disciplined slit of a mouth and feverishly bright eyes. He holstered his pistol, snapped the flap closed, and looked impatiently toward the ceiling.

Father Perecho and Rodolfo were talking quietly above them. First the priest and then Rodolfo, the priest again, and then Rodolfo spoke for several minutes in a near whisper. The priest said something.

The lieutenant glanced at his watch. Martin noticed that the index finger of his left hand had been severed below the knuckle. The rounded stub was pink and glossy.

A rectangular block of light slanted in through a window high on the east wall. Dust specks floating in the light were incandesced to gold. The three bell ropes were like gold braid where the light touched them. On the table were some dirty plates and glasses and worn pornographic magazines. There was a tier of bunks against one wall, clothing lockers against another, and in the corner a fifty-five-gallon drum that served as a toilet. Flies crawled around the hole in the lid. The room stank of excrement and unwashed bodies and sour clothing and animal fats.

"Don't you want to talk to the priest?" a guard asked.

Martin shook his head.

"It can't hurt to talk to the priest. I would. What if they are right? I don't believe in it myself, but still, what if they are right?"

Martin could hear the remote clatter of a helicopter. At first it was hardly louder than the buzzing of the flies. The sound swelled, approached, became a hard thumping clatter that passed overhead and then moved down toward the river. It was the supply helicopter bringing in more guns, more ammunition, more explosives, more tools of death.

"It's that devil Fuerte," the guard said.

The tower door opened and the priest and Rodolfo came down the stairs. Rodolfo seemed even drunker now.

"Okay, let's move," the lieutenant said.

Rodolfo, supported by two guards, went outside. The priest followed.

The third guard and the lieutenant looked down at Martin. Their expressions were quizzical rather than threatening. They weren't angry. They weren't sympathetic. They were curious.

Martin rose from the bench and preceded them out of the room. The sun was warm on his face. He was assaulted by the colors: the dark blue of the sky, the lavender hue of the shadows, the black stones of the church and campanile, the dust as gray and powdery as ashes.

Rodolfo, a few paces away, suddenly bent over and

vomited. The guards jumped back, protecting their boots and pantlegs. Rodolfo convulsed again and again, spewing vomit.

Now the priest took Martin's arm and led him away.

"I've given your letter to a man I trust."

"What?"

"He came to me yesterday. He was in town for only a few hours. He agreed to take your letter and mail it when he could."

"Letter?"

"The letter you wrote to your wife."

"Oh. Yes."

"Martin?"

"I understand."

"If he has a little luck it will be done. Your wife will receive the letter."

"Thank you."

"Martin," the priest said, embracing him.

The lieutenant was cursing when they returned to the group. One of the guards trotted across the churchyard. What was the problem? Ah, the faces, of course, the round brown faces peering over the gate and wall. Children spying on the executions. They must chase away the children.

"Let them watch," Martin said.

The lieutenant stared at him.

Really, he thought, why not let them witness the murders? Maybe anything that would shame us to do in front of children should not be done.

"Bastards," Rodolfo said. "Assassins."

Now the children were gone and the firing squad was forming into a line.

"Do you want the blindfold?" the lieutenant asked.

Martin shook his head.

"All right. Walk it."

They passed through a shadow, cool and dark, and out

again into the burning sunlight. Martin's clothes were soaked with sweat. Sweat burned his eyes. Rodolfo, helped by two of the guards, was nearby. His breathing was fast and rattly. He smelled of vomit. Ahead was the bullet-pitted wall where Major Cabrera and other men had died. There were holes and sprays of fine cracks in the adobe plaster. A stream of ants emerged from one of the holes. Martin felt a hand on his shoulder. He turned.

The guards retreated across the churchyard. The sun was blinding. The guards, the firing squad, the priest, and the lieutenant were faceless shadows, as insubstantial as figures on a film negative in the scintillating glare.

"Martin," Rodolfo said. "Are they really going to do it?"

CHAPTER

1 1

Martin had ceased to believe that time moved point by point into the future and receded equally into the past. No, time was like a cloud that penetrated everywhere and everything. Birth and death were nearly simultaneous. He was being born this instant, wet and bawling; now his blood was clotting in the ashy soil of the churchyard, drawing flies. These few minutes were his lifetime.

On his left Rodolfo hoarsely cried out, *"Viva el Cristo Rey!"* No one noticed him. He was early; the firing squad was not quite ready.

The boys slid back the bolts of their rifles and the lieutenant—was it possible?—was looking into the chambers. To see that each contained a cartridge?

"Viva el Cristo Rey!" Rodolfo cried again, his voice trailing off to a whisper. No one cared about the gesture. He had been preparing his valorous exclamation for days (he'd turned against the revolution that was killing him), and now it was ignored.

The morning was bright, none had ever been more purely brilliant, and yet Martin had difficulty seeing. It was like looking through another's eyeglasses, clear on the periphery but blurred in the center.

The lieutenant, hands behind his back, leather boots, belt, and holster glistening, moved down the line of boy soldiers.

Father Perecho stood ten yards away from the firing squad, reading his breviary. The edges of its pages were gilded. His lips moved as he read. Once he raised his eyes and recited from memory. The skirts of his black cassock were dusty. He wore sandals with tire-tread soles. The priest seemed remote in time and space. They all did.

Martin could hear Rodolfo's rapid breathing, smell his vomit, and smell excrement as well—he had lost control of his sphincter.

A dog limped around the corner of the tower, a yellowish bitch nearly bald with mange. Its ribs and vertebrae were outlined against the skin. It halted and stood splay-legged for a moment, staring, and then, lowering its head and tail, slunk back around the tower.

Now the lieutenant was backing away from the field of fire. Now the priest lowered his breviary. Now the boys were raising their rifles. It was happening at last. It seemed to Martin that he had been waiting for this moment all of his life; it was like the fulfillment of prophecy.

But now there were shouts and curses beyond the wall, blasphemous invocations, and then someone began kicking the gate. Spaced, powerful kicks; a board split lengthwise. The gate shook on its hinges. Then there were two pistol shots, deep cracks that reverberated down the narrow street.

"It's Fuerte, you degenerate slime! Open this gate!"

Martin observed this dully, without curiosity. More madness. He was dead; it did not concern him.

The lieutenant sent one of the guards to the gate; he slid back the iron bolts and was nearly knocked down as the door was kicked inward. A big, bearded man loped into the churchyard. He wore clean, pressed green fatigues with the trousers bloused inside paratrooper's boots. Gold insignia flashed on his shirt's shoulder loops—a colonel. He carried a .45 pistol and screamed, "Who's in command here? What son of a bitch wants to join those men against the wall?"

The lieutenant stepped forward a pace and stiffly saluted. "Colonel Fuerte, I have orders—"

"So it's you, Gabaldon!" the man said, advancing. "I should have known. I find you wherever unarmed men are being shot. By Christ, I think I'll save your honor by sending you to the serious fighting."

The lieutenant fumbled with the button on his breast pocket. "Colonel, I have orders—"

"Signed by whom?"

"Signed by General Gutierrez."

"General Gutierrez," the colonel said scornfully. He began pacing back and forth in front of the lieutenant. "General Gutierrez is in Cuba. Two-thirds of the Revolutionary Council is in Cuba, eating well and manufacturing rhetoric and screwing the whores. Don't talk to me about General Gutierrez, you egg-sucking dog."

He snatched the papers from Gabaldon's hand and turned his back.

It was hot. Needles of light glittered on the church windows and rifle barrels and in the mica-flecked stones. Heat collected in the right angle between the ground and the wall. It was silent now, here and beyond the wall. No one moved while the colonel slowly read and reread the papers.

"Martin?" Rodolfo said. "What are they doing?"

"I don't know."

"I don't understand what this is about, Martin."

Martin closed his eyes for a moment.

"That man is here to save me. I told you it was all a bad mistake."

Now the colonel returned one sheet of paper to the lieutenant, tore the other in quarters, and stuffed the scraps into a pocket. "Shoot the deserter," he said. "The gringo is mine."

"Will you give me a receipt for the prisoner?" the lieutenant asked.

"A receipt? A receipt, you say? By God, you are insolent, Gabaldon! I'll give my boot to your unborn heirs!"

"But, Colonel, my orders . . ."

Fuerte showed the lieutenant and everyone in the yard a broad, artificial grin. He had long, uneven, yellowish teeth. It was a dog's grin. There was more violence implicit in his smile than in his previous rage. And in a soft voice, with an exaggerated patience, he said, "Your orders are stupid, son. You are stupid. The general is stupid. The world is stupid. The stupidity of the world is turning my hair gray and rounding my shoulders."

And then, suddenly furious again, he shouted, "Deliver that man to me immediately or I'll cut off your vestigial balls and feed them to the crows!"

The lieutenant issued an order and a guard crossed the open stretch of ground, moved behind Martin, and unlocked the handcuffs. "I think I'd rather stay here than go off with that devil," he said quietly.

"Martin?"

"Good-bye, Rodolfo."

"What is this about? Herrera? Martin, where are you going?"

"Good-bye."

"Why can't I go with you? Why do I have to stay behind? There's been a mistake. I'm the one he wants. Martin, help me."

Martin unsteadily crossed the churchyard. Each step required concentration.

"Thank you," he said.

"You're a sorry-looking slab of carrion," Fuerte said in English.

"Martin!" Rodolfo cried in a choked voice.

"If I had my way I'd send you off to hell with the other one, but there are fools who think you have value."

"Can you save Rodolfo too? My friend? Please."

The colonel stared at him with loathing. His lips, not quite concealed by mustache and beard, were wide and gracefully curved, feminine, anomalous on that broken face. Martin could see his own face, diminished and distorted, reflected on the lenses of Fuerte's sunglasses.

"Imbecile," he said. "You can return to the wall or you can follow me." And he stalked off toward the gate.

Martin hurriedly followed.

"Martin, good-bye," Father Perecho said. He was smiling and nodding.

"Martin, where are you going?" Rodolfo cried.

"I'm sorry."

"Martin, come back. Please."

They passed through the gate and walked toward the plaza. Fuerte holstered his pistol. Thin children and emaciated dogs scattered and gravely watched them from a distance. Ahead a woman who had been sweeping the cobblestones picked up her bucket of water and vanished through a door. To his right, above the wall, Martin could see the upper level of the bell tower. Two of the window ports were visible from this angle. He realized that the villagers had clearly seen him during those long afternoons when he had looked out at the town. That surprised him; he had vaguely supposed that the observer had remained unobserved.

Three passing soldiers stepped into the gutter to let them pass. Fuerte ignored their salutes.

"Are you hungry?" the colonel asked in a mild tone.

"No. But I'm very thirsty."

Fuerte smiled. "Yes, the prospect of death dehydrates one. We'll stop in a café. We have a little time before they wake up. If you run, Doctor, something will chase you."

They reached the plaza. The trees and fountain had been deeply scarred by the explosion. Rubble from the statue of General Vargas was scattered over the grass and walks. They entered the café where Martin and the priest had breakfasted a few days before.

Colonel Fuerte ordered two bottles of beer and threw a pack of cigarettes on the table. There was a latent violence even in that simple gesture; but he appeared calm now, lazy.

"So," he said. "It was very close. What do you feel?"

"Nothing," Martin said.

"Yes, it takes a while."

"You were almost too late," Martin said.

"I know."

"There were delays. Some children, foul-ups . . . in another ten seconds . . ."

"I understand. We had some difficulties with the helicopter."

"I died. I'm a dead man."

"Nonsense. It was close, so what? You'd do as well worrying about your fate if your mother had had a headache on the night of your conception."

The beer was warm and foamed over the rim of Martin's glass. He drank that glass, poured another, and lit a cigarette. He was proud to see that there was no tremor in his hands.

"Are you going to kill me?"

"Probably not."

"If I had been killed here this morning the entire village and all the soldiers would know. Word would eventually get out. But if you take me away and kill me, without witnesses . . ."

"You have a point," Fuerte said complacently.

"I've heard of you. Fuerte isn't your real name, is it? 'Strong'?"

"It's a *nom de guerre*."

"You have an evil reputation."

"I have earned it." He was relaxed now, slumped in his chair. His eyes were concealed behind the sunglasses. Wiry gray hairs were scattered through his head and beard. There was something cold about the man, frozen; and Martin realized that his earlier rage had merely been a tactic, a performance, a way of instilling confusion and fear in other men. This was a truer Fuerte; calm but not off-guard, intelligent, detached, ironic.

"I'd like another bottle of beer."

"We've stayed here long enough. We'll take food and beer with us."

"I don't have any money."

A brief, mocking smile. "We won't pay. The owner will be happy to see us leave without his daughters."

Martin had just lifted his glass when he heard a volley of shots from the churchyard, a staccato crackling followed by the echoes. He flinched and spilled some of the beer. Vultures left the trees in the park. The village was silent. Both men waited for the snap of the lieutenant's pistol.

They carried boxes of food and beer through the back streets and emerged on the fields south of town. The helicopter, surrounded by children, squatted insectlike in the center of a weedy pasture. One of the boys had climbed onto the tail section. As Martin and Fuerte approached, the pilot stepped out of the aircraft, picked up some stones and began throwing them at the children. The boys danced away, laughing. One boy threw a rock at the pilot, who drew and cocked his pistol. The children, no longer laughing, turned and ran hard for the river.

The pilot's name was Ávila. He wore gold captain's bars on the shoulder loops of his khaki shirt. He had kinky dark red hair and coppery skin, and a teardrop had been tattooed at the corner of his left eye. He studied Martin coldly, contemptuously.

"Is this what you brought us?"

"He was very good," Fuerte said. "He didn't shit his pants, he didn't beg, he didn't fall down. Do you think you'll do as well, Juanito?"

Fuerte and Ávila sat in the front, Martin on a jump seat in the cargo section, among the crates of ammunition and supplies. They rose swiftly through the dust cloud and angled, still rising, toward the village.

The river was the color of strong tea and from a height appeared solid, like a road twisting through the forest. They passed over a patchwork of fields, still climbing, and then they were above the town. Tepazatlán looked clean and orderly from this altitude, a symmetrical array of cubes and rectangles, a pleasing pattern of light and shadow. The town plaza was a perfect square with paths radiating outward from the shattered fountain. The churchyard was empty now. Poor Rodolfo. Poor Cabrera, Martin thought. This was a world in which it was usually impossible to distinguish the patriots from the traitors, the witnesses from the spies, freedom from servitude.

Then they were beyond the village, banking over an uneven quilt of fields and pastures. Narrow dusty roads, a few palms, a crooked grid of irrigation ditches, huts whose corrugated metal roofs flashed sunlight. The land gradually rose to the southwest. Far away the snowy summits of the volcanoes trailed plumes of vapor. Below was a big white house that appeared derelict; there were no men or machines in the fields. The rich landowners had fled this district.

They returned to the river. There was more forest here, fewer cultivated fields, no roads or power lines. The helicopter's shadow preceded them upriver. A great many birds were frightened by the noise and swirled confusedly below.

After thirty minutes the helicopter began to lose altitude. It descended to tree height, banked steeply around a curve in the river, hovered, and then gently settled onto a clearing. The engine was switched off. Martin could hear the purring of the river.

"Out," Fuerte said. "We are going to picnic. Isn't that nice, Dr. Good?"

There was a sandy beach sloping down to the river, a few acres of clearing, and the stone ruins of a small house. Debris was scattered around the area, rusted cans, bottles, bits of brightly colored plastic, rags, a coat hanger, broken glass.

"We'll bathe," Fuerte said when they had emerged from the helicopter. He began to unbutton his shirt. "The water looks dirty, Dr. Good, but it's really quite clean. It's been stained by the soil. We have soap. We do have soap, don't we, Juanito? Yes?"

"I don't want to swim."

"Did you hear that, Juanito? He doesn't want to swim."

"Fuck him," Ávila said. "I don't know why he's here. Let him swim or not swim, it's nothing to me."

Ávila had removed his shirt, unbuckled his belt, and was now lowering his trousers.

"I'm not going to kill you, fool," Fuerte said to Martin. "At least not now. Not before lunch. I only kill women and children before lunch."

Martin began unbuttoning his shirt.

"I kill cripples and old people after lunch."

Birds, silenced by the helicopter, had begun to whistle again back in the forest. The river had a swampy odor and hissed as it foamed around boulders and half-sunken logs.

"I kill doctors and missionaries just before the cocktail hour."

Ávila was naked now. "I don't know what you're doing, Felipe. I don't understand why this gringo is with us. This wasn't my idea. You'll have to answer for this stupid adventure."

"You too, Juanito? Do I have to hear this kind of thing from you too?"

Martin removed his shirt. The sun was warm on his shoulders. He was dizzied by the heat and his fatigue.

"The gringo was sentenced to die. You know that."

"Well, Juanito, you know that I always obey my commanders in the field. But the political cadres can go to hell."

"But what is the point? I object to this." On Ávila's chest there was a welted scar that ran from just below his left nipple to his navel. It looked like an enormous centipede.

"Dr. Good, for Christ's sake, will you stop stalling and get undressed? If I wanted to kill you I would have done it by now. Like this." He drew his pistol, pushed the safety lever forward with his thumb, and said, "Bang."

The barrel was silver where the blueing had worn away, and silver too, a bright ring, around the muzzle.

"Do you believe in the sanctity of human life, Dr. Good? We die like dogs, we die like cattle. And we all rot. Except for saints—I hear they are spared corruption."

"Just shoot him now," Ávila said. "Don't make speeches." He removed his wristwatch, dropped it on the sand, and waded into the river. The bottom shelved steeply; after a few steps the water was waist-deep. He leaned sideways into the current. "It's cold," he said.

Colonel Fuerte pivoted, aimed carefully, and shot the pilot twice in the back, first between the shoulder blades and then a little lower, left of the spinal ridge. Ávila pitched forward, twitching convulsively, and then the current pulled him toward the center of the river. Head first, facedown, he floated away from the beach and downstream, trailing blood that curled like black smoke in the water.

Fuerte holstered his pistol. "I didn't want to shoot him until he'd undressed. You'll need his clothes."

The corpse was mostly submerged now, a pale shape whose arms and legs moved sinuously in the current. Martin watched until the body vanished around a curve in the river.

"What next, Colonel?" Martin asked.

"You're going to bathe and shave and wash your verminous clothes. And then we'll see about luncheon."

The river originated in the mountain glaciers and was still cool at this point. The silt bottom was mushy; he sank into it beyond his ankles. Fuerte would shoot him now, of course. He stood for a time in the shallow water, soaping, and then he dove forward and swam out into the current.

"Not too far, Dr. Good," Fuerte called.

Later Martin hung his wet clothes over a shrub and then dressed in Ávila's khaki uniform. The shirt was tight around the shoulders and the trousers too short, but the boots fit well enough.

"Do you know how to use a pistol?"

"I've done some hunting," Martin replied.

"With a forty-five pistol?"

"I can use a handgun."

"We'll try you out after lunch. And pick up that watch. It's very expensive. Juanito stole it from a corpse. That corpse probably stole it from another corpse. It's yours now."

They sat in the shade of a moss-draped willow. There was beer and sardines and corned beef and bread rolls.

"Why did you save me?" Martin asked.

"Money."

"A ransom?"

"No."

"I don't understand."

"I serve two masters. One master will pay me to save your sorry ass."

"You're Cuban, aren't you?"

"Why do you say that?"

"Your accent. One of my Spanish teachers was a Cuban exile."

"He should have devoted more time to your verbs."

"Where is your home now, Colonel?"

"Hell."

Martin nodded. "Hell is the place where, when you have no other place, they have to take you in."

"Not bad, Dr. Good."

Above them the palm fronds dryly rattled. The river swarmed with slivers of light.

Martin knew that he had changed but he didn't know in what way, to what depth. He understood that he would never again be the same man. Something, his soul, his psyche, his core self, had been shattered this morning in the churchyard while he'd waited to die, and it would eventually reassemble in a new combination. He was different and so the world looked different to him, new, strange, and desperately impermanent. Trees, sand, sky, the wrinkled and hissing river, had a reality that they had not possessed yesterday. They were more real and yet he felt less real, provisional.

"What next, Colonel?" he asked.

"Oh, we must make a visit. And then we'll fly out of this country—the planet's asshole."

"You can fly the helicopter?"

"Oh, yes, I've flown it often. Though never alone."

"I'll be with you," Martin said.

Fuerte showed his ferocious dog's grin.

CHAPTER

1 2

Juan Ávila had flown the helicopter with the casual ease of an expert pilot, never hurried, hardly concentrating, it seemed; but Fuerte's movements at the controls were jerky, indecisive, as if each adjustment were a microsecond late, which required a compensatory adjustment which then compelled another.

The helicopter rose jerkily from the beach and then darted westward above the treetops, still rising.

Fuerte relaxed when the aircraft was several hundred feet above the forest. He pounded Martin's knee with his fist.

"God's wounds!" he said. "I don't like this very much. Maybe I shot Juanito too soon."

Below and to his right Martin could see the river divide around a sandbar. There were palms and olive-green shrubbery and on the beach a speckle of white birds. Even from this height he could see the chevron ripples of the current. The birds flew off, circled back, changed directions once more, looking like confetti in a swirling wind.

"Is it hard to land one of these things?" Martin asked.

"Hard! Hard, you say. It's murder. It's suicide. It can't be done." Fuerte tunelessly sang phrases from *La Adelita*: ". . . if we must die tomorrow, then let us die tonight . . ." He grinned at Martin. It was a complicitous grin; there was no derision in it.

"Open me a beer, Dr. Good. This is thirsty work."

Martin got a bottle of Tecolote beer from the case behind his seat, opened it, and passed it to Fuerte.

Scattered here and there in the forest below were small patches of cultivated land. The river moved through a series of S-curves, like the coils of a snake. Ahead were volcanoes, green on the lower slopes, bare furrowed soil above, and finally the conical white summits. Thunderheads were coalescing beyond the mountains, out over the sea.

Fuerte had finished the beer. "Light me a cigarette, Dr. Good. I don't have nearly enough hands."

Martin lit a cigarette, inhaled once, and passed it to the colonel.

Earlier, on the beach, Fuerte had told Martin that they were flying to a rebel training camp. There was a fuel depot there. The supplies they carried would be unloaded and enough fuel taken on to enable them to fly out of the country. Where? Martin asked. Maybe to Chiapas, in Mexico. Why Mexico? Fuerte knew people there who would buy the helicopter. Is the helicopter yours to sell? You are a strange and innocent man, Dr. Good. God bless you.

Small tributary rivers emptied into the Rio Negro. One of the mountains seemed to separate from the others and gradually expanded; in another thirty minutes, Martin thought, it would fill the windshield. Vapor wound like a spring around the summit cone. In the gaps Martin could see snow, brilliant in the sunlight, boulders that at this distance looked like pebbles but which must be as big as cathedrals, and streaks of a cobalt-blue sky.

"We'll beat the rain," Fuerte said.

"Is there enough fuel?"

"With a teaspoonful left over."

The river was clear as they approached its source. The water was a sparkling blue, and as white as the snow where it curled around rocks or foamed down narrow chutes. And here it backed up into a small lake; ahead it had carved a gorge through the hills. The land inclined up toward the base of the mountain.

The helicopter began losing altitude. "Remember what I told you," Fuerte said.

What did he tell me? Martin wondered. He could not see a landing site ahead, just the gentle forested hills and the twisting, fizzing river that now appeared no bigger than a creek. It might be shallow enough to wade across.

"Where the hell is it?" Fuerte said. "Do you see anything?"

"No."

"Christ!"

They skimmed over a ridge and suddenly a clearing appeared. Fire-blackened tree stumps rose out of the grass. An X, marked with strips of bright orange fabric, marked the landing site. Fuerte worked frantically over the controls. The helicopter hesitated, hovered unsteadily for a moment, then began to settle. "Shit!" Fuerte said. They were descending too fast. The aircraft was canted toward Martin's side. The landscape tilted and slid upward past the windshield. Fuerte regained partial control. The impact didn't come and didn't come and then finally there was a shock that Martin could feel in his belly and head. There was a loud crack as something broke beneath them.

Fuerte turned off the engine. "Son of a bitch," he said.

Martin could taste blood. He had bitten his tongue at impact. Ahead, through the haze of dust, he could see three men running toward them.

"You're a soldier now," Fuerte said. "Don't forget that." He opened his door, got out, and immediately began screaming, "What soon-to-die scum moved the landing site? We're too far from camp! This ground is not level! My machine has been damaged! Look, there are huge rocks! What saboteur has tried to kill me?"

The three men slowed to a walk and after a few more paces stopped. Only one of them wore a uniform. They would not look directly at the colonel.

"Can't you talk? You might have injured Captain Smith. By God, if he has one bruise he'll eat your livers for lunch!"

Fuerte glared at them for a moment longer and then stalked around the helicopter. "I myself," he said in a milder tone, "prefer the ribs of young Indian boys barbecued over hot coals. I like the way the fat sputters in the fire. But"—his voice rising in outrage—"but there's no fat on you three, you're dried out, it would be like eating my boots!"

The men tried to pacify the colonel with their shy smiles and their postures—they posed like children overcome by guilt and shame.

Martin opened the door and stepped out. Some welds on the right skid had fractured. An anthill had been destroyed and thousands of red ants, many carrying what appeared to be larvae, swarmed over the rust-colored soil.

The land was semidesertic; there were cacti and gnarled thorny trees and stalks of yucca, and the yellow grass grew in spiky clumps. The air was dry at this altitude and piercingly clear; each grain of soil was separated from the other, and every pebble cast a tiny crescent shadow.

Fuerte squatted and examined the right skid. "I don't see why she won't fly," he said.

"Bad luck," Martin said.

Fuerte straightened and looked at him. "Are you going to be an albatross tied around my neck?" he asked mildly.

After a few paces he stopped and turned to face the men. "Zombies! Unload the aircraft. If you disturb my personal belongings I'll flay you alive."

They walked west toward the fringe of trees. The land was sculpted into shallow arroyos and conical anthills and thorny hillocks. Swallows flitted erratically over the ground. Rectangular blocks of black basalt were scattered here and there. The blocks and the charred still-standing trees looked like the remains of an old ruin.

"You are Captain Smith," Fuerte said.

"All right."

"An American mercenary."

"Yes. Okay." Martin was aware of the weight of Ávila's pistol on his hip.

"You eat barbed wire."

"And pass nails. Okay."

The land tilted toward the mountain. Martin was aware of the effects of the altitude on his legs and lungs. The volcano filled his field of vision; he felt vaguely oppressed by its mass and weight.

A horse-drawn cart emerged from the woods. There were black oil drums stacked behind the driver and his companion.

"They have a radio here," Fuerte said. "It rarely works. But if it's working now they may have some questions."

"What do we reply?"

"We don't reply. We become indignant. And dangerous."

"Colonel, I'm sorry, but I don't know how to be dangerous."

"Better learn, Dr. Good."

"All right," Martin said.

Beneath the trees Martin could see tents and several

transparent orange fires. He saw men too, briefly and indistinctly; they wore camouflage fatigues and looked like patterns of light and leaf shadow as they moved through the woods.

When the horse cart was a few yards away Fuerte raised his hand. The driver, a thin black youth, reined in the horses. The man at his side had an eye milky from glaucoma. One horse was gray and the other chestnut; both were small, not much bigger than donkeys, and there was a pneumonic wheeze in the gray's exhalations. The horses' skin twitched at flies.

"Did you forget the chamois cloth?" Fuerte said harshly.

"No." The driver held up the cloth.

"That filthy rag! You use that to strain gasoline? Do you want to clog the fuel lines of my complicated machine? Imbecile! Scrub the cloth in the river. Do you hear? Well?"

"Yes, sir."

Fuerte and Martin continued on toward the camp. A streaky mushroom cloud now obscured the volcano's summit and other clouds were boiling in from the southwest.

Two men emerged from the trees and walked toward them. The stout one walked with a limp. They were officers.

"Felipe!" the stout man shouted. "Where have you been, man?"

"Paco!" Fuerte called. "Paco, if you had tits on your back I'd marry you." And then, "Augustin, you renegade Dominican, you priest in military vestment, how is it that you haven't murdered Paco by now?" Fuerte embraced them, fists thumping backs, first the lean man, Augustin, and then Paco. He used the familiar *tu* form.

"I've been sleeping with your wives," Fuerte said. "They smile all the time. Your sons call me 'Uncle'." He gestured toward Martin. "This is Captain Smith. He's a war criminal who learned his trade in Wisconsin."

They walked four abreast toward the camp. A cloud blocked the sun and now the landscape had a submarine aspect; it was like walking over an old seabed. Martin could hear bursts of automatic-weapons fire to the north.

"The Revolution is going well," Fuerte said. "All of the brave men are dead and we are carrying on with cowards and mercenaries."

The tents looked big enough to sleep eight or ten men each. Some were camouflaged and others colored a drab olive. They were widely scattered among trees that looked like eucalyptus, tall, with partly exposed roots and raggedly peeling bark, and with most of the foliage starting near the crowns.

"Augustin," Fuerte said, "you're so thin and Paco so fat. Maybe there is something good to be said for cannibalism. Eh, Paco?"

There were crude wooden sheds among the trees, some pens fenced with chicken wire, a slant-roofed stable, and a corral enclosed by a fence of saplings. Chickens and pigs roamed freely through the woods.

"Smith here is an expert in demolitions. Don't jostle him, he carries detonators and vials of nitroglycerin in his pockets."

There was little undergrowth in the woods, some low ferns, ivy, twisted shrubs of thorn, but mostly the soil was exposed. Some men were cooking over fires; other men rested with their backs against tree trunks or lay supine on the ground.

"Paco," Fuerte said fondly, "you strangler of old ladies, you violator of children, you're giving the Revolution a bad name in Europe and North America. Can't you satisfy yourself with pigs and goats until the war is won?"

Martin glanced at his watch. It was almost one o'clock.

"We're hungry, we're thirsty, we have palpitations. Feed us well. Smith is very close to some members of the Revolutionary Council. He's engaged to marry one of Gutierrez's daughters. The epileptic one. Cristina, is that her name? They'll live together in Wisconsin. Paco, Jesus Paco, you are fatter every time I see you. It's not good for your health. Only the vultures and worms are pleased. Why aren't you more like our friend Augustin, who lives on amphetamines and the prose of Lenin and Marx?"

They were well into the trees now. Pigs and chickens scattered; a gust of wind tore a spiral of sparks off of a nearby fire.

"I should kill both of you," Fuerte said affectionately. "But I can't, I love you both too much."

CHAPTER

1 3

Martin balanced an earthenware bowl of greasy brown stew on his knees. It tasted gamey and contained chips of bone. He chewed carefully. Fuerte, in one of his petty furies, had thrown his own bowl out of the tent opening. But Martin was hungry, he had been hungry for weeks. He soaked the tortillas in gravy. The meat had flavor but required dedicated chewing.

Fuerte and the two officers, Augustin and Paco, were drinking rum and telling lies. Lies about war and lies about sex and lies about the revolutionary leaders they served; this one was a low bourgeois, that one a sodomist, that one certainly worked for the CIA.

A wounded boy lay on one of the cots, naked except for a pair of soiled shorts and bloody bandages wrapped around one thigh. He had accidentally been shot during training. His body was sweaty and he shivered, teeth clicking, and he talked deliriously in some Indian dialect.

It was a big field tent that contained canvas cots, wooden trunks with rounded lids and brass hinges, a gas pressure stove, a radio transceiver, and ammunition crates that served as tables and chairs and cupboards. The tent ballooned and then slackened in the gusts of wind. Raindrops snapped against the fabric.

The man named Paco looked like a fat cheerful bandit. Augustin was pale with sandy hair and hands as soft and slender as a woman's. The wounded soldier resembled the anguished, cadaverous Indian Christ you saw on posters all over the country.

"Did you hear?" Fuerte was saying. "Bolaños tried to assassinate the bishop. He planted a bomb in the bishop's limousine, but it detonated too soon and killed only the chauffeur and the bishop's mistress."

They laughed.

"Yes," Fuerte said. "And so all week the bishop has been interviewing old chauffeurs and young housekeepers."

They laughed again.

Martin scraped his bowl clean with a tortilla, ate that, and then got up and went outside.

Tree branches clattered in the wind. Leaves and scraps of paper tumbled over the ground. Pebbles of hail were mixed with the sparse rain. Men ran back and forth, laughing, collecting weapons and backpacks and carrying them inside the tents. A nearly featherless hen—looking reptilian—pecked at the ground and then paused to stare at Martin with a single cold snake's eye. Through the columns of trees he could see a horse running around the corral, whinnying, trotting in counterclockwise circles. Martin had horses on the farm. He and Katherine rode occasionally, but mostly the horses were for the kids. Placid animals, as horses go, but still with a tendency toward blind panics. He would not let the children ride on a windy day or when a storm seemed imminent.

All around now the smoky clouds were veined with lightning. The complex patterns were for an instant etched into the sky and then existed for another instant in retinal afterimages. The horse, still running, screamed loudly. He'll hurt himself, Martin thought. One of their horses had broken a cannon bone during a storm like this. The leg was bloody and you could see splintered bone. She had limped all the way from the pasture by the lake to the stable. Martin had called the veterinarian and told him to come out right away and put her down. A nice euphemism. Put her down. They nearly put me down this morning.

He returned to the tent. The rum bottle was empty and a new one had been opened. Rain drummed on the tent roof. Clear droplets of water, from leaks and condensation, trickled crookedly down the walls. You could see the flare of lightning through the fabric.

Martin kneeled by the wounded boy. Augustin had called him "Chucho." He babbled softly in a language filled with x and ch and z sounds. There was a clicking deep in his throat on certain consonants. His skin radiated heat. He stank of putrefaction.

A large metal box, like a carpenter's tool kit, lay beneath the cot. Martin opened the double lid: medical supplies, confused, nothing in its place, a loose pile of surgical implements, tape, gauze, bottles and tins, plastic disposable hypodermics, coils of rubber tubing, loose powders and pills. There were no antibiotics.

"What are you doing, Smith?" Fuerte asked. "Praying for him? It's too late."

"I know," Martin said.

The bandage on Chucho's thigh was caked with dried blood and pus. Martin was nauseated by the smells, the infection, the boy's breath, sour-sweet.

"He's going to die, Captain," Paco said.

"Yes," Martin said. "And soon."

He removed a pair of narrow-bladed scissors from the box and began to cut away the mass of tape and bandage.

It looked as though the dressing had not been changed for days; it was filthy and as tight as a tourniquet. Gently, gently, Martin told himself, but it hardly seemed to matter; the boy was unconscious, dying, and mind and body had already been consumed. The bandage was pasted to the wound; he poured some alcohol on the crust, to loosen adhesion, and then peeled it away.

"Christ," Fuerte said. "Let the kid alone."

The storm was almost directly overhead now; there was only a brief interval between flash and concussion.

"Stop torturing him."

Martin had pulled the scab loose and now creamy pus welled up out of the entry hole. It was small, ragged, and only the size of a nickel. But there were other wounds; evidently the bullet had shattered on the femur and fragments of bone and lead had exited here and there on the back of the thigh. Martin sponged up the pus with a wad of gauze. It kept coming.

Chucho lay quietly, still sweating and babbling, making querulous inquiries in his dense language. Martin dressed the boy's thigh, then soaked a ball of cotton with alcohol and bathed his torso.

"After a few years," Augustin was saying, "in time, war ceases to be a means to an end, a purposeful activity; it becomes oneself and one's life. I am war. I mean, Felipe, if this war ends I'll go off and find another. The way you do. War is what I've become."

"That's crazy," Fuerte said. "You damned intellectuals should not be allowed in the field. You belong in cities, in universities, in exile."

Martin picked up some coarse blankets from another cot and spread them over the boy. He splashed alcohol over his hands and went to sit on an ammunition crate. His hands were chilled by the evaporating alcohol.

"But Felipe," Augustin said, "you're an intellectual."

"Don't say that, *hijo*, please. There comes a time in every revolution when the intellectuals must be tortured and shot."

"Sometimes," Augustin said, "I am awakened by a bad dream. The dream is that the war has ended."

"Colonel," Martin said, "the storm is passing. We can leave soon."

"The struggle is beautiful in itself," Augustin said. "It's art and science together. In the struggle we find ourselves, we are ennobled."

"*Hijo*, you're full of shit."

"Don't sneer, Felipe, you know it's true. We learn the limits of our courage and strength and pity. What are you without war, my friend? A criminal, an adventurer, a drunk. What is Paco? Maybe the foreman of a hacienda, maybe the leader of a small, futile union. What am I? A bad priest, a third-rate poet. Ah, but Felipe, with war I am Odysseus. Yes, damn you, I am a hero, I exceed the shitty standards for humanity. And, Felipe—we make the world a slightly better place."

"We have to believe that, don't we, *hijo*?"

"Colonel," Martin said. "The rain has stopped."

Augustin turned. "Captain Smith, what would you be without war?"

"I don't know. Ask the boy that question."

"He can't answer. I asked you."

"The question is stupid."

"Can't you think, man? Why did you leave your fat country to come down here to patronize brown-skinned people? Do you have an ideal, an ideology, a sense of history, of justice, a motivating passion? Christ, man, can't you speak?"

Fuerte laughed. "*Hijo*, he's an American. You know that gringos get along quite well without ideas. Money substitutes for ideas. It's rude of you to force him to think."

"Colonel . . ." Martin said.

"Yes, yes, yes," he said, and then to Augustin and Paco: "He's like a wife."

Augustin and Paco escorted them down to the helicopter. It was after three o'clock. There were thunderheads far to the east but the sun was shining here. The mountain seemed to vibrate in the clear, new-washed air. Fresh snow had fallen on the summit cone. Puddles reflected the sky.

They stopped. "How badly is it damaged?" Paco asked. "Do you think it will fly?"

"She'll fly, by God. I'll make her fly."

Augustin turned. "Good-bye, Dr. Springer."

Fuerte placed his hands on his hips. "Doctor, did you say?"

"Felipe, do you know what you're doing?"

"Yes."

"You killed Juanito."

"No."

"I doubt if he would have willingly given Dr. Springer his clothes, his pistol, and his watch."

"I executed him summarily. He was working for the Americans."

Augustin smiled.

Fuerte was cold sober now, watching them.

"We heard about it on the radio this morning. About Tepazatlán and the doctor here. We were commanded to arrest you if you came."

"Why didn't you?"

"Ah, Felipe, we're old friends."

"We've known each other less than three years."

"Three years of war."

"Yes, that's a long time."

"I wish you hadn't killed Juanito, though."

"I thought it was necessary at the moment. Maybe now

I wouldn't kill him. Why didn't you mention the radio message sooner?"

"I hadn't decided what to do. I didn't decide until the rain stopped. Paco and I had a signal arranged."

"There would have been a fight. I was ready for one."

"Or I could have left the tent to piss and returned with some men. It wouldn't have been an arrest, Felipe, we would have just killed you and the doctor."

"All right. I understand. Why didn't you do it?"

Augustin shook his head. "I don't know. Really. It wasn't because I was afraid."

"I know that, *hijo*. You're afraid of nothing."

"I guess, I guess"—he laughed briefly—"I guess it was because I was enjoying the conversation so much. I kept putting it off." Augustin shaded his eyes with a palm and gazed steadily at the colonel. "What is it about? Money?"

"I'm fifty-two years old," Fuerte said. "I'm tired. I've got arthritis from sleeping on the ground so often. My wounds ache. My liver's bad. I wake up wearier every morning. I've been around too long, *hijo*. I know it's all lies, nothing will ever change. I'm tired of the big words, *hijo*, and the mean petty actions. You understand?"

"No."

"That's because you're basically a theorist. Theory and reality are strangers. Listen, *hijo*, I'm going to buy a house in Fort Lauderdale, Florida, and a boat, a fishing cruiser. I'll fish every morning and nap every afternoon in front of the TV. I'll limp if I feel like it—no more impressing the troops. I'll get fat."

"A fat bourgeois."

"Exactly." Fuerte laughed. "You don't know how good that sounds, I'll walk along the beach and stare at the seventeen-year-old girls in their bikinis. I'll jog, I'll play tennis, I'll try to diet, I'll court rich widows, I'll subscribe to the *Wall Street Journal*."

Augustin shook his head.

Fuerte laughed again. "My life is just beginning."

"You'll shoot yourself within a year."

"Five years."

"You'd better go now," Augustin said.

"Come and see me when the Revolution succeeds or fails. You and Paco. You won't be welcome here either way, you'll have to go somewhere. We'll fish."

"Good-bye, Felipe."

"You'll pardon me if I say that you must return to camp before I start the machine? I trust you both like brothers, but I always cut the cards, I always inspect the dice, I don't eat the stew if I see that my hosts aren't hungry."

Martin and Fuerte stood by the helicopter, watching the two men walk back toward the woods.

"Damn it, you weren't ready, Dr. Good."

They flew east above the river. The land had a glossy lacquered sheen after the rain. Mist crawled through the ravines.

"They were generous," Fuerte said loudly. "Occasionally friendship counts for something."

The river, discolored by soil, was high and swift. In the narrow channels there were rapids where before the water had been smooth.

"We have one more stop, Dr. Good."

"Whatever you say, Colonel."

"You weren't ready. Not for a second. With Augustin and Paco—you weren't ready. You must help me, I can't do it all. You have to be ready, Dr. Good."

"You're drunk, Colonel."

"Am I? Good. Excellent. I can fly this machine much better when I'm drunk."

PART TWO

THE RIVER

CHAPTER

1 4

There was a gate and guardhouse at the entrance to the suburb of Las Lomas, and armed soldiers searched the taxi and driver. The driver, a hungry-looking man with scaly eczematous skin, protested that he had done nothing wrong, never, he was a patriot. The officer in charge was extremely courteous to Katherine, almost servile. Her name was on a list of those to be admitted; she was a guest of Jorge C' de Vaca. "You understand," the officer said. "We don't know this man. He could be a terrorist."

"Or simply terrified," Katherine said. "It's all right. If Mr. C' de Vaca asks I'll tell him that you were polite and quite efficient."

"Thank you." He stiffened and saluted.

She had been saluted half a dozen times during the past few days. It was done reflexively. She was a civilian, a woman—what could they be thinking of?

A sticky asphalt road coiled up through some low ferny hills. It was a misty blue twilight. Fireflies rose like sparks from the grass. Most of the landscape was hidden behind high walls but she briefly glimpsed houses with red tile roofs, topiary hedges, fountains, patches of woods, a pond that reflected the sky and duplicated, upside down, a row of long-necked white birds, swans, she thought. And through a white board fence she saw magnificent horses grazing, licorice-colored, caramel, cream, and strawberry, confectionery horses on a mint-green pasture.

The taxi, a thirty-year-old Chevrolet, could barely climb the gentle grade. Katherine wondered what the driver thought of all this wealth and beauty. Perhaps his wife was ill from too many pregnancies, his many children under-nourished and sickly too, his home a slum shack in a subcity where there was never a moment's peace or privacy. An open cess-trench beyond the door, kids with crooked bones and oozing sores. Was the man filled with hatred, rebellious, ready to kill or be killed? She did not think so. Probably he respected the God-ordered nature of things. A patriot. How could this kind of servitude last for thousands of years unless the great mass of humanity was prepared to submit? By God, she thought, if I were one of them I would sneak up here at night and cut throats. No I wouldn't, I would be nursing two babies and trying to care for several more, and my husband would be half mad and beat me because he couldn't feed us and he had to kowtow to every reptile who wore a uniform or a business suit. Then she thought: Wake up, Katherine. *I* am one of the privileged. There are millions of people in America who wouldn't mind slitting *my* throat.

C' de Vaca's place was near the top of the hill: above there were a few more houses and then on the summit a radio tower with a flashing red light; below and to the east, in bluish shadow, she could see the city, a grid of lights that pulsed like stars.

Katherine tripled the driver's fare, smiled, and quickly walked away from his gratitude. She could hear music and laughter behind the high wall. A soldier opened the gate, grubbed through her purse for a moment—looking for guns, bombs?—and then briskly saluted. It was a large courtyard with trees here and there, palm, hibiscus, mimosa, frangipani, lime, and banks of poppies and bougainvillea. There was a marble fountain acrawl with ugly marble cherubs. A flagstone walk curved into the pool area. Dozens of people were scattered around the patio and there were more inside the brightly lighted house. She immediately glanced at the women and saw that most were dressed in whites and pastels. Her white cocktail dress was all right, though perhaps a bit shorter than was common here.

Poise, Katherine told herself. But it was hard to be poised when you were late, unescorted, and everyone was staring.

The swimming pool reflected the paper lanterns strung overhead on wires, orange and yellow and green blurs, and there was enough breeze to wrinkle its surface. The poolside tiles contained a design that resembled Moslem calligraphy. The people here spoke English mostly, though she heard Spanish and French too. A quartet of musicians, dressed like organ-grinder monkeys, sang a romantic ballad. Electric insect killers periodically sizzled. An old man in a uniform was walking toward her now.

"Bon soir, madame. Attendez-vous quelqu'un? Puis-je vous offrir un verre?"

"Je ne parle pas bien français," Katherine said.

"Habla usted Español?"

"No."

"Do you speak English, then?"

"A little," Katherine said.

"Good."

He wore a starched khaki uniform with brass buttons, a glossy Sam Browne belt and holster (empty), and heaps of gold salad on the shoulders. Katherine thought that Alexander and Napoleon combined could not have earned as many medals and ribbons as were spread over his breast. He had yellowish eyes and the jowls of a bloodhound. Would he salute her? She thought not.

"Who are you, beautiful mystery lady?"

"I wouldn't be a mystery lady if I told you."

"Ah," he said, "if I were ten years younger . . ."

"Or if I were thirty years older."

"Do you bleach your hair?"

"No."

"Good. Prostitutes bleach their hair."

"Do they?"

"Yes. I have been with many prostitutes."

"It isn't necessary to confide in me."

"Do you think that I am intoxicated?"

"Well, yes, I do think that."

"I am not. Prostitutes—forgive the word, my lady—harlots belong to a special category of humanity."

"If that's so," Katherine said, "then the men who patronize them must also belong to a special category."

"You think that I am intoxicated."

"Yes."

"Prostitutes are all right. I like prostitutes. They know what a man likes."

"Why do you want to talk to me about prostitutes?"

"May I smell your hair, pretty lady?"

"No."

"I have a house nearby," he said. "I have old Benny Goodman records. Would you like to come to my house and listen to Benny?"

Katherine laughed. "Well, no, actually."

"Have I offended you, dear lady?"

"Not yet, but I think you will soon."

"Never. I will kill any man who offends you. Tell me.

Show me the man who has offended you and I will kill him."

"You're a perky old general, aren't you?" Katherine said.

"That's true, I am. I'm not like these other generals. But you think I am intoxicated."

"You are."

"Maybe so. But I can still perform."

"Wake up one of the maids when you get home."

"I like you, gentle lady. You know how to tease an old man."

"Tease?"

"Should I go home?"

"Yes. Go home, General."

"Now?"

"Now, yes. You've had too much to drink."

"You won't come with me?"

"I won't."

"By God you are a woman! I'll kill any man who insults you. Where is the bastard? He knows to hide from me. May I touch your breast?"

"Of course not."

"You think that I am intoxicated."

"You're drunk."

"I will go home. You won't come with me?"

"No."

"I am desolated. May I kiss you good night?"

Katherine shook her head.

"Your hand?"

"Okay, my hand."

He bowed and kissed the back of her hand and then, turning it, he licked her palm.

Katherine pulled her hand free.

"I'm sorry. Please forgive me. I couldn't stop myself. I went mad. Don't let me near your feet. I love your narrow feet. The Benny Goodman Quintet. Benny Goodman, Gene Krupa, Lionel Hampton. I forget the others."

"I'm going to faint soon," Katherine said.

He smiled. "Good night, dear sweet lady. I love you, I've always loved you, but I didn't know it until tonight."

"Go away. Beat it, General Smut."

"I shall go home and wake up the maids. All of them. Because you have inspired me." He bowed from the waist, clicking his heels, and then turned and moved away.

It was dark now. The air was perfumed by flowers and there was a faint chemical odor too, insecticide perhaps. The Latino band was leaving their corner now and a group of black men with long-sleeved white shirts and black trousers were replacing them. An ashcan Caribbean rhythms group, judging by their equipment.

A tall man in a white dinner jacket was approaching her now. He carried two flute glasses of champagne. Mr. Harley of the embassy.

"Mrs. Springer," he said. "Good evening."

"Mr. Harley." She accepted a glass of wine and sipped it.

"It's very good champagne," he said. "Moët et Chandon."

"I wouldn't know good wine from bad."

"Have you seen the buffet? Real caviar. I haven't seen Caspian Sea caviar since I was stationed in Iran."

"A long and terrible deprivation."

He smiled. He stood with his legs apart, one hand behind his back and the other holding the glass. His bow tie was askew. He was relaxed and affable and good-looking in a bland way.

"I saw General Hernandez flirting with you."

"He was advertising his potency."

Harley smiled.

"How did he earn all of those medals and ribbons? Participating in coups d' état?"

"No doubt. You know, Mrs. Springer, sometimes I have a hard time seeing you as Martin's wife."

"Do you? Well, I have a hard time seeing you as a spy."

"That's because I'm not a spy, I'm a diplomat."

"What kind of name is C' de Vaca?"

"C for Cabeza. Cabeza de Vaca."

"Head of the cow?"

"Jorge something Cabeza de Vaca. He claims to be a direct descendant of Alvar Nuñoz Cabeza de Vaca."

"Is that good?"

"He thinks so. His ancestor Alvar Nuñoz for years wandered all over the southwestern United States and parts of Mexico. Of course it wasn't the United States then. Didn't you ever hear about the mythical seven cities of gold? They were his invention. Coronado couldn't find them. No one could."

"Why haven't you returned my calls, Mr. Harley?"

"I have. I phoned your hotel twice today and two or three times yesterday. You were out, but I left messages."

"I didn't receive them. What about Martin? What is happening?"

"I can't tell you anything, Mrs. Springer."

"You haven't heard?"

"Mrs. Springer, I advised you to be silent about what I told you. Remember? I said that if you talked it could jeopardize your husband and our friend. Well, you talked. You talked to Dix Stenstrom, and this morning to Vaca."

"How do you know that?"

"You and Dix went to Playas del Óro last night to meet with some punks who pass as revolutionaries. You offered to ransom your husband. The fact is, Mrs. Springer, you're going to foul things up if you keep interfering."

"You know an awful lot for an assistant commercial attaché. So I'm interfering, am I? My husband is captive or dead or lost and you have the gall to tell me that. Why should I trust you people? You have your own—what's the word?—your own agenda. And I have mine. Martin is my agenda—or is it agendum? My husband is in trouble. Please don't tell me that I am going to foul things up."

"I'll tell you nothing now," he said. "Maybe tomorrow or the day after."

"Maybe tomorrow or the day after you'll return my calls?"

"I *have* returned them."

"Well, I think you're the one, Mr. Harley, who may foul things up."

"Don't expect Vaca to help you. He can't. He knows nothing about your husband. We've kept him out of it. Mrs. Springer, please listen to me. I understand what you feel. I think I know what you're going through. But Dix Stenstrom can't help Dr. Springer. Punks like Cortez can't help. Cabeza de Vaca can't help. You can't ransom your husband. *You* can't help him. We can."

"Tell me, just tell me, please."

"I told you too much the other day. I was stupid."

"I don't know what to do."

"Do nothing for a short while."

"I can't. Don't you see that?"

"I believe he will be all right," he said. "I really believe that."

"Introduce me to your wife, Mr. Harley. I'm tired of talking to men. I want a woman's company."

"My wife is in the States."

"Oh."

"I'm sorry that you don't trust me."

"So am I."

"How did you get here? Taxi? I'll drive you to your hotel when you're ready to leave."

"Do you have Benny Goodman records?"

"Pardon?"

"Nothing, a dumb joke. I'm sorry. Thank you, Mr. Harley."

He hesitated, staring at her, and he seemed about to speak, but then he nodded politely and walked toward the house.

And now she saw her host, Mr. Head of the Cow, coming toward her. He walked lightly, smiling, his eyebrows raised in dark semicircles. He wore a cerise blazer, a cummerbund, a ruffled white shirt, and black trousers with silk stripes along the outer seams. The outfit, which would be hilarious in the States, did not seem *too* gaudy here in the tropics.

He shook her hand. "Thank you for coming. I'm sorry there was no one to greet you. I had a man stationed at the gate with orders to bring you to me the instant you arrived, but there was a security problem, a false alarm, and—well, forgive me."

"You're forgiven, Mr. Cabeza de Vaca."

"Isn't it a ridiculous name? Just call me Jorge—pronounce it 'George' if you like. Or just call me Vaca. May I call you Katherine?"

"Yes, all right."

"No, I'll call you Caterina. Your skin, eyes, and hair are Nordic but I suspect that you have the Mediterranean soul."

He, like the general, spoke an almost unaccented English. This morning he had mentioned that he'd attended the University of Arizona as a youth. A short man, he stood very erect, back straight and chin lifted. Katherine, in high-heeled shoes, was two or three inches taller. He was trim and compact. Clean-shaven, dark brown hair, brown eyes, sallow complexion. There was something appealingly boyish about his features and posture. But he was much too confident, too smooth.

"Your glass is empty," he said. "I have eight servants on duty tonight and your glass is empty."

He took her glass, smiled, turned, and walked toward the bar. She saw that his patent leather shoes had two-inch heels. He moved with great authority. There, she thought, was a man who never doubted his opinions and actions; he was right, he would always be right. Katherine knew that many women were attracted to such men but she distrusted them; the world was too complex, human relationships too intricate and ambiguous, to justify such certitude.

Katherine had gone to see Vaca this morning. All she had known about him was that he was some sort of policeman and very powerful in the government. A power behind the scenes, Dix told her, a gray eminence. He had a suite of offices in the National Palace. She had waited for hours, smoking, drinking water from paper cones, paging through picture magazines with names like *Venceremos* and *Nuestro Día* and *Somos*. C' de Vaca was busy, his secretary said many times, very busy, perhaps another day . . . ? But then he had passed through the outer office on his way to lunch, seen her, and halted, alert now and emanating that cloying, formal, predatory Latin American charm. He listened, very grave. "Yes, yes, I understand, of course I'll help you. No, please don't thank me, it's my privilege. But as you see I'm busy, I can't see you today. Would tomorrow—wait! I'm giving a small cocktail party tonight. Will you come? We will find time to talk this evening. I'm very angry that no one has told me about your husband's situation. Will you come to my little party?"

Now she watched him return, bearing the glass of wine like a ceremonial offering.

"Thank you," Katherine said.

"You are probably accustomed to far better wines."

"I'm not, in fact. Can we talk about Martin now?"

"Very soon." He glanced at his wristwatch, a thin gold

wafer. "You understand, as host I must supervise things and chat with the guests."

"Introduce me to your wife," Katherine said.

"My wife and daughters are shopping. In Paris." He smiled. "I'm afraid they're terribly spoiled."

"Mr. Harley said that you didn't know anything about Martin, that you wouldn't be able to help."

"Robert Harley does not know everything. I know a little more about my country and people than Mr. Harley. I made inquiries today after our talk. Your husband is no longer in Tepazatlán as you thought. He's being held in a village called Esperanza."

"Can you help him, Jorge?"

"I'm sure of it. We hold many of their people in prison. A trade is likely."

"Thank you."

"Please don't thank me, Caterina. If your Robert Harley had confided in me earlier I might have sooner rescued your husband."

"But he's safe now, Martin's safe?"

"Yes. You must excuse me now. This cocktail party was scheduled to end at eight-thirty and it's already nine o'clock. The guests will be leaving soon, I'll see that they do, and then we'll talk."

"I have some money, if that will help."

He appeared hurt and a little angry. "I know that you don't mean to insult me."

"Oh no, certainly not. I just meant . . ."

"Be patient for another hour, Caterina."

"Yes. Thank you."

CHAPTER

1 5

From the veranda Martin could see much of the hacienda's holdings. Straight ahead, past an empty marble fountain and weedy flower gardens and overgrown lawns, were the workers' shack village and some equipment sheds. To his left, an orchard; to his right, down a long slope and beyond a fringe of trees hung with Spanish moss, was the sun-burnished river.

Martin opened a bottle of warm beer and bowed his head to drink the eruption of foam. It was late afternoon, 7:20 according to Ávila's wristwatch, and still very hot. There was a sour, burnt taste to the air.

The hacienda had been abandoned two or three years ago. It was virtually worthless now. The house and outbuildings had been looted of everything of value, metals, glass, plumbing, doors, tiles, and furniture. The surrounding fields were fallow, empty now except for a burro that grazed among the weeds. The well was polluted, the pond coated with bright green scum, and the wooden buildings riddled with termites and dry rot. Inside the house he had seen human excrement, fairly recent, and discarded bottles and cans, and filmy nets that bore the weight of spiders as big as mice.

Colonel Fuerte had deserted him here. "Sorry, Doc. He travels fastest who travels alone."

"But we had a deal."

"My deal wasn't with you."

"I thought you were going to take me out of this goddamned country."

"I changed my mind. I'm going to save my neck. You save yours."

"It would be just as easy to take me."

"No it wouldn't. You complicate everything."

"All right," Martin said. "I suppose you're going to shoot me, the way you shot Ávila."

"I might," Fuerte said cheerfully, "if you don't stop complaining."

That was an hour ago. It had been another rough landing; the helicopter descended too swiftly, and tilted, and upon impact more welds on the right skid had broken.

They got out of the helicopter, walked a few yards, and sat on the grass. Martin's nose was bleeding. His face had struck the rim of the control panel. There was a cut on Fuerte's forehead, his beard was threaded with blood, and when he grinned Martin could see that his mouth and teeth were bloody too.

"How are you, Doc?"

"I don't know. Okay, I guess."

"One thing—one thing, you'll never have a Protestant nose again." He laughed, spraying a mist of blood. "Well, I think the machine may be capable of one more landing."

"You fool," Martin said. His voice sounded strange; there was blood in his throat and nasal passages. "I was safer with my back against the wall than flying around with you."

"You probably didn't know this, being educated and a

physician, but a very good remedy for a broken nose is dung. It's a famous folk remedy. You stuff clean dried dung up your nostrils. Do you want me to find some dung?"

"I think I'd like a second opinion," Martin said.

"You're all right, Dr. Good. By Christ, I could have made a soldier out of you if I'd got you when you were sixteen."

Martin lay supine in the tall grass and closed his eyes.

"That's right, you take it easy. I'll see to the machine."

Martin half drowsed in the sun for a time and then, bothered by flies, he got up and walked to the helicopter. His nose was still bleeding. He felt light-headed, and his right shoulder and right lower ribs were beginning to ache. Some things had been removed from the helicopter, a large plastic canister, a duffel bag, and a cardboard box. Fuerte, a cigar in one hand and a bottle of beer in the other, was standing nearby.

He said, "I've left you most of the supplies. I'll be out of the country in a couple of hours. It will take you longer."

"What do you mean?"

"There's a life raft in the plastic container. And you'll find some topographical maps in the duffel, but you probably won't need them. Just stay to the main channel of the river."

"Fuerte, just what is this about?"

"I suggest you travel by night and hide out during the day."

"You're leaving me here?"

And that was when Fuerte said, "Sorry, Doc. He travels fastest who travels alone."

"You son of a bitch," Martin said just before Fuerte left.

Softly, Fuerte said, "I saved your life this morning, didn't I?"

Martin did not reply.

"Didn't I, Doc?" he quietly insisted.

"Okay. Yes, thanks, but—"

"But no buts, I saved your life, now it's up to you to keep it. You've got a good chance of making it out by the river."

Martin nodded. "All right. Maybe I'll visit you in Florida."

"Sure. I'll be like all the retired gringos there. I'll have a wife who can't cook and a mistress who can't screw."

They shook hands.

"*Mucha suerte*, Dr. Good."

"Yeah, good luck," Martin said. "And thanks."

Now Martin finished his bottle of beer, opened another, and kneeled on the veranda to look through the gear. There was a compact raft with an attached CO_2 cartridge, a hand pump, a patching kit, and two aluminum paddles that were assembled by screwing shaft to blade. In the duffel he found the clothes he had worn in the tower, fairly clean now, Levi's, shirt, socks, and jogging shoes; a flashlight with spare batteries; an eight-ounce bottle of insect repellent; a machete and sheath; and a compass and several worn topographical maps. The cardboard box contained some of the items taken from the café in Tepazatlán: a dozen bottles of beer, a pack of cigarettes, melted candy bars, corn chips, canned foods—tuna, corned beef, beans, sardines—and a bag of stale rolls. Not much. Plus he had the uniform he wore, Ávila's wristwatch, wallet, and cigarette lighter, and the .45 pistol with a spare clip.

At dusk, in two trips, he carried everything down to the river. The water was still running high and muddy from the afternoon rains. He could hear frogs and crickets and the high whine of mosquitoes. Clouds of gnats swarmed above the river. A fish jumped in midstream and left a spreading bull's-eye ripple. This was a transitional period between the creatures of the day and the creatures of the night. *Pues*, he thought, I guess I'm a creature of the night now.

He removed the raft from its plastic box, unfolded it, spread it over the sand, and activated the CO_2 cartridge. The rubberized fabric twisted and filled. The raft was bigger than he'd expected; it could easily hold two men plus gear.

Martin loaded the rest of his supplies into the raft and pushed offshore. The current was moving at four or five miles per hour, the pace of a fast walk. It seemed faster, though; the trees on shore flicked past in a jerky procession. He could feel the throbbing power of the river.

He sat in the stern and used the paddle only to align the raft. Let the river do the work. His nose ached, his right ribs and shoulder hurt, and there was now a painful swelling in his right knee. He stared ahead, alert for rocks or snags that might damage the raft. Anything that protruded above the water's surface would change the sound of the river and create a patch of white water. But it was nearly dark now and he could not see much. He supposed that he would not have time to evade any obstruction that lay dead ahead.

The river narrowed and steepened as it passed between shadowy cliffs. Water fizzed white and there were many small waves. The raft bounced through and then the river widened and swept left around a bend.

Individual features of the forest could not be distinguished now. The black river, etched with foam, uncoiled; a strip of star-hazed sky unraveled overhead.

Martin lay the paddle across his thighs, dipped into the cardboard box for a bottle of beer, opened it, and then lit a cigarette. The cigarette coal could easily be seen from shore, of course. Never mind: he *felt* alone.

He would move into the future the same way this river moved into the night. The river would eventually empty into the sea and in a similar way Martin Springer would empty into eternity. Maybe tonight, maybe tomorrow, maybe thirty years from now. His death was a fact not yet recorded.

He found that he was enjoying the night and the river. He was alone. He could not remember ever really being alone. No one knew where he was. He himself did not know. He was a stranger to the world and to himself.

Martin felt that he was being watched by owls, big cats, ferrets, wolves, and ancient warlike gods. And he sensed something new within himself, an unused resource, dark and willing. A nocturnal self.

CHAPTER

1 6

The general was not the only old man at the party. There were others, civilian and military—saurian patriarchs—one a strange man by the name of Javier Solis. He was treated with great deference. All of the guests were dressed semiformally except for Mr. Solis, who wore sandals without socks, white duck trousers, and a loose guayabera shirt that was elaborately embroidered with gold and green thread. A black patch covered his left eye. He looked to be in his early seventies, tall and lean, with silky snow-white hair and mustache and leathery brown skin. He approached her with the ludicrous gallantry that she had come to expect in this country.

He bowed, introduced himself, and said, "You probably wondered who the peculiar old man was who had been staring at you with such intensity and admiration."

Katherine started to joke that, judging by his costume, she'd assumed that he must be the gardener, but she halted. He possessed a definite authority.

"I apologize for my rude staring. But you see, you remind me very much of my first wife. You could be her sister. She died when she was about your age. I remember her as she was then. Of course, if she had lived, she would be old now, nearly as ancient as me."

"You don't seem old, Mr. Solis," Katherine said. And that was true; she was aware of an extraordinary vitality in the man.

They chatted easily for a while and then he bowed again over her hand, wished her well, and left.

Katherine found Robert Harley standing alone at the deep end of the pool. He was a little drunk.

"Who is that man over there?" she asked. "The one talking to Vaca."

"That's Javier Solis."

"I know his name, but who *is* he?"

"Javier Solis is your ordinary everyday Peruvian polo-playing yachtsman multimillionaire. He invests in resort properties. He owns a big percentage of the hotel in Playas del Oro, and other places in the Caribbean. Now, I hear, he's building a new resort somewhere in Yucatán."

"He told me that I look very much like his first wife."

"Yes, well, maybe so."

"How did she die?"

"He killed her."

"My God."

"With a dagger. Because she was involved with another man. Or rather, he *thought* she was. And so to save his honor and her honor he killed her. He didn't kill himself. There are limits to the obligations of honor."

"And he seemed like such a nice man."

"Javier is pleasant, but not nice."

"I suppose there's also a gruesome story about how he was blinded in one eye?"

"Yes. He lost his eye in a duel."

"You mean like sword fighting?"

"Exactly."

"How strange."

"Are you sure you don't need a ride to your hotel after the party?"

"No, thank you."

"I'm not trying to get you into the sack, Mrs. Springer, I'm only offering you a ride. It's a long way to the city."

"I must talk to Vaca."

"Talk to him at his office. Make an appointment."

"I appreciate your advice, Mr. Harley."

He grinned. "Meaning you don't, not at all."

"That's correct."

"By God, you are a woman!" he said, perfectly imitating the voice and accent of the general.

"That's pretty funny," Katherine said, "for an assistant commercial attaché."

The guests began leaving at nine-thirty and by ten o'clock Vaca, standing at the high entrance gate, was saying goodnight to the last of them. Katherine could hear voices and car engines beyond the wall. Servants were cleaning up around the pool area. Some of the guests, men and women, had approached her during the last hour. Their questions were discretely phrased and uttered. Most seemed to think that she was Vaca's new mistress.

Katherine went through the sliding glass doors and into the house. There was a bathroom at the end of the hall. The porcelain—sink, bathtub, toilet, and bidet—was lavender; the taps and pipes were gold-plated.

She exited through a different door and found herself in a large bedroom, a male's room, Vaca's. The bed was round and very big. She could not resist the impulse to look in his closet: shirts, trousers, suits, shoes, ties, several military uniforms. Did Vaca hold rank in the army? Probably, she thought: didn't all of these tin-pot dictator types like to believe that they possessed the military virtues?

One gaudy dress uniform looked like the kind worn by doormen at posh hotels.

Katherine returned to the living room. It was huge, with a vaulted beam ceiling. Most of the furniture had been crafted out of heavy dark woods, but there was a blond television-stereo console, and a white baby grand piano, lid open, in the corner. Pretty Indian blankets were scattered over the tiles. There were ceramic pots and pre-Columbian figures—ugly little idols—on the fireplace mantel (you could walk erect into that fireplace), and other, larger old pots served as planters. A bookcase contained volumes in Spanish and English, most of them concerning the political and military sciences, and the dismal science, economics. High on the wall above the fireplace was a life-sized wood carving of the crucifixion. Crude, gory, ugly. There were paintings, portraits and realistic landscapes, elsewhere on the walls. There weren't enough furnishings and decorations for the space; the room looked cold and bare. She could not imagine Vaca's wife and daughters being wholly at ease in this room, this overly masculine walled-in house.

Vaca entered and smiled at her. His expression was stern, like a resentful boy's, until he smiled.

"I've sent the servants away," he said.

"Why did you do that?"

"So we can talk."

"I don't see how the servants would interfere with our conversation."

"You don't know. They would be everywhere, moving things, breaking things, mopping the floors, cawing like crows. I'm going to have a brandy. Will you have one with me?"

"No, but I'll have another glass of wine."

"Good. Is it too hot in here? We could go outside by the pool."

"Yes. Let's do that."

"Your hair will trap the starlight."

Katherine reclined in a chaise lounge by the water while Vaca, walking stiffly, like a mechanical man, went to the bar. The Japanese lanterns were still burning. There were many stars and a few clouds that had been incandesced by moonlight. It was unnaturally quiet now, no voices, no music, no insect noises, no dogs barking, no traffic sounds—she realized that this was the only silence she'd known since arriving in the country.

Vaca returned, passed her a glass, and sat on a nearby deck chair. "I hope the party wasn't too boring for you," he said.

"I enjoyed myself."

"I was afraid you would not come. And then I saw you standing over there and I was very happy."

"My husband . . ."

"Well, as I have told you, he has been moved from Tepazatlán to the coastal village of Esperanza. Perhaps they fear that we will retake Tepazatlán in our new offensive. We think he has been treated fairly well. I've had my people inquire. There are often channels of communication between enemies, you know. At first the communists hoped for money, a ransom, but now it seems that they're willing to make a trade. We are holding a man named Enrique Carvajal, one of their leaders. Only the details have to be negotiated. That may take time. You understand. They will ask for more. We may have to trade another prisoner or two. But it will turn out fine in the end, Caterina, I promise you."

"Thank you. Is there anything else you can tell me?"

"Not at this moment. But I've told my people to telephone us here tonight if there are any developments."

"Thank you," Katherine said again. "I can't tell you how grateful I am. Everything seemed so hopeless."

"No longer. Did you know that the word *esperanza*—
the name of the town where your husband is held—means
'hope' in Spanish?"

"No, I didn't know that."

"And so now try to relax for a while, Caterina. Enjoy
your wine and this night. Aren't our nights very sensual?
I have visited many countries but nowhere have I seen
nights like these."

"I'll finish my wine and this cigarette and then I must
go. You have someone who can drive me to the hotel?"

"Go?" he said. "I had hoped you would stay here with
me."

"For just a few more minutes."

"I want you to stay with me."

"Stay here tonight?"

"Yes."

"You mean sleep with you?"

"Are you so surprised that I desire you? You are a
lovely woman, Caterina. You must not be shocked when a
man behaves like a man."

"All right," she said. "You've behaved like a man. Now
I would be happy if you'd arrange to have someone drive
me to my hotel."

"You ought to stay with me. You won't regret it. No
woman has ever been disappointed in the lovemaking of
C' de Vaca."

"Are you telling me that you'll help Martin only if I
sleep with you?"

He was annoyed now. "Why do you put it that way? I
want very much to make love to you. I will please you,
I promise that. And I will also do all I can to help your
husband."

"But you'll try harder, do more, if I stay with you tonight?"

"Why are you behaving like merchandise?"

"Why are you treating me like merchandise? I want to go now, Mr. Vaca."

"Caterina, we both know that you are going to spend the night in my bed. You're a mature woman. Too mature to play the coquette."

She watched him.

"I won't deny that a man will work harder to please a woman he has loved than one who has rejected him."

"I understand."

"Only Vaca can restore your husband to you."

"Yes, yes, it's clear enough."

"You are so innocent. It is the way of the world."

"Your world."

"Relax, have more wine, enjoy this night. Love should be flavored by anticipation. By expectation. We shall take our time. We have all night. All of it. I don't think either of us shall sleep much. Love is an art, you know."

"You're not talking about love, you're talking about sex."

"You are acting like a child."

Katherine smiled.

He misinterpreted the smile. "Yes, it's true, a brat, a sulky child. Perhaps you want me to spank you."

"This is a wonderful pool. Let's swim, Vaca."

"Splendid idea. Now you're being reasonable."

"Go in the house and put on your swimming suit. And bring me one. Maybe your wife or one of your daughters has a suit that will fit me."

"Why do we need swimming suits? I want to see your lovely body, Caterina. And I want you to see me too. I am very well endowed."

Katherine laughed. She was genuinely amused, the vain rooster did make her laugh; but at the same time he frightened her. There was something missing in him; or maybe something present that was absent in other men.

"I'll admire your endowment later," she said. "But I want a swimming suit, just for a little while. I'll remove it in the water."

He smiled. "Usually it's the women with ugly bodies who are modest."

"I'm only modest at first. Until I get to know a man."

He stood up. "I have cocaine," he said. "It can be absorbed through the mucous membranes of the vagina."

"Really? I didn't know that. It must be fun."

Katherine watched him circle the pool and enter the house, then she rose, removed her shoes, and ran over to the heavy wall gate. Wait, my purse. She returned to the pool area and hunted frantically. Forget the purse. No, there it was. She snatched it up from the tiles and hurried back to the gate. Oh, God, was it going to be locked? No. She pushed it open, passed through the arch, and closed the gate behind. The latch clicked loudly. She pressed her right eye to a crack just above the middle hinge. And now here came Mr. Head of the Cow, naked as a plucked chicken except for patches of chest and pubic hair, his endowment attentive to the pleasures ahead. Vaca stopped and looked around uncertainly.

"Caterina?"

Katherine picked up her shoes and purse and started down toward the dense spray of lights below. How far was the city? Fifteen miles. A long walk, but she had walked as far in the past and could do so again. It would be painful, though, without the right kind of shoes. But there was a telephone in the guard shack five or six miles down the road; she could call a taxi from there.

The arrogant bastard. There was something psycho about him. Would he follow her? If he did, she could hide in the darkness on either side of the road.

"Katherine?"

She stopped. There was a car parked just ahead.

"It's me. Robert Harley."

"Who?"

"Are you all right?"

"Mr. Harley?"

"Get in the car. I'll drive you to your hotel."

She hesitated for an instant (frying pan into fire?), and then got into the front seat. He started the engine, turned on the headlights, shifted into gear, and pulled away.

"What are you doing here?" she asked.

"Waiting for you."

"Why?"

"Why were you walking barefoot down the road at this hour?"

"Thank you."

"I didn't expect to see you walking. I was going to come in if I heard you scream."

"Thank you."

"You're welcome."

"He's a creepy man."

"He is that."

"Why are the men down here so obsessively randy?"

"I suppose it's the machismo thing. If you don't make a pass at every pretty woman someone might think you're a eunuch. I don't know."

"Why didn't you warn me about Vaca?"

"I did."

"Not explicitly."

"He's an insect."

"And apparently a great friend of the government of the United States."

"He's very useful to us."

"He said he wanted to talk to me about Martin."

"Sure."

"And then I found that he'd dismissed the servants."

"Uh-huh."

"There's something wrong with him, isn't there? Psychologically?"

"You're a quick study."

"Don't be sarcastic."

"I'm sorry." Then he said, "You can smoke if you want to."

"And stink up your upholstery? Never."

"Did he assault you?"

"No, but he would have. I'm sure he would have raped me if I hadn't got out of there."

"Vaca has been involved in a number of scandals concerning women. Wives in the diplomatic community. Schoolgirls. A tourist girl from Minnesota who vanished. He has the reputation of a sort of Bluebeard."

"Now you tell me. Just what does the man *do* in this vile government?"

"He's head of the Bureau of Internal Security, generally known as *Telaraña*. Do you know what *araña* is?"

"No."

"An *araña* is a spider. That's what Vaca is."

"Then *telaraña* must be a spider's web."

"That's right. They regard themselves as an elite, patriotic, piously Catholic cadre, almost a mystical brotherhood, the only salvation of their country and the hemisphere."

"I wish I were home with my kids," Katherine said.

"Where are your children?"

"At home. My mother is taking care of them."

"I'll drive you to the airport tomorrow morning."

"No. I must stay. I must do all I can to help Martin."

"Listen," he said. "Don't repeat this. Don't ask me any questions. I don't have any hard information yet. But I do think—it may be that at this moment your husband is free."

C H A P T E R

1 7

The river had expanded into a crescent-shaped lake that on the topographical map appeared to be about ten miles long. Here in the center the current was slow, barely twisting the water's surface, and the raft completed a revolution every sixty or seventy yards as it drifted downstream. The lake was moon-scaled and the Milky Way was reflected star for star—a duplicate galaxy. Martin could hear the squeaking of bats and see their elusive shadows on the water; and there were larger animals hunting overhead too, perhaps nighthawks. He sprawled in the bottom of the raft, his hands trailing in the cool water. He felt feverish, on the verge of delirium.

It was after midnight now but still hot and very humid. He would not find a better place to swim. Hurrying because of the mosquitoes and gnats, he removed the gun belt, boots, and uniform, and slipped over the side. There was a cold shock at first, he lost his breath, but then he was comfortable.

Water, textured by the current, rippled almost painfully

over his body. He was certain now that he had a fever; his skin was abnormally sensitive and his thinking was skewed.

The lake had a clean astringent smell, and in its surface motion he could hear a hallucinatory hissing and whispering and tinkling. He imagined that below, in the blackest depths, other sounds might exist, an alien music denied to his senses. The water's coolness made him aware of the aches in his right shoulder, ribs, and knee. His nose was swollen and painful too; he could not easily breathe through it.

He wished Katherine were here with him. She loved the water and swam like a porpoise. While underwater her mouth formed a moue and she expelled silver bubbles that ascended in chains and burst softly on the surface. She scavenged along the bottom, finding objects to show him—freshwater clams or snails, a smooth pebble, a lost fishing lure. Here, Martin, see? She would show it to him and then let it flutter back down to the bottom. Katherine had a way of surfacing faceup toward the sun so that her hair fitted like a close sleek cap. Her eyelashes were spiky then and her eyes narrowed as she smiled. The children were good swimmers too; Peter boyishly violent, Mary balletically graceful.

Martin floated downstream for twenty minutes and then, refreshed, crawled into the raft. The forested shores to his left and right were closer, the lake had narrowed, and the current seemed swifter now. Forward he could hear a humming similar to the noise of swarming bees.

The coolness of the water had reduced air pressure inside the raft; the tubes were spongy and buckled slightly beneath his weight. He should have attended to that sooner; it was too late now to find, assemble, and employ the hand pump. He had only enough time to dress and secure the supplies.

He still could not see a flash of white water ahead, although the humming had become louder. The rapid would be situated in the narrows where the lake was retransformed into river. A great volume of water might be funneled into the old riverbed. Very fast and rough, he supposed, but deep too—rocks probably would not be a problem.

Gradually the water's surface was roughened, churned into six-inch-high wavelets that streamed in V's down toward the channel. Moonlight fractured the water into light and dark facets and ignited the bubbly froth, and moonlight rimmed the dark holes—some as big as melons—that swirled downstream. The raft rocked fore and aft and from side to side. The humming had been amplified into a deep crackling roar, like the noise of a great fire, and in the roar he could hear a tinkling like silver bells—altar bells—and a rhythmic throbbing.

Ahead now he saw that over the years a natural dam had accumulated at the narrows, a tangled dark mass that rose at least ten feet above the water's surface. Floodwaters had carried down uprooted trees that had jammed at this place; later floods had brought more trees and tons of silt, ultimately forming the lake.

There was a momentary calm, a pool of fairly smooth water, just above the rapids. It appeared slightly convex. The river had forced a thirty-foot-wide exit through the dam's center. The raft lifted onto the smooth dome of water, hesitated, and in that instant Martin could look down an avalanching chute that ran straight for hundreds of feet and then hooked into the darkness beyond. It looked very steep. A little steeper, Martin thought, and you could call it a fall. But, through a trick of light, the river below appeared frozen solid, crystallized. An ice river, a river of quartz. The light-suffused mist above the water was crystalline too. And the stars. It was beautiful and deathly cold, this mineral universe. And then the raft, jerked violently forward, was glissading down the spillway.

Martin's fever made him feel light-headed and pleasantly detached. He was not afraid. It seemed to him that he was thinking very clearly. But then his feverish lucidity was gone and there remained only a sensed kinetics—violent propulsion, abrupt rising and sinking, spins, torsion, a momentary suspension of gravity. Abstract forces assaulted his body. There was no time now for thought: there was just the erupting phosphorescent river, the wet choking mist, the incessant motion.

Near the end of the rapids Martin was hurled into the river and pulled down through the chop and foam. He fought to remain on the surface. He retched. He floated down the last silver riffles and into the deep water beyond. The surface was still roiled and pocked but no longer white, and not so swift. He was tired. God, he was tired.

The river had broadened and smoothed. Ah well, he thought, let it go. It was painful and ridiculous, humiliating—really, what was the point? Today was his time to die. Haven't you been paying attention? Enough of fear and hope, foolish struggle. He envisioned his body thirty or forty feet below, carried along by the current (his limbs sinuously moving, like Ávila's), touching the silty bottom here, there temporarily snagged by the roots of a sunken tree, lifting in an upswell, sinking again, rolling along the riverbed, borne unceremoniously toward the sea. No sense of sadness accompanied the image.

And then Katherine and the kids were in the river with him. "Martin," Katherine said urgently, "the raft is going away. We're all tired, you've got to retrieve the raft for us, Martin."

The raft, a yellow blur hardly distinguishable from the blurs of moonlight, was slowly receding downstream.

"We'll wait here for you, Martin."

He began swimming. His joints ached, he had been weakened by fever and his exertions, he was unable to establish an effective rhythm. Easy, he thought, pace yourself.

He heard Katherine and the kids shouting encouragement—a trick, a lie from one part of himself to another part. "Go on, Martin, you're almost there!" "Hurry, Daddy, just a little farther!" Hallucinations, he knew, and yet so clear, so accurate in pitch and intonation, that he could not disobey.

The raft was half-filled with water. It nearly submerged beneath his weight. Martin rested for a time and then bailed out the raft. The flashlight still worked. The hand pump had been lost in the rapids, and the spare paddle, the bottle of insect repellent, and most of the food. The topographical map and the bread rolls had been turned to pulp. He wrung out his clothes and dressed.

There were five bottles of beer left. He opened one and drank it slowly. The river was wide and not very fast here. It moved elliptically through the forest, finding its way. Martin finished his beer and opened another. His fever and the beer combined to create a pleasant, dreamy sensation; it was like being suspended midway between sleep and waking.

There was a series of curves and then a straight run, and downriver and to his right, set back in the forest shadows, a light burned. A square light; a window. Weak light, probably from an oil lantern or candles. A military outpost? Martin got out the pistol and worked the slide to inject a cartridge into the chamber. Would the cartridge fire after immersion?

The light seemed to be moving toward him rather than the opposite. When the raft was fifty yards above the light a mule brayed and some dogs began barking. Three or four dogs. He could not see them but judging by the noise they were racing along the bank, keeping pace with the raft. And then in the moonlight he saw that there were a few acres of cultivated land and a hut. The hut's door opened, spilling a crooked rectangle of yellow glow over the ground, and a shadow passed through the light and was reabsorbed by darkness. A whistle, a shout, curses. Dogs, growling sullenly, retreated up the bank. It was only a small farm. The light, the man, the dogs, and the braying mule were left behind.

There would be more farms ahead, and towns, and the war.

Martin sprawled out in the bottom of the raft. The duffel bag served as pillow. He could feel the movement of the river beneath the fabric. That and the motion of the raft gently rising and sinking and sliding downcurrent, the slow revolutions, and the changing patterns of the stars, were very soothing. Everything was all right now. Nothing could happen to him for a while. The river purred and softly chimed.

He awakened. Motion had ceased some time ago. It was false dawn now; the sky was a luminous gray and the air around him irradiated with a glossy sheen.

The raft had drifted up on a sandbar in the center of the river. The channels, curving around to his left and right, were mostly invisible beneath a cobwebby mist. Along shore there was wrinkled grayish sand, scrub brush, and scattered pieces of driftwood as pale as bone. They looked like bones, femurs, fibulas, tibias, ribs. A patch of forest rose in the center of the island; great trees hung with ragged cloaks of moss, ferns, palms, and parasitic vines whose translucent blue-green leaves looked like glass.

The air was heavy and soft and hot. Hot, yet he shivered. His joints ached. His face and hands were swollen from insect bites. Some of the bites were oozing pus. His fever waxed and waned. At moments he was fairly lucid; his life was an orderly chain of actions that had delivered him to this time and place. But at other times the past was jumbled, inconsequential, and he was a stranger to himself and this queer reeking planet. His fever loosened particles of thought and disconnected images that combined in disturbing ways.

The green splash of forest in the middle of the sandbar was about fifty yards away. What was that? A thirty-second stroll. He thought: I must hide, I must rest, a day in the sun will kill me, I must wait for night. Go then. Yes, in just a moment I'll go, I promise. He slept for a time and when he awakened the clouds to the east were glowing neon pinks and oranges and yellows. A flock of long-necked white birds, legs dangling, were flying low up the left river channel. Their wingbeats compressed the air with a crepitant sound and stirred the mist. Martin had dreamed that he lay in a cool aqueous light beneath a grove of palms.

He commanded his body to crawl out of the raft and stand erect. His vision darkened and swarmed with filmy specks like bacteria seen through a microscope. He was astonished by the rapidity and power of his heartbeats; they shook his body, his heart leaped about unanchored. It seemed to Martin that this, simply standing and then dragging the raft over the sand toward the woods, was the most determined act of his life.

He left the raft, pushed through a barrier of thorny shrubs, staggered a few yards into the dimness, and lay down. His bones and flesh melted. It was shady in here, safe, but very cold; he shivered and sobbed from the chill. The fever. Am I dying? He slept deliriously for a time, a minute or an hour, and awakened with the conviction that small needle-toothed animals watched him from the shadows, rats and lizards, serpents, gargoyles no bigger than his hand.

And in the trees were leering bat-winged monkeys and arboreal shrews with tiny human faces. He hoped they were friendly. They might approach while he slept, smelling and touching his body, bringing him water cupped in their wrinkled little palms.

The light was as thick as jelly. There was no nourishment in this air. A winged dog-faced thing glided down from the treetops and began to suck the breath from his lungs.

CHAPTER

1 8

Jorge C' de Vaca managed to restrain his temper until near the end of the interview when, exasperated by the arrogance of the reporter, the hot lights, the swinish technicians (one man casually tossed a fuming cigarette into a valuable pre-Columbian vessel; another spilled coffee on the carpet and rubbed it in with his shoe), he finally snapped. "You are an idiot, Mr. Packard. Do you really believe that if a man did order the torture and murder of other men, that he would appear on camera to confess his crimes?"

Packard did not like being called an idiot; he flushed and flexed his jaw muscles; but he was also pleased by Vaca's outburst.

"Sir, I didn't accuse you of anything. I merely inquired. There have been rumors, you know. Accusations."

"Accusations. I see. Well, have you stopped beating your wife, Mr. Packard?"

"Then you refuse to answer my question, sir?"

How could you deal with this casuistry? By comparison, American television journalists made the Jesuits appear almost childishly candid, and the communists fair, rigorous logicians. It seemed that they studied something called "communications" in college: not history, certainly not the political and military sciences, and not languages— Packard did not know enough Spanish to order breakfast in that tongue.

"Sir?" Packard said, exploiting the silence.

Chinga tu madre, Vaca thought. He tried to smile in an amiable way, and failed: he knew it was his rictal smile, his death's-head smile.

"Mr. Packard, I am a mild man. I am bullied by my wife and daughters, I am persecuted by my servants and my pets. Sometimes I wish I were the kind of man you accuse me of being. If I were—if I were you would have long ago become a martyr to your whorish profession. Good day. That is all. Turn off your fucking machines immediately and get out."

He did not rise from behind the desk. After the men had gathered their equipment and were preparing to leave the office, he said to Packard, "Alvin? I've received reports that the communists have you in mind for some sort of . . . gesture. Your name has appeared in certain documents. It isn't very clear what they intend, but you would be wise to take precautions."

"What?"

"Think about it, Alvin."

Packard, near the door, stared back down the long room. He was carrying one of the sound man's cases; his knees were bent, shoulders a little hunched; one hand extended toward (but not quite touching) the door handle.

"What is this, Vaca?"

Jorge C' de Vaca concentrated on directing his hatred the length of the room toward the complacent Mr. Packard. Yes, and the man *was* afraid: he seemed to have become smaller, maimed, dwarfish—an analogue to his inner state.

Vaca knew that he possessed powers. The powers (and they could be used either benignly or malignantly) had to be projected outward, not diffused, never ever turned against the self, but focused on the object the same way you focus a magnifying lens on dry grass and watch it burst into flame. Your will, your energy, radiated outward and enabled you to either seduce or wound.

"If you'll make a formal written request to my secretary, Alvin, I may be able to assign some men to watch over you."

"Hey, what is this?" Packard asked. "What are you telling me?"

"It's your choice, Alvin. But if I were you I would very quickly return to the United States. But you decide. This is not an expulsion."

"Like hell."

When they were gone, when he was alone, Vaca got up and walked out into the room. The coffee stain was an ugly blotch, still damp. There was powdery cigarette ash in the nap of the carpet and one cigarette, carelessly laid on the edge of a cabinet, had burned through the varnish. Pigs, savages. Another cigarette butt in the pre-Columbian pot, a dirty handprint on the silk wallpaper, cardboard coffee containers, a tooth-indented wad of chewing gum in a decorative porcelain plate, and lingering in the air the stink of unclean bodies and cheap cologne. Vaca had an acute sense of smell: it was a lifelong torture.

He loved this room. Only the president of the republic had a larger office, with a better view, with finer damask drapes, with more gilded fretwork along the baseboards and cornices. Vaca had furnished it partly at his own expense and partly by the confiscation of objects possessed by politically unreliable persons and organizations. His crescent-shaped desk, ornately carved and so highly polished that you could see your reflection on the surface, was larger than the president's. (He would move this desk to the great office when he became president.) A muralist had painted the high ceiling a sky-blue, and there were mackerel clouds sweeping the length of the room, and flying birds, and a hazy indistinct face—composed of sky and cloud mist—that represented the Virgin Mary. She was ethereal, asexual, pure. The Holy Mother. Vaca worshipped Mary. She shined like gold out of the slime and filth of this world. Mother of God. But sometimes he stared at the image on the ceiling for so long that the face dissolved, as in a trick painting, and in its place he saw snarling dogs or a human skull or a copulating pair. Blasphemous images, tricks of Satan.

That afternoon one of his agents, a mongrel named Saavedra, arrived to deliver his report. He was like a dog who had been beaten too often, cowering before the strong and vicious to the weaker. Yet he was good at his job; he hadn't the courage for treachery. Vaca did not invite him to sit down. "Yes," he said. "Go on, man."

Saavedra consulted his notebook. Vaca knew that the man had memorized its contents, but this was a way of avoiding his master's eyes. Saavedra never looked at a man unless his attention was elsewhere.

"The lady ate breakfast alone in the hotel restaurant at eight-forty. She returned to her room until ten o'clock, and then left the hotel by taxi. She visited the anthropology museum, and then walked to the duty-free zone where she entered several shops. She bought alligator shoes and an alligator handbag in one of the shops, a silk scarf from China in the second, and nothing in the third and fourth shops. The lady then went to a bank and cashed a check. After that she went—"

"For how much money?"

"The lady's check was for two hundred dollars."

"Did she receive the money in dollars?"

"No, in our currency."

"Go on."

"Yes, sir. The lady then walked to the cathedral. She gave money to the beggars. She entered the church. She did not dip her fingertips in the holy water. She did not genuflect. She did not kneel. She did not appear to pray. She walked around the cathedral, and looked in all the chapels, and then she returned to the street."

"She didn't pray?"

"No, sir, I did not see her pray. She took a taxi back to her hotel. She went to her room. At twelve-forty she ate lunch in the hotel restaurant."

"Alone?"

"The American newspaperman—Dixon Stenstrom— talked to her but she did not invite him to sit at her table."

"But was she friendly toward him?"

"I did not receive that impression, sir. No."

"What impression did you receive, Saavedra?"

"To me, sir, the lady appeared disdainful."

"You know, don't you Saavedra, that she went with the man to Playas del Oro. Where you and Sosa lost them."

"The vehicle broke down, sir. It was the carburetor."

"Yes. Go on."

"After lunch the lady returned to her room." Saavedra closed his notebook. He did not lift his eyes, but stared down at the carpet.

"So," Vaca said. "She's at the hotel now? In her room?"

"Yes. When I left, sir."

"Who is detailed to watch her this afternoon?"

"Sosa and Peña, sir."

"Is there anything else you wish to tell me?"

"No, sir."

"All right then, Saavedra."

"With your permission?"

"Yes, go," Vaca said. "Wait—what have you learned about this Dr. Springer?"

"Nothing so far, sir."

"Is he being held in Tepazatlán?"

"We don't know, sir."

"Go," Vaca said.

After Saavedra left the room Vaca picked up the telephone and dialed the Hotel Nacional and demanded to speak to Katherine Springer. There were five rings.

"Yes. Hello." Her voice was husky, sleep-thickened.

"Caterina. Did I awaken you?"

"Who is this? Vaca? It's Vaca, isn't it?"

"I'm sorry if I awakened you."

"I was napping, yes."

"Ah, Caterina, I am so sorry about last night. I was a drunken pig. Please forgive me. Please, give me the opportunity to beg your forgiveness."

"Never mind, Vaca. Just forget it."

"Last night, when I realized that you had gone, that I had frightened you away, I nearly went mad with remorse. Caterina. I placed the muzzle of my revolver between my teeth. Yes. But I couldn't pull the trigger—not because of fear, but because I could not die without first apologizing to you."

"Well," she said. "Now that you've apologized . . ."

"How did you get back to your hotel last night?"

"One of your guests drove me."

"Who?"

"Does it matter?"

"I want to thank him."

"I thanked him for you."

"Caterina, listen, I have dispatched a trusted subordinate to contact the enemy. I have authorized him to negotiate in my name. I have exceeded my authority in order to free your husband. I have jeopardized my position. But I made a promise to you. Do you think I could violate my promise?"

"I really don't know. Could you?"

"Listen. Listen, Caterina, I was drunk last night, cruel, selfish. I wanted you too much, it made me crazy."

Silence.

"Caterina? I will continue to do everything I can to help your husband. You have my word."

"Thank you."

"I expect to learn something tonight. A report is due. I am confident that the news will be very good. Do you hear? The news should be good."

"Phone me, will you?" she said.

"I want you to come to my house this evening. We will await the good news together. Please? Somewhere, somehow, my cook has managed to obtain a young lamb. This is not the season for lamb, but my cook is a magician. He's Lebanese, and I don't believe that you have ever tasted lamb as this master prepares it. Will you come?"

"No. I hate out-of-season lamb prepared by Lebanese cooks."

"Caterina. Don't tease me. You will come tonight, won't you?"

"No."

"I'll expect you. My cook will prepare the lamb. The wine you like shall be well chilled. The moon will bless us—I promise you. Eight o'clock. Caterina?"

"Eight o'clock," she said. "Sorry, I have a prior engagement."

"I love you," he whispered.

Silence.

"I am holding myself as I talk to you. I am hard."

"Soften up, Vaca." And she broke the connection.

* * *

She was late. That was to punish him. He expected it. He was amused. They were so predictable. And then she was very late. He listened for the sound of an engine outside the walls. At ten o'clock his wife telephoned from France. She had been suffering from angina; she and the girls were returning home.

"As you please," Vaca said.

Twenty minutes later he dismissed the servants and threw the overcooked lamb roast to the dogs.

CHAPTER

1 9

There were periods when Martin's fever was quiescent and he regained awareness. He did not wholly welcome consciousness; it denied the powerful quirky magic he had discovered in delirium. The music and the voices ceased. His visions dissolved. His voluptuous lassitude was interrupted and he returned to a limited, inflexible world.

Late in the afternoon his thirst forced him out of the woods. His lips were crusted from fever. His saliva was stringy. Martin sat by the raft and drank the remaining three bottles of beer. They did not quench his thirst.

It was going to rain. As he watched, the inky clouds overhead eclipsed the last blue patch of sky. He was immersed in a smoky violet glow. Inverted trees of lightning flickered in the clouds. The air was thick with humidity and herbal scents and the swampy odor of the river and the sharp ozone smell of the storm.

The raft's air chambers had inflated in the heat; the fabric was taut. When Martin felt the first cold pellets of rain he turned the raft over, lay supine, and pulled it over him. There was a soft yellow glow, a pleasant feeling of enclosure, and the smell of the rubberized fabric. The crisp snapping of the raindrops resonated through the air chambers: *tick!* and then *tickatickatick*. Soon the rain came down hard and the ticking turned into a steady rumble.

Martin slept again and when he awakened the rain had stopped. It was stifling beneath the raft. He could smell his stale fever sweat. He lifted an edge of the raft and crawled out. Some tall white birds on a bank across the channel were hanging out their wings to dry. The river was high and turbulent now. It was seven-thirty: he'd slept most of the fourteen hours he had spent on the island. His fever was gone but he remained very weak.

He dragged the raft down to the water's edge, then returned for the paddle, his duffel bag, and the webbing belt with its holster and pistol. It was a mild evening, cooled by the rain, with a sinking orange sun and charcoal clouds and flashes of turquoise sky. He lay prone on the sand and drank deeply of river water (thinking that at this moment dehydration was a greater threat than unknown bacteria), then he loaded his gear into the raft and pushed off. The current swept him past the island. The two channels merged in a foamy chop the color of root beer, and the river curved off into the darkening forest.

Rafting was easy tonight. The current was swift but there were no serious rapids. A steady breeze out of the northwest kept down the gnats and mosquitoes. He felt a little stronger. The river hissed and purled, curved glassily over submerged boulders, ponderously advanced through a series of meandering curves.

At dusk he surprised a large spotted cat that was drinking from the river. A jaguar; what they called *El Tigre* down here. All of the remaining light seemed concentrated on its eyes and tawny fur. It lifted its head and gave him a long yellow stare and then vanished into the forest.

Later the moon rose and its reflection appeared to spin like a catherine wheel in the riffles.

He passed a small farm and then, a few miles downriver, another. Several miles more and he drifted by a village of a dozen huts; in the air there were smells of wood fires and cooking food. A naked potbellied boy, sucking his thumb, watched him from the bank.

The air chambers of the raft had partly deflated, the left more than the right. That loss of pressure could not be accounted for by the coolness of the water alone; there had to be a leak in the left chamber.

He passed another settlement of shacks. Dogs barked, a baby cried, a man on shore shouted drunkenly. A mile or so above the riverside village, situated upon a low plateau, were the lights of a much larger town.

He wondered if he had reached government-controlled territory. It was difficult to estimate how far he had traveled, especially during yesterday's long, fever-crazed voyage.

The raft could hardly support his weight now; the left air chamber was almost completely deflated. He paddled over to the bank and hauled the raft up a muddy slope and into the trees. The ground swarmed with shifting patterns of light and shadow. Wind in the treetops mimicked the sounds of the river.

"Goddamn the luck," Martin said.

His forearms appeared furry: mosquitoes. It did no good to brush them off, there were millions more. Got to get out of here, Martin thought, the bastards will exsanguinate me. And he thought, Christ, malaria, encephalitis, filariasis, equine encephalomyelitis, yellow fever, dengue fever . . .

He strapped on the pistol belt, picked up the duffel bag, and walked north through the woods. After about fifty yards he found a path that tacked through the trees, climbing all the while, which finally ended at a two-lane asphalt road. To his left and below, the town was a crosshatch of lights that outlined strips and rectangles of blackness. The churchyard was a black square close to the large square of the plaza. The campanile rose above the surrounding rooftops. Tepazatlán. Home. Jesus.

As he watched, all but a few of the lights were extinguished. Martin glanced at his wristwatch: ten o'clock, curfew. All civilians and most military personnel were required to carry passes when on the streets after ten. But he was not a civilian, there were captain's bars displayed on his khaki shirt, and he wore a .45 pistol on his hip—an object with considerable authority.

Well, he thought, what the hell. Be bold. He had learned at least that much from Cabrera and Fuerte and a few others during his months in this mad republic—be bold. Mostly it was the timid who perished: they died easily, and their corpses were thrown into the rivers and irrigation ditches or just left in the sun to rot. Let them know that you are dangerous. The crows ate the grasshoppers and let the wasps alone.

Martin, convinced of his logic but not free of dread, started down the road toward Tepazatlán.

The asphalt was still tacky from the day's heat. There were only a few clouds tonight, rows of wispy crescents drifting down from the north. The cambered black road, curving down through low hills, reminded him of the river. There were fields and pastures and patches of scrub forest on both sides of the road. The mosquitoes were a bother but he no longer worried about what diseases they might transmit; that, like so many other bothers, was a problem for the future.

The future—he imagined himself at home with his family during the Christmas holidays. It will be cold and snowing outside, maybe a blizzard, yes. The house smells of food, a goose or a big tom turkey, and smells of pine resin from the tree, and burning oak and cedar. There is a fire, of course, in the big stone fireplace. My daughter is helping her mother in the kitchen; Peter is sprawled out on the floor, doing his homework or maybe watching a football game on TV. And I—I am sitting in a chair by the fire, cracking and eating walnuts and sipping dry sherry.

God, I,wish it were true, I wish it were happening now.

And then he thought, fool, that isn't the future, it's the past, nostalgia. Listen, fool, wishes can weaken and kill you. Lies kill.

He realized that he still had a slight fever, enough to divest the world of cogency. He inhabited a dream. Dreams kill. Pay attention, Martin.

The road leveled and passed over an iron-grid bridge that spanned a ravine. He heard running water in the darkness below. He entered Tepazatlán. The main street was dark and quiet. A few blocks from the plaza he turned north down a narrow cobbled lane. He could smell night-blooming flowers and the smoke from wetted charcoal fires. He walked in silence for half a block and then the dogs started barking. There were dogs behind every wall, in every courtyard, and they barked and growled with an insane fury. Soon dogs were baying all over town.

Martin walked two blocks north and then turned west. Ahead he could see the church tower silhouetted against the stars. A woman and two children were curled up in a door well. One of the children, a small boy, lifted his head and silently stared at Martin as he passed. Further on a piratical marmalade cat gazed down at him from atop a glass-studded wall. "Kitty," Martin murmured, and the cat mewed a complaint.

He paused in front of the church, listening, staring up and down the street, then he swiftly climbed the steps. The big double doors were unlocked. He slipped inside and in his haste closed the door too firmly; the creak of the hinges, the slamming noise, and the metallic click of the lock reverberated through the nave. He moved sideways, pistol in hand, past the font of holy water and the poor box, and halted at the entrance of the left aisle. This end of the church was dark but faint light spilled out of the two side chapels ahead, and a bank of votive candles guttered near the altar. The least sound was amplified and lingered in the corners and around the apse.

Martin waited until the echoes diminished to a persistent throbbing hum, like the music in a conch shell, then he returned to the center aisle and advanced toward the altar. He moved slowly, glancing left and right, down the rows of pews. Candles glowed in each of the small side chapels, and in one he saw a pair of worn sandals on the stone floor. Martin crossed the nave, climbed the stairs, and passed through a gate into the chancel. Vagrant cool drafts of air made the candle flames snap and flutter. Crabs of orangy light scuttled up the brass organ pipes.

There were scraps of paper and balls of dust on the floor of the choir loft. And faintly, like aural hallucinations, he heard violin music: J. S. Bach, *Jesu, Joy of Man's Desiring*. At the rear of the choir Martin opened another gate and went down worn steps and through an open door into a hallway. It was very dark here. The music was louder. He realized that some of the ghostly echoes that he'd heard in the nave had their source in this music. He passed into a fairly large room. The vestry? There was a smell of mice, mildew, and camphor. Across the darkness there was a door; a thin strip of light seeped out beneath. Martin holstered the pistol, wiped his sweaty hand on his trouser leg, and crossed the room.

He knocked lightly on the door, paused, knocked again. The violin music ceased. Father Perecho's voice, on the other side of the panel, said, "Yes? Who is it? It's very late."

"Martin."

"It's late. Please return tomorrow unless it's very important. Is someone very ill?"

"It's me, Father. Dr. Springer."

"Martin?"

"I need your help."

The lock tumblers clicked; the door swung open. "What happened? Why are you here? This is very odd, Martin, very dangerous." The priest wore oversized black trousers and a white sleeveless undershirt. His bare feet were dirty.

"Let me in."

The priest stepped back to allow Martin to enter the room, then closed and locked the door.

"I don't understand," he said anxiously.

The little room was illuminated by half a dozen candles. There was a narrow unmade bed, wooden table and chairs, a desk, cabinets, a wardrobe, and against one wall a church pew. The priest's violin and bow were on the bed.

"I used to listen to you play from the tower some nights," Martin said. "I was surprised when you played secular love songs."

"Martin, you aren't going to tease me, are you? This is not the time."

"Are there new prisoners in the tower?"

"Yes."

"How many?"

"Five."

"Five in that small room? What will happen to them?"

"I don't know. I pray for them."

"Did you pray for me?"

"Of course. Martin, how did you get in here?"

"The front doors were unlocked."

"They were? But I thought ... I must go lock them. Wait here, Martin. Don't do anything foolish."

"Nor you," Martin said.

Father Perecho paused at the door. "How dare you enter my church wearing a pistol. I can't permit that."

"You permit armed soldiers in the church."

"I have no choice then."

"You have no choice now either, Father."

The blades of candlelight thinned and curved when the door opened. It was hot and stuffy in the small room, and smelled of unwashed bedding and hot candle wax. An arch led into a small kitchen and a bathroom ruled by cockroaches. A heavy wooden door bound by iron strips led into the churchyard. Next to it was a square iron-barred window: Martin parted the curtains and peered outside. The campanile was a tall obelisk tilted by his perspective, and beyond it were the moonlight-puddled yard and the killing wall. He saw no movement; no soldiers gathering in the shadows.

A yellowish, flaking mirror hung above the desk. Martin was surprised by his reflection. His nose was crooked and swollen, and there were dark bruises beneath his eyes. He had lost considerable weight during the last few weeks.

The priest entered carrying a candelabrum with three burning candles. He said, "I locked the door. Sometimes drunken soldiers sleep here. Vandals, thieves." He placed the candelabrum on the desk. "Martin, why are you here? Why did you come back?"

"I didn't intend to return."

"Then why did you?"

"Bad luck."

"What do you want?"

"I'd like to stay here for a couple of days. I've been sick. I'm better now but I need to rest."

"Here? Please, you can't stay here. No, that's impossible. You'll ruin my position with the authorities. It isn't that I'm afraid for myself, Martin . . ."

"Naturally you're afraid for yourself. You shouldn't be ashamed of that."

"I have my people to consider, my office and duties, my dear mission."

"All right, just one day, Father. I'll leave this time tomorrow night."

"Martin, please don't do this to me."

"I'm very tired."

"You don't know what you're asking."

"I do know."

"Please don't force me to make this decision."

"Look then, just give me some food and let me sleep here for four hours."

"No longer? You promise?"

"Just that."

"And then you'll go?"

"Yes. And now, for Christ's sake, will you have the decency to offer me something to eat and drink?"

"You've changed, Martin," the priest said quietly.

Father Perecho served him soup and bread and cheese and a cobwebby bottle of musty, sour wine, and then placed a pot of the strong local coffee on the table. "A cigarette, Father?" The priest brought his small hoard of American cigarettes, stale Lucky Strikes, and a nearly empty bottle of brandy.

"Why do you live in these miserable rooms?" Martin asked.

"I used to have a fine house not far from here, with a lovely garden and flower-covered walls. There was a gardener and a cook and a housekeeper. Say what you will about the rich landowners, Martin, they were very generous to the Church. There's no money now. These were the sexton's quarters. He vanished one day. I don't know whether he ran away or was arrested or killed or what."

"Well, the rich landowners will be back someday and your parish will prosper again."

"Why do you think they'll return?"

"They always do."

"But what if the communists win the war?"

"Then there'll be another war."

"Why have you come back to Tepazatlán? What happened to you during these last two days?"

"Has it only been two days? No, it's almost three days. It's a long story, Father. I don't have time to tell it now."

"I suppose you want to sleep. Four hours only, Martin, you promised."

"I'll go now. I feel stronger after eating."

"Where will you go?"

"North, cross-country to the border," Martin lied. Lying was a survival tactic. Trust was a game for victims.

The priest went into the kitchen and returned with a loaf of bread, a block of hard cheese wrapped in linen, some fruit, two liter bottles of water, and a package of cheap cigarettes. Martin packed everything into the duffel bag.

Father Perecho took the candelabrum and led him through the church to the front door.

"Martin, if something happens, if you're captured . . . you won't betray me, will you?"

"I'll try not to. It depends on how much they hurt me. But no, I don't think I'd betray you."

The priest sorted through a ring of heavy keys, unlocked the door, stepped outside, and advanced to the top of the steps. He stared up and down the dark street, then turned and nodded.

"Well," Martin said.

Father Perecho quickly embraced him. "I'm sorry. Good luck. Adiós, Martin."

"Adiós, Father."

Martin descended the steps and walked east down the street. The heavy church door slammed closed behind. Dogs commenced barking.

CHAPTER

2 0

Martin soon became lost in the maze of streets and alleys. He was forced to backtrack several times. He believed that even with the detours he continued to move south toward the river, but he was not certain. Once he heard low voices and breaking glass on the far side of a wall—soldiers looting a shop? The men sounded drunk. Eventually he found himself in the poorest section of town. The cobblestones ended and the street narrowed to a muddy lane, hardly more than a footpath, that tacked through a slum of shacks constructed out of salvaged planks and tarpaper. There was a septic stink here.

Ahead, a dog barked at him, spinning in fury. Martin leaned over and pretended to pick something up from the ground. The dog fled. These dogs had been well trained; every one of them had stopped stones with its ribs. *"Quién es?"* a voice inquired from one of the shacks.

"Shut your mouth," Martin said harshly, and the man was silenced. The poor in this country had been well trained too.

There were fewer shacks, and finally none, but the path

twisted on through corn and bean fields and thorny pastures where cattle bawled and trotted out of his way. Martin passed between the strands of a barbed-wire fence and ascended a rise to a copse of trees. Below was the moon-scaled river. No lights burned among the shacks. He tried to recall how Major Cabrera had described the area when they had discussed their escape plan. The river was wide there. Fishermen and river merchants usually left their boats pulled up on the sandy beach. There was the ferry landing, the stone ruins of an old mill, a village of maybe thirty shacks, and a log building that quartered three or four soldiers who were expected to guard the ferry and monitor river traffic. (But who, Cabrera said, drank rum and piratically extorted bribes from those who had to move up- or downriver. "Drunken swine. They'll be drunk. We'll kill them in their beds.")

Martin started down the slope. The dogs below were already barking. He had intended to sneak down and silently steal a boat. Foolish: you could not be furtive in this country. You had to be bold. He cut diagonally across a field to the dirt road and followed it to the ferry landing. The guard's quarters were just below the landing. The dogs howled and raged.

He walked directly to the cabin and began kicking the door. "Wake up, you drunken filth!" he shouted. "Move, do you hear me? Jump or the pigs will eat your greasy guts at sunrise!" Martin drew his pistol and flicked off the safety.

He heard sounds from within, muttering, a curse, and something—a bottle?—falling on the floor. A few yards away the river hissed against some pilings. Beyond the ferry landing the water appeared convex, arching toward the opposite shore. In one of the shacks a baby started crying.

Martin kicked the door again. "Can't you hear me? I'll

cut off your fucking ears!" He stepped to a small window
that was opaque with dirt and cobwebs, and rubbed the
heel of his palm against the glass. A spark flared in the
cabin's interior. The spark bloomed and a thin orangy light
pulsated through the room. A naked woman was crawling
beneath one of the bunks. Martin glimpsed only her legs
and buttocks before she vanished into the shadows. Above
her, on the bunk, a fat man was trying to arrange the covers so that she would be concealed. The kerosene lantern
had been turned too high and was smoking; a man, one leg
bare and the other thrust into a trouser leg, was reaching
out to lower the flame. A young mestizo with a bowl hair-
cut and a weedy mustache was buttoning his trousers as he
approached the door.

The door opened and Martin stepped sideways and
framed himself in the light.

The mestizo was very young, a boy.

"Identify yourself!" Martin screamed, and then without
permitting time for a reply, he placed his left hand against
the boy's chest and shoved him deep into the room.
"Scum! Rabble!" He entered, violently kicked the door
shut, and shouted, "You miserable riffraff, don't you know
how to salute an officer?"

The mestizo, the fat man in the bunk, and the man with
one leg in his trousers hastily saluted.

This is funny, Martin vaguely thought. Someday, if I
live, when I'm safe, I'll tell this story and it will seem hilarious.

The room reeked of sour bodies and sex and smoke
from the lantern. The woman's dress had been carefully
folded over the back of a chair; her red plastic shoes were
placed below.

"You," he said to the mestizo. "What is your name and
rank?"

"Sergeant."

"Sergeant what, idiot?"

"Vasquez."

"Señor?" Martin inquired softly.

"Señor Capitán."

And now, imitating Fuerte, Martin became dangerously gentle. He holstered the pistol. He smiled, and thought that in the dimness and with the tension he had created his smile might appear as mad as Fuerte's.

"Are you boys happy?" he asked softly. "Are the rations adequate? Do you miss your home villages? Do you miss your dear mothers? Are the whores good to you?"

And then, in a harder tone, he said, "Come with me, Vasquez. Bring the lantern. Never mind your boots and shirt." To the others he said, "You pigs stay here. Entertain your guest."

Martin and the sergeant went outside, turned left, away from the ferry landing, and walked along a steep sandy beach overhung with mossy trees.

"Hold the lantern higher," Martin commanded.

The boats had been pulled up on the sand: there was a flat-bottomed barge, several dugout canoes, an aluminum dinghy, a square craft that looked like it had been assembled out of packing crates, and half a dozen old wooden skiffs. Two of the skiffs had modern outboard engines cocked up in the sterns.

"I'll take this one," Martin said.

The skiff was about fourteen feet long, painted green, with an absurdly high prow and a low square stern. The engine was too small for the weight of the boat but it looked clean and fairly well maintained. And there was an extra five-gallon can of the gas-oil mix, and a set of oars.

"Push this one into the river," Martin said.

The sergeant hesitated. His smooth young face looked Oriental in the lantern's glow.

"I remember," he said. "You're the gringo doctor."

And now Martin recognized him: this Vasquez was a member of the firing squad. He had been among those who had shot Cabrera and Rodolfo, and would have shot Martin too if Fuerte hadn't arrived.

"You don't have to obey me," Martin said. "I can easily launch the boat. You can die for the Revolution. Maybe they will write a song about you. Maybe your mother will receive a small pension."

The sergeant hunched over and began pushing the skiff. It moved slowly, heavily down through the thick sand. Pebbles scraped against the keel. When all but the skiff's bow was afloat, Martin placed his hand on the pistol butt. I should kill him, he thought. Major Cabrera would kill him. Rodolfo would want me to kill him. Vasquez straightened and waited placidly. Felipe Fuerte would certainly kill the boy now.

"I want fifteen minutes," Martin said. "If I let you live, will you promise to give me fifteen minutes to get away?"

"Yes."

"You understand what I'm saying?"

"Yes. I understand."

"You swear you won't act until I've been gone fifteen minutes?"

"I swear."

"You swear to God?"

"I swear to God and Jesus and Mary and all the saints. I swear on my mother's soul."

"Get out of here," Martin said.

Vasquez picked up the lantern and started toward the cabin.

Martin pushed the boat offshore and clambered aboard. He lowered the engine, shifted into neutral, and pulled the cord three times. The motor sounded dead; there was no indication of a spark. He opened the choke and pulled the cord again; it stuttered, almost caught, and then died with a whine and a puff of oily smoke. (Now Vasquez, carrying the lantern, had passed through the trees and was climbing the bank above the ferry landing.) The skiff had drifted twenty yards offshore. Martin pulled the starter cord again and again until finally the engine, spewing smoke, was running fairly smoothly.

There was a clanking noise as he shifted into reverse and backed out into the river; another when he shifted into forward and headed toward the center. He closed the choke and advanced the throttle. Glassy waves peeled off the bow and the propeller churned up a seething wake. The motor was not smoking as much now. The skiff was more stable and faster than he had supposed. The speed increased when he reached the main current.

Here the Rio Negro was broad and deep. The surface whorls and ripples barely hinted at the enormous power below. The center appeared higher than the shadowy, equally distant shores. Ahead a low sandbar split the river. Martin aimed toward the right channel.

And then, above the buzzing of the engine, he heard a queer fluttering sound and immediately afterward a distant echoing crack. He twisted and looked back over the fizzing wake. The ferry landing and the shack village were indistinct shadows in the chiaroscuro of night. Now a spurt of flame and another sharp crack. More flashes from the darkness beneath the trees. The bastards were shooting at him. On the soul of your beloved mother, Vasquez, you son of a bitch!

Martin did not believe that even an expert rifleman would be accurate at this range, in the deceptive light, and with a moving target. Even so, they shouldn't be given any free shots, should they? They weren't members of a firing squad now. No free shots. Martin drew his pistol and squeezed off three rounds at the next muzzle flash. Only a freak shot would hit one of them. Still, they were shooting at a man who was now shooting back.

"*Chinga tu madre,* Vasquez!" Martin screamed. They would hear his voice but fail to understand the words. Even so. He emptied the clip into the boxy shadows of the ferry landing and mill. "On the soul of your mother, the maggoty, syphilitic whore!" The skiff entered the right channel and slipped behind the sandbar.

"Asshole," Martin said to himself. He had not been able to kill the boy. Fatuously, he had extracted a promise ("Give me fifteen minutes to get away") from a savage moron who no doubt *volunteered* to shoot helpless men. Martin knew that he could kill Vasquez or someone like him now, easily. He apologized to Rodolfo.

Martin ran the engine at top speed. He calculated that the skiff, with the help of the current, was moving at about fifteen miles per hour. He did not think that there would be pursuit but it was possible that soldiers downriver might be alerted.

The first can of gasoline lasted ninety minutes; the second can a little less. Say three hours, forty-five miles. Surely he had escaped rebel-controlled territory by now.

When the gas was gone he fitted the oars into the locks and commenced rowing. The current seemed slower here. Martin rowed until his hands were blistered and the muscles of his lower back spasmed, then he brought the skiff to shore. He changed into his own clothes and buried Ávila's uniform and boots. He ate a cheese sandwich and two oranges, and lay down to sleep. The ground seemed to undulate.

The sun was well above the horizon when he awakened. Ten-thirty. A grimy steel barge was slowly pushing upcurrent. Its bow wave washed high on the beach, wetting his legs. A big bare-chested seaman, smoking a cigar, stared at Martin until the barge passed around a bend in the river. A dozen goats, tended by a small boy, grazed on the opposite shore. He thought: stay here a while, warm your blood in the sun like a lizard.

Martin peeled and ate an orange, then lit a cigarette, his last. He was cold and stiff and very tired. And still anxious: he knew that he was not yet safe; this was government territory, controlled by an ally of the U.S., but here too there were uniformed men who possessed weapons and the cruel indifference that weapons conferred. No, he would not relax until he reached the capital and once again became Dr. Martin R. Springer, physician and surgeon, a man of some wealth and influence, too important to casually imprison or murder.

Martin finished his cigarette, stood up, dizzy for a moment, and then he launched the skiff. He fitted the oars into the locks and rowed out toward the current. His palms were raw from last night's rowing. His back ached. Now his heart paused for an instant and then leaped—a premature ventricular contraction. One more day.

He reached the center of the river, shipped the oars, leaned back, and watched the landscape revolve as the skiff drifted downstream. The wilderness was behind now. This was a tamed land, the forests long ago cut and burned, the hills furrowed by erosion, the fields divided into small irregular plots of corn and beans and peppers. He passed clusters of shacks, a mill, and little farms with palm-thatched huts and skeletal dogs and doll-like brown kids. He floated by a small town and beneath an iron-grid bridge that vibrated from the weight of cars and trucks. Farther downriver there was a town large and prosperous enough to have some paved streets and a baseball park with lights.

He rowed ashore just below the municipal dock. Nearby there was a marine supply store whose employee filled the

two cans with a gasoline-oil mixture. He paid with the
money he'd taken from Ávila's wallet. Another store sold
him bread, cheese, fruit, cigarettes, and four bottles of cold
beer. He was hungry for a hot restaurant meal but there
would be police in town, and probably a unit of the militia, and he was a foreigner, without papers or sufficient
bribe money.

There was considerable traffic on the next stretch of
river, barges, tugboats towing strings of cargo rafts, even
some small rust-streaked freighters whose props churned
up huge boils of cloudy water. Martin stayed close to the
right shore, just outside the mud banks and the tangled
beds of water hyacinth. The outboard engine ran smoothly.
He ate and drank beer and smoked. An old fisherman told
him that he was about twenty miles from the capital.
Twenty river miles and an airplane ride away from Katherine and the children, home.

It was midafternoon when the river at last curved out of
the agricultural plains and entered the city. On both sides
there were warehouses and concrete wharfs and dismal
brick factories. The mouths of pipes, four feet in diameter,
spewed sewage and industrial wastes into the river. Here
the river died. Dead, it viscidly meandered down to the
sea. There were bridges every few blocks; he could hear
the rumble of traffic overhead and smell the bitter ex-
hausts. The skiff sliced through iridescent oil slicks and
evil-smelling chemical foams.

When he was halfway into the city he cut the engine
and let the skiff drift into a rickety wooden pier. He tied
the bow line to a cleat. He threw his duffel bag onto the
pier. He climbed out of the boat, picked up the duffel, and
wearily started up a steep narrow street named Calle Subir.
The buildings on both sides were abandoned—condemned,
the signs said. There were other, crudely stenciled signs:
¡Comunismo Sí! and *¡Pan o Sangre!* Bread or Blood. On

his right was a three-story building with all of the windows broken and the doors missing. A derelict or a corpse lay on the concrete ramp. Pigeons strutted high on the window ledges.

Martin climbed the hill and walked through a district of fire-charred shops and rubble-filled vacant lots. Dirty, cheerful boys were playing soccer in the street.

He waited by a newspaper kiosk. A taxi stopped at his signal.

"Dónde?"

"Hotel Nacional," Martin said.

PART THREE

THE CITY

CHAPTER

2 1

"I'm so ashamed," Katherine said.

"It was spectacular."

"I made such a fool out of myself. Screaming and falling down in the middle of the lobby."

"It was fine to see, Kit. You got a little shorter with each stride. It looked like you were going down stairs."

At first she had not quite recognized him; he'd been shabbily dressed, sunburned and unshaved, limping, with a bruised, crooked nose, and as slim as the Martin of fifteen years ago. It was the way he held himself, his carriage and walk, that identified him; that and his grin when he saw her. She had screamed "Martin!" and started toward him, her knees buckling more with each step. The next thing Katherine knew, she was lying supine on the carpet, a circle of curious faces looking down, and Martin kneeling at her side.

"I've always been contemptuous of women who fainted," she said now. "I thought they were faking."

"The vapors," Martin said. "Well-known Victorian ailment. We seldom see it nowadays."

"I think I'm going to cry again."

"Don't."

"Women cry when they're happy too, you know."

They were in bed, naked beneath a sheet. The television, sound turned off, flickered in the corner; it was showing an old Spanish-dubbed version of *Gunsmoke*. The telephone worked now too. The air conditioner blew cool air into the room. Martin had growled to the management this afternoon and within half an hour everything had been repaired, even the leaky faucet in the bathroom. And he had retrieved from storage some clothes and two cartons of medical supplies.

"I'm hungry," he said. "Would you like a snack?"

"Martin, we had a huge dinner less than two hours ago."

"I'm still hungry."

"I can see why. Poor baby. You're half starved."

"Maybe ten pounds below my ideal weight."

"More," she said. "You're skinny. Different in other ways too. It was like making love to a stranger."

"What do you know about making love to strangers?"

"What I read in romance novels."

"And what's it like in romance novels?"

"Divine usually, but occasionally hideous."

"Damn, I'm hungry."

"What time is it?"

"Almost eleven," he said.

"You'd better order, the kitchen closes at eleven. Where did you get that watch, Martin? It looks very expensive."

"It belonged to a man named Ávila. Before that it belonged to someone else, I don't know who. Now it belongs to me."

"Was it very bad, Martin?"

"I almost died, Kit. They were five seconds away from shooting me. Five seconds. Rodolfo—another man—was shot. And Cabrera."

"Tell me about it. Please."

He sat up on the edge of the bed and pulled on his shorts. "Do you want another drink?"

"I'm still woozy from the last one."

"So am I, but I want to get a little woozier."

"Make me a very weak one."

He walked to the dresser where there was a bucket of ice, a bottle of soda water, a lemon, and a nearly full bottle of Cutty Sark scotch. *Escocés*, it was called down here, and it was very expensive. Japanese "scotch" was cheaper, Martin had said, and it wasn't *too* bad; but he would start drinking scotch distilled in Japan at the same time as they started brewing sake in Inverness.

Katherine watched him scoop ice out of the bucket and pack their glasses full. He poured the whiskey, a little for her and more for himself, and then added soda and lemon twists. He was so lean now, youthful, and his face, neck, wrists, and hands were burned dark by the sun.

There were new scars on his face and body, and lacerations and ulcerated insect bites that would soon become even newer scars. His fine straight nose was ruined. Poor Martin. He had suffered. He had changed. He had been cheerful all afternoon and this evening, frivolous even, but she had observed the changes. Martin had always possessed a quiet authority—all good doctors do—but now he seemed domineering in a falsely polite way. Politely he issued commands. Politely he rewarded or condemned you with a glance. He was colder and harder and more secretive than the Martin she knew so well. She was no longer able to sense what he was thinking and feeling. There were wounds that she could not now reach, touch, heal.

This afternoon he had spent half an hour exploring the hotel, locating the service elevator, the fire escapes, and every exit including those in the kitchen and on the roof. On the streets or in public rooms he stared rudely at policemen and soldiers; he watched people's reflections in store windows; he presumed they were being followed. There was something feral about Martin now, half wild, and perhaps dangerous.

Tonight, before going out to dinner, he had slowly dismantled a huge pistol, oiled and polished the parts, and then reassembled it. And God, he had carried it stuck in his trousers, covered by a sports coat, out to the best restaurant in this blighted city. That wasn't right, normal. It was a little crazy.

Wait, Katherine thought, just wait. I must be patient. Wait and it will be all right, he will eventually repudiate his fear and wildness.

"Christ," he said. "I'd pay twenty dollars for a pizza. A slab of goo. Could you eat pizza, Kit?"

She accepted her drink. "No. Martin, just call room service before the kitchen closes."

He sat on the edge of the bed and lit a cigarette.

"Let's quit smoking again," she said.

"Right. As soon as we get out of this hellhole."

"This is a bad place, Martin."

"Evil," he said. Then: "Pizza, or one of those toxic ballpark hot dogs. Or a bucket of terrifically greasy fried chicken."

"The restaurant here serves fairly good cheeseburgers."

"I don't believe it. But we'll see." He picked up the telephone, dialed room service, and ordered a cheeseburger and an order of french fries.

"You haven't told me how you escaped, Martin."

"Long story. I don't want to think about it just now. I want to drink good scotch and eat bad foods. And make love, both divine and hideous."

She laughed. "Did Vaca's people help you to escape?"

"Vaca? Which Vaca?"

"Cabeza de Vaca."

"That creep. How do you know Vaca?"

"I went to the National Palace to ask him to help you. No one seemed to be doing anything. People told me that Vaca had a great deal of power and influence, and a spy organization of some kind. I went to see him at his office, and later at a cocktail party at his house. And he told me that he would help. He promised. It was complicated—but he said that he would trade some political prisoners for you."

Martin, smiling faintly, shook his head.

"I had to do *something*, Martin."

"Did you give him any money?"

"Certainly not."

"Vaca doesn't help anyone free of charge. He's the most rotten and corrupt of the whole rotten and corrupt bunch."

He wanted sex, Katherine thought, he wanted me. But she did not think she should tell Martin that. "I know he's a creep," she said. "But I believed him. He really did seem sincere."

"Oh sure, Vaca can be charming in that greasy way when he smells a dollar or an advantage."

"He said you were being held prisoner in a place called Esperanza, on the Pacific coast."

"Well, he was mistaken. Or more likely he lied. Probably he was just stringing you along, Kit, until the bills came due. There are unexpected expenses, Mrs. Springer, wire the bank, cash in your stocks and bonds, sell the farm."

"Were you in Tepazatlán, then?"

"How did you hear of Tepazatlán?"

"A man from the embassy told me you were being held there. He said that he was arranging your rescue."

"What man?"

"His name is Robert Harley."

"Never heard of him."

"He's the assistant commercial attaché."

Martin was silent for a time, then he got up and mixed another scotch and soda.

"Don't get drunk, Martin."

"I'll get drunk," he said. "But not too drunk."

He returned to the bed and said, "A man called Fuerte busted me out of Tepazatlán. He said that he was being paid to do it. He saved my life, Kit. He later abandoned me in the middle of nowhere, but by Christ, he did save my life. He might have been this Harley's man. But why would they bother to help me?"

"For propaganda purposes. Because of the massacre."

"Massacre? Katherine, what are you talking about?"

"He—Mr. Harley—said that most of the inhabitants of a village where you worked were slaughtered. And the communists arrested you and were going to kill you because you witnessed the whole thing."

He was smiling at her.

"Am I being stupid again?"

"Go on."

"Well, Harley told me that he—his friends—were going to arrange your escape so that you could tell the whole world about the communist atrocity. Wasn't there a massacre, Martin?"

"I suppose. There always are, in war. I heard rumors. But nothing like that happened in my district, not that I know of."

"But then why did they arrest you?"

"I'm not sure. It was stupid of them. I was the only doctor in the area. I treated the guerrillas as well as the villagers. They needed me too. I don't know—war is the business of paranoids. They might have suspected that I was a spy. I suppose some politician, some theoretician safe in Havana or Mexico City, issued the order for my arrest."

"Mr. Harley seemed absolutely certain that you witnessed a massacre."

"Maybe I should be grateful that he thought so."

"Do you believe that his people arranged your escape?"

"Kit, I don't know."

"Could it possibly have been Vaca, then?"

"Not if he thought I was in Esperanza."

"Oh, Martin, I've been so stupid, I've done everything wrong since I arrived here. It's been a nightmare. I've been such an awful damn meddling fool. I could have gotten you killed with my foolishness."

"Who knows? You might have saved me."

"I would like to believe that. But I don't."

There was a knock on the door. Martin pulled on a pair of trousers, opened the door a few inches, and accepted the tray of food from a bellman.

"It looks like a cheeseburger," he said. "It smells like a cheeseburger. It's well cooked—most of the parasite eggs and lethal microorganisms have been stunned, at least. But the fries smell like fish that have been left out in the sun."

"Martin. Can we go home soon?"

"You bet. How does tomorrow morning sound?"

"Wonderful, just wonderful."

"Don't cry."

"I'm not crying."

"I'll just finish this sandwich and hop back into bed. How do you want it this time, divine or hideous?"

CHAPTER

2 2

Martin paused on the hotel veranda. It was early and clear and fairly cool. The streets were still wet from last night's rain, and in the little park across the street the trees, grass, and flowers had a lacquered gloss. Dix was sitting at a bench in the center of the park, at the X formed by the convergent flagstone walks. He waved and shouted something that Martin could not understand.

Martin waited for a taxi to pass, then crossed the street and entered the park. Nuggets of bronze gleamed in the wet grass. Nearby were the ruins of the statue's pedestal; one of the horse's rear legs and half a haunch remained absurdly erect, like a flat. Here, unlike the engagement in Tepazatlán, General Vargas had been the only casualty.

"You're up early this morning," Dix said. "Has the second honeymoon ended?"

Martin sat on the bench. "Give me a cigarette."

"I thought you quit smoking."

"I did. A cigarette please, Dix." After lighting it he said, "You'd better get out of here. You've gone native, voluntarily smoking these cigarettes. They're mostly dung and pesticides."

"I've gone native in other ways. I drink water from the tap. I drink unpasteurized milk. I eat those killer pork *carnitas* from dirty carts you see parked by the curb. I lie with raddled whores."

"I wish I was the beneficiary of your insurance."

"I won't be bullied by a doctor who smokes cigarettes."

They sat beneath a tree that was colloquially known as the "tree of fire." It blazed and crackled now in the breeze. Across the park an old woman was digging through a refuse can, and on the street behind her boys sold newspapers to the drivers of cars halted at the traffic light.

"Are you making any progress?" Dix asked.

"I wonder if we'll ever get out of this goddamn country. I get the same old bureaucratic shuffle every time. No one has any authority. I've been to six government offices during the last week, and everyone shrugs and apologizes and says go see the minister of X department. Yesterday I ended up at the Department of Agriculture."

Dix smiled.

"At first they wouldn't let me leave because I didn't have a passport. The bastards knew it'd been taken by the rebels. But that doesn't count. No passport? 'Señor, you're lucky you aren't in jail.' So the embassy issued me a new passport. And the clowns look at it, scowl and say, 'But, Señor, there is no entry permit.' Without an entry stamp I'm not officially in the country. And if I'm not officially in the country then I can't very well be issued an exit permit. It's been nine days."

Dix nodded. "You're like a character out of Kafka. Martin S., mysteriously persecuted by anonymous officers of unknown bureaus."

A small boy carrying a shoeshine box trotted across the

park and kneeled at their feet. "*Limpiar, Señor* Dix? Shine, mister?"

Dix gave the boy some money and told him to go to the bakery and buy half-a-dozen doughnuts, a quart of milk, and two large cartons of coffee.

"How is Katherine taking this enforced exile?"

"Not very well."

There were more people in the park now: other shoe-shine boys, peddlers of fruit drinks and ices, a pair of old men who silently played dominoes on the rim of the fountain, a man carrying a large cage (elaborately constructed out of twigs and string) full of brightly plumed tropical birds, a few soldiers, a pair of sullen policemen. A wedge of sunlight had pushed the shade to the east side of the park. Martin removed his jacket and folded it over the back of the bench.

"It's much too hot here to wear a suit," Dix said.

"A suit impresses the bureaucrats a little."

Martin watched the boy return across the park with two paper bags. He was an ugly child, stunted, with protruding ears, bad teeth, and a scalp patchy and scabby from some infection. But his smile was radiant as he approached—errand completed. Dix divided the food: two doughnuts each, the quart of milk for the boy, and coffee for himself and Martin.

"I call him Shine Mister," Dix said.

"What's his real name?"

"I don't know. He's just another Third World kid—Shine Mister."

Shine Mister lay sprawled in the grass, eating and drinking, watching them.

"Have you complained to the embassy?" Dix asked.

"Sure. They don't seem terribly interested."

"I don't know what to tell you, Martin. This seems very odd to me."

"And to me. I hate like hell to bribe any of these swine. Apparently that's what they want."

"No. This isn't the standard graft. I mean, you aren't some punk kid down from the States to make a dope buy or smuggle out pre-Columbian artifacts or play Ché Guevara up in the hills."

"All right, what is it about, then?"

"I don't know," Dix said. "But it may be that *Telaraña* is involved."

"Vaca?"

"It's got that dirty secret-police smell about it."

"But why?"

"That I can't guess."

"It doesn't make sense, Dix."

"Well, you can't expect sense—ordinary logic or action—from a paranoiac, can you?"

"Is Vaca paranoidal?"

"Yes, but then so are all the best cops, spies, and politicians. And some of the worst too, of course."

"I've got to get going. Thanks for the breakfast."

"Martin, I can shake you and Katherine loose from this place. Just let me write the story."

"I don't want to do that. Not just yet, anyway."

"Let me write it, the whole thing. Your primitive clinic out in the bush, your arrest by the commies. The weeks in that church tower, the abuse, the death sentence, the wall. Escape, and then finally you're back safe and the fucking government—a corrupt, fascist ally of the Washington clowns—won't let you leave. I'll have Burke take some pictures of you and Katherine. After my story is in print we'll turn you over to the television people. We'll burn their asses. You'll be out of here damned quick."

"Thanks, Dix. I don't know."

"People like Vaca hate publicity. They hate publicity like mushrooms hate the light."

"Can I borrow your car, Dix? Katherine's going stir crazy in the hotel. I thought I'd take her out for the day."

"Good idea." He offered the keys. "There's plenty of gas. You might want to check the oil."

Katherine was tired. Makeup and careful grooming could not conceal her fatigue. She missed her children, her home, her happiness; she was, she'd told him, always afraid. It was a quiet, persistent dread, a sense of impending disaster, a daily gnawing of her spirit. "I sometimes feel that I'm slowly vanishing, Martin. Becoming less real every day."

But this morning she seemed cheerful, glad to escape the claustral hotel room, and glad to be with him—she had complained that he spent too much time at the Center, away from her.

He drove east down the boulevard. The traffic was light at this time of morning, taxis, buses, and trucks that fouled the air with bitter blue smoke.

"I've got to stop off at the Center, Kit," he said.

"Why?"

"I left something there last night. I'll only be a minute."

She was quiet for a time, then said, "Martin, I've been thinking. Maybe we ought to have a baby."

"Well. I don't know."

He stopped at a red light. Eight or ten small, scruffy children left the sidewalk and swarmed around the car, pleading with them to buy chewing gum and candy and newspapers and flowers, and one held aloft an ordinary gray bird in a twig cage.

"I'm only thirty-three. That isn't too old."

"I don't know what to think. This is a surprise to me. What made you decide you wanted to have another child?"

Katherine bought a bouquet of bright red flowers from

a girl. The light changed and the children ran back to the sidewalk.

As he pulled away from the intersection, Katherine said, "Those children made me decide. I mean, all the children you see here. The little boys and girls shining shoes and selling flowers. They're beautiful, don't you think? Their lives are so hard, but they're always cheerful and . . . and none of them have a chance."

In the rearview mirror Martin saw the familiar black car, or another just like it. A black sedan with tinted windows and a tall radio-telephone antenna at the rear. Police, Vaca's men, probably. He and Katherine had been under surveillance for days.

"I don't quite understand, Kit. You want to adopt one of these kids?"

"No, I didn't say that. I just think that we should have a baby. We can easily afford another child, Martin. We can give a child every opportunity, every advantage, while these poor sweet kids . . ."

Martin turned off onto a side street. The black car drove on past the intersection. Maybe the police had not been following them after all. Maybe, he thought, his belief that he and Kit were being observed was false, a symptom of his anxiety.

"Well, sure," he said. "We ought to consider it."

She smiled. "Really? You'll think about it?"

The Center was located on the south side of the river. Martin pulled into the parking lot and switched off the engine.

"Do you want to come in?"

"Oh, no. I'll stay here, thank you. There are a thousand plagues inside that building."

He smiled. "It's perfectly safe."

"It isn't perfectly safe, and I don't like you working there."

It was a fairly new, three-story building. There was no one in the reception area. The Center was funded by a big German pharmaceutical company. A sign on the wall above the desk read:

BRANDT-BREIDENBACH
CENTER FOR THE STUDY OF
TROPICAL DISEASES

When the receptionist did not appear, Martin went behind the desk and wrote his name and the time in the ledger, then took an elevator to the third floor.

An old man was on his hands and knees, repairing a broken tile. A radio played loudly in one of the laboratories (trypanosomiasis); and behind the door of another, where Weiler cultivated colonies of liver flukes, a woman laughed.

Martin went to the end of the corridor and entered Tetz's office-lab. Lothar, leaning back in his swivel chair, had his feet on the littered desk. He was sixty, with lank, silky white hair and an angular, unsymmetrical face.

"You're late," he said.

"I'm through, Lothar. Thanks for the temporary employment."

"Did you learn anything?"

"A little."

"What about your cultures?"

"Maier can finish up."

Tetz removed his feet from the desk and sat erect, shuffling through some papers, and then he looked up. "We received a threatening note in the mail, warning us to close down immediately and leave the country. We are accused of, let me see, yes, '. . . preparing and stockpiling vast quantities of deadly biological and viral plagues to be employed by the fascist government in its campaign to terrorize and destroy the freedom-loving peoples of this suffering republic.' Et cetera."

"Is that what you're doing here?"

"The trouble, Springer, with studying tropical diseases is that you often must live in tropical countries."

"What are you going to do?"

"Increase security."

Martin laughed. "You can start by posting someone at the front desk."

"Is Francisco AWOL again?"

Martin nodded. "I'll probably see you before I leave for the States."

"Unless they blow us up."

"Right."

Martin walked halfway down the hall and entered what Dr. Tetz called the "delirium tremens ward." The door was unlocked. Increase the security, indeed. This was Dr. Shumacher's domain. Snake venoms were a distinctly minor interest of the pharmaceutical company; but they had vague hopes of discovering and patenting a poison-based drug as medically useful as curare or atropine. There were glass terrariums on the floor and on the shelves that circled the room; each contained a species of venomous snake. Some had charming common names, fer-de-lance, black mamba, green garden creeper. Coiled serpents dozed, others sluggishly weaved through the sand in their cages, and one, his forked tongue flicking, attempted to climb the glass wall, fell back, tried again. Deadly reptiles, but not ugly: Many were brightly colored, reds and blues and yellows and soft pastels, and Martin wondered again at how nature granted so many deadly animals, reptile and fish and insect, an extraordinary beauty.

He got his pistol from the desk drawer, removed his satchel from another drawer, dropped in the pistol, and zipped the satchel closed. Objects were safe here.

Shumacher had spread the rumor that some snakes had escaped from their cages. None of the native custodial crew would enter the room. Theft was reported elsewhere, but not in the delirium tremens ward. The slumbering snakes, the tangled snakes, the weaving snakes, protected this room more effectively than any security guard.

The black car was parked across the street when Martin stepped outside. He could see shadows behind the tinted glass.

"How long have they been here?" he asked as he got into Dix's car.

"Since a few minutes after you went inside," Katherine said.

"Christ."

"Martin, I am so tired, so weary of this political and social hell."

"Dix wants to start a kind of publicity campaign. He thinks it will embarrass the government enough to shake us free."

"Let's do it. But, Martin, where is *our* government? What are *they* doing to help us?"

He started the engine and drove out of the parking lot. In the rearview mirror he saw the black car pull in behind them.

"They're trying, I suppose."

"Maybe a little. An inquiry here. A suggestion there. But they aren't really trying or we'd be home now. They aren't very interested in us. We're little. They're interested in big things."

Martin turned onto an iron bridge that spanned the river. Below he could see the water, muddy brown, foul, barely reflecting the sunlight.

"But Dix's publicity might get them interested," Katherine said. "If it embarrasses a few of our bureaucrats, we'll be home soon."

They left the bridge and drove down a narrow street. A building on the corner, a post office, was a charred ruin. A mailed bomb had exploded prematurely. The black car was not following them now. It had turned off after leaving the bridge.

They went to the old section of the city, the *Zona Histórica*, and toured the archaeological museum, some galleries, the old church, an open market, and then walked the streets until they found a restaurant that looked interesting. The menu in the window featured Italian food. It was a quiet, clean, pleasantly decorated place. The food smells were appealing. There was the main room at street level and a stairway that led up to a loft. They asked to be seated in the loft.

Katherine was relaxed now. She did not look so tired. She was interested in the decor and the people at the other tables and the menu.

They ordered cocktails and a bottle of wine to be served with lunch.

"This is nice," Katherine said.

The room was carpeted, there were good paintings on the walls, the utensils were sterling and the glassware crystal, and each white-clothed table had a spray of fresh flowers. The customers were well dressed, prosperous, refined. "Not a bully in the lot," Katherine whispered.

"Maybe I'll have twins," she said later. "It's possible. You know that twins do run in my family. My sister had twins, and a cousin. Wouldn't twins be nice, Martin? One labor, two kids."

The waiter brought their plates of antipasti.

"We can name them Tweedledum and Tweedledee," she said.

"Or Act In Hate and Repent At Leisure."

She laughed.

Looking down over the railing, Martin could see them

enter the restaurant: five of them, three men in dark suits and two uniformed policemen. They paused to talk to the maître d'. The maître d' pointed, and the five men looked up toward the loft, toward Martin and Katherine.

"Or how about," Katherine said, "Hermes and Aphrodite?"

"Hermaphrodite," Martin said.

The pistol is in the car, he thought. Locked in the car.

The five men paced aggressively across the floor below, weaving among the tables, and began climbing the stairs.

"Try the Bruschetta Toscana," Katherine said. "It's very good."

The five men moved with the authority of the righteous. Their exalted state was evident in the set of their shoulders and the brusque way they advanced.

"The sottaceti's not too hot."

Katherine made a small cry of surprise when the five men circled their table.

A tall black-suited man bowed to Katherine. He wore insect-eye sunglasses. There was a crusted white material at the corners of his mouth. In careful English he said, "Excuse me, Señora. I am so regretful. We disturb your food this way. But you must come with us please."

Katherine, eyes wide, looked at Martin.

"Get out of here," Martin said to the man.

"Sir," the tall man said, "no. Pardon. Sit down. Please. Yes, it is the lady. Not you. The lady is taken. For questions, you understand. Nothing very far. Come with me please, lady."

"Sit still," Martin said. To the tall man he said, "You are making a big mistake. The American Ambassador will arrive any moment. He is meeting us for lunch."

"Sir. There will be no more. Not. You understand that, not. The lady is arrested. No more. Get up, lady. Pretty lady, rich lady, nice lady. Yes yes yes, get up, walk please, lady."

"I'm warning you," Martin said.

"No. No, sir. I warn you. Shut it. Now you shut it. Okay?"

"Andele," the tall man in the black suit with the insect-eye sunglasses said, and the two uniformed policemen grabbed Katherine's arms and roughly pulled her to her feet.

Martin grasped a fork and, quickly rising, leaping, thrust it toward the tall man's eyes. He didn't think about the sunglasses. It was an instinctive attack. The fork tines glanced off the man's sunglasses and gouged a bloody hole in his cheek. Martin thrust again, but the others had him then, dragging him into the aisle, and he was being twisted and pummeled, and then he was on the floor and the tall man kicked him once, twice, three times. The air exploded from his lungs. He could not breathe. He curled up tightly on the floor. He could hear Katherine's cries. She was down the stairs now and on the ground floor. Martin, still unable to breathe, squirmed over to the railing and looked down. They were dragging her through the restaurant, knocking over chairs, scattering the diners, and Katherine was screaming, "Martin! Please help me! Please, Martin!" The tall man was holding a bloody napkin to his cheek. He slapped Katherine. Martin still could not breathe. The front door was opened and they were out on the sidewalk. Katherine continued to struggle. The restaurant was silent.

Finally Martin inhaled, it was like a sob, he exhaled, inhaled again. Faces in the room below stared up at him. Men were cursing. They had saved their curses, reserved their anger. On this level, he waited for someone, man or woman, to approach and offer him a sip of water, a warm hand, a sympathetic word, but no one came. He was a pariah. He was a victim of the police and so a pariah.

At last he was able to rise and walk slowly toward the stairs. The diners watched him warily. At the door the maître d' said. "Sir? Your check?"

Martin limped out onto the sidewalk. Here, on the streets of the city, he did not attract much attention. There were wounded men and women everywhere, and children. Lame, halt, blind.

By the time he reached the car he felt a little better. His chest ached. Maybe a cracked rib, he thought, maybe torn cartilage. He got into the car. Katherine's bouquet of red flowers was already wilted, crushed. He opened his satchel and took a Percodan tablet. He lit a cigarette even though his lungs hurt. Poor Kit—Jesus, she'd already been near the limit of her strength.

All right, he thought. We'll see. Yes, we'll see.

CHAPTER

2 3

Martin had not been injured. He'd raised his fist. He was free. He would help her.

Vaca's goons had taken her to a large red brick house a dozen blocks away from the downtown section of the city. There were flower boxes on the window ledges and brightly patterned curtains. The front door opened into a big room with a bar and bandstand and dance floor. Tables were arranged around the room's perimeter. A caged parrot greeted her in Spanish: *"Bienvenidos."* Welcome. Upstairs there was a long hallway with doors on both sides. They had locked her in one of the rooms.

At first Katherine did not understand. She was furious and frightened and confused. She did not want to understand. It was just a large bedroom. There was a double bed with a tufted pink bedspread, a dresser, desk and chair, and gaudy throw rugs scattered over the hardwood floor. An ordinary bedroom, really, except for the mirror, which ran the length of the bed along the left wall.

She tried the door again. Locked, locked, locked. No windows. It was very hot and the room smelled of pine-scented disinfectant. There was a plastic glow-in-the-dark crucifix hanging on the wall above the bed, and elsewhere framed photographs clipped from slick magazines—the sea at sunset, sheep grazing in an alpine meadow, the Pope, snow falling over what appeared to be a New England village. There were no clothes in the closet; the dresser drawers were empty except for some hairpins, a comb with half of the teeth missing, and some thumbtacks.

Katherine sat on the edge of the bed. It was impossible. A whorehouse. Vaca couldn't, no, he wouldn't dare. It was just a cruel joke.

They had not taken her purse. Money—perhaps she could bribe someone. Passport, checkbook, makeup kit, keys, a half-written letter to the children, cigarettes, a plastic butane lighter. I'll burn the place down. Breath mints—a whore mustn't have breath that smells like carrion.

There was a noise out in the hallway, the sound of a key fitted into the lock, and then the door swung open and Vaca entered the room. He was carrying a bottle of red wine and two glasses.

"This isn't funny, Vaca," Katherine said. "Not at all."

He uncorked the wine, filled the glasses, gave her one, and sat next to her on the bed.

"You're sick," she said.

He said, "There will be a man watching over you. He'll see that no one hurts you."

"Not funny at all."

"And he'll also see that you are not *too* popular. A blond gringa will attract a lot of lovers."

"Please," she said. "Don't."

"One night only, Caterina. Tomorrow you and your husband can return home. But every natural whore should spend at least one night in a whorehouse."

"You're insane."

"There will be no brutality or extreme perversions. Ordinary copulation, oral sex, anal sex perhaps—nothing beyond that."

"Now I'm starting to cry. I didn't want to let you make me cry."

"The wine is very good," he said. "Try it."

"Enough is enough, Vaca. Too much. Let me go now. You've frightened me half to death."

"One night only. I promise you."

"Your promises are worthless. We both know that."

"I'll personally drive you to the airport, if you wish."

"You're kidding, aren't you, Vaca? Please tell me that you're kidding."

"You'll be expected downstairs at eight o'clock. That's when your evening will commence. I suggest that you shower and wash your hair soon, and after that rest. Someone will bring you a pretty gown before you go to work."

"But why? *Why!*"

He said, "In ancient Babylon every woman had to spend a few days in the temple brothel before her marriage. There were no exceptions. Any man could buy her. The lowest citizen could, if he had the money, use the body of a princess. A salutary custom, don't you think? Every male could satisfy his passion for the delectable young virgins, and at the same time the girls would learn how to please their future husbands."

He smiled. "And you know, Caterina, good women, women with high moral standards, even wives and mothers like yourself, have spent a few days in a whorehouse and then declined to leave. They liked the life. They chose to stay. It isn't uncommon."

"I don't believe it."

"One girl, an American, stayed here just one night and decided to remain a whore."

"No."

"Yes."

"Where is this girl now? Is she here?"

"No. She stayed here for a year. She drank too much and lost her beauty. She's now working at a less exclusive whorehouse."

"The girl was destroyed by the experience. She had no self to return to."

"She realized that she was born a whore. All she needed was the opportunity to find that out. I gave her and others the opportunity."

"This is insane. Things like this don't happen."

"They do happen. It is happening to you now."

"Please, why are you doing this?"

"You need to be humbled. You are too proud."

"But that's crazy. What's wrong with pride that you want to punish it? You're proud enough for a thousand men."

"Who knows, Caterina. You might enjoy it here. You may wish to remain."

"You're filth."

He stood up and placed his glass on the dresser. "I'll leave you the wine," he said. "Do you need anything else? Are you hungry?"

"Just go."

"There are a shower, toilet, and sink behind that partition at the rear of the room. Someone will be along to explain the little details of your profession."

"Cripes," she said, starting to cry again. "Who turned over your rock?"

He smiled. "I might even be one of your late customers."

"Please," she said, crying, "I'm particular about my clientele."

"Are you? Then you're very lucky. I could have sold you to a fifty-cent crib in the slums. You'd turn fifty tricks there in a night. But here the customers are military officers and businessmen and foreigners—journalists and members of the diplomatic community. This is a quality whorehouse, Caterina."

"I suppose I should thank you," she said dully.

He smiled again, a cadaver's rictus. "You'll be home with your children in Wisconsin—the Dairy State?—by tomorrow night. Unless you decide to stay."

"Pimp," she said. "Slimy pimp."

"Whore. Tonight you will be literally a whore."

Katherine drank half of her wine, blotted her lips with a touch of her horizontal forefinger, and said, "Well, this is all very interesting, Vaca, but no. I refuse to play your game. No sir. Katherine isn't going to participate in any of Head-of-the-Cow's sick fantasies. So there. I'm not playing. Tell my suitors that Katherine is indisposed."

"I admire your courage."

"No you don't. You hate courage, because you have so little. That's why you're such a creepy little sneak manipulator."

"Of course you have the option of saying no."

"You bet."

"You *do* have a choice. Spend the night here as I have described or elect to have your face slashed to ribbons."

"Oh no."

"Oh yes."

"You aren't serious."

"Look at me."

"I don't want to look at you."

"Look at me, Caterina. Am I serious?"

"Can't you go away now? Haven't you tortured me enough?"

"See you later," he said, and he opened the door and stepped out into the hall.

She heard a key turn in the lock. She heard Vaca dancing lightly down the stairs. She heard, in the room adjoining this one, music playing on the radio. The scent of Vaca's cologne lingered in the air. This was not real. This was a mad prank, and when she was sufficiently frightened and humbled Vaca would have her released. Wasn't that the truth of it? A sadistic trick.

Katherine finished her wine, set the glass on the bedside table, and lay back. The ceiling was high and there were brass light fixtures. A whore's view of the workplace. Lying down on the job.

The doorknob turned. Katherine swiftly rose to her feet. An old, stout, flat-faced woman entered bearing a tray upon which were some folded towels, a bar of soap in its wrapper, a box of condoms, and a jar of petroleum jelly. She set the tray on the dresser and, without looking at Katherine or speaking to her, left the room. It's too realistic, Katherine thought.

She went behind the partition at the rear of the room. A toilet, a shower stall, sink, a vanity with an oval mirror that slightly distorted her reflection, and a cabinet beneath which she found cleaning supplies and a tin basin. There was a small plastic bottle of shampoo and a safety razor in the shower stall. There, I can always cut my wrists.

She returned to the bedroom and poured another glass of the wine.

Again Katherine heard a key in the lock; the door opened and a young woman entered the room. She wore a belted housecoat and furry slippers. Her hair, bleached almost white, was wet. Perhaps she would be pretty when her hair dried and she put on some makeup—she was awfully pale.

The woman said, "They told me that there was an American in here who didn't know what it was about."

"You're American?"

"South Dakota. There's another American girl here too,

a nigger from Florida. My name is Roxanne. Most people call me Roxy."

"Roxanne. Is that your real name or your prostitute name?"

"It's Roxanne, that's all."

"I'm Katherine. I have a husband and two children and I don't belong here."

"You are here, though," she said with a brief, malicious smile.

"I am here, yes. I was taken here by force."

"Sure, but it's only for one night."

"You know that?"

"It isn't a secret. Everybody knows. Anyway, Jorge has brought other decent women here for a night or two." The word *decent* was ironically emphasized.

"He's forced other women to come here and . . ."
Roxanne nodded.

"I can't believe this. This is insane, it ghastly."

"Can I have some of your wine?"

"Go ahead."

The girl poured wine into Vaca's glass. She studied Katherine for a time and then said, "We're about the same size. I can loan you a nice dress."

"A ghastly nightmare."

"Oh, come on, you probably won't be doing anything tonight that you haven't done before."

"Madness. I'm not a slut, a whore."

"Well, you certainly are Miss Pure," Roxanne said dryly. "I can see why Vaca wanted to soil you a little."

"Go away."

"You'll learn something about the world tonight."

"Not *the* world, *your* world."

"Your world and my world aren't so far apart—a taxi ride."

"Ridiculous. What is going on? Is everyone crazy? What kind of man is Vaca?"

"Vaca is a pig."

"Yes," Katherine said. "He's a pig, all right."

"All men are pigs."

"Well, Lord, if you believe that why are you here instead of in a convent or lesbian commune?"

"Can I have one of your cigarettes?"

"All right."

Roxanne lit the cigarette, formed her mouth into a moue, and blew a series of tiny smoke rings. "Aren't you going to drink any more wine?"

"Oh, go ahead, take it."

"Thanks."

"Listen here, Roxanne, you seem fairly intelligent. What are you doing here? How did you become a whore? And why, for God's sake?"

"Those are the same questions the tricks ask."

"I'm not a trick, I'm a woman, like you."

"*Not* like me, you've been saying all along."

"Were you forced into this life?"

Roxanne laughed. "You're not real."

"But you are real. And Vaca is real. This is reality."

"Can I finish the wine?"

"Take it." And then Katherine quietly said, "Roxanne, will you help me escape? There must be some back doors or windows. Or maybe you could distract everyone while I ran out the front door into the street. You could start a fire up here, say."

"Wow, and you think I'm goofy."

"Won't you please help me? I have money, not very much with me, but I can pay you very well. How much money do you want?"

"What do you think would happen to me if I helped you?"

"Would they hurt you?"'

"I guess they would!"

"We'll escape together. All right? You can leave this awful place, return with me to the States."

"For what? They treat us pretty good here. They keep out the creeps. The money's good. When I go back to the States I'm going to have a lot of money and I'm going to open a business, maybe two businesses. A beauty parlor and a Laundromat. I'm going to be my own boss."

"I'll give you money."

"Look, no more bullshit, lady, okay? They told me to explain things to you and that's what I'm going to do."

"I could pay you five thousand dollars. More."

"Just listen now. They keep out the rough ones but there'll be someone out in the hall if you need help. Now, you got to make sure they're not diseased. Peel back the foreskin if they got one. Look for discharges, or any kind of sores or ulcers or blisters."

"I think I'm going to puke."

"Pay attention. If they're sick, you tell them that they got to go. If they look okay you wash them in warm water with that bar of antiseptic soap. You wash them yourself to be sure. They'll cheat. Okay? Give them a towel. You can try to get them to use a rubber but they don't have to if they don't want. Most don't. They pay downstairs. The guy downstairs will tell you what for."

"For nothing. I'm not going to play Vaca's game."

"A lot of places, they have an extra bed or even a table like you see in doctor's offices for examinations. Here, you have to sleep in the same bed, but you'll get clean sheets."

"I've never been with any man except Martin," Katherine said softly.

"What?"

"My husband is the only man I've ever slept with."

"You're kidding. You never ever fucked anybody else?"

"No."

"As pretty as you are?"

"Only Martin."

"You'll have variety tonight. God yes, you will!"

Roxanne stubbed out her cigarette in the ashtray, finished the glass of wine, and went to the door. "We all have to be downstairs at eight. Nothing much is doing that early, but sometimes."

"Roxanne, do you really believe they would slash my face if I refused? Vaca said they would."

"You're very pretty."

"Would they?"

"Like carving a turkey," Roxanne said.

CHAPTER

2 4

Martin drove carefully through the city. He remained within the speed limit and obeyed each traffic signal. He did not challenge the aggressive taxi drivers; he conceded them the right of way at intersections. He was losing minutes, but if he were involved in an accident or stopped by the police he might lose hours, lose everything. Make haste slowly, Martin told himself. Think coldly, like a surgeon at work or a veteran criminal; ruthlessly suppress the imagination and emotions. Freeze your heart.

Traffic thinned at the western edge of the city. The street cut through a sprawling slum and then emerged into agricultural country. The land was flat here but ahead he could see the green hills of the Las Lomas residential section. The hills rose one behind the other, each series higher than the last, finally culminating in a cone—misty in the heat haze—upon which a red light flashed at night. Rivers and lakes of shadow lay in the folds and gullies of the hills.

Martin increased his speed to the legal limit. Here the road was paved with asphalt and there were light standards every fifty yards. A Mercedes Benz going in the opposite direction passed, then a Porsche. Martin wished he had a better car than Dix's battered old VW. At least, though, he wore a good suit and clean white shirt.

Martin ignored the signs warning of the roadblock. He drove straight at the barrier and then at the last instant braked.

A young officer emerged from the guard shack and, moving with exaggerated slowness, displaying his authority, circled the car and stopped by the driver's window. He stared at Martin. Clearly, he was too important to speak first. The contempt he felt for the car and the gringo stranger who drove it was apparent in his eyes and the twist to his mouth.

"I'm Dr. Smith. I'm on an emergency call." Martin gestured toward the medical satchel on the seat. "Lift the gate immediately."

"Let me see your identification."

"I told you this is an emergency. Now get out of my way and raise the fucking gate."

A soldier, rifle slung over his shoulder, appeared in the doorway of the guard shack. He was an Indian, very short and broad, whose round face was riddled with acne scars.

The officer was uncertain now. He said, "I have my orders. Who needs a doctor? I must telephone to confirm this."

Martin twisted the ignition key. He loosened the knot of his tie. The engine creaked and ticked in the silence. Blurry heat devils distorted the air above the road.

"Very well, Lieutenant," Martin said. "Take your time."

"I have my instructions."

"Of course. A soldier must obey. It's dangerous to think. Maybe the mother will stop her efforts to resuscitate her child and run from the swimming pool to the house.

But more likely one of the servants will answer the telephone. You can ask the servant to fetch her mistress."

"Doctor, please, I am only doing my duty."

"Could I have a glass of water, Lieutenant?"

"If you will only please cooperate!" the officer said, his voice rising. "Your papers, please!"

"It's possible that your obedience to orders will be rewarded." Martin removed a package of cigarettes from his shirt pocket ("Of course, if the child . . ."), lit the cigarette and inhaled deeply (". . . *dies* because of your stupidity . . ."), exhaled and picked an imaginary fleck of tobacco from the tip of his tongue (". . . then the remainder of your life will be brief and painful").

"Raise the gate!" the officer angrily told the Indian.

"Do you have water, Lieutenant? Or maybe a cup of coffee?"

"Go!" he shouted. "Get out of here!"

The gate was lifted. Martin started the engine and pulled away. In the rearview mirror he saw the two men standing in the center of the road watching the car recede. Just before entering a curve he saw the officer turn and viciously kick the Indian.

It was cooler up in the hills and very green. This area received more rain than the plains below. Rain clouds were gathering now; the summit cone with its radio tower was being obscured by flat crawling layers of mist. Martin could hear the remote percussion of thunder in the west.

Vaca's place was named Villa Mariposa. Hummingbirds and butterflies swarmed around the flowering vine-covered walls. He saw, above the glass-encrusted top of the wall, red tile roofs and Moorish windows and little balconies enclosed by wrought iron. There was a small bronze bell above the gate. It briefly reminded Martin of the bells in the tower at Tepazatlán and the deafening clangor when the guards rang them. He pulled the bell rope and waited, the medical satchel in his left hand, unzipped so that he could get to the pistol quickly.

A middle-aged woman, a servant, opened the gate. Martin said that he would like to see Señora Vaca. The señora was not home. Where was she? At the park with her children; the girls were playing tennis. Where was this park? Not far, down the road one kilometer, on the right. Martin thanked her. *"De nada, señor."*

The tennis courts were a mile below Vaca's house, set back in a parkland of lawns and topiary hedges and great trees shrouded by moss. Martin turned right onto a gravel road that crossed a steel cattle guard, a wooden bridge spanning a creek, and then curved into a parking lot.

There were only two vehicles there, a battered pickup truck—the groundsman's?—and a Volvo station wagon. He backed into a slot next to the Volvo.

He left the car and walked down a path between flower beds that had been planted in the shades of the spectrum, reds fading to yellows deepening to blues. He passed a weedy pond upon which swans floated like exiled nobles. There were picnic tables, a rock garden, a bronze monument, and then the path rose to an arched wooden footbridge. The creek below was swift and clear and looked like good trout water.

There were four wire-screened tennis courts scattered around the grounds; three were empty now, but in the fourth two girls were engaged in a baseline rally. At this distance the popping of the struck ball reached him an instant after the actual impact, and the player's frantic motions appeared absurd, a purposeless pantomime. The taller of the girls hit the ball into the net, threw up her arms and shouted angrily (the sound reaching him after the gesture had been half completed). A woman sat on a bench outside the court. Vaca's wife. Two men were working on a flower bed at the eastern boundary of the park.

Martin returned to the parking lot and let the air out of the front tires on both the truck and the Volvo. He got his satchel from the car and started down a flagstone path toward the tennis court. His shirt was soaked with sweat. He could not imagine what he would do if the Vaca women refused to be terrified of him and the gun.

Vaca's daughters were changing sides now. Both were suntanned and wore white tennis dresses. One was tall and slender with short raggedly clipped hair in the gamine style; the other was smaller and younger.

The tall girl served with an easy, fluid motion, followed to the net, and volleyed away the return. The short girl claimed that the volley had gone out. *"Merde,"* the server said, and then as she was returning to the baseline, "Bitch." She stared hard at Martin for a moment and then prepared to serve to the ad court. She was about fifteen and physically a woman, but still with an adolescent's softness around her mouth and eyes. Her sister was perhaps two years younger.

Martin walked slowly beneath the big shade trees. Mrs. Vaca looked at him. She had dark hair and eyes and a round pretty face, but she was twenty pounds overweight. There were cans of tennis balls, spare rackets, a thermos jug, and warm-up clothes on the grass next to the bench.

He stopped. "Señora Cabeza de Vaca?"

She nodded.

"I'm Dr. Martin Springer."

"Yes?"

"I'm sorry."

"Pardon?" She was not alarmed, only curious and perhaps a bit impatient. Her daughters were rallying from the baselines; Martin could hear the squeak and scrape of their shoes and the spaced popping of the ball. She did not wear makeup. Her eyes were large and humid, with long black lashes.

"I'm sorry, but you must come with me."

"What is this about?" Mrs. Vaca asked.

The rally ended on the court behind him and Martin heard the taller girl say, "Oh, *merde*, it's hot." He half turned and said, "Girls, come over here."

"Dr. Springer, what—"

"One moment," he said.

The tall girl was going to be a beauty in a year or two; now she was just a little too gawky and sullen. Her sister had heavy legs and wore braces on her teeth.

"Would you both come through the gate, please," Martin said.

"I demand an explanation immediately," Mrs. Vaca said.

"Shut up," Martin told her. It was time to start behaving like a terrorist.

"Don't tell my mother to shut up," the tall girl said.

Martin withdrew the pistol, showed it to them, and returned it to his satchel.

"Oh, God," Mrs. Vaca said softly.

"Come on out here," Martin said to the girls. "Now."

The younger girl immediately came through the gate; the other hesitated defiantly for a moment, then shrugged and followed.

"Sit down."

They sat on the bench, one on each side of their mother. Three faces tilted up toward him; three pairs of rounded, frightened eyes.

"Listen to me. Don't ask any questions. Don't question, plead, protest, or weep. This afternoon, less than an hour ago, Jorge C' de Vaca forcibly removed my wife from a restaurant and took her away."

"But," Mrs. Vaca said, "my husband is a policeman, it's his—"

"Silence! I told you to listen. Your husband has my

wife, Mrs. Vaca. I have you. You are my hostage. You won't be harmed if my wife is not harmed. Is that clear?"

"My mother has a bad heart," the tall girl said.

"Oh, shit," Martin said. He looked closely at the woman; her lips did appear slightly cyanotic. "Do you take medication?"

"Yes."

"Do you have the medication with you?"

"In my purse."

"Let me see it."

The woman, her hands trembling, opened her purse and removed a small jar.

"Throw it to me."

Martin caught the jar and looked at the label: the drug was nitroglycerin, an antispasmodic commonly used to relieve angina.

"Christ," he said. "Well, I'm sorry, but you'll have to come with me anyway."

"I'll be your hostage," the tall girl said.

"No, Selene!" her mother cried.

The girl stood up. "It's all right, Mother. This man would not dare harm me."

"No, Selene!"

"Yes," Martin said. "It's better this way. I'll take your daughter." To the girl he said, "Put on your warm-up suit."

"It's too hot."

"Put it on."

She shrugged scornfully and picked up her warm-up outfit.

"Now, Mrs. Vaca, listen very carefully to me. Your daughter's life depends on how well you listen. Thirty minutes after we have left here, you and your daughter are to return to your home. Tell no one there what has happened. Get in touch with your husband. Don't explain anything to his secretary or any of his aides, no one, wait until you see or talk to Vaca himself. Get a telephone number from him. I'll telephone you later at your house for the number, or talk to Vaca if he's there. Do you understand this?"

"I think so." Mrs. Vaca's right hand was splayed over her breastbone.

"Are you in pain?" Martin asked.

"Yes."

He returned the jar of nitroglycerin pills to her. "Take your usual dose."

She shook two of the pills onto her palm and placed them beneath her tongue.

"Mother, did you understand his instructions?" Selene asked. She had dressed in the warm-up suit and was now combing her short, sweat-dampened hair. "Mother?"

"I think I understand."

"Repeat what he told you, Mother."

Mrs. Vaca slowly, in broken phrases, repeated Martin's instructions.

"Lisa," she said to her sister, who was weeping quietly. "You understand too, don't you? You must tell no one about this except Father."

Lisa wiped her eyes and nodded.

"Let's go, then," the girl said to Martin.

He nodded. She was a cool, brave, insolent kid.

"Don't worry, Mother, I'll be all right. Father is just having one of his little affairs and this husband has over-reacted." She kissed her mother on the cheek, then her sister, and then walked with Martin around the back of the court and down the path beneath the trees. The sky had darkened and scattered raindrops snapped against the leaves overhead. Now that the girl walked at his side Martin could see that she was not as tall as he'd supposed, maybe five feet six or seven. Her slimness made her appear taller. Her cheeks were still flushed and sweaty from the tennis.

"How old are you, Selene?" he asked.

"We aren't going to be chums, are we?"

"I guess not."

They got into the Volkswagen. Martin placed the pistol beneath his left thigh. It was almost six-thirty.

He drove very fast. Raindrops spattered against the windshield. He braked and downshifted entering the curves and then accelerated through them. On one curve the rear end slewed off the pavement and gravel rattled off the underside of the car. There were no railings. A vehicle that left the road would finish forty or fifty feet below in a gully.

"Slow down," the girl said. "Do you want to kill us?"

"I want to get down into the city before your mother or sister can reach a telephone."

"My mother isn't stupid. She'll do what you told her. And so will my father."

"You speak almost without accent."

"Lisa and I had an American tutor for years. Miss Phillips. Please, you must slow down."

"You'll have to help me get past the gatehouse, Selene. Remember, I have the pistol."

"You're scared, aren't you?"

"Not for myself."

"For your wife."

"And for you," he said.

"You've got to slow down. Please. Your wife will be all right. I'll help you, I promise."

Martin pumped the brakes lightly and coasted through the next curve. It was raining harder now.

"We're almost down now," Selene said. "When we reach level ground blow the horn. Everyone does that. The gate will be lifted by the time we get there. The guards are paid to keep people out, not in."

The road dropped into a shallow valley, continued to descend for half a mile, and then leveled out. Ahead there was another curve, the one that opened onto the guard shack and the plains beyond.

"Horn," the girl said.

Martin pressed the horn button. Now they were on the straightaway and ahead he could see the gate slowly lifting. Beyond, the tall buildings of the city were indistinct in the heat haze and smog. The Indian was outside, hauling on the gate's counterweight. Martin did not see the officer. He accelerated past the shack and then began to weave the car from side to side, from shoulder to shoulder. The officer was still not visible. Perhaps he was inside the shack with a rifle. Several hundred yards down the road Martin relaxed.

The girl said, "They wouldn't dare shoot at the car with me in it. They aren't that stupid."

"Selene, for every inconceivably stupid action there is an inconceivably stupid man eager to perform it."

"Yes? Like kidnapping the daughter of Jorge C' de Vaca?"

"Like kidnapping the wife of Martin Springer."

"My father is anything but stupid."

"He has just done a very stupid thing. We should both hope that he's smart enough to recognize a stalemate."

"I don't believe that he forcibly took your wife. That doesn't make sense. She went with him willingly. Lots of women do."

"Not this one. Not this time."

"Probably she was arrested."

"I suppose so, technically."

"Listen," she said, leaning toward him with an impulsive feminine sympathy. "I'll help you get your wife back. I'll be your hostage. Okay?"

"You have no choice," Martin said.

"You wouldn't hurt me. I can tell. You're not that kind of man."

"You don't know anything about men."

"You're a doctor. You're a good man, I can tell. You would never hurt me, would you?"

Martin took her left hand in his, held it lightly for a moment (a damp, soft, brown hand with bitten nails), and then he squeezed until she screamed and recoiled against the door. Her lips thinned; she clenched her teeth. Her eyes were narrowed as she stared slantwise at him. She did not cry.

Martin thought that maybe his sudden violence, the pain he'd inflicted, would frighten the girl into docility and obedience during the hours ahead; he hoped so, because he knew he was incapable of hurting this girl twice.

CHAPTER

2 5

At first Katherine decided that she would simply remain locked in the room. All right then, I'll stay. I'll refuse to leave here until I'm given my freedom. They'll have to carry me screaming down the stairs. Just see if the goons slash my face.

But then she thought: Here I am, trapped in this little room that smells of chemicals, no windows, one door and that locked from the outside. There is no way to escape from this nightmare except by going downstairs at eight o'clock. Downstairs there are doors and windows, and people, human beings, witnesses. Perhaps I can dash through a door and out into the street. Or it might be possible to bribe someone. Or maybe someone will help me just because it's right. You would not find the most chivalrous of men frequenting a whorehouse, but they could not all have hearts of stone, could they?

Katherine poured out the last few drops of wine, lit a cigarette, and sat on the edge of the bed. Across the room, in the wall mirror, her double satirically mimicked her glances and postures.

Later there was a thunderstorm that shook the building and temporarily cut off the electricity; and it was still raining at eight o'clock when a man rapped on the door and said, *"Cinco minutos."*

Five minutes. It was like a stage call. Five minutes, darling—break a leg.

One of the whorehouse's thugs escorted her down the stairs. She thought of him as the "Frogman." He was very fat, with short bowed arms and legs, a wattled neck of larger circumference than his head, warty skin, and a wide bullfrog mouth and bulging ("exophthalmic," Martin would say) bullfrog eyes.

The downstairs dance hall was busy: a man was setting up the bar; some musicians tinkered with their sound system; the eighteen or twenty women scattered around the room were talking, smoking, laughing. Katherine noticed that most of them were fairly attractive; two or three were beautiful. All were well groomed and nicely dressed, as if for a cocktail party or dinner out at a special restaurant. Decorum, gentility. Prom night at the brothel. Oh, this was much too ridiculous.

Roxanne, unsteady on her high-heeled shoes, was approaching with a smile that looked more malicious than friendly. She wore a black knee-length dress, black shoes, and black gloves that stretched above the elbows.

"How are you feeling?" Roxanne asked.

"I feel like a debutante," Katherine said wryly.

Roxanne's smile increased; yes, it was malicious. "Come on, I'll introduce you to the girls."

"No. Thanks all the same, but I don't want to meet the girls."

"You think you're better than us, don't you?"

"Yes," Katherine said. "I do think I'm better. I *am* better."

"Yeah, see if you still feel like a debutante at three this morning."

Katherine sat at a small table near the door. It was still raining, though not as hard as before. On the table was a not-very-clean pink tablecloth, a candle—unlit—inserted into a brandy snifter, and an ashtray that contained a book of matches. There was printing on the back of the matchbook. *Casa de Amor*. An address, a telephone number. Well, then, I am a prisoner in *The House of Love*.

Don't cry, she thought. Don't cry don't cry don't cry for God's sake don't cry anymore. Tears do not evoke sympathy in this milieu. They might, rather, trigger a feeding frenzy.

The Frogman and another thug were standing by the door. Every now and then he glanced at her, and once he winked.

C H A P T E R

2 6

Martin could not find the street—Calle Subir—in the storm. It was early evening, not yet seven-thirty, but the sky seethed with low black clouds. Cloud mist obscured the tops of the tallest buildings. Some of the wind gusts were so strong that the rain was driven horizontally for a moment. The streets in the old section of the city were uncambered and drained poorly; in places the water flowed six inches deep. He drove slowly, in second gear, careful not to stall the car.

"What are you looking for?" the girl asked. She had been quiet, though not in a sullen way.

"Calle Subir."

"I don't know it."

It was hot in the car and the insides of the windows were steamy. The buildings lining the street were indistinct; blurred, colorless façades studded here and there with splashes of yellow light and neons that were duplicated on the wet concrete.

"I'm looking for the river," Martin said.

"We're close. It has to be that way—to the right."

Ahead, a police car slowly approached. Its front tires threw up curving sheets of water. Its headlights were on bright, frosting the Volkswagen's misted windshield—Martin was half blinded. He reached over and grasped the girl's wrist.

"That's my sore hand," she said quietly.

The car passed. The policeman had not seemed interested in them or their vehicle.

Martin turned right onto a flooded narrow street. The water flowed swiftly and choppily toward the south, the river. He stopped at an intersection.

"Can you read that street sign, Selene?"

The girl wiped the side window with her palm. "No. No—wait, I think, yes, Calle Subir."

He engaged the clutch and eased the car forward. There was another intersection and then they entered a block of mostly empty buildings and rubble-filled lots. The water was not deep here; it was draining too rapidly toward the river to flood the street. They passed a junkyard with the shells of cars stacked five and six high. Some of the buildings, though still standing, had been gutted by fire.

"Where are you taking me? This is a terrible place."

"Right, urban cancer," Martin said. "We'll be safe here for a few hours."

"*You'll* be safe."

"Hush."

The grade abruptly changed: for an instant they were staring straight ahead at the buildings on the other side of the river, and then the car pivoted forward on its axis and they looked down a long, very steep incline to the rain-frothed Rio Negro. Martin quickly shifted down to first, grinding the gears. The street was like a waterfall; half an inch of water rushed down the pavement and poured off the quay into the river. Martin touched the brakes. The rear end of the car slewed and he corrected by turning the wheels into the direction of the slide. A mistake now and they'd be launched into the river.

Below, at the base of the hill on his left, he saw the vacant warehouse. The signs were still there, warning of danger, of the penalties of trespass, and the announcement that the building was soon to be demolished. And there was the graffiti, stenciled and freehand. Martin pumped the brakes gently, swung wide to the right and then sharply back to the left, accelerating to climb the ramp. The muffler scraped and then they were inside, headlights sweeping cement walls smeared with slogans and crude drawings. He circled the perimeter counterclockwise and parked at the juncture of the north and west walls, facing toward the doorway and ramp.

"We'll stay here for a little while," Martin said.

The headlights illuminated the rain-puddled floor and the graffiti on the far wall, most of them obscene, one a monstrous depiction of the male and female genitalia. Martin switched off the lights and ignition.

It seemed that the core of the thunderstorm was directly overhead now. He could not recall a storm more violent—incessant lightning and thunder, and gusts of wind that he feared might bring the rotten building down on them. Selene was hunched against the door, shivering.

"Don't be afraid," he said.

Lightning flashes penetrated the doorway and glassless window high on the walls, and filtered down through square holes cut in the centers of the three floors above. The holes were all that remained of the elevator shaft: the motor, the cables and gears and pulleys, the elevator car itself, even the walls that had enclosed it all, had been removed. Raindrops, briefly frozen in the strobes of lightning, fell from above. A leaky roof, or possibly no roof at all.

"We're safe in the car," Martin said. "The lightning can't harm us here."

"I'm not afraid of the storm," she said. "I'm afraid of you."

"I'm sorry I hurt your hand, Selene."

"I don't believe that my father arrested your wife. You just said that. How do I know that it's true?"

"It's true."

"You're probably a political enemy of Daddy's."

"Yes, I am, in fact. But that isn't what this is about."

"You're probably a pervert. You probably kidnap young girls all the time and bring them here and rape them and murder them and then throw their bodies into the river."

"Remember, I was going to take your mother. You volunteered to be my hostage."

"I was a fool. My mother's old and has a bad heart. She's lived long enough."

Martin laughed.

"Well, it's true."

"I won't hurt you."

"You already hurt me."

"Let me examine your hand."

"Don't touch me."

"I did hurt you before, and I'm sorry."

Martin got out his pack of cigarettes.

"Give me one of those."

He gave her a cigarette; in the match flare he could see crooked tear-trails on her cheeks. Her lips were puffy. She did not inhale the smoke.

She said, "Think how you'd feel if someone did something terrible to your daughter."

"I do have a daughter," Martin said. "And I know how I would feel."

"You're really not a pervert?"

"Really not."

"Are you actually a doctor?"

"Yes."

"A medical doctor, not some kind of quack?"

Martin saw a shadow scuttling near the far wall and quickly flicked on the headlights: a rat, wet and big, as big as a domestic cat, with glowing yellow eyes. He switched off the lights.

"What was it?"

"A rat."

"Oh, lovely."

"You were very brave earlier."

"I didn't *believe* in this earlier. It was like a movie."

"But you feel okay now, don't you?"

"I guess."

The storm had moved away to the east. They could still hear a distant reverberant thunder but there were no more close lightning flashes. The air was cool and fresh-smelling, with an autumnal tang.

She crushed her cigarette in the ashtray. "I hate cigarettes. I try to like them but I can't."

"Stop trying."

"You're a doctor and you smoke."

"Everyone likes to remind me of that."

"How long are we going to stay in this sewer?"

"There is still an hour or so of daylight left when the sky clears. I'll wait until night."

"Yes, and then what?"

"I need to make some telephone calls. That won't be simple. Public telephones are as rare in this country as just men."

"I know a place. We'll go to my aunt's condominium. She went with us to Europe and is still in France."

"Your mother's sister?"

"My father's."

"I don't know."

"Her place is on the sixth floor. There's a telephone, and probably some food, and safety for you—no one would ever think of looking for us there."

"What about servants?"

"They don't live in."

"Security?"

"There are always guards in the downstairs lobby. Two of them at night usually."

"Is there any way we can get past or around them?"

"They know me. I can get us through."

"Young Selene taking an older man up to her aunt's vacant condo?"

"Let me think." She ruffled her hair.

"Is there a fire exit, an outside stairway?"

"Wait. The service elevator. I'll go through the lobby, take the regular elevator up to the sixth floor, go down the hall to the service elevator, and ride that down to the alley and let you in."

Martin smiled. "You won't be long, will you, Selene?"

"Trust me. I can do it, honestly. I'll tell the security guards that I'm waiting in the apartment for my father. I'll say he's working late. I'll be a cold haughty bitch and they won't dare question me."

"Okay," he said. "But I can't trust you, Selene."

"Why not? I'm trusting *you*, aren't I?"

"Before you go into the building I'll give you an injection of a drug that in twenty or thirty minutes will cause a severe hypoglycemic reaction that can quickly lead to shock, coma, and death. Unless, Selene, unless I'm there to administer an ephedrine or corticosteroid. Do you understand?"

She made a face. "I hate needles," she said.

CHAPTER

2 7

The young Venezuelan spoke as little English as Katherine did Spanish; their conversation was an unbroken series of non sequiturs. He, she guessed, was praising her hair and eyes and skin; she was telling him that she was a good girl and had no intention of entertaining him upstairs. The man had liquid soulful eyes and square teeth that looked as if they had been carved out of elephant ivory. He seemed a nice young man. The establishment had extorted twenty dollars from him for a split of cheap champagne, the price for chatting with one of the whores. It tasted like warm bitter ginger ale.

They were sitting at a table near the door. She could feel an exhalation of cool air when the door was opened to admit another—what were they called?—john, trick. It was dark outside now. The rain had stopped. The goon stationed at the door was watching her. Slow Tuesday night at the whorehouse.

The Venezuelan got up from the table, walked over to the bar and gave the Frogman a sheaf of currency, and then returned. He smiled down at Katherine and said something in Spanish. When she did not respond he said, "You come. Yes. *Sabes tu?* Okay."

"It is *not* okay," Katherine said. He grasped her left hand and tried to lift her erect. She resisted. He became puzzled, then exasperated, and finally angry. He did not seem like such a nice young man when he was angry. He stalked over to the bar and in a loud voice began haranguing the Frogman.

Well, there you are, Katherine thought: by now it must be clear that the lady does not intend to, shall we say, screw.

The whores and the few other patrons seemed spitefully amused by the Venezuelan's predicament. Can't get laid in a whorehouse.

Katherine lit a cigarette and finished her glass of fake champagne. She felt a faint shiver of exhilaration: I won't, you can't make me, go to hell, Vaca.

The band was now playing "I'll Be Seeing You." The singer did a fair imitation of Johnny Mathis. The Frogman gestured to Roxanne, who got up from her table and walked clickety-click on her high heels to the bar. They huddled. The Venezuelan looked both furious and hurt, like a little boy. Tut tut.

Now Roxanne separated from the group, crossed the room, and sat down next to Katherine.

"Are you crazy?" Roxanne said.

Katherine smiled.

"You've got to be crazy, that's all."

"I'm thirty-three years old," Katherine said. "I've been married for twelve and one-half years. I've been absolutely faithful to my husband. I have two children. My life has been very ordinary. Except that a few hours ago I was kidnapped by a fascist lunatic and taken forcibly to a whorehouse. And now one of the whores tells me that *I* am crazy."

"You are crazy."

"The question is—should I believe the whore, or should I trust the experiences of my thirty-three years, my life, my heart."

"You should believe the whore when the whore tells you that it's crazy to be stinking crab food in the river when you can go home. You got a home. It's just one night. Can't you do one night, honey?"

And now Katherine was scared because she could see that Roxanne was honestly scared for her.

"You got a home, an old man, kids—aw baby, don't lose it all. Your pussy don't know the difference between one cock and the next. You're stupider than any whore if you let your pussy think for you. Are you gonna get cut up, are you gonna die, for the sake of your holy pussy?"

"Go away. Leave me alone."

A few minutes earlier, Katherine had seen the Frogman leave the bar, circle the bandstand, and pass through a red swinging door into the kitchen. Now he returned with a slender young girl who wore a white apron and had her black hair massed beneath a hairnet. Even at this distance Katherine could tell that there was something wrong with the girl's face—it looked like two different faces cemented together along a vertical centerline. Different foreheads, eyes, jawlines, mouth . . .

"Lupe," Roxanne said quietly.

They weaved their way among the tables: the Frogman sat on Katherine's left, the girl called Lupe directly opposite.

"Mira," the Frogman said.

Roxanne said, "Guillermo says 'look.' "

The girl's face had been slashed, the left side more terribly than the right, and the cuts very poorly sutured. Twisted wounds with uneven, puckered lips; fairly recent wounds, still a glossy pink; dozens of cicatrices crawling over her face like insects. Nerves had been severed: the left side of her face was paralyzed; the eyelid, mouth, and skin on that side pale, drooping, and empty of expression. Her eyes were alive though, small, bright, and hateful.

"What did she do?" Katherine asked.

"She tried to castrate a drunken colonel."

The Frogman said something in rapid Spanish.

"I didn't get all of that," Roxanne said. "But I think Guillermo was saying that the same thing would happen to *your* face if you don't do as you're told. The same or worse."

The Frogman put out his cigarette, removed a straight razor from his pocket, opened it, and placed it on the table. The handle was inlaid with mother-of-pearl. An overhead fan caused spokes of light to spin on the blade. Katherine looked in the Frogman's eyes. Zeros. Zero eyes and a wide wet pink frog's mouth. Katherine stared into the zeros that were his eyes and was seized by terror and despair.

"Please," she said. "Roxanne, tell him to please not hurt me. I'll do it. He won't have to slash my face or kill me."

"I was afraid you'd never wake up," Roxanne said.

"I'll go upstairs. I won't be difficult anymore."

"Sure. It's just for one night. Look at it as rape if you want to. Guillermo's got a razor at your throat. It's a kind of gang-rape situation, Katherine. You can't fight them."

Katherine, despairing, crossed the big room (the whores and tricks watching) and started up the narrow stairway. The Venezuelan, murmuring incomprehensibly in Spanish, followed close behind. She entered the room; the Venezuelan shut the door and turned. *"Querida,"* he said.

Katherine began to undress. She felt queer, numb and sleepy, remote. The Venezuelan sat on the edge of the bed, took off his shoes, socks, and shirt, and then stood to remove his trousers. His bikini briefs were made out of a silky, translucent gray material. He pulled them down. He had not been circumcised. Naked now too, Katherine went behind the partition and filled the basin with warm water. She felt nothing; an emotional circuit had been broken. She glanced at her reflection in the mirror.

Poor Katherine. But she felt nothing at all. She returned with the basin, a towel, and the bar of disinfectant soap. She examined his genitals for sores or discharges, as Roxanne had advised, and then washed them. He quickly became erect. Katherine dried her hands on the towel and gave it to him. Well. And now. She moistened herself with petroleum jelly, got into the bed and lay supine, lifted her knees and spread them. He crawled on top of her. He smelled clean at least, at least that. She guided his penis inside her. There. It really was very simple. He moved gently at first, and then began thrusting hard and deep. Katherine felt impaled. She did not think it would last long at this rate. Bodies clashing, an exchange of juices. Nothing much (then why this sense of horror postponed, revulsion impending), just a synchronic pounding and hot sticky skin and deep moist gliding and then his spasms. He lay heavily on top of her, breathing hard, and then rolled away.

Katherine got rid of him and then quickly showered and douched. She stared at her face in the mirror: was there something blurry, indefinite in her reflection? She hoped it was just the poor quality of the glass and not a correlative of a loss of self. Would she become more and more insubstantial until finally the mirror refused to surrender an image?

Someone pounded on the door. Time is money. Katherine dressed and went back downstairs. The room was crowded and noisy now. The band was playing jazz, poorly, and one of the whores was clowning around in a parody of striptease. Roxanne, sitting at a table with two men, smiled and waved.

CHAPTER

2 8

One wall of the living room was glass; French doors opened onto a balcony that looked over rooftops and beyond the cathedral's dome toward the sea. There were two bedrooms, a living room, a study, a kitchen, a dining room with a long refectory table, and vacant servants' quarters in the rear. The furniture was new but had been designed and crafted to look very old.

Martin quickly explored the apartment and returned to the living room. Selene had removed her warm-up outfit and now stood in the center of the room in her tennis dress. Her feet were apart, toes pointing outward, and her hands were cocked on her hips. She smiled impudently.

"Did the security guards give you any trouble?"

"Certainly not," she said.

"We should pull the drapes. And then I'll give you a shot of ephedrine."

"Oh boy," she said, "you must think I'm pretty dumb."

"What do you mean?"

"All of that medical mumbo jumbo."

"You didn't believe that the injection was dangerous?"

"No. What was it?"

"Gamma globulin. It can't hurt you, and it will help if you have been exposed to viral hepatitis or measles or some other diseases."

"I knew you wouldn't poison me."

"You're a strange girl, Selene. You could have easily escaped."

"But it's just getting interesting now."

"I guess you could say that."

"Anyway, I couldn't be really sure about the injection, could I?" She pointed. "There's the telephone. Over there is a liquor cabinet. I'll have a glass of dry sherry. I'll go and see if there is any good food in the freezer." She pivoted like a dancer, her short skirt spinning, and went toward the kitchen.

Dusk was rapidly deepening into night; lights were coming on in the windows of the apartment building across the street. Martin pulled the drapes, turned on two more lights, poured three ounces of scotch into a highball glass, and filled a liqueur glass with sherry.

Selene returned. "I've found some food in the freezer."

"What's your home telephone number?"

"Five two nine nine four." She accepted the glass of sherry.

"Stay here. You should speak to your mother. She must be very frightened for you."

Martin dialed the number. It was answered midway through the first ring; Mrs. Vaca had been waiting by the telephone.

"This is Dr. Springer."

"Yes. Please, is Selene all right?"

"Do you have a telephone number for me?"

"The number is five seven three five one."

Martin handed the receiver to the girl. In Spanish she told her mother that she was all right, she had not been hurt, truly, she should not worry about—

Martin pressed his index finger on the lever, breaking

the connection. He said, "We can't give them time to trace the call."

Selene nodded.

"Do you recognize the number five seven three five one?"

"That's my father's private office number at the National Palace. It doesn't go through the switchboard."

He dialed the number. It rang six times and then a man's voice said, *"Digame?"*

"Vaca?"

"Who is this?"

"Who is *this?*"

"Caceras. What do you want?"

"You know what I want. Put Vaca on the line."

"I'll try to find him. He may be with the president."

"Listen, Caceras, you son of a bitch, I'll call one more time, just once, and Vaca better answer the telephone himself." He hung up the receiver.

Selene looked at him. "What was that about?"

"Your father is playing games."

"He wouldn't do that, not when I'm involved."

"Yes he would. He can't do anything else. It's his nature."

"You don't even know my father."

"I've heard plenty."

"All lies."

"Your father is a bad man, Selene."

"My father has many enemies who are bad men, communists and traitors. Sometimes you have to do bad things when you fight the bad, but it doesn't make you the same."

"But it does."

Solemnly she said, "You say my father is bad. He kidnapped your wife, you say. But you threatened me and my mother and sister with a gun. You took me away as a hostage. You hurt my hand. Are those bad actions justified by my father's bad actions?"

"Probably not."

She gazed at him for a time and then turned and walked off toward the rear of the apartment.

Martin sipped his whiskey. Selene was partly right, of course, but mostly she was wrong. Vaca kidnapped Katherine; Martin took Vaca's daughter hostage; so therefore Vaca and Martin were equally malign.

How had he and Kit become involved in such a mess? It didn't make sense; it seemed that effect had been severed from cause, and action from consequence. Exactly how had this situation occurred? Katherine a captive and Martin a captor. Ridiculous. All of the laws and beliefs that he and Katherine had lived by had been abruptly canceled. What could he do? Keep rolling the dice. Continue living heartbeat by heartbeat until the thousand possibilities had been reduced to one or two.

Martin crossed the room, slipped inside the blackout drapes, opened the French doors, and stepped out onto the small balcony. There were some potted plants, an iron railing, a rolled-up awning on the façade above the doors, and white-painted wrought-iron table and chairs that in the dimness looked like they had been fabricated out of lace. The air was still damp and cool. The street six floors below glistened wetly. A corona of moths swarmed around the sodium vapor lamp on the corner. There was no vehicle traffic on the street, no pedestrians. Music floated up from one of the apartments beneath.

He returned to the living room and dialed Vaca's private number. It rang three times.

"Yes?"

"Vaca?"

"Yes."

"You know who this is."

"Yes."

"I have your daughter."

"I know."

"You have my wife."

"Let me speak to Selene."

"After I've talked to Katherine."

"She's not here."

"Where is she?"

"I've sent for her. She should arrive here very soon. Let me speak to Selene."

"I'll call you back."

"Wait!"

"Where is my wife?"

"She has been placed under arrest."

"Don't tell me why, I don't want to hear any of your lies."

"She's involved with the communist terrorists. Not long ago she and Dixon Stenstrom met with some of them in Playas del Oro. They gave them money and information."

"Lies. I'll call you back in twenty minutes."

"Wait. I want to talk to Selene."

"After I have spoken to Katherine." Martin broke the connection.

Selene was watching him from the doorway.

"Your father is still playing games, still testing me."

She shook her head. "Really, I'm sorry, but you're no match for Daddy."

"We'll see."

"The food is ready."

She served the meal at the refectory table in the dining room. Martin's steak and peas were still half frozen. A bottle of 1968 Romanée Conti stood on the table along with a couple of tulip glasses.

"Your aunt will kill you for taking that wine."

"Why? Is it expensive?"

"It's precious."

"It tastes like any old wine to me."

"That's because you're a savage."

She was pleased. "Yes, and I hope I'll always be a savage."

After eating, Martin returned to the balcony. The street was empty as before, but soon he saw a car turn the corner to his right and cruise slowly down the centerline. It looked like one of the black unmarked sedans used by *Telaraña*. There was a long whip aerial at the rear. The car halted at the end of the block. Now a black delivery van, lights off and tires hissing on the wet pavement, turned the same corner and pulled into a parking space directly below and across the street. It had a pronged antenna. The windows were darkly tinted. Martin could not see the occupants of either vehicle from his perspective. He waited. No one emerged from the van or the car. The engines had been switched off. No doubt there were other vehicles in the area. The equation had changed: Vaca knew that he and Selene were here. Maybe the telephone calls had been traced; maybe the security guards in the lobby had been suspicious of Selene and phoned her father.

He returned to the apartment and dialed the number. The phone rang only twice.

"Vaca."

"Tell your friends in the radio van that if they look out the window in two minutes they'll see your daughter splash onto the street." He slammed down the receiver.

He slid the sofa and a heavy chair in front of the door. That would slow them a little if they attempted an assault. He checked the pistol to make sure that there was a cartridge in the chamber.

Selene returned. She wore a silk bathrobe that was too big for her slender build.

The telephone rang. Martin lifted the receiver.

"I've ordered the van to leave," Vaca said.

"And the cars?"

"Yes."

"You are a fool."

"Let me speak to Selene."

"Where is Katherine?"

"She'll be here very soon."

"Fine. Call me then." He hung up.

"What is it now?" Selene asked.

"Your father is still playing games. Very dangerous games. He doesn't seem to mind risking your life."

"You could give up, you know."

"So could he."

"Daddy will win, he always wins."

"It seems that way because people have let Daddy establish the rules."

CHAPTER

2 9

Two of the men sat in the backseat with her, the Canadian on her right, and the small Negro drove the car. A rosary and some religious medallions hung from the rearview mirror. The big man on her left removed a flat leather case from an inside jacket pocket and opened it. Lined up on velvet were a gold toothpick, gold fingernail clippers, a file, and a tiny gold spade—an earwax cleaner? He selected the toothpick and began probing his teeth.

All of the streetlights and neons were still burning. The traffic was heavy. It was not much after ten o'clock. Was that possible? Had her watch stopped?

"Where are you taking me?" Katherine asked.

"To the National Palace," the Canadian said.

"Why? What's happened?"

"It's not for me to tell you."

"Why did these brutes beat up that boy in the room?"

He shrugged.

"Who are you?"

"Me? A nobody. An employee."

"Vaca's employee. You don't care who you work for, do you?"

They were passing the cathedral now; its central dome, gold painted, was spotlighted. At a traffic signal some children rushed out into the street to peddle chewing gum and candy and cigarettes. The light changed and they pulled away.

"Look," the Canadian said, "no one hurt you back there. You'll get over it."

"Will I?"

"Sure. You'll be all right."

"You really think so?"

"You probably didn't do anything you haven't done before."

Katherine stared out the side window at the pedestrians.

"How many tricks did you turn?" he asked.

"Don't expect me to satisfy your filthy curiosity."

"Sex is sex," he said, "whether in a whorehouse or the bridal suite. Did you ever come?"

"Whores don't come," Katherine said.

"Like hell they don't."

"What's your name?"

"Jim."

"You're pretty slimy, Jim. Did you know that?"

Guards armed with automatic weapons waved the car past the palace gates. They drove down a long tree-lined avenue and stopped in front of the main entrance. More soldiers, some of them with leashed attack dogs. The Canadian escorted her into the ground-floor reception hall. It looked, Katherine thought, like the lobby of a nineteenth-century opera house; pinkish marble, functionless Doric columns, a parquet floor, gilt and velvet and crystal chandeliers, and on the walls dozens of hideous portraits—a rogue's gallery of dictators and thieves and murderers.

They took an ancient slow elevator up to the top floor

and then walked down a hallway to a big carved door. Vaca's door—she remembered it from her previous visit. There were shiny brass locks and hinges and doorknob, and a Christ had been carved into the dark wood.

In the outer office there were spindly antique chairs and settees. A male secretary—was his name Caceras?—sat behind a desk. She remembered him from her prior visit. He looked at her steadily for a moment and then rose and guided the Canadian into Vaca's office.

A big, shaggy, sloppy man with a beard and aviator-style sunglasses sat sprawled on one of the settees. His cheap suit was much too small for his shoulders and belly. He wore leather sandals with tire-tread soles. A cigar fumed in an ashtray. There was a satiric insolence in his nod and smile.

Katherine sat in a straight-backed chair. On the opposite wall there was a large oil painting of Vaca mounted on a great horse. He wore a polo outfit and held the mallet cocked over his right shoulder. It had been painted and hung so that no matter where in the room you sat, Vaca stared down at you.

"He looks eight feet tall in that painting, doesn't he?"

Katherine ignored him.

"Actually, he wanted to be painted in a suit of armor, holding a lance, but even the artist thought that was absurd. And that artist is obviously without taste. Sir Jorge Cabeza de Vaca—a noble, chivalrous knight. Don't you think he's chivalrous, Mrs. Springer?"

He had a beat-up satyr's face and a snaggle-toothed smile. Another cold, mocking bastard.

"I met your husband not long ago," he said. "In one of the western provinces. I had to leave him there in a bad situation. I doubted that Martin possessed the resources to survive. He didn't seem strong enough. I was wrong. Dr. Good has done very well."

"Who are you?" Katherine asked.

"I'm sometimes called Fuerte."

The name was familiar. This man was a thug, of course, but he seemed more intelligent than the others. And—she could not be sure—there might be a queer kind of sympathy buried in his irony.

"Will you tell me what is going on?"

"Your husband has kidnapped Vaca's eldest daughter, his angel, his darling Selene."

"I hope Martin cuts her throat," Katherine said.

"A simple task for a surgeon."

"Fuerte," Katherine said. "Felipe Fuerte, Colonel Fuerte."

"The same, I confess."

"My God, you're the man who rescued Martin from that town."

"Tepazatlán."

"And . . . murdered your pilot."

"Something the Springer family will not let me forget."

"And you abandoned Martin in the middle of nowhere."

"It seemed necessary at the time."

"But I thought. . . . What are you doing here with Vaca?"

"I'm not sure, Mrs. Springer. I think I may be half a prisoner and half a comrade."

"Did Vaca hire you to free my husband?"

"No, certainly not. No, another person hired me to help Dr. Good escape, though I'll never see the money."

"Why do you call Martin Dr. Good?"

"The name isn't appropriate anymore, is it? Maybe I should call him Dr. Bad from now on. Especially if he slits young Selene's throat."

"I really didn't mean that about cutting the girl's throat. But I'd burn candles and sacrifice goats and dance in Vaca's blood if someone would cut *his* throat." Katherine was alarmed by the strangled quality of her voice, and the hatred—a witch's curse.

"It's a pretty picture," Fuerte said mildly. "I'm tempted." And then, smoking his cigar, head tilted back to study the painting of Vaca, he said, "Speaking of blood, your left wrist is bleeding."

Katherine looked down and saw that she had picked the thin scab.

"I couldn't do it. I really wasn't trying hard. I couldn't."

Mockingly, exhaling smoke, he said, "Then it isn't quite what we've been told—a fate worse than death?"

"Do you think that what's been done to me is amusing?"

"Indeed I do not."

"Really, wasn't it more than just a nasty practical joke? Send the haughty bitch off to a whorehouse for the night. Pretty funny. It won't hurt her any and it might do her some good."

"It's your husband's job," he said lightly, "but I'll kill Vaca if you wish. Tell me."

"Send the cunt off to a whorehouse, teach her a lesson. Is that all it was? Nothing serious at all. Not like soul murder. She probably won't have to do anything she hasn't done before. So what's the difference? Put her on her back for a night. What she needs, the bitch needs a thorough fucking."

"You seem close to the edge, Mrs. Springer. Very close. Is there any way I can help you?"

"Yes, oh yes! Leave me alone. Don't talk to me. Don't look at me. Don't even think about me. Pretend I don't exist."

"But you do exist. Be glad that you exist. I'm glad, and Martin and your children will be glad you still exist."

Katherine was silent for a time and then, her voice normal, she said, "I don't care about your greedy motive, I don't care if you're murdering slime—I must thank you for saving Martin. That act might have redeemed your entire miserable useless life."

Fuerte laughed. "You're welcome," he said.

The door opened: the Canadian, with a sly glance toward Katherine, went out into the hall; Caceras rudely gestured to Katherine. She remained seated. He gestured again, jerking his thumb toward the open door. You'd expect a gigolo to look like this Caceras. He resembled the young bisexual television soap-opera actors. He wore a black suit with a row of military ribbons above the handkerchief pocket. He had been exceedingly polite the last time Katherine had been in this office—but now he was dealing with a whore. Go to hell. He was surprised and annoyed that she refused to obey his rude signal.

Fuerte said, "You know English, Caceras. Courteously inform the lady that she has been invited into the sanctum sanctorum."

The secretary shot a glance of loathing toward Fuerte and then coldly said, "Mrs. Springer."

"Not good enough."

"Maybe I should go in," Katherine said.

"Not until this lout treats you with respect."

Caceras was confused and angry. His power—his master's power—had been challenged. Both master and servant were diminished. He turned away from Fuerte's malignant smile. He bowed. "Mrs. Springer, will you come this way please."

It was a sneering parody of good manners, but Katherine picked up her purse, rose, and walked past Caceras into Vaca's office. The door closed behind her. It was a big rectangular room, a rococo travesty of luxury, with a gaudy fresco on the ceiling and, many yards away, at the far end, an enormous desk behind which sat Vaca. He rose. You stand when a lady enters the room, don't you? Katherine concentrated on walking straight and gracefully; she didn't want him to know how bad she felt, how sad, how hurt, how lost.

She sat on a straight-backed wooden chair situated at the right corner of the desk. Vaca remained standing for a moment, smiling, said, "Caterina," and then settled into his own chair, a leather-upholstered throne. "Cigarette?"

She nodded.

He pushed a gold cigarette box toward her. There were several brands inside; she selected one with a filter tip and leaned forward to greet the flame from his lighter.

"A drink?"

"Yes," she said, exhaling smoke.

"Wine, sherry, port, cognac, or scotch?"

"Cognac."

He went to a drink cart, poured some brandy into a crystal snifter, presented the glass to her, and then sat down again.

"Caterina, we are waiting for your husband to telephone. I have work I must attend to. Perhaps you would like to watch the television while you wait."

"No," she said.

"You might enjoy this program," he said. "It's special."

She knew immediately. Of course. It had been a two-way mirror.

There was a cabinet in the corner behind Vaca's desk. The doors opened to reveal a large television screen. Vaca turned on the television, inserted a cassette into the VCR, and returned to his chair. He lowered his head over a sheaf of papers. The picture fluttered for a moment and then settled, and she watched herself washing the Venezuelan's genitals.

Both were naked. The picture was surprisingly clear: the light was adequate; the colors fairly true; the camera steady, probably mounted on a tripod. The sound was poor, though, dull and rather faint, with cavelike echoes and a periodic crackling like static. But the picture was clear, far too clear, horribly clear.

Katherine was afraid that she would vomit. She sipped the brandy. Vaca was pretending to study the papers before him. He had already viewed the tape, of course, he and the smirking Canadian who had brought it and her from the whorehouse.

"No," the Venezuelan said. He was refusing a condom.

Now on the television Katherine moistened herself with a finger smeared with petroleum jelly, got into the bed, lay back with her knees lifted and spread, and received the body, the penis, of the man. He began moving on top of her.

Katherine closed her eyes, but the noises persisted, the thumping of the bed, their labored breathing, sounds—though imperfectly transmitted—nearly as graphic as the images. Fucking. That was the right word, the only word—fucking.

She opened her eyes and saw Vaca staring intently at her. The irises of his eyes were surrounded by white.

"Turn it off," she said.

He smiled faintly.

"I don't have to watch this. I was there, remember."

"You're a good whore, Caterina."

"I was raped," she said. "Seven times."

"You appear to be enjoying it."

"You are disgusting."

Katherine wanted to leave the room but her legs failed; she was sick, paralyzed—and Martin would telephone soon, she must be here to speak with Martin. She could endure this videotaped version of tonight's events: hadn't she endured the night itself?

The pounding ceased. The Venezuelan withdrew from

her. The picture faded into darkness and then almost immediately brightened again.

The big man from Illinois. He sold farm equipment. He had played professional football for a few years. He called her "baby." He carried a silver pint flask of whiskey in the inside pocket of his suit jacket, and poured it into the two wineglasses. They drank. Katherine smoked. He disapproved of her smoking. "Listen, baby, I got asthma." He said he earned sixty to eighty thousand dollars per year selling farm equipment in Latin America. He disapproved of Katherine drinking her whiskey so fast, just gulping it down. "Do you know what they charge down here for the stuff?" He was an American: Katherine tried to tell him what was happening to her, but he cut her off. "No, baby, forget it, no way. I got to do business here." He had a huge, plump, nearly hairless body. While she examined and washed his genitals he said, "Do they let you out of here? I mean, can you date regular?" "I told you, I'm a prisoner." "Sure." He asked her to take the top position. "I'm pretty heavy." He was, several inches over six feet and very heavy, though not grossly fat, just a huge man.

Katherine watched her image crawl onto the bed and sit astride the salesman from Illinois; she watched herself, her palms spread flat on the bed, slowly settle on him, impaling herself. During coitus he said, "Can't you move a little more, baby?" Both were sweating. Katherine's hair veiled her face from the camera. "I'll never get off if you don't move and squeeze. Squeeze, baby, can't you squeeze?"

When the screen went dark Katherine said, "When did Martin take your daughter hostage?"

"Late this afternoon."

"When did you hear of it?"

"A little before seven."

"Seven o'clock? And even so you made me . . . ?"

He nodded.

"Then that man wouldn't have slashed my face, he wouldn't have killed me."

"That is correct."

"God, you're cruel," she said. "I never harmed you, Vaca. How can you be so cruel?"

Now she was with the third man, a jovially drunken junior army officer. They were naked on the bed; Katherine was fellating him. This too was rape although you could not see the Frogman or his razor. The officer spoke a little English. He apologized for being so slow. "I am very drunk, I think."

She could not turn away from the television. She felt herself divide into this Katherine and that Katherine. She repudiated that Katherine, the victim, the whore.

How long did it last in real time? Not long, not more than five minutes, surely. Five mindless minutes and the officer ejaculated.

"Well done," Vaca said.

It was after this, when the officer had gone, that Katherine went into the bathroom and tentatively drew a razor blade across her wrist. She was certain that she would escape this place only through death. Vaca had lied about releasing her tomorrow (when had he ever told the truth?); Martin would not find her; she would never see him or her children again; she would remain here, a whore, until she gathered the courage to kill herself. A thin red line appeared on her wrist and then beaded with droplets of dark blood. She had not tried to kill herself; no, it was only an experiment, a practice run, to see if she might be capable of it later when life became insupportable. Her despair was not yet complete. She'd stanched the bleeding with tissue and gone back downstairs.

"You have a talent," Vaca said.

Katherine knew that Vaca was trying to break her down, shame her completely, ruin her, corrupt her soul. And this videotape was more damaging than the actions it recorded. Because eventually this night would have been half forgotten and wholly forgiven. But to *watch* yourself do these things and have those things done to you, to see it objectively (with no Frogman in sight), was too brutally real and permanent. How could these images be forgotten? They were indelible now. That is my body, that is me. That is Katherine.

"I would like another brandy," Katherine said.

"I'm sorry. I didn't notice that your glass was empty." He got up, poured a few ounces of brandy into the snifter, and returned to the desk.

"Push the cigarettes and lighter toward me."

He complied, and once again returned to the pretense of studying the sheaf of papers. But no, she knew that he was alert, acutely sensitive to her mood, intuiting and absorbing her emotions, entering her mind, her heart.

The fourth man was a middle-aged diplomat from the East German Embassy. He was the only man to use a condom. He was silent: silent downstairs, silent during coitus, silent afterward. Standard sex, missionary position, a coupling so cold and indifferent that it scarcely seemed an intimacy, another outrageous violation—just a discomfort to get through.

Who was next? She could not remember. She waited. The door opened and then Katherine and two men entered the room. Yes, her fifth trick was a "double," although she had sex with just one of them while the other, also naked, sat on the edge of the bed and watched. She thought that they were probably homosexuals. The younger man fucked her while the gray-haired man, smiling faintly, closely and curiously observed. The man on top of her was lean and sweaty and, it seemed, in a frantic hurry to end it. The gray-haired man smiled benevolently. Once he reached out and delicately touched her knee. Then he stared into Katherine's eyes until it was over. The two men, laughing and talking excitedly in Spanish, dressed and left the room.

It surprised Katherine that she had not been self-conscious while being watched that way; she'd begun to regard her body and its uses with contempt. In order to preserve some remnant of pride, of sanity, she had attempted to sever her body from her mind—her soul. If she despised her body sufficiently then she would not care so much what was done to it. She *had* ceased to care then, but now, sitting in the room with Vaca, watching herself on the television, she realized how dismally she'd failed in the severance.

Vaca had again abandoned his pretense of work and was watching her. She turned to meet his gaze. Something burned in his eyes, hatred, humor, lust, madness—she could not tell.

Katherine sipped her brandy. She was a little drunk now. That made it easier. She had been more than a little drunk at the whorehouse after the tractor salesman's whiskey, and desperately drinking more whiskey downstairs with the men. The alcohol had partly anesthetized her, helped her then as it was helping her now. She, who rarely drank at home, who had drunk more alcohol in the last week than in the previous year, was grateful for its effects.

You could tell that *that* Katherine was drunk when she entered the room with the local businessman, a banker named Aguilar. She was more talkative than with the others, slurring her words some; and she moved differently, looser but with an evident concentration. Her face had changed too; her features were more mobile and expressive now. Aguilar had paid for a "half and half," fellatio and then copulation. Katherine gave him release without herself feeling much more than impatience and disgust. Her despicable body performed its tasks while her soul remained inviolate. That's what she had thought at the time. Now she knew better.

The television screen darkened. Katherine lit a cigarette. The soccer player was next. Number seven. It would be over soon. Was it really only seven? It seemed like an endless procession of men, pendulous genitals, glandular sweat, rasping beards, hard flesh. God, how she hated men, greedy greedy men. Yes, and now the screen brightened and the door opened and they entered the room, Katherine and the pretty, narcissistic boy named Raul. He was nineteen. It was absurd. He wanted to seduce Katherine, he was not satisfied with buying her. He was teasing and lighthearted and seductive. He tried to kiss her. She turned aside while continuing to wash his genitals. Their voices sounded strained and unnatural on the tape. Raul was a professional soccer player; he had played the game in America and Great Britain and Australia. That was why he spoke English so well, he told her in broken, nearly incomprehensible English. He made funny faces, he petted her, he sought her true inner consent. "Rubia," he crooned. "Blondie." It was a seduction. He demanded her complicity. "Dulce. Sweetie pie." She finished washing him. "You are a foolish boy." He took her hand and placed it on his erect penis. "Is that a boy?" He kissed her mouth.

She twisted away. "You don't kiss whores." "Let me kiss your other lips." He was insistent but not rough. He really did seem to like her, like the real Katherine. At least he was human. He ruffled her hair. (Katherine, watching the television, recalled what she had decided during that instant: this Raul was decent and bold—perhaps he would help her if she pleased him; he would go to the Hotel Nacional tonight and tell Martin where she was. Or he could simply anonymously telephone Martin. He would do that if she pleased him, if, whorelike, she made him happy.) Katherine, dizzy from alcohol, lost her balance for an instant. "Do you really like me?" "I love you." "Liar. But maybe you'll help me." Katherine broke away from him and moistened herself with the petroleum jelly. "This is what you want." "Yes!" "It's yours, you paid for it." She took his hand and guided him to the bed. She lay down and lifted her knees. She'd consented, yes. Did it matter? He was going to fuck her anyway, he had paid the fee. But he would help her, she knew that he would. He was human. Katherine intended to fake a lust equal to his own. She guided his penis inside her. There. Go on, then, it wasn't important, merely genital friction. She was so desperately alone, and he was comical and decent (and he would help her), and he really did seem to like her, and his youth made this act seem simple and innocent, even a kind of solace.

And so Katherine consented, she accepted his tongued kisses, she greeted his thrusts, she surrendered. Whorelike, she acquiesced. The camera lewdly observed, changed angles and focus, established evidence of her self-betrayal.

The telephone rang. Grinning, Vaca lifted the receiver, listened for a moment, and passed it to Katherine.

"Hello," she said. "Yes? Martin?"

"Kit?"

"Oh, Martin!"

"Are you all right?"

"I don't know," she said. "I don't know."

"Speak up. I can't hear you very well."

That Katherine was writhing. She moved with him easily and naturally, as if they had been lovers for years.

"Katherine?"

"What?"

"I asked if you were all right."

"Martin?"

"For Christ's sake, Kit, what's wrong with you?"

The camera slowly traversed the length of their bodies.

Damp flesh, white and brown, tangled damp hair, explosive breaths, a steady cadence.

"Katherine, please," Martin was saying.

"What?"

"Are you all right?"

"Yes."

"You don't sound like yourself."

"Really, I'm fine, honest."

On the television screen *that* Katherine arched her back, arched and cried out, convulsed and was still.

"What was that noise? Was that you?"

"It was the television, Martin."

He rolled away. They lay side by side. The camera slowly, satirically explored their bodies. It was so quiet now that you could hear a faint whine of spinning tape. Katherine stared vacantly, stupidly, up toward the ceiling.

"Kit, I'm going to free you. It won't be long."

"That's good," she said. "That's what I want."

"You haven't been hurt, have you? Did they hurt you?"

"Help me, Martin."

She was unable to cease watching the television. He abruptly left the bed. Katherine watched herself watching him smear jelly on his penis. Raul returned and roughly moved her over onto her belly. She did not resist. She was too heavy, too slow-thinking to fight. Vaguely, she'd assumed that he intended to enter her vaginally from behind. She felt his weight. She felt him spread her buttocks and before she could cry out or twist away he had entered her anus. It hurt, it hurt terribly.

"Kit? It's going to be all right."

"Do you think so, Martin? I hope that's true."

"I promise."

Vaca took the telephone receiver from her hand. "Dr. Springer," he said. "Your wife is fine. She has not been harmed. She is just upset and exhausted."

It hurt. She'd known that if she screamed the Frogman or someone would rush into the room to help her, but she remained silent, she did not know why. Maybe because there was still a chance that he might telephone Martin later. Or maybe because she felt deserving of this pain and humiliation.

"Yes," Vaca was saying. "Now let me talk to my daughter. Wake her up, then. Wake her up and call me back. Yes." He lowered the receiver into its cradle and smiled at Katherine.

That Katherine faced the mirror, the camera. You could see the pain in her face. She licked her dry lips. Her eyelids fluttered. Her body was compressed beneath his weight. (Watching now, Katherine felt permanently defiled, hopelessly profaned.) The poor woman licked her parched lips, lifted her eyelids briefly, exposing a gleam of light, then closed them. She bit the tip of her tongue.

And it was then, actually and now on the television screen, that she heard voices in the hallway. Several men talking softly at first, then with hard authority. (Odd, wasn't it, that the boy had not even hesitated?) And then the door was violently kicked open and three men in suits rushed into the room. Two of the men dragged the soccer player off Katherine's body; they pinned him against the wall and smashed their fists into his face and abdomen. Katherine screamed. She'd screamed then, she screamed on the television, and she now screamed silently inside. They dragged him naked from the room and down the hallway.

The third man remained. He looked down at her curiously for a time, said, "Get dressed. You're leaving here." She thought he was American but later he said he was from Canada. "Come on, come on." His voice was distorted on the tape. He was a stocky man with a cherubic face and indifferent eyes. "Get dressed." "I have to shower," Katherine said. "I have to get myself clean." "We don't have *that* much time," the Canadian said. It was a joke. He smiled.

Vaca turned off the television, ejected the cartridge, and returned with it to his desk.

"All right," he said. "You have talked to your husband. The whore has permission to leave."

Katherine stood up.

He reached out and placed the cassette on the edge of the desk. "Take it. Show it to your husband, your children. Let them see the slut, the whore. You know what you are. Show them the evidence of your whore's soul."

Katherine picked up the cassette.

"Wait." Vaca withdrew some American currency from his wallet and tossed it on the desk. There were seven one-hundred-dollar bills. "Pick it up, Caterina. You earned it. It belongs to you."

"You might need it. The money." She cleared her throat. "To bury your daughter with."

"Take the money!"

Katherine picked up the currency and placed it and the cassette into her purse. "For the fund," she said. "To hire someone, Vaca. Hire someone to kill you."

Smiling, he leaned back in the swivel chair, unzipped his trousers, and lifted out his penis.

"Come here, Katherine."

"Die," Katherine said, and she turned and left the room.

CHAPTER

3 0

He found Selene in one of the small servant's rooms, curled tightly on the bed, sleeping, her cheeks flushed, her dark hair feathery. In repose she looked perfectly youthful, perfectly beautiful, perfectly innocent.

Martin hoped that he would not murder the girl tonight. Two hours ago he'd been certain that he could not harm her no matter what happened to Kit; now, harming her did not seem impossible; by morning it might appear inevitable. For months Martin had been learning to adapt to an increasingly capricious and hostile world, to necessity. Jorge C' de Vaca was no more and no less than a different aspect of necessity.

He raised the pistol and aimed at the moist wisps of hair curling over the girl's temple. Could he pull the trigger? God no. An hour from now? Maybe—let's see what I have become during the next fifty-nine minutes.

Martin permitted the sleepy Selene to talk with her father for half a minute and then he broke the connection.

"You didn't have to do that," she said crossly. Her hair was tousled and there were pillow creases on her cheek.

She remained there for a while, complaining vaguely, and then wandered back toward the other rooms.

Martin dialed the number again.

Vaca said, "Dr. Springer. This has become very annoying. When I become annoyed someone is usually made very sorry."

"You've been jerking me around all night. I don't like the way Katherine sounded. I don't like your cute games. A few hours ago—"

"You are dead," Vaca said. "You have executed yourself."

"Did your men report that I was at the Center this morning?"

Silence.

"Good, they told you. Did they also tell you that I left the building with a large black satchel?"

Silence.

"Good, they told you that as well. You know what kind of research is done at the Center, don't you, Vaca? Of course you do. It's valuable work, but it's dangerous, too, because those laboratories contain the cultures of many deadly diseases, killer toxins. Viral, bacterial, mycotic, protozoal—they've even got a room full of lethal snakes. Are you listening, Vaca?"

"Yes."

"I walked out of the Center this morning with some very nasty potions in my satchel. Eight little bottles. Killer soups, Vaca. A satchel full of nightmares. I've got one," Martin continued, inventing wildly, "that acts strangely. The body goes on quite well but the brain is destroyed— memory gone, cognition gone, soul gone. But the body remains for years and years."

"What is the point of this?"

"A few hours ago I gave Selene an injection. I'm not gong to tell you what it was. It might be a virus, like rabies. Rabies—I doubt if there is a more agonizing death. It could be bacillary, clostridia, say, tetanus or botulism. It's none of those things but it works something like them. There is an incubation period during which the disease can be effectively treated. If the treatment is delayed or insufficient the disease is fatal. Are you listening, Vaca? I'll make it clear. Unless I tell you within a couple of days what specific disease Selene has been infected with, she will die, and die in extreme and prolonged agony. Now you think about this. Think about it, and if you decide your daughter's life is more important than the defense of your vanity, call me. You know where we are. You have the phone number."

Martin hung up the telephone. He noticed that his hands were trembling. Extraordinary. His hands had not trembled on the morning of his scheduled execution at Tepazatlán; his hands had never trembled during a crisis in the emergency or operating rooms; and yet this creep Vaca had the power to provoke in Martin a rage so deep that his stomach knotted and his hands shook.

It was ten minutes before the telephone rang. "Yes," he said.

"All right," Vaca said.

"Good."

"You swear that the disease is no danger to Selene."

"There is enormous danger to Selene if anything happens to Katherine or me, or if you continue playing games."

"What do you want?"

"I want to get out of this country."

"All right."

"Tonight. Tomorrow morning at the latest."

"I don't know. That might be difficult."

"Vaca, get it through your skull, we aren't negotiating

now. There's not going to be any give and take, no compromises. My wife and I and Selene will fly out of—"

"Selene!"

"You will procure an aircraft, a private charter. I will not accept a commercial or military flight. Only four persons will be permitted on board excluding the flight crew. Me. Katherine. Your daughter. And a man selected by you to participate in the exchange."

"I will come."

"No you won't. You will designate a man to accompany my wife on board the aircraft. He may be armed. I'll certainly be armed."

"I'll see what I can do."

"Call me back when you've made the arrangements," Martin said, and he replaced the telephone receiver.

Selene was standing in the doorway. She had changed into a dark blue dress that was too small for her, too tight. She wore a pearl necklace, pearl earrings, and a ring with a large stone. And Selene had been experimenting with her aunt's makeup, lipstick, mascara, eyeliner, and eye shadow.

She said, "It isn't very smart to talk to my father that way."

"It isn't smart to know him."

"You can't *talk* to Daddy that way. No one can."

"Kid, your daddy doesn't understand any other kind of talk. Your father doesn't pay attention unless you've got thumbs hooked in his eye sockets and a knee in his groin."

She smiled faintly.

"How much did you hear?"

"All of it. You were shouting. I heard you tell him that you had injected me with rabies."

"I didn't say that, exactly."

"No, you mentioned tetanus too."

Martin smiled and nodded.

"Is it true that you injected me with a terrible disease?"

"What do you think?"

"I believed you before when you said you injected me with gamma—what?—gamma . . ."

"Globulin."

"Now I don't know. It scares me. Did you inject me with AIDS?"

"No."

"With what, then?"

"Gamma globulin, that's all, and it's harmless. Beneficial, even, as I told you before."

"Why should I believe you?"

"Selene, do you really believe that doctors carry vials of the AIDS or tetanus viruses in their medical satchels?"

She grinned, relieved. "No. I believe you. Did you talk to your wife earlier?"

"Yes."

"You told my father you didn't like the way she sounded."

"That's right. I didn't."

"Why?"

"She was very emotional. Distracted."

"Distracted. Probably she was in bed with my father."

"No."

"That's one of Daddy's favorite tricks. I mean, to have a woman talk to her husband on the telephone while he's in the bed with her. He does that pretty often, I've heard. He'll telephone one of his subordinates like, say, Caceras, and talk to him about something while he's *doing* it to her. Or he'll have the woman talk to her husband while he's doing it. So, if your wife sounded strange on the telephone it's probably because Daddy was fucking her at the time."

"No, Selene."

"Really, that's what all of this is about. Just some hot dirty sex but you panicked and kidnapped me and injected a deadly substance into my body."

"Sometimes you seem a woman," Martin said. "And at other times a very young child, possibly brain impaired."

"I *am* a woman," she said.

"No."

"I *am* a woman, Doctor. There was a boy in Paris, a student at the university. We fell in love. We slept together my last night there. So, you see, I am a woman."

"You're a child with a ruptured hymen. Now go away and wash that nasty grease off your face."

CHAPTER

3 1

Martin took a narrow, meandering country road to the airport. The road's surface, an ocherous clay, was like concrete when dry but a deep and slippery mud now during the rainy season. He drove slowly. He could feel the rear of the car sliding a little on the curves. A mistake and they would be stuck out here—a small dread to add to the larger ones.

The air was sultry, misty, a richly scented tropical fog that Martin doubted would ever be totally eliminated from his nostrils, his mind.

The wind had died and the palms drooped against the red glare of dawn. There were palms and eucalyptus and, far out in the fields, willows marked the course of a river. The road, the fields, and the river were all the same ocherous yellow. Alongside the road there were shacks and patches of cultivated land, and livestock—spavined horses, cows, hogs, goats, turkeys, and chickens (the cocks crowing). All the animals (the people too) were small, dwarfed by generations of malnutrition and disease; they were like new subspecies.

No cars were visible on the road ahead or in the rear-view mirror; if they were being observed it was at a considerable distance. But then there was really no need for Vaca to track their movements; he knew the destination.

The girl sat sleepily and sulkily next to him. She glanced out the side window, buried her fingers in her hair and yawned, softly murmured the words to a song. Selene still wore her aunt's dress and jewelry. She had not removed the makeup. The scent of perfume was strong. In her fatigue, dressed and painted as she was, she looked younger and yet more sexual, a corrupted child, a debauched adolescent.

She said, "I don't think this road will take us to the airport."

"On the map it does." He had found a road map in the glove compartment of Dix's car.

"Oh, the map," Selene said. "You can't believe our maps."

That was true: the cartographers were obedient to the wild pledges of politicians and so they put roads, bridges, harbors, and airports where there were only forests and silted bays and pestilential swamps. In this country the illusion of progress often seemed preferable (and was nearly always more profitable) than progress itself.

The girl was slouched low in the seat, her bare feet propped against the dashboard. Her toenails had been painted carmine. There was a smudge of dirt between the heel tendon and ankle bone.

"Do you know Javier Solis?" Martin asked her.

"I've met him."

"What do you know about him?"

"He's very rich."

"And?"

"He used to be one of the greatest polo players in the world."

"What else?"

"They say he murdered his first wife. They say he's killed men in duels."

"Is Solis a good friend of your father's?"

She hesitated. "Not really. I think my father would very much like to be the friend of Javier Solis, but he isn't. Everyone wants to be Javier's friend. It's like—everyone is the very good friend of Javier Solis, but Javier Solis the friend of no one. Do you know what I mean?"

"Yes."

"He's very charming. I love him. But I wonder. I think maybe you can't be that charming unless you don't care about people. Is that dumb?"

"No."

If everything went smoothly during the next few hours they would fly to the Yucatán peninsula in the private aircraft of the Peruvian named Javier Solis. "They" were Solis himself, his pilot, his copilot-engineer, his steward, Martin and Selene, Katherine, and Vaca's representative. The hostages would be exchanged during the flight. Their destination was a small town, Templo, in Quintana Roo not far from the coast. It was agreed that Selene and her protector would debark first; ten minutes later Martin and Katherine might leave the plane. There, at the airport or in Templo, they could hire a driver to take them to Mérida, a few hours away by automobile. There were many commercial flights from Mérida to cities in the United States; no doubt one to Chicago, a mere two-hour drive from the farm.

So there it was. Martin and C' de Vaca had disputed the details over the telephone and their final arrangement was not much different from the original proposal. They'd quarreled pettily, incessantly, out of a mutual loathing, and finally reached an accord. Martin did not like the agreement or trust the negotiator, but what could he do? Vaca held all of the cards except one, Selene. And Martin still wondered if he were capable of killing the girl, as a reprisal, out of blind fury, panic, desperation. He figured that living for months among extremes had radically changed him; pushed him far beyond his old limits; erased the future insofar as he was no longer able to predict his own behavior; and given him an appetite for nihilism, perhaps for death. The .45 pistol was a comfort to Martin. He was always aware of it. Its weight was actual and metaphorical. The pistol compensated for his loss of faith in civilization. You have ceased to have faith in the essential decency of Man? Well then, Brother, believe in the efficacy of Colt.

Ahead now, set in the center of the ocherous plain, was a grove of dusty palms, a dozen adobe buildings melting back into earth, and a crossroad—according to the map a left turn would take them north to the airport. Martin slowed the car. There were pigs and dogs and children in the street. Vultures sat on the cornice of the one commercial building. Vultureville, pigville, muttville, bratville. Villorio was actually the name of the place, and it meant hamlet or, contemptuously, hick town. Idiotville— an adolescent who looked hideously and comically like a large fetus was staring at them from beneath the portico. He was evidently the product of long and enthusiastic inbreeding. Incestville.

Martin stopped the car, got out, walked past the goggling fetus, and entered the store. He waited as his eyes adjusted to the dimness. Clumps of bananas as tall as a man hung from the rafters. There were bins, rows of barrels, honeycombs of boxes, and shelves sparsely stocked with jars and cans. He inhaled smells of woodrot, decaying produce, rat feces. Behind the counter stood a woman who could not be much more than four feet tall. There was a familial resemblance to the fetus outside on the porch.

Martin bought cigarettes, matches, half a dozen oranges, and two bottles of warm Coca-Cola.

Martin got into the car, drove to the crossroad, and turned left. Far ahead they could see the silvery glint of an airplane, its lights blinking as it steeply descended.

Selene was smiling, and when Martin looked at her she broke out in laughter. "Did you see that strange boy?"

"Yes."

"I shouldn't laugh. But he was so loathsome."

"It's all right to laugh."

"Do you think people like that have souls?"

"If I knew what a soul was maybe I could tell you."

"I don't pity him. To me he's just loathsome and comical. Does that make me bad?"

"You aren't bad, Selene."

The aircraft, named *Ascenso de Peru* (with a fierce Harpy eagle painted above the script lettering), was a commercial twin-engine jet that had been converted to private use. Behind the flight deck, in the space generally reserved for first-class seats, a lounge had been installed that contained fluffy peach-colored carpeting, a walnut bar and walnut-veneered cabinets and paneling, a compact galley, and a large oval table around which were five black leather chairs.

They passed through a curtained hatch into a compartment furnished with a desk and chair, bookcases, a pair of half-sofas, and a stereo-TV console. Half a dozen abstract paintings had been fixed to the bulkheads, and a small, lighted ivory Madonna rested in a glassed-over niche. Music—Chopin, Martin thought—issued from concealed speakers.

They sat together on one of the sofas. It faced forward and was equipped with seat belts. Behind them was a closed door that Martin assumed led to the lavatory and a bedroom.

Selene lifted the window shade. Looking past her, through the tinted glass, he could see a stretch of concrete, a steel-link fence surmounted with concertina wire, and beyond a few buildings set among some dusty palms. The airplane had been parked well away from the tower and passenger terminal.

He heard male voices forward in the lounge; the curtain parted and a small black man, wearing white trousers and a short jacket, came toward them. The steward. He halted a few feet away and apologized for the extreme heat; the air conditioner would be turned on soon. In the meantime would the gentleman or the little lady care for a cold beverage?

Selene asked for a glass of iced orange juice.

Now, through the window, Martin saw a black Dodge van with dark windows and a radio-telephone antenna pull up and park beneath the wingtip. The rear door opened and Katherine and a big shaggy man in civilian clothes (could he possibly be Fuerte?) got out. She looked exhausted. Martin had never seen her so tired. There were sooty crescents, like bruises, beneath her eyes. Her skin was grayish and shiny with perspiration. Her lips were puffy. The man (yes, it was Fuerte) leaned over and talked to the driver of the van. Katherine, docile, stood next to him, staring dully—stupidly—down at the oily concrete. Her dress was wrinkled, her hair was mussed, and there was an expression of pain around her eyes and in the curve of her lips. So then, she was not merely exhausted, she was hurt or sick.

She did not move until Fuerte took her arm and then she obediently walked with him toward the boarding stairs. The black van made a U-turn and swiftly drove away.

A moment later he heard voices from the lounge, though not Kit's, and then the engines were started. Puffs of warm air issued from the air-conditioning vents. Selene had finished her orange juice and was now chewing an ice cube.

"Is she your wife, Martin?"

"Yes."

"Is she much older than you?"

"No, she's a year younger."

"She's very pretty," Selene said politely, insincerely.

"She's beautiful," Martin said. "But not today."

"You aren't going to kill anyone, are you, Martin?"

"I don't know. I don't think so."

"Don't. Your wife and kids need you."

He told her to fasten her seat belt.

The airplane halted at a juncture of runways, swiveled and turned west down the bumpy concrete, lifted, rose steeply, lowered a wing and banked, straightened and continued to climb above some green fields, a white scythe of beach, and then the land was gone and below was the sea, blue-black and flecked with foam, studded with green islands, the reef, and then even the sea vanished as they entered a great lobed cloud.

When they emerged from the cloud the airplane was ascending less steeply. The curtain forward divided and Katherine stepped into the compartment. She took a few hesitant off-balance steps and then halted. Fuerte, framed in the doorway behind her, was grinning madly.

"Now?" Selene asked.

"Yes."

She unbuckled her seat belt. She stood up, started forward, then impulsively returned and kissed him twice, on the cheek and again at the corner of his mouth.

" 'Bye, Martin."

Katherine and Selene paused for an instant in the center of the compartment, gazing curiously at each other (behind them, huge and rumpled, Fuerte grinned at Martin); and then they separated, Selene walking forward to the lounge, and Katherine, pain and confusion in her eyes, came to Martin and sat at his side.

"Thank God," she said hoarsely. "Thank God, at last."

"Are you all right, Kit?"

"I feel awful, Martin. Terrible. You don't know. You just can't know."

"We're together now. It's over."

"You don't know, Martin."

The air-conditioning was functioning now and Katherine began to shiver. The sweat on her forehead was chill. He got a thermometer from his satchel, removed the sterile wrapper, shook it down, and inserted it between her lips.

"Do you feel dizzy, faint?"

She nodded.

"Nausea?"

She nodded again.

"Any vomiting? Diarrhea?"

"No."

Her respiration was faster than normal. Her lungs sounded clear of fluids. Her pulse was fast, ninety-nine, but regular. Her temperature was one hundred and two.

"You have a fever."

"Oh, Martin, I can't cry. I've wanted to cry but I can't."

"Is there pain in your joints? Pain anywhere? Your abdomen?"

"Everything is so filthy, so vile, so grotesque."

"Things often seem that way with a fever. I had a fever myself a while back. Is your throat sore, Katherine?"

"Vile, filthy, vile, filthy, vile vile vile."

"Katherine?"

"Was that smug little thing Vaca's daughter?"

"Katherine . . . ?"

"I don't have a sore throat."

"Who is up front? Fuerte, I know. Selene. The steward. The flight crew. Did you see anyone else?"

"Solis."

"Is he dangerous, do you think?"

"What are you talking about, Martin? Everyone is dangerous."

He pressed the service button and a moment later the curtain parted and the small black steward approached.

"Bring a bottle of mineral water," Martin said. "A glass, no ice. Don't open the bottle, I'll do that. And bring a blanket for my wife."

"Yes, sir."

"Let me tell you what happened to me," Katherine said bitterly.

"Later, Kit, not now."

"Katherine had a very nasty time, Martin. Listen to her."

The steward arrived carrying a wool blanket and a tray upon which were balanced a bottle of water, a glass, and an opener. Katherine half rose and wrapped herself mummylike in the blanket. Martin opened the bottle and poured half of the water into the glass. He dismissed the steward.

"Kit, take these aspirin. They'll help reduce your fever."

She obeyed, shivering and perspiring. Her eyes were glittery; her puffy lips were dry. She stared silently ahead, whimpering, and then abruptly opened her purse and withdrew a plastic cassette.

"Here."

"What is it?"

"A videotape. Take it."

"What is it for? What's on it?"

"Oh, you'll see, Martin, you'll see." She spoke in a tone and cadence he'd never heard her use. She dipped into the purse again and removed seven one-hundred-dollar bills. "Here. Take it. Martin and Katherine will buy something pretty for their children."

CHAPTER

3 2

The runway at Templo was new and long enough to accept the largest jet aircraft: *Ascenso de Peru* required less than half of the length for its landing. The runway seemed much longer than necessary for the town which, from the air, looked provincial and decayed. On the outskirts there were some mills with huge slag piles, open pit mines, and patches of agricultural land. Beyond in all directions there was forest. Not far to the east the forest abruptly ended at the sea, pastel greens in the shallows, deepening to indigo farther out.

The plane stopped in front of the uncompleted passenger terminal. There were workmen on the roof. Three men waited behind the tall chain-link fence: Vaca; a tall man in a silver-gray uniform; and a few yards away, a plump man with a round face and a Salvador Dali mustache.

"Who are those men with Vaca, Kit?"

"The one in the uniform in Caceras, Vaca's secretary, chief aide, head flunky—lover, for all I know. I don't know the other man."

Vaca, small and trim, very erect, wore a dark suit with

a white shirt and red-striped gray tie. He held a Panama hat at his side. His eyes were concealed behind sunglasses. The officer, Caceras, shifted his feet, shaded his eyes with a palm, grimaced into the sunlight; but Vaca remained absolutely still. He had a straight-lipped mouth and a clefted, jutting chin. Martin hated him, knew he would hate him more after hearing Katherine's story, but at the same time there was something in the man's face, his stance, his stoic immobility, that made Martin fear him as well.

Now Selene was walking alone toward the gate. Sunlight glazed her dark hair, made it appear silvery. Slender and pretty, unusually poised for her age and recent experience as hostage, she walked without urgency toward her father.

"She's a perky little brat," Katherine said.

Selene passed through the gate. Vaca moved then, finally. He took two quick steps forward and fiercely embraced his daughter. It looked, from a distance, in its suddenness and intensity, like an act of violence. They remained locked together for maybe twenty seconds. When they separated Martin saw that Selene was smiling. Caceras, and then the other man, stepped forward and shook her hand. Vaca removed his sunglasses, furtively rubbed the back of his hand beneath his eyes, and then turned and stared long and hatefully toward Katherine and Martin.

Now Fuerte and a tall white-haired man with a black eyepatch were walking across the concrete.

"The old man is Javier Solis," Katherine said.

The six of them shook hands all around and then entered the terminal.

"I'm sick, Martin. I feel awful."

"I know."

"I'm spoiled, Martin. They ruined me."

"Hush," he said. "You've got a fever. It's the fever talking."

"I'm rotting inside."

Katherine was very weak and Martin had to help her down the steps and through the gate and into the terminal. Carpenters were working inside the building. There were no customs agents, no policemen or soldiers. Katherine was saying, "Stop, I've got to rest, please let me rest, Martin." Bearing much of her weight, Martin led her across the terminal and outside into the sun glare. "Let me rest, oh please let me rest a moment." There were several battered taxis parked nearby. The driver of the first in rank jumped out and opened the rear door. When Martin and Katherine were seated inside he slammed the door and trotted around and got in behind the wheel. He was a bony mestízo with wild hair and two gold incisors. The usual religious medals hung from the rearview mirror, and a printed card on the sun visor read, *"Este Hogar Es Católico."* His English was unintelligible.

"We'll speak Spanish," Martin said. "Can you drive us to Mérida?"

"Cómo no?" He would certainly try. However, much of the road leading to the north-south highway was unpaved. It was often a difficult passage in the rainy season. They might get stuck. Certainly some cars and trucks were getting through. The road was scheduled to be paved next year, or maybe the year after that. As long as the señor understood the situation . . .

Katherine was slumped in the corner. Her eyes were closed. "No, Martin," she said. "Don't make me travel."

Martin asked the driver if there was a hospital in Templo. There was not. There were doctors but no hospital. However, the governor of Quintana Roo had promised that construction on a new hospital would begin before the next election.

"What's the best hotel in town?"

The Hotel Templo. It was a hotel that would not be ashamed to be sited in Chetumal or Campeche or even Mérida. The executives and engineers of the mining companies stayed there when they were in town. There was a restaurant and a modern cocktail lounge and fancy shops. There were telephones and televisions in every room.

"Take us there."

As they circled the plaza he saw two banks, a movie theater, a pharmacy (where, if necessary, he could buy drugs for Katherine), shops, stores, restaurants, and several hotels. The Hotel Templo was the largest, four stories high and with a triangular bank of steps leading up to the lobby doors.

Katherine managed, with his help, to make it up the stairs, and she sat quietly in a lobby chair while he registered, but in the elevator she suddenly slumped to the floor and voided her bowels.

The elevator door slid open. He helped her to her feet and down the hall to their room. There were no windows, but it was big and clean and comfortable, and it would take a battering ram to break through the heavy door.

Martin wet a towel in the bathroom and went out to the elevator and scrubbed the carpeting. When he returned to the room he found Katherine sprawled on the floor of the shower stall. A hard spray of cool water pounded down on her. He turned off the water, helped her to her feet, and dried her with a towel while she supported her weight by hanging on to the shower's curtain rod.

Martin carried her into the room, put her on the bed, and pulled the sheet, blanket, and bedspread over her. He got another blanket from the closet. She was shivering. Her wet spiky hair was spread over the pillow. It was not yet ten o'clock.

He examined her briefly and then sat at the writing desk

and lit a cigarette. Her temperature was the same, one hundred and two. Accelerated respiration, no rales or apparent accumulation of fluid in the lungs. Heartbeat rapid and strong. Her breath was sour, not acidotic. It could be anything: amoebal, bacterial, fungal, viral, the bite of a poisonous insect or spider, the inhaling or ingesting of a toxic substance, a parasitical infection. Wait and watch. It was not yet serious. If her symptoms increased in severity he would try a broad-spectrum antibiotic.

Katherine had tossed off the covers and was moaning and writhing. In his own febrile dreams Martin had seen gargoyles and bat-winged monkeys and human-faced rodents. What was Kit seeing?

He got up and went to the bed. Her body glowed with sweat. The long muscles of her inner thighs stood out rigidly. There were some specks of blood on the sheet. He examined her more closely, ignoring her muttered protests. She was bleeding slightly at the anus. Furiously, with surprising strength, she twisted away and turned over onto her back. Her eyelids lifted. "Martin?" The pupils were dilated. "Where were you?" she said. "Where did you go? I was alone." He smelled her skin and then her breath. Still that faint sour odor. She said something that he could not understand, a slurred garble of words. He palpated her abdomen. The liver did not seem enlarged; there were as yet no signs of jaundice. Hepatitis was still a possibility. He felt in her armpits and at her neck to see if the lymph glands were swollen. They were not. "Don't touch me!" There were bruises on her breasts and thighs, and a series of bruises, like fingerprints, on her upper right arm.

Martin pulled the covers over her but by the time he reached the desk chair she had thrown them off.

She was quiet for a time and then again she began writhing and whispering. Sibilant whispers, lisping complaints. He fell asleep in the chair and when he awakened

Katherine was shivering. He could hear the clicking of her teeth. He drank three glasses of *agua pura*, undressed, and crawled in beside her. Eyes closed, neither awake nor asleep, she sniffed his skin (as earlier he had smelled hers), and then she entwined him with her sweaty arms and became still.

Martin awakened at two o'clock. The covers were on the floor. It was very hot in the room. There was condensation on the mirror. He and Katherine were still entwined, their skin slippery with sweat, each inhaling the other's breath. She was awake. He got up and drank a glass of water, then brought her a glass. She asked for another. She observed him intently, without expression.

Martin showered, dressed in his soiled, wrinkled suit, and took the elevator to the lobby. There was a shopping arcade where he bought Katherine a terry cloth robe, underwear, and a white sundress spattered with red and yellow flowers. He stopped at the desk and told the clerk to have the restaurant send food to his room: orange juice, soft-boiled eggs, toast, and coffee.

Katherine was asleep. There were flecks of fresh blood on the sheet. The bruises were dark, purplish, on her fair skin, and slightly swollen. They would turn green and yellow as they faded. The psychic bruises would not heal so quickly. Martin was sure that she had been sexually used, raped.

A bellman arrived with a wheeled food cart. Katherine could not eat more than a glass of orange juice and a piece of toast. Martin was not hungry either, but he forced himself to eat. He would have to kill Vaca, of course, somehow, now or later. That was not an action he would have considered a few weeks ago. It might prove difficult to kill Vaca tactically, but not emotionally: Martin no longer considered himself a civilized man. The consequences didn't matter much. He had left consequences behind at the wall

in Tepazatlán. He did not fear imprisonment; and he had
died once—a second death would not be as hard.

He slept and when he awakened the bed was vacant and
he heard the hissing rush of the shower. A few minutes
later Katherine emerged from the bathroom, walking delicately, as if on ice. She had not toweled herself; her body
was beaded with water and her hair was dark and sleek.

"How do you feel, Kit?"

"A little better. But very weak. I still have a fever."

"Let me take your temperature."

"No." She sat on the edge of the bed, watching him, and
then she lay back, supine.

"Can you eat now?"

"No."

"Go back to sleep."

"I want to talk while I'm fairly lucid."

"All right."

"I spent part of last night in a whorehouse, Martin. I
was a whore. Seven men. They did what they liked with
me: A vicious man at the place said he would mutilate my
face with a razor if I didn't ... cooperate. I was scared,
Martin, I thought they would kill me. I didn't want to die.
I didn't want my face sliced and scarred ..."

"Not now, Katherine. Tell me later, or never say another
word about it."

"I want to tell you."

"All right. Go on, then."

She took a deep breath and slowly exhaled. "So," she
said, "I fucked them."

"Try to sleep."

"Seven men."

"Katherine ..."

She sat up so that she could see his eyes. "It's all on
that cassette I gave you. Vaca had a man filming it from
behind a two-way mirror. Isn't that banal, isn't that fun,

Martin? You can watch me being a whore. We can view it at home on special occasions, our birthdays, Christmas Eve, the Fourth of July, Memorial Day ... And then of course we'll go to bed and I'll show you my whore's skill."

He did not know what he could say that might reduce her bitterness and self-loathing.

"I earned seven hundred dollars in just a few hours. That's peanuts to a doctor but it isn't bad for a woman without a degree or talents approved socially. We can add a solarium to the house, Martin. We can send the kids to college without much sacrifice. I really think that I may have three or four years of maximal earning power."

"Listen to me, Kit—it's going to be all right."

"No, it will never be all right. I can smell them, Martin. I can't scrub them off. Whenever I fall asleep they're on top of me, in me, they'll never go away."

"Can you sleep now?"

"Yes."

"Sleep, then."

Later the telephone jangled. Martin snatched up the receiver before it could ring again. Katherine stirred but did not awaken.

"Yes," he said.

"Springer? This is Major Caceras. I am Colonel Vaca's aide."

It was "Colonel" Vaca now.

"What do you want, Caceras?"

"I have a very grave matter to discuss with you. I am down in the lobby. May I come up to your room?" His voice was toneless, uninflected, perhaps the voice of a man who is trying to conceal extreme emotion.

"I'll meet you in the cocktail lounge," Martin said. "Are you alone?"

"I am alone. I am not armed."

Martin hung up the telephone, dressed in his wrinkled suit, tucked the pistol in his belt, and buttoned his jacket over it. There was a cartridge in the chamber; all he would have to do was release the safety with his thumb and pull the trigger. He knew that if Caceras had lied, if Vaca was downstairs, he would kill him.

He went through the lobby and into the lounge. Caceras was standing at the bar. He still wore his silver-gray uniform with a glossy Sam Browne belt and calf-high leather boots. A rainbow of ribbons were attached to his tunic above the breast pocket. There was no one else in the lounge except for the bartender, a waiter, and a shoeshine boy.

Caceras, without speaking or offering to shake hands, went to a semicircular booth against the far wall.

Martin sat across from him. "What do you want to drink?" he asked.

"I will not drink with you," the man said. "I will complete my task and then go."

"Fine," Martin said. "Keep your hands on the table." His own right hand grasped the pistol butt. "Talk."

The man was extremely agitated and trying to conceal it with an exaggerated dignity and formal diction. He sweated despite the air-conditioning.

"I am here on behalf of my superior officer and good friend, Jorge Cabeza de Vaca, to issue a challenge to meet him on the field of honor."

"In ordinary English, I am being challenged to fight a duel."

"That is correct."

"I accept."

"I personally would shoot you like a rabid dog. The field of honor is for gentlemen. Your crime is that of a coward and degenerate and pervert. If you refuse this generous offer other means will be found to punish you for your crimes."

"I told you that I accept."

"You have soiled the honor of a great man, a great family."

"I suppose I'm permitted to have an advocate? A second?"

"Yes."

"Is Felipe Fuerte still in the area?"

"Yes."

"Have Fuerte come to see me as soon as possible."

Caceras removed several paper napkins from the dispenser and wiped his face. His hand trembled. The whites of his eyes had become bloodshot in these few minutes, and his mouth tensed in an involuntary rictal grin. It was curious: clearly, the man so despised Martin that his body rebelled. I cause an allergic reaction in this fool, Martin thought. Soon his sinuses will commence draining.

"I have advised Colonel Vaca that—"

"Shut up. Get out of here. Have Fuerte see me."

Caceras glared hatefully at him for a moment, then rose stiffly, his back straight, and walked with a military bearing out of the room.

Katherine was still sleeping. Her fever had not abated. She had a wasted appearance; Martin could see what she would look like when old.

PART FOUR

THE BEACH

CHAPTER

33

Felipe Fuerte filled the lounge with his bulk and loud voice and violent gestures. He had cowed the barman and the waiter and a young couple that nervously smiled at him from a corner. "Dr. Good!" he shouted. Martin offered his hand but Fuerte contemptuously brushed it aside and enfolded him in a crushing embrace. He thumped Martin's back with his fists. It was a form of intimidation, of course. Fuerte grinned slyly when they separated. "I hope that is a pistol beneath your belly and not . . . but no! You do not care for Fuerte in that way!" They went to a booth and sat down. The young couple left the room without finishing their drinks.

"Pues," Fuerte said, *"Pues,* Dr. Good."

"Do you want a drink?" Martin asked. "Caceras wouldn't drink with me."

"I will drink with anyone who pays."

Fuerte ordered a double tequila from the waiter, Martin a bottle of beer.

"So? What is this they tell me? You are going to fight a duel?"

"That's right."

"Why do you want to see me?"

"I want you to be my advocate."

"Why me?"

"Why not you?"

"Indeed, why not me? Except that this would compromise my position with Vaca."

"Vaca will be dead soon. You'll have no position."

Fuerte showed his teeth in a dog's grin. "Oh my, the good doctor has become a macho loco in just a few days."

"Have you ever fought a duel, Felipe?"

"Do I impress you as a romantic fool?"

"In some ways, yes."

"Really? But not so romantically foolish that you would expect me to be killed in such a stupid ritual. Please, Doctor."

"You'd rather shoot a man in the back," Martin said.

"Certainly."

"As you shot Ávila in the back."

"Precisely. Ávila was a hard man. He might have killed me in a fair fight." He contemptuously added, "A *duel*!"

"At least I won't have to listen to any crap about honor from you."

"No, I leave it to serpents like Vaca and Caceras to discuss honor."

"Will you help me?"

"No."

"I've heard that duels are often fought in Latin America."

"Yes, by parvenu swine who imagine themselves to be seventeenth-century aristocrats. They like to kill newspaper editors and minor politicians who have publicly insulted them. They don't take chances."

"You don't believe that Vaca is taking a chance now?"

"Vaca is a competent marksman. He's also taken fencing lessons for years. That's what they do, these Vacas, they prepare themselves to kill nearsighted newspaper editors and simpleminded physicians. Unless you were a champion fencer in college, I advise you to select pistols. You might get off a lucky shot, a happy ricochet."

Martin nodded. "Let's have another drink."

"One more and then I must go. My master awaits."

"Of course, I'd be willing to pay you well for your services."

"Well," Fuerte said. "It's true that I am a mercenary. That should not be forgotten."

The waiter brought their drinks, a plate of cooked squid and tiny shrimp, and a bowl of crackers.

"I have some cash," Martin said. "Nearly four thousand dollars. I visited some banks during the week. I thought I might have to do some serious bribing. I can pay my bills here with credit cards."

"You could also have more money wired down from the U.S., couldn't you?"

"Yes."

"You are a successful bourgeois, a rich man."

"Not rich."

"No checks," Fuerte said. "Cash. Ten thousand dollars."

"Four thousand dollars in advance. The rest afterward."

"What are you paying me to do?"

"I want you to be an advocate. My second. And if there's treachery, a double cross, then you'll fight with me."

"Mercy."

"How do these things work?"

"I don't know. I've never read the Code Duello."

"I was the one who was challenged, so I get to dictate the weapons and details of the combat."

"No, I think that has to be negotiated."

"I want the fight to take place in an open area."

"Good thinking," Fuerte said dryly. "Ideally, duelists should not hide behind rocks or trees. Listen, my friend, forget all of this. You and your wife should get aboard an airplane tomorrow and fly home. Take a vacation. Take the children to Disneyland, go to Las Vegas, see the Grand Canyon—have gringo fun. What does it matter? You'll be alive and your kids will have a father."

"It's that easy?"

"Yes."

Martin leaned over the table. "Do you know, do you know what Vaca did to my wife? Do you know?"

"I know."

"Then you understand. I'm going to kill him."

"All right."

"Wouldn't you do the same?"

"Certainly, but not in this stupid way."

"But I don't want to murder him, Felipe, I just want to kill him."

"The distinction is too fine for me."

"Will you help me?"

"Do you trust me, Doctor?"

"I'd like to have you on my side."

"That wasn't the question."

"I *do* trust you."

"That hurts," Fuerte said.

"I trust you. The ten thousand dollars is merely a token of my esteem."

"I understand that. But oh, Doctor, if Vaca kills you there won't be ten thousand dollars, there'll be only four thousand."

"Your arithmetic is sound," Martin said.

Fuerte speared three of the shrimp with a toothpick, dipped them in sauce, and ate them.

He said, "For fifteen thousand dollars I'll kill Vaca for you. I'll bring you his head tonight."

"No."

"All right. I'll go talk to Caceras now."

"Why not go directly to Vaca?"

"It isn't done that way. Arranging a duel is like the old-style courting of a virgin—there are proprieties that must be observed."

"Meet me here at the hotel when everything is settled."

"These shrimp have been dead for a long time."

"Felipe?"

"Yes, yes, yes."

"And listen—what is really the point of this challenge? I kidnapped Vaca's daughter, that's true. But look what he did to Katherine. There seems to be an element missing."

"Caceras didn't tell you?"

"Tell me what?"

"That you brutally and repeatedly raped young Selene."

"Did I?"

"Oh yes, it's a squalid tale of bestial lust," Fuerte said cheerfully, "the defilement of innocence, forced sexual congress, and hideous perversion. I'll tell you about it for the price of another drink."

They were staying, Fuerte said, at a hunting-fishing lodge owned by Javier Solis. A vast pristine beach just outside the front door; a forest containing crumbling Mayan ruins in back. It had of course been designed by a famous architect. You can imagine the place: a fake-rustic mansion with great airy rooms, parquet floors, furniture like medieval instruments of torture, modern sculpture and paintings everywhere—as vulgar as only money and exquisite taste can make a place. Liveried servants glided around the halls and grounds like zombies.

Vaca, Selene, and Caceras had been given rooms in the lodge while Fuerte ("because I am a ruffian with no lies to tell about the distinction of my ancestors") had been banished to a cottage a rifle shot away from the main structure. Other courtiers were already in attendance when they arrived from the airport: Solis's personal physician; a Mexican artist who had been commissioned to fashion a mosaic; an expatriate poet from Chile; a former president of the republic; and an American writer-photographer team who claimed to work for *Architectural Digest*, but who were probably just freeloading.

Fuerte had received most of his information from the American woman, a formidable slut who had wheeled her way into weepy Selene's confidence in the name of female solidarity, and of course the virago had immediately betrayed Selene.

They had eaten breakfast on the terrace and then dispersed. Vaca had gone off with Selene. He had commenced interrogating his daughter. He was a policeman, after all. Selene had initially denied having been molested by Dr. Springer. She had been very frightened at times, yes, and injected with a substance that she had later been assured was harmless, and he *had* hurt her hand. But he had not raped her. This Vaca found hard to believe. They were in Selene's room. Vaca was shouting and Selene weeping and protesting that she had not been sexually assaulted. Vaca then summoned Solis's personal physician, Dr. Jaramillo, a monkey-faced quack who, the American woman said, periodically injected Javier Solis with hormones extracted from the glands of goats or ducks or something. With Vaca present, Dr. Jaramillo performed a careful gynecological examination: he attested that Selene was not *virgo intactus*—she had been fully penetrated, her hymen broken, recently, in his opinion. The doctor was dismissed.

Vaca then resumed his interrogation. He was relentless: it was not for nothing that the blood of inquisitors ran through his veins. He did not beat Selene; you don't have to beat someone who loves you. She finally confessed.

Once you start confessing it's hard to stop. She replied "yes" to each of his questions and elaborated when commanded to do so. Yes, Dr. Springer had repeatedly raped her. How many times? Three times. Yes, he'd forced her to fellate him. How many times? Twice. Yes, he had once forced her to submit to cunnilingus.

"It was when I heard your list of crimes, Dr. Good, that at last I began to admire you."

"Withdraw your admiration. I never touched the girl."

"Alas. Then old Dr. Jaramillo is the only man who's had sport with Selene's bottom."

"No. There was a boy in Paris. She mentioned her adventure to me."

Fuerte nodded slowly and then smiled. "So then—*reductio ad absurdum*—this fight, this duel to the death, is about the real and imagined abuse of female genitalia." He abruptly got to his feet and, roaring with laughter, hurriedly left the room.

Late that afternoon he met Fuerte on the hotel rooftop where there was a small swimming pool, its surface sooty from windblown mill dust; a bar and grill, and half a dozen umbrellaed tables. No one was swimming: a few women lay sunning on lounge chairs and a few more sat at the tables. From this height you could look over other rooftops to the scarred hillsides. The air had a sharp chemical odor. A large parrot slept with his head tucked under a wing. They sat at a table near the parapet.

"All right," Fuerte said. "I did well. There will be six of us present. You and me, Vaca and Caceras, Javier Solis, who is to serve as a sort of referee, and Dr. Jaramillo."

"Fuerte, how can we have a referee who right now has one of the principals as his houseguest? He's friends with Vaca, isn't he? He's got to be biased in his favor."

"Don't worry about Solis. He's a vain old man, an addled Quixote. He's another one who's very serious about honor. It isn't likely that his sense of honor would permit him to participate in a massacre."

"If he's so fucking honorable, why is he attending a duel between a white slaver and a child molester?"

Fuerte laughed.

"Go on."

"It's like this: we'll drive out to a remote beach early tomorrow morning. There will be two identical Beretta pistols, each with just three cartridges in the clips. That's to your benefit—with just three bullets Vaca will be forced to move close to you before he fires. With a full clip he could afford to try a few shots from a distance. You will choose your pistol. Don't select the one containing blank rounds."

"I assume that's a joke."

"I think so," Fuerte said. "Okay. You will separate and walk down the beach, Vaca to the north and you to the south. The sun shouldn't be a problem for either one of you."

"All right."

"You will continue walking in opposite directions until Solis calls halt. You'll be about fifty meters apart then. I specified fifty meters. You will turn. The referee will say, 'Commence.' Either of you may then fire your pistol. Or you may advance and close the distance. At any time, Dr. Good, you may, at your discretion, stop and fire your pistol. Both men may advance and fire at will. However, there is this caveat—if one man discharges his three cartridges, the other man may not advance farther. He must halt and shoot at whatever distance remains between them."

"You sound like a bureaucrat, Felipe."

"At the moment I am a bureaucrat," he said. "Your hired bureaucrat. Now. No quarter is to be given. I mean, if Vaca shoots you through the lungs with his first shot, he is permitted to shoot you through the brain and the balls with the next two, as long as he does not advance after the initial wounding."

"That's sporting," Martin said.

"You won't think this is so droll when the sun comes up tomorrow morning."

"I've been through one of those sunrises. Has Vaca?"

"I'll pick you up in front of the hotel at four A.M." He started to rise.

"Felipe," Martin said. "How did you get mixed up with Vaca? Were you working for him all along?"

"I had trouble with the helicopter when I left you," he said. "It was running very poorly. I doubted that it could make it out of the country, so I flew directly east and landed at a government airfield, and told them I had defected from the communists with a valuable machine. They wanted to kill me. When confused, kill. I screamed like a maniac, I cursed them, I knocked down the soldier most eager to shoot me. I was scared, Dr. Good, but convincing. I believe I even foamed at the mouth. They took me to see the base commander, whom I persuaded to telephone Vaca. So, there you are."

"And Vaca wanted to see you?"

"Certainly. I am a high-quality turncoat."

"Have you betrayed your comrades yet?"

"No, I have lied. God, how I have lied! I very well may be the world's most vicious liar. The angels weep every time I open my jaws. It's a terrible thing to be such a liar—no one trusts me."

"As I said, Felipe, I trust you."

"You are not an insignificant liar yourself," he said.

Martin lay on the bed next to Katherine. She was sleeping peacefully at last. The room was black except for a crack of light shining beneath the bathroom door. Down the hall someone was showering; he could hear a rush of water through the pipes. It was after midnight.

Martin vaguely recalled reading about a young French mathematician, Évariste Galois, who had spent the night before a duel jotting down some of his ideas. He knew he was going to die. He was killed, and the mathematicians of today were still working on the ideas hinted at in those scrawled notes. Yes, and of course the scoundrel Aaron Burr had killed Alexander Hamilton in a duel. And another Alexander, the great Russian poet, Alexander Pushkin, had been killed at twenty-nine by a vain, worthless army officer.

Martin stared into the darkness: he thought it was probably not intelligent to sympathize with losing duelists at this time.

CHAPTER

3 4

At four o'clock Martin got out of bed and quietly dressed. He stuck the pistol inside his belt. It was too hot for a suit jacket but he needed it to conceal the gun. He removed the safety chain and set the regular lock to engage when the door closed.

"Martin?"

"I didn't mean to wake you."

"You didn't. Where are you going?"

"I'll be gone for a few hours, Kit."

"Will you come back?"

"Yes," he said. "I promise. I'll come back."

"Kill him," Katherine said.

"You're ill, Kit. You have a fever. Try to sleep."

"Kill him, Martin," she said. "Kill him."

He went down the stairs and into the lobby; it was empty except for the desk clerk and an old man dozing in front of the TV.

Fuerte's rental car was parked at the taxi station. Martin opened the door, glanced at the floor behind the front seat (no hidden passengers), and then at Fuerte.

"I wondered if you had lost heart," Fuerte said.

Martin got into the front seat and slammed the door. "I wondered if you had changed employers. Let's go."

They drove down the main street of town and then out onto a paved highway that ran parallel to a railroad line. There was no traffic. Martin saw shacks and patches of cultivated land along the road. The air blowing in through the windows was soft and warm and spicy smelling. After twenty minutes Fuerte turned left onto a narrow road that cut through a thick forest. The road had been surfaced with a thick layer of seashells—thousands of tons of seashells, stretching all the way to the coast, perhaps a million generations of clams and oysters and snails and conchs. The shells had been crushed into crystalline fragments and reflected the headlights with a phosphorescent glare. The road was mostly white, near-blinding white, but here and there Martin saw flickers of pink and blue and ocher.

"You didn't forget the money, did you, Dr. Good?"

"I have the first part."

"Four thousand dollars?"

"And small change, Colonel."

"You have purchased the services of a zealous advocate. And the rest of the money is to be paid today, after the duel?"

"Yes. If I am alive."

"Of course. By God, if Vaca harms you I shall wrench off his balls and roast them on a sharp stick."

"What time is the fight?"

"At dawn, naturally. Do you think we are dull yokels, Dr. Good? We are not without a sense of tradition and ceremony. It is important to die correctly."

"How many will be there, did you say?"

"You and me, Vaca and Caceras, Javier Solis and a doctor. Just six, I hope. I would take it as an evil portent to arrive at the site and find twenty or thirty armed men waiting."

"You're very droll tonight, Felipe."

"I am always droll when I send other men into mortal combat."

Ahead now there was a sign, an S-shaped arrow, and the word ¡DESPACIO! spelled out in red reflectors. Beyond, on a straight stretch of road that linked the two curves, was another sign that designated the area as an archeological site and warned against trespass. Martin briefly glimpsed three or four massive, shadowy pyramids rising out of a clearing. Temples to forgotten gods. Ceaselessly, old gods were dying and new ones being born. Fuerte drove swiftly through the curves and accelerated down the straightaway.

"That was a good spot for an ambush," Martin said.

"I thought so too, General," Fuerte said.

After a few miles Martin could smell the sea, tart and salt; another mile and the road abruptly ended on the fringe of a vast white beach.

The sand sloped downward and away to an indigo expanse that flashed here and there with breaking waves. The tide was coming in now, the surf was high and thundering against a reef a hundred or so yards offshore. Wind rattled through the palms and speckled the windshield with a fine mist.

"A beautiful place to die, no?" Fuerte said. He removed a bottle of dark rum from the glove compartment, unscrewed the cap, and offered it to Martin.

"A seashell road to nowhere," Martin said.

"Now, don't get metaphysical," Fuerte said. "The road has a purpose. A huge resort hotel is going to be built here soon. Javier Solis is a major investor. Your compatriots will jet down for weeks of sun and fun. Fat white people will issue commands to emaciated brown people."

"Don't go Third World on me, Colonel."

Fuerte laughed and slapped his shoulder. "I like you, Dr. Good. But by Jesus you are slow to drink."

Martin swallowed some rum and passed the bottle.

"Are you scared?"

"No."

"You lie."

"I lie," Martin said.

"Fear's natural, Dr. Good, but it must be controlled. Your mind must be very clear and cold, concentrated. The fear has to be ignored. No, mastered."

"I know."

"You know," Fuerte said scornfully. "How do you know? This must be your tenth duel."

"I'm a doctor," Martin said. "We're trained to disregard our emotions, to be dispassionate."

"That's all very well, but how many patients are trying to open your abdomen while you're opening theirs? How many patients are shooting at you while you're practicing emergency medicine? Not nearly enough, if you're typical of the physicians I know."

"Let's take a walk," Martin said. He felt the car, removed his shoes and socks, and rolled up his trouser legs. The sand was thick and warm on the surface; damp and cool beneath. A thin crescent moon dimmed and brightened behind lines of scudding cirrus. The surf was very high; there was a storm out there somewhere. They walked down the beach. Fuerte smoked a cigar and carried the bottle of rum. They reached cool wet compacted sand and halted. Every ten or fifteen seconds a big comber detonated against the reef. Imperceptibly the light had changed; details of the landscape were emerging from the darkness, and Martin noticed a sandy promontory to his left and, dimly, another far to the right. So this was a large bay. He tried to imagine a hotel complex here, and a marina, tennis courts, a golf course, terraced restaurants under

the palms, swimming pools and expensive shops, and
people—a thousand guests and half a thousand more to
serve them. It was impossible to visualize. Surely this wild
coast would always remain exactly as it now was. (As in
the same way the church tower and killing wall at
Tepazatlán would never change, nor the town, the priest,
the river, Cabrera and Rodolfo, the particular quality of the
light that morning when he was scheduled to die—those
things were unalterable. At this instant and forever he
would be standing in the shadow of that wall; and standing
here on this windy beach with the smells of sea and rum
and cigar smoke. There was something in him—in
everyone—that rebelled against the logic of time and
change and death.)

"Look," he said, "if it goes wrong, see that my wife
gets safely home."

"I'll do more than that," Fuerte said cheerfully. "I'll
court and marry the widow. I'll raise your children as if
they were my own. Pedro and Maria."

The light had increased enough so that Martin could
clearly see Fuerte grinning around his cigar.

"And I'll take over your medical practice. I'll continue
to exploit the diseased for profit."

Martin heard the distant hum of an engine and turned. A
car, headlights burning, was proceeding down the road toward them. Shells crunched loudly beneath its tires. Now
he saw that another car followed a considerable distance
behind.

"Give me the money," Fuerte said.

Martin removed the roll of bills from his pocket.

"And your pistol."

"Shouldn't we wait a bit?"

"I'll give it back if it looks like trouble. But Solis will
confiscate all the extra weapons. Fine, he can take your
pistol. I have another."

Martin took the pistol from his belt and gave it to Fuerte.

"Okay," Fuerte said. "Now take this."

"What is it?"

"Take it."

It was an ammunition clip full of cartridges.

"Nine millimeter," Fuerte said. "The clip should fit the Beretta you'll be using. If things turn ugly you'll have it."

"All right." Martin put the clip in his rear pants pocket.

"Now, Dr. Good, Solis will try to settle this without a fight. You'll have a chance to back down."

"I won't back down," Martin said. "Maybe Vaca will."

Fuerte showed his leering dog's grin and roughly slapped Martin's shoulder. "By God, you have become a monster. The devil's own chap. Good. In twenty minutes you'll be drinking Vaca's blood. But here, first have a swallow of rum."

"No. I don't need it."

"I love you," Fuerte said. "By God, let's team up and fight duels all over the world."

CHAPTER

35

The first car, a coral-colored Rolls Royce, halted at the edge of the beach. The headlights were switched off. Two men got out of the car and walked toward them. The sun had not yet risen but light was rapidly increasing. Javier Solis wore a collarless silk shirt, tan riding breeches, black boots that came to the knee, a black beret, and a black eyepatch. In his left hand he carried a briefcase—the guns? With Solis was a short, fat man who wore a rumpled tan shirt. He carried a medical satchel. They came down through the deep sand and then halted.

"Don Javier," Fuerte said. "This is Dr. Springer."

"Yes. Good morning, Doctor." His handshake was slack and brief.

The other car pulled up to the beach. The occupants remained inside.

"This is Dr. Jaramillo," Solis said.

Dr. Jaramillo's hair was black and straight, his brown face lumpy, and he wore a greased thin mustache that curved upward at the tips. He did not offer to shake hands.

Solis turned. "Damn you, Felipe, give me that cannon in your belt."

"When Caceras has been disarmed," Fuerte said.

Now Cabeza de Vaca and Caceras emerged from their car. The doors were slammed shut and they walked slowly down the beach. Vaca was wearing black suit trousers and a white shirt open at the throat. He moved stiffly, mechanically. He was a ferocious little man. Martin wondered what the source was of his infinite malice.

"Colonel Vaca," Solis said. "Caceras."

"Don Javier," Vaca said. "Can we proceed at once?"

Vaca was very pale. His lips were pink, as if rouged, in the pallor. He had shaved not long ago but his beard was visible beneath the waxily translucent skin. Martin wondered if his own face was as bloodless.

"Gentlemen," Solis said. "Jorge. Dr. Springer. You both are brave men. You both have grievances. But let me remind you that even grave differences can be settled without bloodshed."

"Let's proceed," Vaca said.

"Both of you have families. They need you. Your children need you. Please think of your families for a moment before continuing."

Now Fuerte, grinning satirically and brandishing his cigar stub, said, "You are putting my principal to sleep with all of this genteel horseshit. We're here to fight. Let's fight. Someone has to die. Vaca, you must die—Dr. Springer is a champion pistol shot. He won a silver medal at the 1988 Olympics. So for Christ's sake, man, shut up and die."

"I will not have this, Colonel!" Javier Solis said in a hard voice.

Solis was a dandy, Martin thought, even effeminate, but probably tough enough beneath his greasy veneer of cultured gentleman.

Vaca coldly glanced at Fuerte. Caceras took two steps to the side.

"Stop!" Solis said.

Suddenly Dr. Jaramillo, in a soft furious voice, said, "This is stupid, insane. Fools, all of you." And to Martin: "And you, a physician!"

"I have been asked to conduct this *affaire d'honneur*," Solis said. "And by God I shall see that it is done properly. My reputation is at stake here too."

"If we don't get going soon," Fuerte said with a crazy grin, crazy eyes, "I'll kill all of you. This isn't a parlor game, it's death, so one of you please have the decency to die. Stop boring me."

"That's enough," Martin said. He understood what Fuerte was trying to do—inspire confusion and terror, as usual—but he didn't appreciate it even though it was being done for his benefit.

This duel was absurd, Martin knew that, and comic too if viewed from the right perspective, and he had long ago realized that there was no special dignity attendant upon death. Still, violent death was in the air now, with its bitter stink of blood and viscera, and even this sleazy kind of quasi-legal homicide was deserving of more than Fuerte's buffoonery.

"Will you give us the pistols now?" Martin asked.

"Do you both understand the terms?" Solis said.

"Yes. Will you give us the pistols?"

"Please," Solis said. "Is there anything I can say to persuade you gentlemen to pause, to reconsider, to negotiate an honorable agreement?"

"No," Martin said. "My pistol, please."

Vaca, his eyes and skin shining feverishly, said to Martin, "I'm going to soak my handkerchief in your blood and give it to Selene."

"The pistols," Martin said to Javier Solis.

"The pistols, for Christ's sake!" Fuerte shouted, and he laughed his calculated, maniacal laughter.

"You are all mad," Dr. Jaramillo said furiously. "You are despicable. I despise all of you."

"The pistols!" Fuerte shouted. He drank from his bottle of rum. "To death!" he cried. "How could we live without it?"

"Give me a pistol, please," Martin said.

"The pistols!" Fuerte screamed, laughing.

Martin accepted his pistol, returned Javier Solis's grave nod, then pivoted and started south down the beach. It was a hot, very humid morning. The air was sharp with the scents of salt and iodine and vegetal rot. Some stars were still visible overhead. He did not think he was afraid: tense, yes, very nervous, but there was not that nauseating fear that he had experienced in the churchyard at Tepazatlán. He'd been paralyzed then, without hope or will, without self. Now, though, he was alert, his senses abnormally acute; he was "high." That feeling, no doubt, was due to the adrenaline being released into his bloodstream.

To his left were the gleaming wet sand flats left by the previous high tide; and the sea, purple in this light, extending on toward Africa; and the rising carmine sun. Gulls and pelicans cruised above the ruffled lines of surf. To his right the broad yellow beach sloped up toward a wall of green. Slim coconut palms arched above the forest. A few simple bright colors, green, yellow, and shades of blue, a pattern that seemed about to dissolve into abstraction—color without form, shape without content.

Before him, on the sand, he saw the tracks of sandpipers, spiral shells, sand dollars, washed-up crabs and shellfish, driftwood, clumps of sour-smelling seaweed, and a glass fishnet buoy.

Martin listened for the command to halt. Surely he had

walked more than twenty-five yards. He released the pistol's safety and cocked the hammer.

"Bastante!" The voice of Javier Solis.

Martin turned. Vaca was a small man, and at this distance, fifty-some yards, he looked like a boy. His features were a blur except for arched black eyebrows. The other men, Solis, the doctor, Fuerte, and Caceras, had moved up the beach, well away from the line of fire.

"Avanzar!"

Vaca began walking toward him. Martin remained frozen for a moment, his mind utterly blank. What the hell . . . ? And then he stepped forward.

The physical world evaporated. He was no longer aware of the hard geometry of sea and sky, the mosaic of colors, the smells, the thunderclap of surf and the catlike mewing of the gulls. And he was now unaware of his body: he floated through a sphere of pure light and absolute silence. Impending death had obliterated his rational consciousness; he existed now on a more primitive plane. Even so, his mind was clear as a hypnotic's or somnambulist's mind is clear. It was exhilarating in a queer way, perhaps like the onset of madness.

The distance between them closed to about forty feet. Vaca stopped. Martin took two more steps and then halted. Sweat burned his eyes. Vaca tried to grin. Was that a sign of weakness or of strength? Vaca's eyelids fluttered; his mouth turned down at the corners.

Martin turned in profile and raised his arm. Jesus, the gun was heavy. He did not intend to fire. He didn't feel confident at this distance but he hoped to upset or hurry Vaca's aim.

Wait, Martin thought, wait. He didn't want to shoot but he felt the butt of the pistol jolt in his hand, not just once—two or three times, he was not sure. And at the same time he realized that Vaca had fired; Martin hadn't heard the reports, they were simultaneous with his own shots, but he had seen the muzzle flashes.

And then Vaca fired again, his hand levitating with the pistol's recoil, and Martin, without willing it, discharged his last shot. Now Vaca, taking his time, standing erect, sighting carefully, his right eye staring down the length of his arm and the pistol's barrel, squeezed the trigger. Nothing. The slide was locked open.

They stared at each other. Martin wondered if he had been hit. He knew that gunshot victims were often not immediately aware of their wounds.

Was it over?

He waited, returning Vaca's stare, and then he pivoted and walked up the sand. His intense concentration had dissolved. The world returned to focus. He stumbled while passing from the smooth wet sand to the dry beach. Ahead, Fuerte was puffing on a fresh cigar, a nebula of smoke coiling around his head. Caceras and the doctor were still, impassive. Javier Solis smiled and nodded when he accepted the pistol.

"Bien hecho," Solis said.

Fuerte laughed. "Indeed, well done. The seagulls were in greater danger than those two men."

"I was talking about courage," Solis said coldly.

"I was talking about competence."

"You are all fools, idiots!" Dr. Jaramillo said with a quiet fury.

Vaca had remained behind for a moment; now he rejoined the group.

"Well done," Solis said to him.

"The trigger pull is too fine on your pistols," Vaca complained.

"I'm very proud of you both," Solis said. "Señor Cabeza de Vaca. Dr. Springer. It was beautiful. We live in a time made for and by cowards. It was good to see two brave men. Neither of you flinched. I'm glad no one was hurt. Blood means nothing. Courage is everything."

"Fools," Dr. Jaramillo said. "Lunatics."

"I am not satisfied," Vaca said.

Fuerte laughed.

"I demand another opportunity."

"Honor has been satisfied," Solis said.

Vaca would not surrender his pistol. "I insist," he said. "I have the right. It is my right, my duty. There has been no blood. My honor depends upon the spilling of his blood."

Javier Solis, with elegant distaste, said, "Stop. This is ugly, it's shameful."

"You have no right to interfere, Don Javier."

"I do," Solis said. "By God, I do."

"Load the pistols, please," Martin said.

Solis looked at him.

Martin nodded.

"Full clips," Vaca said.

Fuerte removed the cigar from between his teeth and drawled, "We agreed. Three cartridges in each pistol."

"That is correct," Solis said.

"Just load the damned guns, will you?" Martin said.

The pistols were reloaded. Martin walked down to the wet compacted sand and followed his footprints to the south. The sun was above the horizon now and had lost color. Another sticky hot morning, heavy air, glittering sun and sea, a stink of dead fish and rotting seaweed. Surf periodically cracked against the offshore rocks. The particles of spray left dim rainbows in the air. A wave, larger than most, rushed up to within a few yards of him, then clawed back down the slope, chased by nervous sandpipers.

He reached the limit of his footprints, stopped to lever a cartridge into the pistol's chamber, then turned. Vaca was waiting.

"Advance!" Solis called.

Martin started forward. The sole of his right foot hurt; he supposed that he had cut it on a seashell or piece of glass. He welcomed the pain. He increased it by refusing to limp or favor that foot. Pain slightly reduced the unreality of this moment. He noticed that his strides were longer, his heel prints deeper than before. Both he and Vaca were walking faster this time. Eager to finish it. Surf cracked against the reef and a moment later he felt cool wind-borne mist on his cheek.

They went beyond their previous marks, out onto the smooth undisturbed sand. Remember the light trigger action. Remember not to hurry too much—make haste slowly. Kill him, kill the son of a bitch.

Both men stopped. They were about thirty feet apart. Could you miss at this distance?

Vaca, hissing between his teeth, turned in profile and raised his pistol. Martin mirrored the position. Hurry! he thought, and the pistol jolted in his hand, and the sharp cracks blended together in a brief stutter. His gun was empty. So was Vaca's. So they would have to do it again. But then C' de Vaca slowly bent over, clutching his middle, and he sat back on the sand. His eyes were round. It seemed that he looked up at Martin without recognition or understanding. Then he squeezed his eyes shut, drew up his knees, and rolled over onto his left side.

Martin approached. The right side of Vaca's shirt was bloody, and as he watched the stain slowly expanded. Evidently the bullet had entered just below his rib cage. Vaca was unconscious now. His face and hands, so pale before, now looked chalk-white. Shock, Martin thought. Maybe the liver. Internal bleeding, rapidly falling blood pressure, coma. Comatose, Vaca looked young and piteous, innocent.

"Get away from him!" Dr. Jaramillo said furiously. He kneeled on the sand.

Nearby, Javier Solis was saying, "This is very unfortunate. Why did he insist? Honor has been satisfied."

"You were hit," Fuerte said to Martin.

"Where?"

"Your leg."

Martin looked down. His right pant leg was bloody. There was no pain until he probed with his fingertips. A bullet had passed through the mass of muscle a few inches below the curve of buttock. He lowered his trousers. There was a lot of blood but the femoral artery had not been touched.

"I'm all right," he said.

"Are you sure?" Fuerte asked. "You look old, you look like your own grandfather."

"Shock." He felt weak. He could not think clearly. He sat down on the sand. The entry hole was small and ringed by a dark bruise; the exit hole was larger and ragged with shreds of flesh. But what luck—the femur, the femoral artery, and the major tendon had not been touched; and the trajectory was straight, the bullet, entire, had exited; it wouldn't have to be dug out of the living tissue. Martin felt sick and dizzy from the shock, but it would be all right, he'd be fine.

He looked up. Fuerte and Caceras were carrying Vaca toward the cars. Solis and Dr. Jaramillo followed them. Caceras emotionally cursed and wept. How strange, Martin thought: you hated a man, for you he was the personification of malignity; and then you learned that by some he was respected, highly valued, loved, even.

There was not much bleeding now; he was coagulating very well. He did not disturb the jellied blood. He would clean and dress the wound back at the hotel.

But the pain was becoming serious now. Very smart: the

doctor goes off to fight a duel and he doesn't even bring along two or three aspirins.

Sun seemed to fill the sky. He could feel its pulsations on his shoulders and neck, but he was aware of a small chill in his guts.

He heard car tires crackling loudly on the seashells. Fuerte was walking down the beach. His shirt had been stained with Vaca's blood. He had lighted another cigar.

"Assholes," he said as he approached. "Have you ever met such supreme assholes? That Solis—he's half fag, isn't he? Why do women like half fags so much? How is the leg?"

"Okay," Martin said.

"Of course, he's very rich. That counts for something. Stop brooding about those holes in your leg."

Something moved on the periphery of Martin's vision: he turned. A man emerged from the trees and was walking toward them. He wore a holstered pistol, and a rifle with a telescopic sight was slung over his right shoulder.

"Give me my gun," Martin said.

"I'll deal with this *pendejo*."

The word *pendejo* signified a fool or jerk; literally, it meant pubic hair. Martin felt delirious, a little crazy, sitting on the sand and oozing blood while the sun cooked his brain.

The man wore a soiled khaki police uniform. There was a tarnished brass badge on his cap and another pinned to his shirt pocket. He stopped a few feet away. His black shoes, punctured with a pattern of holes, were worn without socks. His ankles were dirty, his trouser cuffs were frayed, there were old acne scars on his dark, thick-featured face. He looked part Negro. His eyes were dull, filmy, they seemed not to reflect light. The man wanted his money. He was sullen, menacing. I want my money. *"Chinga tu madre!"* Fuerte said furiously. "What did you

do? Nothing. And you want to be paid? Get the fuck out
of here, you stinking bandit!" I want my money. I want my
money. "You didn't shoot. Did you shoot the first time?
No. Did you shoot the second time? No." I killed him. I
want my money. "Look at my champion there, bleeding to
death on the sand. He was murdered because of your fail-
ure. And you want to be paid! Get out of my sight." The
man continued to stubbornly demand his pay. He uttered
threats. "You lie!" Fuerte shouted. "Do you hear me? I say
you lie. What do you say?" The man quickly backed
down. Martin saw the surprise on his face, and then the
fear—a bully meeting an even greater bully. He was stupid, Martin thought, dumb as a steer, but not so stupid that
he did not realize what kind of man he was facing, or the
danger of his situation here on this desolate beach. Well,
he said, perhaps it was true that his rifle had not fired. The
firing pin might be defective. Or maybe it was because the
ammunition was old. It wasn't his fault. He had squeezed
the trigger both times. He deserved at least part of the
money.

Fuerte showed the man his most ferocious canine smile.
"Go," he said. "Leave your rifle and pistol here. You can
collect them later."

The man protested, whining, trying to save face, but finally he left his weapons on the beach and walked back
into the forest.

"I should have killed him," Fuerte said. "I would have
killed him except I know you disapprove of casual homicide."

"You wouldn't collect the rest of the money unless I
survived."

"That's true. But also, I like you, Dr. Good. You're my
fool."

"Thank you."

"He was highly recommended. He's the local assassin."

"A cop?"

"Well of course a cop. Who's better suited to the work?"

"But he tried to cheat you. He didn't shoot."

"Yes." Fuerte laughed wildly. "Oh, Dr. Good, don't we have fun?"

"We do, Felipe, we really do," Martin said. "But now will you help me to the car?"

The seashell road glittered blindingly in the sunlight. The forest began to emit a foul smell. It was hot, humid, rank, a primeval morning. They rounded a corner and slowly passed the archeological site. The temples were disappointing in daylight: three roughly pyramidal hills thickly grown with shrubs and ferns and weeds. A facet of the tallest had been excavated down to the shattered limestone steps, and the platform on top—the altar?—restored. A smoky line of fire extended the clearing toward the east. As the car passed Martin saw a chubby blond woman in boots and khaki shorts and a khaki military-style shirt. One of the archeologists. And there were small brown men scattered over the site, digging, sifting, lifting, crouching, trundling wheelbarrows, cutting brush, laboring in the sun. "Look at the monkeys," Fuerte said. They did look like monkeys at a glance. Mayans, descendants of the people who had erected these temples to the glory and honor of gods long extinct.

Two cars were stopped on the shoulder of the road a mile beyond the archeological site. Fuerte pulled in behind them. Javier Solis got out of his car and walked back. He leaned over and looked in the open driver's window.

"Cabeza de Vaca is dead," he said.

"Rest his bones," Fuerte said.

Solis looked past Fuerte to Martin. "I will attend to things here," he said. "I have influence. But even so you should leave this country as soon as possible."

"Yes," Martin said. "Can you loan us your airplane? I mean, could your crew fly us to Mérida where we can pick up a commercial flight to the States?"

"Yes. Certainly. The airplane will be ready. Yes. Adiós, Dr. Springer. Good luck, sir." He hesitated: it seemed that there was more he wished to say, but then he merely nodded and returned to his car.

There was a little rum left; Fuerte drank and then passed the bottle to Martin.

"Well," Fuerte said. "How does it feel to have killed your first man? Outside the operating room, I mean."

Martin finished the rum. "I'm sorry," he said. "Because it means that I can't kill him tomorrow."

Fuerte laughed.

Martin immediately regretted his cheap remark. He supposed that he would carry Vaca's corpse around for the rest of his days.

PART FIVE

THE FARM

CHAPTER

3 6

It was a dry October and there were several hard frosts. The leaves turned gold and amber and scarlet and mauve. Each leaf was a translucent flame incandesced by sunlight. Old men, holding their rakes like tridents, burned dead leaves in the gutters; maple seeds descended like tiny propellers; boys punted footballs through the smoke; carillon bells chimed in the villages.

On his rare free days Martin took his discontent on long bicycle rides. One Sunday he rode out to a bleak pastel country where it seemed that he could observe the curvature of the earth. He pedaled down dusty roads lined with poplars and barbed-wire fences, alongside bare pastureland and convex fields of corn stubble and vacant, vandalized farmhouses.

There were only a few big trees out here, delicate cloud forms against the crow-dotted horizon. He ate lunch by the algae-scummed pond of an old mill. A weasel curiously watched him from among some cattails, and emerged to eat the food scraps he tossed its way. The weasel's brown fur was turning white. Martin felt excluded from the natural world—exiled. He had died and been resurrected to a world he failed to recognize. Nothing was familiar. He could not resolve the contradictions; he was unable to reconcile the opposing forces. It was the same for Katherine; she was as lost as he.

November was windy and rainy—mud and sodden leaves and bare rain-blackened trees. V's of geese flew overhead, honking their wild flight songs. Some of them rested on the lake at night and at dawn went off to forage in the cornfields. There were ducks too, mallards, teal, and pintails. A pair of peregrine falcons preyed on the migrating waterfowl: the male swooped low over the water, flushing the ducks, and the larger female dived on her prey. And flocks of blackbirds, gathering for migration, swarmed crazily over the bare earth, combining and recombining. It seemed to rain every afternoon. Katherine rarely left her bed. The children whispered and went clandestinely about their business. "Sneaks," Katherine said. But no, they were just reacting to the misery in the house.

In mid-December the wind shifted around to the south and for three days the weather was mild. It rained all night of the third day, then the north wind returned, the sky cleared, and it became very cold. Heavy tree limbs cracked beneath the weight of the ice. The sun rose on a world turned crystalline. Everything had frozen to a glitter that hurt his eyes. In the great oaks and maples ice tinkled like wind chimes. Sunlight ignited the frozen drops, creating tiny prisms that flashed amber and rose and violet. This was the planet in a new aspect, bright and purified. Martin felt as though he had received some kind of cosmic absolution.

It began snowing on the afternoon of January fifth and was still snowing the next morning, big mothlike flakes that endlessly fluttered down out of the mist. Martin got up early and went outside. Some crows, high in an oak, mocked and reviled all that was not crow. He shoveled a path to the barn. The horses' shaggy coats steamed in the cold. They impatiently stamped their hooves and rolled their eyes. Martin broke the shells of ice that had formed in the water buckets; dumped a quart of grain into each trough, and then broke a fresh bale of hay and gave each of them a slab. After the horses ate and drank he let them out into the corral. He cleaned the stalls and put down fresh straw. He liked the smells in the barn: the clean smell of horse and horse manure, straw, hay, and the smell of oiled leather from the tack that hung from nails driven into the wall.

He returned to the house and had cinnamon toast and coffee in the kitchen. The kids were awake and rowdy in an upstairs bedroom. He waited, listening, and then heard Katherine screaming at them.

Martin went back outside. Snow was knee-high off the path and almost as deep as he was tall where it had drifted against the barn and sheds and along the fence lines. The lake and woods were invisible in the snow-haze. The air smelled like iron. Martin felt encapsulated in a dim globe of light.

He fixed chains to the rear tires of his car, just in case. In case the hospital called, a seriously ill patient called, a colleague, unable to travel because of the storm, called.

Next he attached the snowplow to the small tractor and cleared the yard from house to outbuildings, and then he plowed the long driveway out to the edge of the county road. There had been no traffic. They were isolated here for a day or two if the snow and wind continued.

The mailbox, a five-gallon oaken keg fixed to a post, was nearly buried in snow. He had not collected the mail yesterday, and Kit rarely traveled this far from her bed. He got down from the tractor, waded through the drifts, opened the cask's lid, and removed the contents. Junk mail, bills, an article refused by the *New England Journal of Medicine*, and two letters, one from Dix.

When he returned to the yard the children were playing in the snow, and the setters, Yin and Yang, spun and leaped ecstatically. They ignored him, kids and dogs—natural allies.

Martin went into the kitchen and poured a cup of coffee. He skimmed Dix's letter; he would read it carefully later. Enclosed were two photographs: one of Dix seated at an umbrellaed table, sea and palms behind him; the other of a thin, dark young man wearing black trousers, a white shirt with black tie, and a short red waiter's jacket. *"Cortez, the famous revolutionary,"* Dix had written on the back of the second photo. The young man had been photographed while bearing a tray of food, and appeared frightened by the camera.

"The son of a bitch is a waiter in a flashy restaurant in Playas del Oro, can you believe that? Our Cortez—our Lenin and our Ché, Katherine. Do you remember? 'We must feed the babies.' He's feeding babies, all right, me and Burke among them. The Limping Man is a dishwasher in the same establishment.

". . . and, Martin, down here they are still fuming and blustering about extraditing you for your 'cowardly assassination' of the beloved national hero and martyr, Jorge Cabeza de Vaca. I'm sorry to say that the demise of Vaca has not improved things in this scorpion's nest; Vaca's replacement, Sr. Caceras, is almost as bad.

". . . yes, I can probably arrange to have a letter delivered to Selene. Write it, and we'll see. But Martin, I don't think that she's the same girl you knew. From all I see and hear she became a raving fanatical Harpy after her father's death. She leads a movement whose name can roughly be translated as 'Youth Who Bathe in the Blood and Tears of Christ.'

"I inquired about your chum Fuerte. He is fighting in Chile, or maybe Peru, he is retired in Miami, he is in Co-

lombia and deeply involved in the drug trade, he is in Washington with the CIA, he has entered a monastery, etc.

"After the rainy season, the government finally mounted their big offensive. Tepazatlán was a major target. Poor little Tepazatlán. I heard that it was devastated. Enormous civilian casualties, many atrocities, a blood frenzy. And I'm sorry to tell you, Martin, that the priest there was murdered, yes, crucified, nailed to a tree in the churchyard. I don't have his name, but unless there were two churches in Tepazatlán, two priests, it must have been your friend Father Perecho. It is all so ugly. Wouldn't it be swell if the murderers on one side were just slightly more decent than the murderers on the other side? One could hold one's nose and choose, in that case. . . ."

The other envelope was battered and dirty, covered with illegible scrawls and foreign, pastel-colored stamps. He studied it. The letter was addressed to Katherine. There was no return address. It had been postmarked in four countries. Then he realized that, of course, this was the letter he had written to Kit in the tower at Tepazatlán, and passed on to the priest. Martin supposed that he ought to destroy it.

Martin got up, fried bacon and two eggs, made toast, poured orange juice and coffee, put everything on a tray, and carried it upstairs. He kicked the base of the door. You had to seek admittance; Katherine became furious at any violation of her privacy these days.

"Yes?" she called. "Martin? Come in."

Katherine lay supine in the big bed —her bed now, not theirs. Pale face, shadows beneath her eyes, unwashed hair, an expression of extreme fatigue. She was a robust woman, an athlete, but now you left her half convinced that she was truly frail, an invalid.

"Thank you, Martin. I'll drink the coffee and juice—I can't eat."

After Katherine's initial fear of venereal disease had passed, she became obsessively convinced that she suffered from cancers of the female organs, the ovaries, the cervix, the uterus ... One of Martin's partners in the clinic, a gynecologist, had examined her and failed to eliminate her fears. Nor did she believe an oncologist who practiced at the university hospital in Madison. *She* knew that she was rotting inside. She despised Martin, all of them, for suggesting that she seek psychiatric help.

"Why are you home?" she asked.

"Day off. Phil is covering for me at the hospital."

"Is it still snowing?"

"Yes." He had to remind himself to speak in a normal voice, move in his usual brusque way. Invalids, genuine or neurotic, tended by their own soft voices and languorous movements to blackmail the visitor into a kind of reverence.

"There's a letter from Dix," he said.

"Oh? What does he have to say?"

"I'll bring you the letter."

"Yes."

He watched snow falling past the window. "Kit. Last night the kids told me that you've hit them."

"Oh," she said.

"They wouldn't lie about that."

"Oh, Martin, please, I'm sorry, I know I shouldn't, I mustn't, I hate myself for it—I slap them. I don't mean to. It's just that they're *mean* to me, they provoke me, and then I slap them. Not hard, really. I don't decide, it just happens, I slap them and afterwards I'm horrified. Do you understand, Martin?"

"No."

"Do they hate me?"

"You're losing them."

"You bastard. You didn't have to say that. Please get

out. Leave me alone. I know you all hate me. No! Don't touch me! Get out!"

The kids were waiting for him outside. Perhaps they had heard their mother shouting. Walls couldn't contain her shrill invective. The children's eyes, their mouths, and their postures accused him. You failed again. Why don't you *stop* her?

"Dad, what's *wrong* with her?" Peter asked, trembling from the cold or from his anger.

"I told you. Your mother is ill."

"Yes, but what's *wrong* with her? You're a doctor—what's *wrong* with her?"

"I'm sorry," he said. "You'll have to be patient. I'll see that she doesn't hit either of you again."

"She's such a bitch!" Mary blurted, her face contorted with scorn; and then her eyes lensed with tears.

Martin did not reproach her. He said, "What do you guys want to do? Do you want to ski through the woods, get out the toboggan, or go ice skating?"

They wanted to do all of those things.

He said, "Go get your skates. I'll clear a patch of ice."

Martin drove the tractor down the slope and out onto the lake. The ice sagged in a rubbery way and there were shrill pinging sounds as cracks radiated out from beneath the weight. It held, though; it was good hard ice, about six inches thick. And the lake was shallow here—if he went down it meant nothing worse than a damaged tractor. He cleared a rectangle as big as a hockey rink. The ice was translucent; you could see patterns of light moving on the bottom. It had stopped snowing, and great lateral rips had opened in the cloud cover. Blue sky in an hour or two. And tonight a cold that would burn exposed flesh like acid, fifteen or twenty degrees below zero, maybe more.

He parked the tractor in front of the house and went up

to Katherine's room. She had been crying. Her voice was hoarse.

"I'm sorry," she said.

"I know," he said. "It's tough."

"Martin, it's like there's another person inside me, like I'm possessed. I hear horrible words, the vile tone, and think—it isn't *me*. But it is me, I guess. I'm sorry. I apologize now, but I'll probably be the same way tonight or tomorrow. I can't stop this new person inside of me."

"I cleared snow off the ice," Martin said. "It's stopped snowing. The sun is out. Get your skates, Kit, and come down to the lake with us."

"Oh Martin, I'm sorry, I want to, there's nothing I'd like more. But I can't. Don't ask me why, I don't know, but I just can't."

"Here's the mail," he said. "The letter from Dix and a letter from me."

"From you?"

"Yes. It's an old one."

The kids were already out on the ice when he walked down to the lake. Their skate blades left cryptic streaks on the dark ice, runic forms, unsolved alphabets. The sun shone brightly, dimmed behind some fast-moving clouds, appeared again. Martin brushed snow off the bench and began lacing up his skates. The kids were showing off: Mary was gracefully trying the figures her mother had taught her last year; Peter was all speed, windmilling arms, power undisciplined by technique. The dogs, barking, sliding and falling, were chasing Peter. Chaos, the disorder under which children and dogs and lunatics thrived.

Martin went out onto the ice. He had not completely forgotten how to skate; the muscles and tendons and bones remembered. Yes. He was pleased by the way his blades carved white commas into the ice, the crisp sound, the smooth weightless gliding. "We'll get out the hockey sticks and a puck later," he called to Peter. The boy did not reply: he skated wildly, furiously. His sister performed her delicate figures over and over again, seeking a different kind of perfection.

Martin's ankles were sore. He wished that he had brought a brandy-spiked flask of coffee.

Then Mary paused, lifted her arm, and pointed up toward the house. "Oh, no, she'll ruin everything."

Katherine, wearing her skates, was tiptoeing down through the snow. Her long blond hair had been frizzed and dyed a rich green. A food dye? She wore black tights and a pair of Martin's baggy blue tennis shorts. And she had on a zebra-striped sweater that Martin could not recall seeing before. Colored scarves, red and blue and yellow, had been tucked here and there in her clothing, the ends free and moving in the wind. They watched her tiptoe down through the deep snow. She had powdered her face white—flour?—and smeared her mouth, chin, and nose tip with lipstick. A clown, a fool. Martin glanced at the children: their faces were bitter, contemptuous. They were not going to be seduced by this pathetic display.

Katherine descended the embankment and began skating. She was a very good skater but now she was deliberately awkward, the clown, always on the verge of falling. Her eyelashes were thickly mascaraed. Her lipstick hooked upward at the corners of her mouth in a goofy smile, but her lips were not smiling. Her eyes, as she passed Martin, were serious, pleading. She fell on purpose, then slid ten or fifteen yards, then twisted and rose before momentum ceased. She was skating backwards now. It was a good trick. Martin looked at the children. Give in, he thought. But they refused to cheer, or even smile.

Katherine swiftly circled the ice, now skating backward, now forward, her speed astonishing in relation to the leisurely motion of her limbs. The colored scarves fluttered.

She skimmed dangerously fast around and around the rink. Her blades grated on the ice and left curving white scars. Was there something abnormal—mad?—about this wild performance?

And then she lost her balance, threw out her arms, nearly recovered but caught a tip in the ice and fell hard. Her speed hardly diminished. She slid swiftly over the ice on her back, completing a single slow revolution, and then she struck the snowbank left by the plow, lifted into the air with her limbs loose and awry, and entered the deep soft snow beyond. She was nearly buried. She did not move. Mary gnawed anxiously on the thumb of her mitten. Peter stood quietly, staring, and then started forward. "Wait," Martin said.

Katherine stirred, slowly stood up. Her clothing and green hair were powdered with snow. Her clown's makeup was smeared. She slowly clambered over the snowbank and skated toward them. There was no blood. Her limbs articulated normally. She was just very tired and maybe a little stunned.

Katherine was solemn but her clown's mask grinned madly. She stopped, spraying ice, and embraced the boy. He did not resist. His face appeared asymmetrical. She released him (leaving smears of makeup on his cheek), skated a few yards, and fiercely hugged the girl. "Baby," she said softly.

And then Katherine skated over to Martin and elaborately curtsied. His return bow was equally grand. She offered her mittened left hand. He took it in his left hand, gently turned her so that they faced in the same direction, and placed his right hand on her right hip. *"Ein, zwei, drei,"* he said, and they began a slow, stately circuit of the rink. Katherine nasally hummed a waltz, something by Strauss, and Martin chanted, *"Ein, zwei, drei . . . ein, zwei, drei . . . Ja, gut!"* They skated around and around while the dogs barked and the children pelted them with snowballs.

Turn the page for a preview of

Ron Faust's thrilling new novel

WHEN SHE WAS BAD

Coming in March 1994 from Forge Books

An imprint of Tom Doherty Associates, Inc.

ISBN 0-312-85164-2

The first we saw of Nativity Shoals was breakers to the northeast, stained by the rising sun and periodically issuing thunderous cracks. The misty air, as well as the foaming seas, was a rich pink, the color of cotton candy.

We had lowered the sails and were proceeding under power, running under the lee of the shoals. Christine was forward, alert for changes in water color. The seas were mottled with many hues of pastel and milky greens, and blues like ink washes.

I was in the cockpit, steering and cursing quietly. The chart was spread out in the cockpit well, and the depth finder ticked off glowing red digits: *51, 50, 49, 37, 35.* The chart had the soundings marked in fathoms and the sonic device computed in feet, so I had to multiply the latter by six to correlate them. I was warily trying to navigate by depth, pinpoint our position on the chart. I didn't wholly trust it; the survey would not have been nearly as exhaustive and accurate as, say, a chart done of a harbor or along a busy coast.

Christine gestured to the right, and I hesitated for an instant, reluctant to go further inside the reef, but then I obeyed and the depth sounder rapidly clicked down to a frightening 9. There was now a little more than four feet of water beneath the keel. I could see mushroom-shaped coral heads below.

"You're going to wreck us!" I shouted.

But then the depth gradually increased. When it reached sixty feet I put the engine into neutral and yelled to Christine to drop the anchor.

"I'll make coffee," she said, walking aft. "Are you hungry?"

"No."

I remained on deck, nervously checking the anchor to make sure that it was not dragging, and then I turned off the engine. In the ensuing silence, the resonant cracking of surf to windward seemed louder and more violent, like an artillery barrage.

And then later, when the diesel fumes cleared away, I could detect a new scent in the air, the sweet rich odor of land and vegetation. The nearest palms were about two hundred yards away, looking like frantic punctuation marks amidst the expanse of blue sea and sky. Beyond, not clearly visible at this angle, were the white lines of surf.

Christine returned to the deck with a thermos and two cups. We lit cigarettes and sat in the cockpit, smoking and drinking the coffee.

"It seems secure here," she said. "Don't you think? We're leeward of the worst of the shoals, and if the weather turns bad we can simply run toward the west."

"I want to put another anchor out," I said. "It wouldn't do to go exploring the reef and return to find *Cherub* gone." Then: "Chris, those breakers on the southeastern side of the reef look bad. I don't know how we can possibly find *Petrel* there, let alone work efficiently enough to salvage the keel."

"But this is low water now, isn't it? And these are the spring tides, with a large differential between low and high water. When the tide comes in there may be very little surf over there."

"I'll check the tide tables again."

"Anyway, I don't believe that the *Petrel* went down over there. I was terribly disoriented that night, of course, but remember—I didn't say that the boat was in the breakers, only that I could see and hear them."

"Okay. I'm not trying to throw cold water on your hot plans, only trying to be realistic."

Later, I put the second anchor in the dinghy, rowed it out, and set it. When I returned we ate a light breakfast, and then she went swimming while I mounted the little Seagull outboard on the dinghy and fussed with it until it started and ran smoothly.

I was, almost unwillingly, beginning to share Christine's excitement and confidence. This was a beautiful and lonely place, with tiny islands to explore, water the colors of precious stones, reefs abounding in fish and shellfish, burning days and indigo nights—every northern man's dream of paradise. And there was a "sunken" ship to be found, "lost treasure" to be recovered. I felt like Huck Finn. Huck Finn on vaster waters, with a mature woman for a companion. I figured that this kind of life, like most others, would become a deadening bore after a while, but not soon.

Christine packed a lunch, and we took the dinghy out to explore the Gothic architecture of the reef. The dinghy, with engine shaft, only drew about eighteen inches, so we were able to leave the labyrinthine channels and skim over the coral spires and domes and parapets. It was like ghosting over an ancient, submerged city.

As much as possible I guided the boat on a grid pattern, searching the water to port while Christine looked down over the starboard side. The water was so clear that it was difficult to estimate depths; details were as distinct at thirty feet as at five.

When the sun was high it spread a glittery film of light over the water's surface, closing off the submarine world. I ran the dinghy a quarter of a mile to the largest of the cays. It was not quite the enchanted isle it appeared to be from a distance; small, hardly bigger than a supermarket parking lot, there was nothing there but sand and broken chunks of coral, yellow weeds, thornbushes, and a half-dozen stunted palms, and the rusty light mechanism up on the thirty-foot-high "summit."

We prowled around the cay, looking for a source of fresh water. There wasn't one. The ground-nesting birds were remarkably tame; they opened their beaks and cocked their heads, watching us with glittering black eyes, but did not fly away.

The light looked like a rusted heap of junk, the kind of mysterious mechanical construction you might see around old mines or railroad yards. It was a cylindrical monolith about six feet high, with a thick lensed "head" and, when I opened the hatch, guts composed of greasy gears and levers and wheels, and a large fuel tank that replied "empty" when I tapped it. The flame, when it burned, would not be much bigger than a candle's, but the lenses would enormously increase the light's power.

"Looks like it hasn't worked for years," I said, closing the door.

She was silent.

"I suppose you're thinking that if the sons of bitches who are supposed to tend this light had done so, everything would be different."

"No," she said. "I was thinking about lunch."

We ate with our backs against the light cylinder. The tide was in now and the sea was smooth except for occasional white bursts which spread out like spilled milk and then fizzingly dissolved.

Later we swam, and then made love on the sand. Our lovemaking was always a little like collaborative vandalism, a psychic as well as physical assault.

We searched the reef nearly all day everyday. More and more of the chart was pencil shaded, until after a week we had covered more of the south-facing shoals (the *Petrel* had been sailing north) than remained to be investigated.

The other two cays were smaller than the first we had explored, and the easternmost was hardly more than a sandbar which permitted the existence of a few dwarfed palms. The little islands had gradually been formed by the action of wind and sea; and it seemed likely that one day a hurricane would come along and obliterate all three.

The weather remained fair except for a couple of vicious afternoon squalls. Thanks to the steady trade winds, it was never intolerably hot, and the late nights and early mornings were cool.

The days passed, one like another: blue mornings with the deck slippery with dew; afternoons when, sun-drugged, we napped on one of the cays and swam in pools colored like exotic fruit drinks; and hushed nights when the stars vibrated and fish made phosphorescent splashes in the dark water.

I often went spearfishing, never without luck, and Christine caught crabs and lobsters in the tide pools, and collected mussels from rocks in the littoral. We ate the seafood with warm wine or beer.

We both got million-dollar tans, and my hair became crisp and tipped with yellow. We worked, swam and fished and dived, ate and drank, listened to music and made love during the long nights. Day and night, awake and asleep, I felt that I was continually on the edge of a great revelation. Harmony lay just a few steps into the future.

* * *

We located the wreck of the *Petrel* quite by accident. Rather, she revealed her grave site to us. Without that piece of luck we never would have found the boat, for she lay in an area we had arbitrarily eliminated from the search.

All along we had been alert to the possibility of finding some debris, flotsam; there were many bouyant objects that should from time to time have broken loose, floated to the surface, and then been carried to shore. The boat itself was of wood construction, and there were life preservers, cockpit seat cushions and bunk pads, foam rubber fenders, blocks, papers, bottles, cans. But we had found nothing more than a few bits of wood and plastic that might have drifted in from anywhere.

We were on the largest cay, resting beneath the canopy of a sail that I had erected by stringing the three corners to palms. The hottest and brightest hours of the day were usually spent there; we ate lunch, ventured down to the sea for a swim, rested, sometimes slept.

On this flaming afternoon I was watching some large, awkward gray birds which were floating about a half mile off the northern—the "wrong"—side of the island. Occasionally one would attempt to fly, sort of running on the water and flapping great frazzled wings in what appeared to be slow motion. There was not enough wind to aid them in takeoff. I was following one of them with the binoculars. He ran and flapped for about fifty feet, almost lifted off, and then fell back with a splash.

Christine was lying nearby, her eyes covered with the back of one hand.

The bird looked as though he might be getting ready for another try. And then, behind the bird and to one side, I saw an object rise straight up out of the water for a few feet and then fall back. For an instant I assumed that it was the bill of a swordfish or marlin; but then the object, horizontal now, rose to the top of a swell. An oar.

"Chris! There it is!"

She sat up. "What?"

"Go down to the dinghy and get the compass and chart. Hurry!"

"What do you see?"

"Emeralds. Move!"

I kept the oar sharply focused in the glasses, and when she returned I took a quick bearing on it, ran to the east end of the cay, searched for the oar, found it and took another compass bearing, and then ran past our camp to the western edge and did it all over again. I wanted the sighting points to be as widely separated as possible.

We spread out the chart and I drew three ruler lines angled at the degrees taken from the compass; the *Petrel* should lie where the lines intersected. Close to that point, anyway. When we took the dinghy out there I could reverse the sightings. We would find it.

Now it was I who was optimistic and Christine advising caution.

"It can't be," she said. "*Petrel* was sailing *north*. She had to wreck on the south side of the shoals."

"No, she sailed right through. Look at the soundings on the chart. She passed between here and Little Cay, see the channel? The *Petrel* damned near made it through by blind chance, but then—here, you see?—she went aground. Another thirty feet and she would have been clear. All that good luck, but it wasn't quite enough."

She studied the chart. "The water shelves off steeply out there. Fifty fathoms—three hundred feet. How can we dive so deep?"

I ran the pad of my index finger over the chart, skimming low numbers, fives and sevens and nines. "No, it's here. You told me how fast she went down. Remember?

You said that it was like the boat's spine had been broken. You had only enough time to inflate the raft. *Petrel* is here, by Christ."

She nodded then. And slowly smiled.

The *Petrel* was on the bottom at eight fathoms, about fifty feet. We snorkeled over the wreck, studying it until the light began to fade. She was lying over on the curve of her starboard bilge. The mast, probably broken off by the initial impact, was still attached by a wiry tangle of shrouds and stays. The bottom had been smashed open. Various kinds of shellfish and weeds had attached themselves to the hull. The round, brass-rimmed portlights stared up at us like dead eyes.

We returned to the *Cherub*. It was dark by the time we had our gear properly stowed away, and I sat on the deck with a glass of bourbon and watched the stars abruptly appear in dense clusters, as if some minor deity were running around and pulling celestial switches.

I was tired, my sunburned skin felt gritty with salt and sand, and I was sorry that we had finally located the *Petrel*. My mood had turned. The whiskey hit me quickly, and I sentimentally mused that our search for the *Petrel* had been a quixotic quest, a kind of metaphor, and now everything would change. We had ceased questing, and that altered our lives in a thousand minute ways. All the frequencies had been changed. A quest had become an economic venture. An end to the gratuitous, and therefore the innocent. We weren't kids anymore. It was the old world again, profit and loss, business is business, the bottom line.

I could hear the sizzle of fish frying below in the cabin, and smell its iodine odor. *Cherub* rocked ponderously to the swell, tugging at its anchor warps and groaning faintly.

Christine passed up the dishes, fish and boiled potatoes, bread and butter, the last bottle of wine.

We ate in silence, smoked in silence. Divided.

"Chris," I said. "Let's sail away at dawn."

She did not reply.

"We'll sail to Panama. I'll work there for a while, and then we'll reprovision, go through the Canal and into the Pacific. The Galápagos—haven't you always wanted to see the Galápagos Islands? Marine iguanas there, tortoises almost as big as Volkswagens, birds—no animals there have enemies. They're all tame as angels."

She was listening carefully, watching me.

"The Galápagos, and then down the trades to the Marquesas, the Society Islands—Tahiti. Samoa, Fiji, Australia."

She lit another cigarette.

I said, "Leave the emeralds here. They're only stones, bad-luck stones at that. They have worth, but they aren't worthy."

I thought she nodded then, but I wasn't sure.

"I think we've found something, *almost* found something, and it isn't wealth. I've felt recently that we're almost there. I mean, I can't explain it, *there!* I'm ahead of you now, but I know you're catching up, we're almost together, almost free. If we sail away from these emeralds . . ."

And then stupidly, cravenly, I stopped talking, partly because I believed that Christine might regard persuasion as domination, partly because I was aware that what I was saying was irrational by all the standards we both blindly accepted. And partly too because I was greedy; those emeralds burned a hole in my character.

I awakened before dawn and lay quietly in the darkness for twenty or thirty minutes, until Christine stirred.

"Awake?" I asked.

"Sort of."

"The emeralds aren't in the lead keel, are they?"

"No."

"Where?"

"There's a five-gallon can of fuel alcohol in a locker below the sink. The emeralds are in it."

"Why did you lie? Again?"

"I didn't trust you."

"Do you trust me now, finally?"

"Yes."

"Let's get ready. The sun will be up soon."

When I reached the *Petrel* I turned and looked up toward the surface fifty feet away. The sunlight, shattered by the refractive lens of water, was composed of needles and points and blurs of pure light from the short end of the spectrum, a quicksilver fire shot through with iridescent veins of gold and violet. And I could see the bottom of our dinghy and its columnar shadow. Oar blades fractured the lens above me, entered my world briefly, were withdrawn.

I pulled myself along the *Petrel*'s steeply canted deck, paused to look in through a portlight. The bronze rim was still bright, unaffected by immersion, but the glass was coated with a gray-green slime. Inside, an impression of chaos; pale floating objects catching a fragment of light, drifting shadows, slowly ascending and descending blobs—gravity nulled.

I swam back toward the main hatch. Clouds of small bright fish exploded and reassembled a few feet away; a fierce crab, pincers lifted like a boxer's hands, backpedaled along the deck; nearby a barracuda effortlessly adjusted his angle, his jaws pointing at me like the muzzle of a gun.

My face mask had fogged a little around the edges. Inhalations hissed in my ears; each exhalation expelled plastically distorted bubbles which wobbled away toward the surface. I felt myself enclosed in a globe that was bright in the center and tended toward inky blues at the perimeter.

I hand-walked down the ladder into the dimness of the cabin. Small darting fish, a snowstorm of particles, obscurity. But I had no trouble finding the oven, the locker beneath it, the can of alcohol. I shook the can and heard a rattling inside. It should not have been so easy.

Back at our little camp on the cay, I pried off the can's lid, poured out the alcohol and the stones. They looked like melted green bottle glass, crystalline and brown-veined. Most were large.

Christine counted them aloud, put them back in a single pile, and counted them again. There were eighteen.

She laughed and hugged me. That wonderful laugh, irresistible because it had been so long dammed—it carried her away. I was not happy for her. She kissed me, and then, an act of generosity which I could not forgive, she gave me three large stones. I accepted them and took three more from the pile. "My share," I said. I didn't want her emeralds; I wanted to hurt her.

I lost her then. She was hurt by my apparent greed, deeply hurt, I could see it clearly. She did not understand what I was doing, and neither did I.

Christine made two dives to bring up some of her personal possessions. We returned to *Cherub* and ate a cold meal in the cockpit. I returned the six stones but I did not explain or apologize.

"We sail tomorrow morning," I said.

"All right."

"I'm not going to try to fight the head winds back to Florida now."

"Of course not."

"I'll drop you off, and store the boat. Where do you want to go?"

She thought about it. "I have the stones . . ."

"I know, but that's the smuggler's burden."

"Mexico, I guess."

"Okay. I'll take you to Progreso or Cozumel. You can catch a flight back to the States."

"Fine," she said.

At dusk she cooked a fish stew that tasted like varnish remover. I threw most of it over the side.

"I think I'll get drunk," I said.

"If that's what you want."

"I want."

"Fine, good, but you ought to collect all of our things from the cay first. If you intend to sail in the morning."

"Right."

I got in the dinghy, started the engine, and buzzed toward the cay. Moonlight splintered the dark water and, behind, the propeller carved out spiraling funnels of green phosphorescence.

I pulled the dinghy up on the beach. What had gone wrong? Me, I guessed. She had gone through hell, she was ill, and I had pushed too hard, or hadn't pushed hard enough, or . . .

The dried palm fronds crackled in the breeze. I walked up the hill, feeling both sad and self-righteous. Maybe we can patch it up. Whatever *it* was.

I turned when I reached camp.

She was a competent sailor now. She'd brought in the two anchors, or cut their lines, raised jib and main, and was now sailing out of the shoals.

I sat on the sand and watched. Moonlight filled the sails. One could imagine, from this distance, that it was moonpower driving the *Cherub* rather than wind. A fine little boat, pretty as a picture as she sailed away in the moonlight, the precise image of romance.

* * *

Cherub's sails gradually shrank, became as dim as candle flames guttering in the distance, and then were extinguished by the night.

She'll come back, I told myself. Maybe she was a little crazy, narcissistic and impelled by strange dark motives, but she wasn't capable of abandoning me here, especially not after what she herself had recently endured.

Jesus, she had used me, probably in the same way she'd intended to use Doug Canelli until someone dumber came along. Until I popped in the door with wine and credulity. It wasn't even close; she had been three moves ahead of me from beginning to end.

When the first of the cramps hit me I realized that she would not be returning. The first was like a fist blow, and then they got worse, sharp jolts that extended hot nerve tentacles into my arms and legs. I vomited until there was nothing left, and still the convulsions bent me double. The vomit scorched my throat. In it I could smell a faint, familiar odor, a caustic solution used to dissolve verdigris.

My extremities were numbing. I staggered downhill to the nesting grounds. The birds croaked softly and ruffled their feathers.

I ate half a dozen raw eggs, promptly vomited, ate some more and this time managed to keep them down. I looted the nests of six more eggs and carried them back uphill.

My legs had gone completely numb, were paralyzed, and I had to crawl the last few yards into the campsite. Two of the eggs were fertile; I tossed them aside and ate the others. I hoped that the sticky albumen would coat the lining of my stomach and esophagus, halt the burning.

I did not sleep that night. Certain that I would soon die in one way or another—poison, thirst, starvation—I considered suicide.

I felt somewhat better at dawn. My guts were still on fire, but except for a tingling numbness in my hands and lower legs, the paralysis was gone. I worried more about my eyes now; every image had a ghostly double hovering nearby.

I looked up at the sailcloth canopy. It had collected several quarts of rainwater during a squall three days ago; we had used it for washing. Perhaps . . . I clumsily rose to my feet and peered over the edge. A few ounces of water had collected in the center and hundreds of dewdrops were slowly trickling down the slopes. There, survival! Oh yes, I was going to make it.

Fresh water. Dew accumulated in the sail at night, and during the day I could rig a solar still—several more ounces. One good squall would give me quarts of the stuff, gallons.

Food. No problem. Fish were plentiful in the tidal pools, and there were clams and mussels. Bird's eggs. The birds themselves. Seaweed, plankton.

Fire, signaling fire and cooking fire. Easy; I would break the light's thick lens and use a piece as a magnifying glass, focus the sun's rays into flame. Fuel was limited, though, driftwood and the dried palm fronds. Okay, raw fish and shellfish and eggs, cooked bird.

Rescue. We had seen no passing ships or airplanes, but that did not mean that none would appear in the future. I could signal by smoke or by flashing a piece of the light's reflector backing. Perhaps the Honduran light tender would call here on its next run to put the Nativity Shoal's light back in service. And Christine had mentioned turtle fishermen. I had seen only a few sea turtles (more potential food), but this was probably not the breeding or egg-laying season. The turtle fishermen would show up eventually.

What did I have, then? A little fresh water and plenty of food; fire; adequate shelter; a kindly climate. What more did Stone Age man have?

Oh, I was going to make it, all right.

* * *

Rescue came sooner than I had any right to hope, and from an unimagined source: sixteen days after Christine had sailed, an old ninety-foot motor yacht anchored two miles off Nativity Shoals. The boat, *Mayapan*, out of Cozumel, Mexico, had been chartered by a group of amateur ornithologists from all over the States. They had been to Panama, where they had visited the Darien rain forest, Guatemala, and Honduras. Nativity Shoals had been on their schedule (they had great interest in the birds whose nests I had regularly plundered—a rare species), but they were running late—the hurricane season was rapidly approaching—so they had almost canceled the stop. My stop.

I greeted the small motor launch while standing thigh-deep in the sea. There were ten or twelve persons aboard, most of them elderly, all staring at me with concern and alarm. Who was this half-naked savage?

I was trying to hold myself together, get through this encounter with a little style. I didn't want to babble, gush, pour gratitude over their heads like syrup.

An old woman sitting forward in the boat, everyone's favorite granny, recoiled as I grasped the bow painter; and a big man stood up and looked at me with what I believed to be loathing.

I said, "Sabu welcomes the white chiefs."